ANGEL
of the
COVE

SANDRA ROBBINS

HARVEST HOUSE PUBLISHERS
EUGENE, OREGON

All Scripture quotations are taken from the King James Version of the Bible.

Published under representation of the Natasha Kern Literary Agency, Inc.

Cover by Koechel Peterson & Associates, Minneapolis, Minnesota

Cover Photos © Koechel Peterson & Associates, Inc; iStockphoto / rcimages; iStockphoto / Thinkstock

ANGEL OF THE COVE
Copyright © 2012 by Sandra Robbins
Published by Harvest House Publishers
Eugene, Oregon 97402
www.harvesthousepublishers.com

Library of Congress Cataloging-in-Publication Data
    Robbins, Sandra (Sandra S.)
    Angel of the cove / Sandra Robbins.
        p. cm. — (Smoky Mountain dreams ; bk. 1)
    ISBN 978-0-7369-4884-5 (pbk.)
    ISBN 978-0-7369-4885-2 (eBook)
    I. Title.
    PS3618.O315245A84 2012
    813'.6—dc23

                                                            2011043839

Printed in the United States of America.

        12 13 14 15 16 17 18 19 20 / LB-CD / 10 9 8 7 6 5 4 3 2 1

To Shelley
For the love you've brought to our family

～

Chapter 1

*M*ountain air was supposed to be cool. At least that's what she'd always heard.

Anna Prentiss couldn't be sure because she'd never been this far into the mountains before. But if truth be told, they still had a fair piece to go before they reached the hills that rolled off into the distance.

The narrow dirt road that led them closer to those hills twisted and bumped its way along. The June heat had dried out the winter mud in this part of Tennessee and produced a dust that threatened to choke her, roiling up and around the buggy. Anna covered her mouth with the lace handkerchief her mother had tucked in her dress pocket and sneezed. The smudge left on the cloth made her wonder what her face must look like.

She glanced at Uncle Charles, her father's brother, who sat beside her on the leather seat of the buggy. Perspiration had cut meandering, dusty trails down his cheeks, but he didn't appear to notice. His attention was focused on trying to avoid the holes that dotted the road.

She wiped at her face once more before stuffing the handkerchief back in her pocket. It really didn't matter what she looked like. There was no one to see her. The only living creatures she'd seen all day were some white-tailed deer that had run across the road in front of them and a fox that had peered at her from his dusky hiding place beside the road. In front of them trees lined the long roadway that twisted and turned like a lazy snake slithering deeper into the mountain wilderness. She'd come a long way from the farm in Strawberry Plains.

A twinge of homesickness washed over her. She closed her eyes and gritted her teeth. The uneasy feeling lingered a moment, but with a determination she'd only recently acquired, she banished thoughts of those she'd left behind to the spot in her heart where her grief lay buried.

Just then the buggy hit a hole, and Anna grabbed the seat to keep from bouncing onto the floorboard. Uncle Charles flicked the reins across the horse's back and glanced at her, his spectacles resting on the bridge of his nose. Wispy gray hair stuck out from underneath a black hat.

"Hold on. These roads can be a little rough. We had a hard winter up here."

Anna nodded, straightening herself on the buggy seat and studying her uncle's profile. How many times had he ridden this way to take care of the mountain people he loved? He looked every bit the country doctor. His smooth hands, so unlike her father's work-roughened ones, gripped the reins tighter as he grinned at her.

The corner of his mouth curled downward when he smiled, just as her father's had always done. That was the only similarity she'd ever seen in them, though. Uncle Charles used to say he got the brains and Poppa got the brawn. When she was a little girl, she wondered what he meant. But she knew no matter what it implied, the two brothers shared a bond like few she'd ever seen. And they were the only ones who'd ever encouraged her to follow her dream of becoming a nurse.

Anna took a deep breath and inhaled the heavy, sweet smell that drifted from the forests on either side of the road. She turned to Uncle Charles. "I've been noticing those white flowers that look like shrubs growing along the road. What are they?"

"Those are our mountain rhododendron," said Uncle Charles. "There are also pink and purple ones. Sometimes in the summer you can stand on a ridge and look across the mountains at the rhododendrons blooming, and it looks like somebody took a paint-brush and colored the world. It's a mighty beautiful sight."

Anna swiveled in her seat again and looked at Uncle Charles. "Thank you for working out this trip for me."

A grin tugged at his mouth. "How many times would you say you've thanked me today?"

"Not enough yet."

A sudden breeze ruffled the straw hat her mother had given her, and Anna grabbed the wide brim. After a moment she released it and pulled the handkerchief from her pocket again. Grasping it with both hands, she twisted the cloth until it stretched taut between her fingers. "I hope I don't disappoint Mrs. Lawson."

He didn't take his eyes off the road but shrugged. "I wouldn't worry about that. She's been delivering babies in Cades Cove for a long time, and she's glad to have an extra pair of hands. It'll be good experience before you leave for nursing school in the fall."

The old anger rose in Anna's throat. "Only if Robert agrees." She spit out the barbed words as if they pierced the inside of her mouth. "Why does he have to be so selfish?" She clenched her fists tight together. Ever since their father's death Robert had assumed the role as head of the family, and he took his responsibilities seriously. Too seriously, if you asked Anna. He never missed an opportunity to tell her how their father wasn't around anymore to cater to her every whim. The first time he'd said that she felt as if he'd shattered her heart. The pieces had never mended as far as her relationship with him was concerned. But if things went as planned, she would soon be free of his authority.

"I don't want you to be angry with your brother, Anna. You may not understand his reasons, but he's trying his best to be the head of your family. He's still young and has a lot to learn, but he loves you and wants what's best for you."

Anna crossed her arms and scowled. "All he wants is for me to stay on the farm and marry somebody *he* thinks will make a good hus-band." Anna shook her head. "Well, that's not what *I* want. Poppa promised me I'd be able to go. Robert has no right to keep that money hostage."

"I know. Your father would have been so proud to know you've been accepted." Uncle Charles's shoulders drooped with the sigh that drifted from his mouth. "Try to see it from his perspective. You've led a sheltered life on the farm, and Robert feels like you aren't ready for what you'll see and have to deal with in a big hospital in New York. You think you'll be able to assist injured and dying people, but it's different when you're right there with somebody's life in your hands. If you find you can't do it, then Robert is out the money for your tuition, not to mention travel and living expenses." He cocked a bushy eyebrow at Anna. "And he doesn't need to be wasting money that can be put to good use on the farm."

"I know. He's told me often enough." Anna smoothed out her skirt and straightened in her seat. "I'm just thankful you came up with a plan that Robert agreed to. Spending the summer with Mrs. Lawson ought to prove I have the grit to handle New York."

"Remember you'll need a good report from Granny Lawson."

Anna smiled. "You don't have to worry about that. I'm going to listen to her and do everything she tells me, no matter how distasteful I think the task is." She clenched her fists in her lap. "When I board that train for New York in the fall, it will all be worth it."

Uncle Charles shook his head and chuckled. "I'll leave New York and all its hustle and bustle to you. I prefer to spend my time right here in these mountains."

Anna let her gaze rove over the trees on either side of the road. "Still, maybe you'll come visit me someday. I can show off the maternity ward!"

He flicked the reins across the horse's back. "I've read a lot about that ward. First one in the country. You'll be fortunate to work there. But don't forget you may see a lot of babies born this summer while you're at Granny's cabin. And there's not a better place in the world to learn about nursing. She can teach you things you would never learn at Bellevue. Listen to her and do what she says and you'll be fine."

Anna nodded. "I will." Her hat slipped to the side, and she reached up and straightened it. "I really can't thank you enough, Uncle Charles.

Everything's coming together just the way I planned it, and nothing—not even Robert—is going to stand in my way."

Uncle Charles sucked in his breath and directed a frown at her. "Nothing? We can only follow the plan God has for us, Anna."

She settled back on the seat and cast her eyes over the hazy hills in front of them. "But that *is* God's plan for me."

"And how do you know?"

"Because it's what I've dreamed about all my life. God's never tried to change my mind."

"Maybe you've never listened to Him." Uncle Charles stared at her a moment. "Like I said, pay attention to what Granny says. She'll teach you how God uses those He's chosen to take care of the sick. It isn't all done with medicine, Anna. A lot of my medical successes—and Granny's as well—have come about after a lot of prayer."

The buggy hit another bump, and Anna bounced straight up. As far as she could see, the rippling Smoky Mountains stretched out toward the horizon. A plume of wispy fog hung over the valleys. A strange world awaited her out there.

Mrs. Johnson, the owner of the inn where they'd stayed in Pigeon Forge last night, had taken great pleasure in warning her of what she might face in Cades Cove this summer. Anna clasped her hands in her lap and glanced at Uncle Charles. "Mrs. Johnson said the folks who live in Cades Cove don't take to strangers."

Uncle Charles nodded. "That doesn't surprise me. What else did she say?"

Anna took a deep breath and brushed at the new layer of dust on her skirt. "Oh, not much. Just that everybody knows it's a closed society in the Cove, but it doesn't matter because no sensible person would want to live there anyway. She called the people there a strange lot."

Uncle Charles cocked an eyebrow and chuckled. "Is that right? I hope you didn't believe her. I know every family in the Cove, and some of them are my good friends." He hesitated a moment. "Of course you're going to find some who cause problems—just like you would anywhere else."

"Like the moonshiners?"

He turned to stare at her with wide eyes. "What did Mrs. Johnson tell you about moonshiners?"

"She said all the men were moonshiners. Are they?"

Uncle Charles threw back his head and laughed as if he'd just heard the funniest joke of his life. After a few seconds he shook his head. "Nothing could be further from the truth. There may be a few who give the Cove people a bad reputation, but most of the men work too hard to waste their time on such nonsense." He reached over and patted her hand. "I wouldn't leave you in a place where you weren't safe. Mrs. Johnson may run a good inn, but she's the worst gossip in these mountains."

Anna heaved a sigh of relief. "I guess I'm just a little nervous. I want everybody to like me."

"They will. Just be yourself and they'll all love you."

Uncle Charles meant well, but doubt still lingered in her mind. Would the people of the Cove accept a stranger into their small community? And if they didn't, what good could she possibly do in this place?

She had to succeed. Her future depended on it. She squared her shoulders. There was no turning back.

As the day wore on, they found themselves deeper in the hills. As they did, a slow awakening began to dawn in the deepest corner of her soul. She'd never seen anything as beautiful as the lush growth that covered the vast mountain range. The air now grew cooler, just as she'd expected it to be, and the sweet smell of mountain laurel mingled with the rhododendrons. As her uncle's horse, Toby, plodded along the rocky trail that grew steeper with each step, she saw the world through new eyes and stared in awe at the wonders of nature unfolding before her.

For the last hour she'd sat silent and watched the shallow river that flowed beside the road. The water bubbled over rocks like huge stepping-stones scattered across its bed, and the rippling sound had a lulling effect. She wished they could stop so she could pull off her shoes and wade in the cold mountain stream, but there was no time for such fun today. She turned her attention back to the steep hillside on the other side of the road.

"It's beautiful here."

Uncle Charles glanced at her. "We're just about to Wear's Valley. When we get there, we'll be close to Cades Cove."

Anna wondered if Uncle Charles was tired of her questions about the Cove. She hoped not. She settled in her seat and said, "Tell me more about Cades Cove, Uncle Charles."

He pushed his hat back on his head and stared straight ahead. "Well, if you've noticed, we've been following that stream as the road's climbed. Pretty soon now we're gonna reach a place where we turn away from it and head into a flat valley right in the middle of the mountains. That's Cades Cove. It's almost like God just took His giant hand and tucked a little piece of heaven right down in the Smokies. The land's fertile—not so many rocks you can't farm—and completely surrounded by mountains. You're gonna love it when you see it, Anna."

"How many people live there?"

He pursed his lips and squinted into the distance. "I'd say there are about two hundred fifty scattered throughout the Cove nowadays. Some left for town life—better work there, you know—but they'll never find a place that's as beautiful as these mountains."

"How far is it from Mrs. Lawson's house to where you live?"

He thought for a moment. "It's not that far as the crow flies, but it takes me almost three hours going around these roads."

A lump formed in her throat. Now that they were closer, she didn't want him to leave. She scooted a little closer to him on the bench of the buggy. "Will you stay at Mrs. Lawson's tonight?"

He shook his head. "No, I'll have enough daylight left to get home. But don't worry, I'll come to the Cove from time to time to check on you. Granny does a good job of taking care of the folks there, but she knows when it's serious enough to send for me."

Anna clasped her hands in her lap to keep him from seeing them tremble. The time had come to begin the test. She *couldn't* fail. She squared her shoulders and lifted her chin. She dredged up all the determination she could muster. No, she *wouldn't* fail.

"How long before we get there, Uncle Charles?"

"Not much longer. The entrance is up ahead."

~

Simon Martin squinted his eyes against the afternoon sun as he tied the reins of his horse to the tree in Granny Lawson's yard. He took off the hat he wore and slapped it across his legs. The dust that billowed up from his pants threatened to choke him. Summer was just beginning and the roads in Cades Cove had already dried, an indication that another hot season lay before them.

He stepped onto the porch of the small house and knocked on the open door. When no one answered, he stepped up closer and peered inside. "Granny, you home?"

For a moment he didn't think she was there, but then he heard a voice coming from the back of the house. He stepped off the porch and hesitated, then smiled. It was Granny's voice, and she was singing. The words drifted on the air like a melody straight from heaven.

He followed the sound. Granny Lawson sat in a straight chair in the shade of the oak tree behind her house, a basket of June apples at her feet. Her forehead wrinkled as she concentrated on peeling the plump apple in her hand. The knife she held made a circular path, and the skin of the fruit dangled below her fingers in one continuous spiral. The words of the hymn the congregation had sung the Sunday before poured from her lips and rang across the yard.

He listened for a moment, watching her. Lines that told of hard work and a difficult life covered the leathery skin of her face. She sat hunched slightly forward, her concentration so focused on the apple that she appeared oblivious to anything else.

Life in the Cove was hard on women. They worked alongside their men, eking out a living in the mountain valley soil and bearing their children. Some buried their babies along the way. He wondered how many funerals of children he'd conducted since he'd come back to the Cove. His mother had buried two before he and then John were born.

No doubt about it. Life in the Cove was hard. But no matter what happened, the people knew there was one person they could always count on—Granny Lawson. Whenever a need arose, she was there.

His gaze dropped to her strong hands—healing hands, they were often called. There was something about her fingers that always caught his attention. Everyone who shook hands with her was surprised to discover she had the grip of a man. Yet those same hands dispensed tenderness and love to all she came in contact with. No woman in the Cove would think of giving birth without Matilda Lawson at her side.

He remembered his grandmother talking about the first white settlers that came after the Cherokee were forced out of their mountain homes. The most loved and respected among them had been the midwives—the granny women of the Cove, as they came to be called. And now Granny Lawson carried on a tradition that had begun many years before. His heart warmed with love for this woman who'd always been like a second mother to him. He cleared his throat and stepped closer. "Making a pie for supper?"

Startled, she looked up and smiled. The delight that flashed in her eyes made him forget his weary afternoon in the saddle and the disappointment he'd had when he tried to talk to Luke Jackson about his need for God in his life.

"Well, it if ain't the preacher come a-callin' to keep me comp'ny," she said.

He walked over to where she sat, reached down in the basket, and pulled out a round green apple. He rubbed the smooth skin across his shirtsleeve and looked up at her. "Mind if I help myself to a bite? I've been riding the Cove all afternoon, and I'm getting mighty hungry."

She motioned toward the house with the hand that held the knife. "Help yourself. Go in the kitchen and git you a chair. Then come set a spell with me. The breeze is nice under this here tree."

Simon shook his head and sat down on the dirt. "The ground is fine. Don't have much time. John and Martha are looking for me to stop at their house for supper. Don't want to be late."

Granny smiled. "How's your brother and that sweet sister-in-law doin'?"

"Fine. Fine. Martha seems to be making it all right."

Granny dropped the peeled apple into a pan at her feet and reached for another one in the basket. "Reckon I'll be makin' my way over to their farm purty soon now." She stopped and thought a moment. "Should be in about two months, I'd say."

Simon nodded. "That's what they tell me."

Granny hesitated before she started on the next apple. "Simon, when you gonna find a nice girl and settle down like John? You need a good woman."

He laughed and chewed on the bite in his mouth. "I'm making it fine by myself, Granny."

A sad expression darkened her eyes. "You kin tell yourself that, but I know better. I see the loneliness in your eyes." She glanced back down at the apple she held. "What ever happened to that gal you was sweet on when you was in school?"

He shrugged, hoping to look as if he'd put the whole matter behind him. "When I had to leave school because my folks were sick, she turned to a good friend of mine. Well, they're married now, and he pastors a church in Knoxville."

She reached out and patted his arm. Leave it to Granny to know the hurt was still fresh. "Then she wasn't the one God has for you. I hope you're not still a-pinin' over her."

"It's not her, Granny. It's just that sometimes I wonder where I would be and what I would be doing if I hadn't come back home."

Granny pinned him with a steady gaze. "You done what you had to do at the time, Simon, and you cain't keep a-worryin' about it. Things happen in God's own good time." Her mouth curled into a smile. "That's why I know there's a girl somewhere out there for you."

Simon leaned over and chucked her under the chin. "Aw, Granny, you know I want a girl just like you. Since you're a little old for me, I guess I'll just have to wait for the next angel to come to the Cove."

Granny laughed and tossed a long strip of apple peel at him. "Hush your mouth, preacher boy. You say that because you know nobody ever moves to the Cove to live, but the Lord's gonna find you somebody. I been a-prayin', and He done told me He's a-workin' on it."

Simon stood up and dusted off the seat of his pants. He frowned and turned his head when his horse nickered in the front yard. "That sounded like a buggy stopping. You expecting anybody today?"

Granny stood up and set the pan aside. She wiped her hands on the apron that covered her long dress and smiled. "That must be Doc Prentiss. He's a-comin' back today from visitin' his brother's family over close to Strawberry Plains. And he's a-bringin' me a new helper, his niece. Come on. Let's go meet 'er."

Granny, her feet raising a little dust cloud, hurried around the side of the house as Simon followed after. As he stepped into the front yard, he stopped and stared. Doc Prentiss had just finished tying his horse to the tree beside Simon's mare. Now the doctor turned toward the young woman who sat in the buggy and offered her his hand. With a smile she hopped to the ground and glanced around at her surroundings. She looked so small standing there, a smile on her lips, her hands clasped as her gaze swept across the mountains surrounding the Cove.

Her blonde hair was pinned underneath a hat with a brim that shaded her face, but Simon could see her blue eyes. She turned back to her uncle, her lilting voice drifting toward him. "You were right, Uncle Charles. This is a beautiful place."

Simon's breath caught in his throat. He'd never seen anyone as lovely in his life. She tilted her head, smiled, and held out her hand as Granny approached.

His heart pumped in his chest and he struggled to breathe. He swallowed and walked toward the young woman. *I think I've just seen an angel*, he thought to himself.

Chapter 2

*A*nna smoothed her dress into place after jumping from the buggy and studied the woman walking toward her. She had imagined her as short and stout with rosy cheeks, but Granny Lawson couldn't have been more different. Her straight back and lean body gave evidence of having known physical labor in her life, and her stride matched the length of any man's. A smile lit her face as she stopped in front of Anna.

Granny Lawson ignored Anna's outstretched hand and her arms encircled her, engulfing her in a tight embrace. "Well, bless my soul. If you're not the purtiest little thing I've ever seen."

"Th-thank you." The hat perched on Anna's head threatened to fall off, and she pried one arm loose to catch it before it toppled to the ground.

Granny Lawson took a step back and held her at arm's length. "Doc Prentiss, you shore was right. She's a-gonna fit right in around here."

Uncle Charles put his arm around Anna's shoulders and smiled down at her. "I think you're right, Granny."

"Oh, thank you," Anna gasped. She grabbed the brim of the hat and pulled it back into place. "Thank you, Mrs. Lawson. I'm so happy..."

"Miz Lawson?" Granny's eyes crinkled at the corners from the grin on her face. "Darlin', don't nobody around here know who

Miz Lawson is. I'm Granny to ev'rybody in these here parts, and I'm Granny to you too."

Anna felt a smile curling her lips. "All right, Granny. And I'm Anna."

Uncle Charles stepped to the back of the buggy and reached for her trunk. "We stayed over at Mrs. Johnson's inn at Pigeon Forge last night. We would have been here earlier, but we didn't get as early a start this morning as I'd hoped."

"And how was Miz Johnson?" Granny's eyes sparkled. "I hope she didn't scare Anna off from comin' here."

Her uncle chuckled and hoisted the trunk to his shoulder. "It would take more than Mrs. Johnson's warnings about the strange folks in the Cove to change Anna's mind." He inclined his head toward the trunk. "I'll take this inside. Where do you want it, Granny?"

She waved her hand toward the house. "Put it in the back room off the kitchen. That's where Anna's gonna be sleepin'." Granny turned and glanced over her shoulder. "Simon, git that there valise and take it inside for Doc Prentiss, but come on over here 'fore you do and meet Anna."

For the first time Anna noticed the young man standing behind Granny. Dust covered his pants and shirt, and he clutched a misshapen hat in his hands. His dark eyes peered at her from underneath long lashes and his dark hair tumbled over his forehead. Her face warmed at his intense stare.

He took a hesitant step forward and stopped in front of her. "Good evening, Miss Prentiss. Welcome to Cades Cove. I know you're gonna like living and working with Granny." He turned to Granny, his white teeth appearing behind his smile. "She was just telling me how glad she was to have a helper."

"Thank you, Mr...."

"Martin. Simon Martin."

She smiled at him. "Thank you for taking my valise inside, Mr. Martin."

"Brother Martin," Granny corrected. "Simon's our preacher."

Anna felt her eyes widen. "You seem so young to be a preacher. And you already have a church?"

Simon laughed, his eyes twinkling. "Yes, but that may be because I grew up in the Cove."

"He don't like to brag, Anna, but he's a real good preacher. And he watches out for the folks in his congregation." Granny's eyes softened, and a smile pulled at her lips. "Don't know what I'd do without him."

Simon reached for the valise and grinned at Granny. "She's one of my biggest supporters, Miss Prentiss, and I have to say I love it."

Granny grabbed Anna's arm and steered her toward the front porch. Inside the house Anna stopped and let her gaze rove over the interior. The sparsely furnished room—perhaps a sitting room?—was a far cry from her mother's parlor at home. Two rockers faced a stone fireplace, and several straight-backed chairs sat to the side of the hearth. But it was the long table against one wall that drew her attention. Dried herbs hung above it on a rope stretched across the wall, and various bottles with medicinal terms painted on the sides lined the back of the table. She picked up one and studied the word printed on it—*morphine*. She held the bottle in front of her eyes and looked at the shape of the pills inside. She set it down and stared at the next two—laudanum and quinine.

Granny Lawson stepped up beside her and picked up the container of laudanum. "This can be mighty helpful when somebody's suff'rin'."

Anna nodded. "I've heard of these drugs, but I didn't think about you having these to work with."

Granny smiled and set the bottle back on the table. "It may look like the folks in the Cove be cut off from the outside world, but we still got the mail a-comin'. And Doc brings me drugs from over to Pigeon Forge or Gatlinburg when he's a-passin' by."

"Oh, I see." Anna turned her attention to the dried herbs hanging above the table. She reached up and touched a bundle. The leaves crunched in her fingers. "How do you know which ones to use?"

Granny chuckled. "It takes a lot of studyin' to know 'em apart, and which ones need boilin' or which need seepin'. My mama taught me, and hers before taught her. I'll be a-workin' to get you able to tell 'em apart 'fore you go out alone."

The words surprised Anna, and she turned to face Granny. "Alone? Surely you won't send me without you."

Granny tilted her head. "Never can tell. We may have two folks needin' help at the same time." She reached for Anna's hand. "But don't go a-worryin' about that now. We got a lot of work to do first."

At that moment Uncle Charles walked back into the room. Her uncle stopped beside her and put his arm around her shoulder. He motioned to the young man she'd just met. "Simon and I got your things settled in the room, Anna. I'd better get on home. I may have messages from patients needing me to come."

Suddenly she didn't want him to go and leave her alone with these strangers. She swallowed her fear and forced herself to remember why she had come. Anna threw her arms around her uncle's neck. "When will I see you again?"

He hugged her. "Granny knows how to get in touch with me if I'm needed. You listen to her and do what she tells you, and you'll be fine." He turned to Simon. "You get by here more than I do, Simon. Hope you'll keep a watch over my girl."

Simon glanced at Anna and smiled. "I'll be glad to help out any way I can, Doc."

Uncle Charles leaned down and kissed her on the forehead. "I'm leaving you in the care of two very trusted friends, Anna. They will take care of you like you're family."

Her lips trembled. "Thank you for everything, Uncle Charles."

He released her and headed toward the porch. Anna followed but stopped at the top of the steps as he untied his horse and climbed into the buggy. She stood there unmoving until he was out of sight. She almost wanted to call him back and tell him she'd made a mistake. Her first glimpse of the drugs and herbs she would be working with made it clear that working with a mountain midwife wasn't for the faint of heart. She was going to be responsible for helping women at the most crucial point in their lives—when they put their own lives at risk to bring new life into the world. Would she be able to do it?

Granny stood beside her and put her arm around Anna's shoulders. "Don't worry. You gonna be fine."

A strange sense of calm settled over Anna, and it seemed to flow from the woman standing beside her. Anna swallowed and managed a weak smile. "I know. Thank you for taking me in."

Granny squeezed Anna's shoulders. "Tell you what. You go on in the house and rest 'til suppertime. You must be pert near worn out from that trip."

Anna shook her head. "I couldn't rest."

Across the road from Granny's house a wildflower-dotted field stretched into the distance. Clouds of the wispy fog that gave the mountain range its name floated on unseen breezes above the gently rolling hills. Anna's heart thudded in her chest. "I've never seen anything so beautiful in my life."

Granny nodded. "I'm glad you like our mountains. Sometimes when I'm tired, I just set out here on my porch and soak 'em up. Then after a while of thinkin' about how God made them a long time ago and left them here for me to look at, I git to feelin' so good I think I can do anything I set my mind to." She glanced at Simon and grinned. "Even run a footrace with Simon."

A surge of energy shot through Anna. "I know what you mean. I can feel it too. But please, let me help you with whatever you were doing when we got here."

"Well, I was a-peelin' some June apples out back."

Anna looked down at the dress she wore. The dust of travel still clung to it. "Let me change my dress, and I'll do that for you."

Granny nodded and glanced at Simon, who had stood silent while Anna studied the beauty around her. "I left the pan under the tree. Simon, you want to keep Anna comp'ny whilst I start fixin' supper? You can tell her about the folks 'round here."

Simon smiled at Anna. "Be happy to, Granny."

Anna glanced at him. "Thank you, Brother Martin."

His face broke into a big smile, and he threw back his head and laughed. "Just call me Simon. Everybody else does."

Anna smiled at him. "All right. Simon, then."

Granny had turned to reenter the house, but she stopped and faced them. "Say, preacher boy, we don't want to make you miss supper over at John and Martha's."

He waved his hand in dismissal. "Oh, they never know if I'll be there or not. I get delayed all the time."

"Well, in that case, wanna stay for supper here?"

"I'd like that, Granny."

She arched her eyebrows and motioned for Anna to follow her inside. "I figured you would."

~

Simon sat on the ground, the knife Granny had given him in his hand, and concentrated on the apple he was peeling. He stole a glance at Anna every once in a while and studied her face as she worked. He'd never seen a complexion so creamy in his life. Her skin didn't have the weathered look of the women who lived in the Cove.

His gaze drifted to the apple in Anna's hand, and for the first time he noticed dark stains on her fingers and around her nails. She glanced up, saw him staring at her fingers, and blushed. "Mama and I picked strawberries and made jam the day before I left home. I tried rubbing vinegar on my hands, but I couldn't get rid of the stains."

"My mother used to make blackberry jam. She'd always say her stained hands were a sign of hard work for the people she loved the most."

Anna smiled. "That's a lovely thought." She paused before continuing. "You speak of her as if she's no longer with you."

He shook his head. "She died three years ago." Simon smiled as he thought of her. She'd stood less than five feet tall, but she worked from sunup until long after dark taking care of her family. She'd been the one to read the Bible as they sat at the kitchen table, the oil lamp casting its glow across the pages of the book her parents had passed down to her.

Simon shook his head. This was no time for remembering the past. Lately, though, his memories had come more often. He cleared his throat and picked up another apple. "So, Miss Prentiss, what made you come to Cades Cove?"

A smile pulled at her lips. "Miss Prentiss? How do you expect me to call you Simon if you're going to call me Miss Prentiss?"

He tried to ignore the teasing quality in her voice. He frowned, directed his gaze to the apple, and sliced into it. "I didn't want to take that liberty unless you approved. After all, we just met."

She laughed, and the tinkle of it sounded like bells chiming in the trees. "We did indeed, but please call me Anna. I hope we're going to be good friends."

"I do too." The blade nicked his finger and he dropped the knife. Blood trickled from his finger, and a sharp intake of breath escaped his lips.

Anna set her pan of apples on the ground and reached for his hand. "Let me see."

She bent closer to look and her fingers curled around his hand. Her hair gleamed in the sunlight, and the urge to touch the spun gold before his eyes welled up in him. Suddenly she straightened. "That doesn't look too bad." She reached in the pocket of her dress, pulled out a handkerchief, and wrapped it around his finger.

Her action shocked him. He tried to pull away, but she held his hand tight in her grip. "It's bleeding," he said. "You'll ruin your handkerchief."

"Don't worry. I have others." Her long eyelashes flickered as she gazed at him. "I suppose you're my first patient."

His heart fluttered at the touch of her fingers wrapped around his. He slipped free of her grasp. "Then I'm honored to have your hand-kerchief wrapped around my wound. I'll testify to all the folks in the Cove that you're going to make a mighty fine nurse."

She gave the bandage one last inspection before she picked up the pan again. "I have to confess I'm a little scared about meeting every-one. I hope they'll like me."

He was thankful for the distance she'd put between them. It was hard to think clearly when she was touching him. He took a deep breath and willed his heart to return to its normal beat. "I'm sure they will. The folks around here have a reputation for not accepting outsiders, but they just want strangers to prove themselves first. Show them you're not afraid of hard work and you'll earn their respect. Once they get to know you, they'll open their hearts and homes to you. Especially the women, when they need you."

Her eyes grew bright. "Then I suppose I should get ready for some hard work."

Simon tightened the handkerchief on the cut and glanced back at her. "You never did answer my question about why you came to the Cove."

She hesitated for a moment, a distant look clouding her eyes. Then she let out a long breath. "There's a hospital in New York—Bellevue Hospital—with a nurse training program. My father told me he'd pay for me to attend, so I applied there two years ago but didn't get accepted. This year I reapplied, and I've been accepted for the fall."

"Congratulations. You must be excited."

Her frown deepened. "Well, things have changed in the last two years. My father died, and now my brother is head of the family. He doesn't think I have what it takes to make it in a big city like New York, and he won't give me the money for school."

"So what does that have to do with you coming to Cades Cove?"

"Uncle Charles talked him into letting me spend the summer with Granny to see if she thinks I'll be able to stand up under the pressure of a big city hospital. If she gives me a good report, Robert will give me the money and I'll leave for nursing school."

For some reason her words saddened him. He pulled up a blade of grass and stuck it in his mouth. "So you're only here for the summer?"

Anna dropped the apple she'd just peeled into the pan. "Yes. Then I'm off to New York. I'm hoping I'll get to see Granny deliver at least one baby while I'm here. And after I graduate, I would love to work in the maternity ward at Bellevue."

The muscle in Simon's jaw twitched as his fingers tightened around the fruit in his hand. "It seems you have your life planned out."

Her eyes narrowed as she stared toward the mountains in the distance. "I do. I'm going to show my brother he's wrong about me. I do have what it takes to be a nurse. I've known it ever since I was a little girl." After a moment, she took a deep breath and directed a smile at him. "And what about you? How long are you going to stay in Cades Cove?"

The question surprised him, but it was the answer that rankled his spirit. "I doubt I'll ever leave."

She looked at him in surprise. "You don't sound too happy about that."

His face grew warm, and he directed his attention back to the apple he held. "I didn't mean to sound that way. You couldn't ask for a more beautiful place to live."

"You're right about that. Where's your home?"

"About a mile from here. My brother and I both have homes on the farm our parents left us. John and his wife live in the house where we grew up, and I live in what was supposed to be John's honeymoon cabin."

Her eyes grew wide. "Honeymoon cabin? What's that?"

The shocked expression on her face made Simon laugh. "It's been a tradition in the Cove for families to build a cabin near their house for their children to live in when they get married. They're called honeymoon cabins, and Pa had just finished one for my brother when he and Ma died. After John and Martha married, they took the main house and I moved into the cabin. I expect you'll be meeting my brother's wife soon. Granny's been tending her, and her time's coming up in about two months. Maybe you'll get to help when their baby is born."

Anna dropped another peeled apple in the pan. "Maybe so. Your family must be excited about the arrival of a new baby. But tell me about your wife."

Simon swallowed and glanced away. "I don't have one."

She let out a choked cackle before she dissolved into giggles. He stared into eyes that sparkled with a mischievous glint. "An unmarried man living alone in a honeymoon cabin? That's the funniest thing I've ever heard."

A sheepish grin pulled at his lips. "I suppose it is." He debated on whether to ask the question that had been in his mind since he first saw her. Licking his lips, he spoke. "And you? Is there someone special in your life?"

Anna wiped at the tears of laughter at the corners of her eyes and shook her head. "No. My brother and mother wanted me to marry the boy who lived on the next farm. He practically grew up at our house, but I knew I wasn't cut out to spend my days on another farm. New York is where I want to be. They have electric streetlights and there are people everywhere. I want to be able to choose which store I shop in and which restaurant I eat in. I can't imagine living anywhere else."

He had never heard such determination in anyone's voice before, and he hoped she would be as happy in the city as she thought she'd be. But experience had taught him reality didn't always live up to expectations. He'd wanted to pastor a church in a city, but God had brought him back to Cades Cove. In so doing, his dream of preaching to large congregations and bringing many souls to God had vanished. "I hope it works out for you."

Anna opened her mouth to speak, but before she could respond Granny Lawson appeared at the back door. "You two got enough ready so I can cook some pan-fried apples for supper?"

Anna grabbed the pan and jumped to her feet. "Sure, Granny. I'll bring them."

Simon watched her run toward the house and struggled to calm his racing pulse. A warning to tread carefully where Anna Prentiss was concerned flashed in his mind. He'd just met her, and yet he felt drawn to her like no other woman he'd ever known.

The fact that he was a preacher was probably the reason for this strange feeling that filled him. It was his job to help all the people in the Cove. For the next few months she would be attending his church, and he hoped he could provide her with any spiritual guidance she needed—just as he did for everyone else in the Cove.

But even as he tried to convince himself that his interest in Anna was related to his calling to serve God, he knew it wasn't true. The feelings she'd stirred in him weren't the same as he'd experienced when helping others in his congregation. He felt something different for Anna Prentiss. Something new.

Chapter 3

*A*nna scraped the last bite of supper from her plate and popped it in her mouth. Maybe it was the mountain air or the long trip, but the simple food had been better than she could have imagined. Mountain cooking might be different than her mother's, but Granny's meal ranked right up there with the best she'd ever eaten. She laid the fork on her plate and pushed back from the table. "Granny, that was delicious."

Granny chuckled. "Twarn't nothin' fancy."

Anna glanced at the empty bowls on the table and smiled. Nothing could have topped the fresh mountain greens Granny had gathered from the surrounding hillsides. The pan-fried apples, sweet corn relish, and greens cooked with hog jowl had made a meal fit for a king. "If this meal is an indication of what you have, then I'm in for a treat this summer."

Granny pushed to her feet and began to stack their plates. "Well, I reckon we make out all right when it comes to eatin'. The good Lord's done provided us with game to hunt and fish in our streams, and we spend the summer a-layin' up food from our gardens. But them fresh greens shore did taste good after eatin' canned food all winter."

Across the table from her, Simon leaned back in his chair and patted his stomach. "Granny's one of the best cooks in the Cove. You can always depend on a good meal at her house."

Granny arched an eyebrow and turned toward the dry sink. "Is that why you always come a-visitin' late in the afternoon? So's you can eat?"

Simon rose from his chair and gathered up several bowls. He winked at Anna. "I guess she's caught on to me."

He stopped beside Granny, and she reached up and patted him on the shoulder. "You come anytime you want, preacher boy. I'll share whatever I got."

Anna studied the two as they joked back and forth. It was plain to see they shared a special relationship. They had kept up a lively conversation throughout supper, no doubt to make her feel welcome, and it had worked. Uncle Charles had been right about this being a peaceful place. The only sounds she'd heard since arriving were the birds that flew into the trees around the cabin and Granny's horse in the ramshackle barn behind her home. With a full stomach and the quiet night surrounding the cabin, she had a feeling she would sleep well.

Anna jumped to her feet, picked up the pitcher from the table, and carried it to Granny. "Let me help wash the dishes."

Granny turned from the dry sink in the corner of the kitchen and glanced back at the table. "Simon, if you'll bring the rest of the dishes from the table, I'll wash 'em and Anna can dry. Won't take but a few minutes with all of us a-workin'."

And indeed, it wasn't long before Granny was handing the last pot to her. Anna dried it and set it on the table with the other clean dishes. "If you'll show me where these go, I'll put them up."

Granny shook her head. "No need for that. Won't take me but a minute to put 'em away. You and Simon take a seat in the other room. I'll be along 'fore you know it."

Anna glanced at Simon and then headed to the room where the dried herbs hung. As they entered the front room, as Granny called it, Anna noticed the door that had been open when she arrived was now closed. Simon stopped beside her and motioned to one of the chairs. "Have a seat, and I'll see if I can stir the fire up. It may be June, but it still gets cool at night. Our fireplaces will be burning for a few weeks yet."

"I noticed someone had closed the door."

He picked up a poker, knelt in front of the fireplace, and began to stir the embers that smoldered there. "In the summertime, the cabin doors are left open during the day to let the air circulate through the house. At night we close them." He glanced up and grinned. "We don't want any bears walking in while we're sleeping."

Anna stiffened and stared at him. "B-b-bears?"

"Oh, yes. They're all around here. But don't worry. They're almost as afraid of you as you are of them." He pulled the poker from the fireplace and pointed it at her. "Remember I said *almost* as afraid."

"I will."

He chuckled. "Don't look so scared. You probably won't even see one this summer." He turned back to the fire and nestled a log into the glowing embers. Flames began to lick at the underside of the wood.

"Did I hear somebody mention bears? Simon, you tryin' to scare Anna on her first night here?" Granny wagged her finger at Simon as she entered the room.

Simon flashed a grin in Anna's direction, but she caught the mischievous glint in his eye that he couldn't hide. It reminded her of how her brother used to tease her when they were younger. "Sorry, Anna. I'll be nice."

Granny walked to the fireplace and turned her back to it. She held her hands behind her toward the flame and smiled. "That feels mighty good."

Simon placed the poker back on the stone hearth and pointed to the other chair. "You and Anna can sit here and get acquainted. I need to be getting on home."

Granny glanced from him to Anna. "Don't go rushin' off on my account, boy."

He shook his head. "It's late, and I'm supposed to go hunting with Will Parrish tomorrow morning. If I kill a rabbit, I'll bring it to you to cook." He stepped to Granny and gave her a kiss on the cheek. "Thanks for supper."

"My pleasure, but you don't have…"

"Granny, I need help!" A fist pounded on the front door, and then there came a scratching sound as if someone was pulling on the latch.

Fear rose in her throat and Anna gripped the edge of the chair. Granny's mouth turned down at the corners, and she shook her head. "That sounds like Luke Jackson. What's he wantin' this time of night?"

Simon's hands balled into fists and he strode toward the door. "I don't know. Let me handle this."

Anna jumped to her feet and whirled at the moment Simon pulled the door open. His back filled the opening, and she couldn't see who stood on the porch. She inched closer to Granny, who reached out and grasped her hand. "It's all right, Anna. Jest one of the Cove fellers. Must be hurtin'."

"What do you want, Luke?" The sharp edge of Simon's voice sent chills down her back.

"I got hurt. I needs to see Granny. She here?" The words were so slurred Anna had trouble distinguishing one from the next.

Her mouth dropped open, and she directed a wide-eyed stare toward Granny. "Is he drunk?"

Granny's grip on her hand tightened. "Yes, but don't worry."

"How'd you get hurt, Luke?" Simon asked.

"This feller thought I was a-cheatin' him and pulled a knife."

"You've been playing cards and drinking over at that tavern at Wear's Valley again, haven't you? Just this afternoon I talked to you about staying away from that place, and you said you had promised Naomi you wouldn't go back there."

"I know, Simon. I shoulda stayed home like you said. I tried to leave, but one of 'em held me whilst t'other one cut me. Honest, Simon. It weren't my fault." Now the words were not only slurred but had a whine to them.

"It never is to hear you tell it, Luke." A sigh rippled from Simon's mouth.

Granny let go of Anna's hand and walked over to Simon. "Let 'im in. I'll see what I can do."

They stepped away from the door and a man staggered into the room. One eye was swollen shut, and underneath the other was a nasty-looking gash. Blood covered the front of his shirt and dripped onto the dirty pants he wore. Anna's stomach roiled at the smell of whiskey and cheap perfume that filled the room.

He only made it a few steps into the room before his legs gave way and he sagged downward. Simon caught him before he hit the floor and pulled him to his feet. Granny grabbed the other arm and helped support his weight.

"Let's put 'im on the kitchen table," she said. She glanced at Anna. "There's water in the kettle on the stove. Pour some in a pan and git some cloths out of that chest in the corner of the kitchen. I'm gonna be needin' you to help." Anna stood frozen in place as Simon and Granny pulled the man forward. Granny frowned at her and jerked her head in the direction of the kitchen. "This man's a-bleedin' bad, Anna."

Anna took a deep breath and ran to the kitchen. Behind her she heard them enter the room and the thud of the man's body tumbling to the top of the table. She didn't look around until she had the pan of water in her hands and the cloths draped over her arm.

Simon had positioned himself at the man's head, but Granny stood beside the table as she cut the man's shirt from his body. Anna stepped to the other side and held the water for when Granny needed it.

When Granny pulled the shirt free, she muttered something under her breath. Then she took a deep breath. "It 'pears that Luke took quite a beatin' tonight. You think he'd learn his lesson."

Only then did Anna glance down. Blood matted the black hair that curled across his chest. His rib cage rose and fell with each breath. And with each pump of his heart, fresh blood poured from a gaping wound that ran from the edge of his right armpit to his navel. Her fingers tightened on the warm pan of water in her hands and she swallowed back the bile that rose in her throat. She swayed on her feet.

"Are you all right, Anna?" Simon's concerned voice floated to her from far away.

She nodded and directed her attention back to Granny, who

glanced up at her. "I'm gonna have to sew this here cut up. Whilst I'm a-gettin' my kit, you wash this wound out real careful, Anna. I kin see all kinds of trash down in there. They must've rolled 'im on the ground after they cut 'im up. I don't want to git nothin' in there that'll make infection set up." She paused and studied Anna's face. "Kin you do that?"

Anna tried to force a smile to her face and nodded. "Yes."

Setting the water on the table near the man's head, Anna dipped the cloth in, squeezed it, and inched it toward the open wound. She leaned closer to study the gash and began to wipe at the blood that poured across her fingers. A piece of what looked like tree bark lay inside the wound, and she caught it between the thumb and index finger of her left hand.

A growl followed by an angry curse roared from the man's mouth as she pulled it free. His eyes flew open, and he glared at her. He exhaled a deep breath, and the sour smell of whiskey that drifted up made her retch. Before she could move, his eyes narrowed, and his left hand circled her wrist in a vise-like grip.

"What you tryin' to do, woman? Kill me?"

Anna gritted her teeth and tried to jerk free, but she only succeeded in knocking the pan of water to the floor. Simon's hand snaked across the table and pried the man's hand from her arm. "Let her go, Luke."

The man's fingers loosened, and his head lolled to the side. "Sorry, Simon. Didn't mean no harm."

Simon released his grip. "Yeah, that's something else you always say." He glanced at Anna. "Are you all right?"

She shrank against the pie safe on the wall behind her, rubbed her wrist, and nodded. Tears flooded her eyes and ran down her face. She glanced back at the man on the table, then to the blood on her hands, and backed away. Nausea rose from her stomach. She grabbed one of the cloths from the edge of the table and clamped it over her mouth.

Turning, she ran out the back door into the cool night. She made it to the side of the cabin before she could go no further. She gagged but couldn't repress the sick feeling any longer. Minutes later she sagged against the side of the house, her stomach now empty of the supper she'd enjoyed.

There was a sour taste in her mouth, but worse than the taste of bile was the shame at what had happened in Granny's kitchen. How would she ever face Granny and Simon again? After a moment she pushed away from the house and stumbled toward the well.

She drew a bucket of water and set it on the ground. Bending over, she cupped some water in her hand and rinsed her mouth. Then she scooped up a handful and splashed it in her face. After another drenching, she turned back toward the house but stopped.

She couldn't go inside as long as Simon was here. She didn't want him to hear the things Granny was going to say to her. Walking to the tree where she and Simon had sat earlier, she dropped to the ground, circled her knees with her arms, and pulled them up under her chin. Maybe her dress would be dry by the time Simon left.

How long she sat there she didn't know. What seemed like hours passed before she heard footsteps leaving the kitchen and the sound of voices from the front of the house. She stood up and crept toward the back door in hopes of entering the house undetected. The kitchen proved to be empty and she slipped inside.

Tiptoeing to the door that led to the front room, she listened to Granny and Simon talking on the front porch. "You sure you kin make it home with 'im on his horse?"

"I'll have to. I keep thinking if I had stayed longer at Luke's house this afternoon, he might not have gone over to Wear's Valley. Maybe I could have kept this from happening."

A snort of disgust rumbled from Granny's throat. "You gotta quit thinkin' like that, Simon. Luke is a grown man, and he makes his own decisions. All you kin do is talk to 'im and pray."

"I do pray for him, and I pray for Naomi and the children too. She'll be worried if he doesn't come home."

"I reckon she will be, but land's sakes, I don't know why. This man gives her more grief than any woman ought to have to live with."

"I know, Granny, but he's her husband. Tell Anna goodbye for me, and tell her I'll see her tomorrow."

"I'll do that."

Anna turned and ran to her bedroom. She didn't want to hear Granny tell Simon what a disappointment she was. Granny probably already regretted allowing her to come. Closing the bedroom door behind her, she threw herself on the bed and buried her face in the goose-down pillow.

A breeze blew through the open window, reminding her of other summer nights when she was a child and she would be tired from playing all day. She would fall asleep on the parlor sofa and Poppa would pick her up in his strong arms and carry her to her bedroom. She wished she could be a little girl again. She had been happy then. She'd thought she could accomplish anything she dreamed about. Tonight she had learned that wasn't true.

A soft tap at the door made her sit up on the bed. Granny's voice drifted through the door. "You all right, Anna?"

"I…I'm fine."

"You sleep well, and don't worry 'bout tonight. We'll talk in the mornin'."

"You sleep well too."

Fresh tears rolled down her cheek. She could imagine what they would talk about in the morning. Granny would tell her she wasn't cut out to be a nurse, and she would send for Uncle Charles to come take her home. Then she'd have to face Robert and tell him he'd been right all along. She didn't have the grit it took to be a nurse.

That thought sliced through her heart, and she fell back on the pillow and buried her face again. She wanted to learn to help people who were hurt and sick, but tonight she had failed in her first attempt. If by some chance Granny let her stay, which she hoped with all her heart she would, she had no idea if she could do what was expected.

In the front room herbs hung on the wall, and drugs she would never be able to tell apart sat on the table. She'd thought she would only be watching and learning, but Granny had hinted that she might have to perform procedures by herself. *I'm not ready for that*, Anna thought. *I'll never be ready for that.*

Perhaps the most troubling thing about her failure tonight was the fact that Simon had witnessed it. There was a quality about him that had made her like him from the very first moment they met. She'd never talked as freely or felt so at ease with any man as she had when they sat under the tree and peeled apples.

She thought of his cut finger and how she'd held his hand. Even though she'd told him he was her first patient, her racing heart was not that of a nurse helping someone in pain. That emotion scared her more than anything else that had happened tonight.

If Granny did let her stay, and she was prepared to beg for the chance, she had to be careful. Right now the most important thing she could do was salvage what was left of her dignity and work to prove her brother wrong. She couldn't afford to let anything else distract her.

Chapter 4

*A*nna had been awake for an hour, but she couldn't make herself open the door of the room where she'd slept. The smell of
baked biscuits drifted from the kitchen, and her stomach growled
with hunger. She closed her eyes and leaned her forehead against the
door. At some point she was going to have to face Granny and take
the tongue-lashing she deserved. She couldn't put off the inevitable
much longer.

What had made her think she could be a nurse? After her complete
failure to help with an emergency last night, she feared Robert was
right in refusing to let her go to New York. If Granny sent her packing today, she would have to put up with his I-told-you-so for the rest
of her life. Facing Granny couldn't be worse than living with Robert's
smug attitude about her failure.

Robert had no regard for her wishes or what she thought. She'd lost
count of how many times he'd told her he knew what was best for her.
Even Mama had been unable to make him see that at times he went
too far in his attempts at assuming Poppa's role.

If Granny sent her home, she knew what her fate would be. With no
money of her own and no way of escaping the farm, the only thing left
for her to do was marry whomever Robert picked out. Anna shook her
head. She *couldn't* go back to that way of life. No, she *wouldn't* go back.

She opened her eyes, straightened to her full height, and clenched
her fists at her side. It was time to face Granny's wrath and try to

persuade her that last night would never happen again. No matter how frightened she was, she had to convince Granny to let her stay, and the conversation could be put off no longer.

Anna took a deep breath and pushed the door open. From where she stood she could see Granny bent over the iron cookstove. A soft hum from Granny's lips rode the stove's heat waves radiating throughout the room, and the sound drifted to Anna's ears. As she listened, the mellow tones encircled her and wrapped her in what felt to her like arms of love. The fear from just moments ago vanished, and in its place Anna felt a yearning like she'd never known.

She didn't want to go home, not just because it meant she would have to face Robert but because it would mean leaving Granny. From the moment she'd walked into this small cabin and spied the herbs on the wall, she had sensed there were great mysteries about healing to be learned here. If she left, she would never get the chance to glimpse the vast knowledge Granny had acquired as she tended the sick and dying. She would never see babies born or give comfort to those sick and dying. Birth to death and all that came between. That's what she yearned for more than anything else in her life.

Easing into the room she stopped beside the kitchen table, already set for two people. A plate of biscuits and a jar of molasses sat in the middle of table where Luke Jackson had lain last night. Anna swallowed back the nausea that roiled in her stomach at the memory of what had occurred here. How long had it taken Granny to scrub the table clean of Luke Jackson's blood? Anna shivered at the thought. She should have helped with the task. Instead she had cowered in her room, afraid to face Granny's wrath.

Now as she studied the woman who'd taken her into her home, she realized she should have recognized the understanding and concern she'd heard in Granny's voice last night when she stopped outside the door to tell her goodnight. A lump formed in Anna's throat. She reached out, wrapped her fingers around the back of one of the chairs, and took a deep breath. The events of last night couldn't be undone, but now she had to concentrate on a new beginning in Cades Cove. "Good morning, Granny."

Granny glanced over her shoulder and smiled. "Good mornin', Anna. These here eggs will be ready in a minute. Go ahead and take a seat."

Anna slid into the chair where she'd sat at supper and waited for Granny to join her. The hunger she'd felt a few minutes ago had now dissolved into cold fear flowing through her veins. Granny set a platter of ham and eggs on the table between them and took her seat.

Granny opened her mouth to say something, but before she could speak, Anna interrupted her. "Granny, I'm so sorry…"

Granny's eyes widened, and she held up a hand. "Whatever you've got to say can wait until after we say thanks. After all, the good Lord's done blessed us with this here food today, and I'm feelin' mighty thankful for it."

"Yes, Granny." Anna swallowed the words she'd intended to say and bowed her head.

"Dear Lord," Granny began, "we thank You for this here food You gave us to eat and all the other blessin's You done given us here in the Cove. I thank You, God, for a-bringin' this fine young woman to my cabin. I know she's got a lot to learn, but her uncle's done told me she's got the gift of healing in her hands. And I believe that, Lord, because You done told me the same thing in my heart. I know I ain't as smart as the teachers she's gonna have in New York, but I know with Your help I can teach her how to trust herself when she's in bad situations like the one we had last night. I believe You have big plans for Anna, Lord, and I pray we can help her overcome her doubts and get her started on her way to makin' a mighty fine nurse. Amen."

Anna sat in stunned silence, unable to open her eyes or lift her head. After a moment she glanced up at Granny, who was concentrating on spreading some blackberry jam on a biscuit. Anna cleared her throat.

"I…I don't know what to say. I expected you to send me packing this morning. I was prepared to beg you to let me stay."

Granny placed the biscuit on her plate and smiled at her. "Darlin', I started helpin' the folks in Cades Cove when I was younger than you. My ma was a midwife, and she taught me everything she knew. The first time I went with her to help birth a baby I ran out of the house and went home. I dreaded facing my ma because I'd shamed her in front of folks, and I was afraid she'd never forgive me."

"What happened?"

Granny smiled. "When she got home, I was a-layin' on my bed cryin'. She came in and sat down beside me and stroked my head. She said she knew how hard it was for a young girl to see what I'd seen that day, and she said she did the same thing the first time she helped her ma."

Anna's eyes grew wide. "She did?"

Granny chuckled. "Yeah. I told her I didn't have no gift, and I wasn't goin' back to no birthin' agin. She jest laughed and said I would because the need to help folks was in my blood, and I couldn't git rid of it no matter what I did." Granny's eyes softened. "And we gonna find out if it's in your blood too, Anna."

Tears welled in Anna's eyes. "Do you think it is, Granny?"

Granny leaned back in her chair and tilted her head to one side. "I cain't rightly tell yet, 'cause I ain't a-judgin' you on what happened last night, but I'll know by the time you leave here. If you really want to be a nurse as bad as you say, then you have to believe in yourself. You have to understand there's gonna be some tough times down the road, and you have to trust in the good Lord to help you face those times."

A tear spilled from Anna's left eye and trickled down her cheek. "Then you're not giving up on me yet and sending me home?"

Granny threw back her head and laughed. "'Course not, child. I ain't in the givin' up business. We gotta git you ready to go to New York."

Anna jumped to her feet, darted around the table, and knelt beside Granny. Tears gushed from her eyes as she bent over and laid her head in Granny's lap. "Thank you. I promise I won't let you down again."

Granny's hand stroked Anna's head, and her touch reminded Anna of how her mother had comforted her in the past. She'd always wanted to please her mother, and now she found herself determined to please a woman she'd known for less than twenty-four hours. Something told her, though, that this midwife who lived in a small cabin in a remote valley of the Smoky Mountains might turn out to be the person who influenced her life more than anyone else.

Anna raised her head and stared at Granny, who smiled down at her. "Those biscuits smell good, and I'm starved."

"Then let's eat, and then we'll get to work. We got lots to do if'n we gonna get you ready to go to New York, and time's a-wastin'."

～

Simon stopped at the front door of Granny's cabin and peered inside. He raised his hand to knock but stopped at the sound of laughter coming from the back of the house. The voices of Granny and Anna drifted from the kitchen, and Simon sighed with relief.

All the way to the cabin, he'd wondered what he would find after the events of last night. He knew Granny would do everything in her power to encourage Anna, but he had no idea how Anna would react. She might even want to leave. That thought troubled him, and he had no idea why it should. After all, they'd only met yesterday afternoon, and he barely knew her. But his heart told him he wanted to get to know her better.

He said a quick prayer that God would allow him to do that and took a deep breath. "Granny," he called out, "it's Simon. I brought a rabbit for you."

Footsteps shuffled on the wooden floor and Granny appeared in the doorway. She smiled and wiped her hands on her apron. "Come on in, preacher boy. Me and Anna's havin' us some breakfast. You can eat with us."

Simon shook his head. "No, thanks, Granny. I ate a long time ago, but I would like to have a cup of coffee if you've got any."

Granny chuckled and motioned for him to come inside. "There's a pot on the stove. Pete Ferguson brought me back some when he went over to Pigeon Forge a few weeks back. I been savin' it for when Anna got here, and you can help us drink it."

He held up the burlap sack he carried. "I killed you a rabbit this morning. I'll take this around back and wash up at the well before I come inside."

Granny nodded. "Fine. Come on in the back door when you git finished. We'll be in the kitchen."

Simon hurried to the smokehouse and set the burlap sack inside before he went to the well. He glanced down at the dirt-streaked pants and shirt he'd worn into the woods this morning and frowned. He looked a mess, not like a man who hoped to impress a woman.

His hands froze in midair, and the water he'd scooped up to wash his face trickled between his fingers. Impress a woman? He had no idea where that thought had come from. There was no reason to believe Anna Prentiss could ever be interested in him. She'd told him right away what her plans were, and he could tell from the determination on her face that nothing was going to get in her way. If he had any thoughts about her, he'd better get them out of his head right now.

The only problem was…he didn't know how to do that.

He recalled the scene in the kitchen the night before and shook his head. She wasn't like the other women in Cades Cove, whose harsh life had made them strong. Maybe it was best if she did leave the Cove. He doubted if she had what it took to survive here.

Scooping up more water, he doused his face and slicked back his wet hair. He'd go in the kitchen, have a cup of coffee with Granny, then be on his way. He had more important things to do today than worry about a spoiled woman who couldn't stand the sight of blood.

He strode to the kitchen door and stopped before he entered. Anna, holding a cup of coffee in her hand, sat at the table. She was smiling up at Granny, who stood beside her. The laugh he'd thought sounded like tinkling bells drifted to his ears.

Simon didn't move as his gaze roved over Anna's face. His heart raced and his chest tightened. In that instant he knew it didn't matter whether or not Anna was spoiled or if she wasn't like the other women in the Cove. There were unfamiliar feelings taking root in his heart, and they had to do with Anna. Looking at her stirred him in a way he had thought was for other men, not for him. Now he knew differently. He'd never met anyone like Anna, and he prayed she wouldn't leave before he could come to grips with his feelings.

~

Anna set her coffee cup down and glanced toward the back door where Simon stood. The intensity in his eyes made her face grow warm, and she wondered if he was remembering how she'd run from the kitchen the night before. She forced a smile to her face. "Good morning, Simon. I hear you've killed a rabbit."

He stepped into the kitchen, glanced at Granny, and nodded. "I left it in the smokehouse. I'll dress it for you before I leave."

"Then you'll come back and help us eat it tonight?" Granny grinned at him.

Anna laughed at the flush in Simon's cheeks. He turned to her and chuckled. "So you think that's funny, Miss Prentiss? Well, just for that, I'll be here."

"I didn't doubt that for a minute, Reverend Martin." Anna tilted her head to the side and a grin tugged at her lips. She walked to the door and picked up the basket that hung on a peg on the wall. "This man looks like he had to chase that rabbit down a creek, Granny. You feed him, and I'll go gather the eggs for you."

She glanced over her shoulder before she stepped outside and chuckled at how the flush on Simon's face had deepened. Swinging the basket in her hand, she fairly skipped across the backyard to the henhouse. She didn't know when she'd ever felt so good in her life.

A few minutes later she stepped out of the small shed that housed Granny's few chickens. Simon, his arms crossed, was leaning against the side of the building. He straightened when she exited and smiled. "So you think I look like I've been wading in a creek. And after I spent all morning trying to put food on your table."

Anna let her gaze drift over his dirty pants and shirt. "Then I suppose I should thank you instead of making fun."

"You should if you don't want me to think you're an ungrateful woman."

His eyes twinkled as he spoke, and the way he looked at her made her heart skip a beat. Then she remembered what had happened last night. Her eyebrows drew down across her nose. "I'm not ungrateful, Simon, but I am sorry about the way I acted last night. And I'm especially sorry you had to see me like that."

His smile disappeared, and he shook his head. "Granny told me the two of you had talked about it this morning. Don't think about it again. Try to focus on what's ahead of you here, not what's behind you."

She nodded. "I'm going to try to do that. I don't want to let Granny down." She took a deep breath. "And not you either. I wouldn't want to disappoint you."

His dark eyes bored into her. "You could never disappoint me, Anna. If I can help you in any way while you're here, let me know."

"I will. It's good to have a pastor who is also your friend."

His shoulders slumped, and he exhaled. "I hope..." Surprise flickered on his face as he gazed past her. Before she could ask what had startled him, he sidestepped her. "Matthew, what are you doing here?"

Anna whirled to see a young boy walking around the side of the cabin. His black hair hung over his ears and down his neck. He looked as if he hadn't had a haircut in a long time. His dark eyes flitted from Simon to her and then back to Simon. He held a basket in his hand.

"Ma sent Granny a fresh loaf of bread."

The boy moved closer, and Anna thought something about him looked familiar. Simon nodded. "That was mighty nice of your mother. Granny's in the kitchen. Do you want to give it to her, or do you want me to?"

He glanced at the back door. "Thanks, but if it's all the same to you, I reckon I better give it to her myself." He took a step toward the house but stopped and turned back to Simon. "Ma said if'n I ran into you I was to thank you kindly for bringing Pa home last night."

Anna sucked in her breath. Now she knew why the boy looked familiar. He was Luke Jackson's son.

Beside her, Simon spoke. "I was glad I could help. How's he feeling this morning?"

Matthew shrugged. "Not good, but I reckon he's gonna live." He turned an expressionless face toward Anna and stared at her for a moment. His intent gaze suggested he was trying to make up his mind whether or not she belonged in the Cove. Maybe he and his father had already had a good laugh about how she had run like a scared rabbit the night before. On second thought, she decided that couldn't be. This boy didn't give the appearance of one who found too much to laugh about. Whatever he was thinking, his somber gaze told her his life hadn't been easy. It was as if an invisible veil covered his features and blocked the escape of any inner emotion.

With a glance at Simon, he stepped to the back door. "Granny, it's Matthew Jackson."

Anna waited until the boy disappeared into the cabin with Granny before she turned to Simon. "He's the son of the man who was here last night?"

Simon nodded. "Yes."

Something akin to despair spread through Anna's soul. The look in Matthew Jackson's eyes haunted her. She felt as if she'd just encountered an old man in a young boy's body. "How old is he?"

"I think he's almost ten," Simon said. "Matthew is a good boy. No thanks to Luke. It's Naomi, Matthew's mother, who deserves all the credit for taking care of her family."

"Did she send that bread to Granny to pay her for taking care of Luke last night?"

"Yes. Folks in the Cove pay their debts with whatever they've got." Simon stared toward the door Matthew had entered and frowned. "And knowing how Luke doesn't see to the needs of his family, I expect Naomi's payment was a sacrifice."

Anna stared in the direction of Simon's gaze and remembered how Luke had frightened her the night before. She couldn't imagine any woman living with a man like that or allowing her children to be subjected to a drunken father. Now his wife and son had given her a different perspective on their family, and this made her wonder about the other people who lived in the Cove. What would they be like? Would they accept her or would they study her with the same wary expression as Matthew Jackson had?

If she wasn't accepted in the close-knit society, it certainly wasn't going to be for lack of trying.

Chapter 5

"I wondered where you'd gone off to."

Anna looked up from the table where she sat making drawings and notes about the herbs on the wall and glanced over her shoulder at Granny. "I was trying to remember everything you've told me, but it's all running together in my mind. I'm afraid I'm a hopeless case when it comes to your herbs."

Granny eased into the chair next to her and set three glass jars on the table. She pulled a root from one of them and laid it in front of Anna. "No, you ain't. You already know more than you did 'fore you come here four days ago." She pointed to the root on the table. "Now, which one is this?"

Anna pursed her lips, narrowed her eyes, and examined the root carefully. "Um, I think that's sweet gum."

Granny's face broke into a big smile. "That's right, darlin'. See, you gonna learn all my yarbs and how to use 'em. Don't you fret none."

Anna smothered the giggle she felt bubbling up inside her each time Granny referred to the herbs as *yarbs*. Granny's mountain speech might be different from what she'd heard all her life, but if she hoped to fit in with the people in the Cove, she'd better learn their ways. She pushed her hair back from her face and glanced at Granny. "I hope I can get them all straight and remember what they're used for."

Granny dismissed her fear with a wave of her hand. "Well, we gonna start with somethin' easy today. We gonna gather sweet clover blooms. Now I know you can tell them apart from anything else."

"Clover? Oh, yes, I know what that looks like. We had lots of clover at home. But what are we picking it for?"

Granny stood up and stretched her back. "I make my whoopin' cough syrup out of the blooms. I make a big batch this time of year jest in case we have little'uns get sick this winter. Ain't nothing worse than seein' a child a-chokin'."

Anna closed the journal and jumped to her feet. "I'm ready. Let's go now."

"Well hold your horses, missy. I ain't as spry as I used to be." She pointed toward the bedroom. "Go git your bonnet 'fore we go. I don't want you to come back in with a freckled face 'cause you been out in the sun too long."

Anna ran to do as Granny said and hurried back to the kitchen where Granny waited with two large baskets in her hands. She held one out. "Take this here basket. We gonna need both of 'em."

Anna pushed the back door open and hopped down the steps to the yard. "How far are we going?"

Granny chuckled. "Look in front of you, darlin'. We jest goin' right behind the house."

Anna stared in wonder at the field that stretched from Granny's henhouse toward the mountains. Red clover blooms dotted the area and waved in the breeze. It looked like a sea of red covered the field all the way to the base of the mountains in the distance. Why had she not noticed this before? Maybe because it was hard to take in all the beauty that surrounded her in the Cove. Each day she saw something different she hadn't noticed before.

The sight of the clover field and the mountains in the background took her breath away. "Granny, you've got the makings of your cough syrup right in your backyard. I wouldn't have thought about it being so close."

Granny studied the field before her. "I learnt a long time ago God gives us lots of things we don't see 'cause we're too busy looking in the wrong places. Sometimes He's got a real blessing right under our noses." Granny pointed to the blooms. "Come on, darlin'. Let's us go pick us some clover."

The blossoms brushed against her legs as Anna stepped into the clover patch. Within minutes her basket was half full, and she straightened and stared into the distance. She'd often heard Uncle Charles speak of how the mountain folks used home remedies, but she'd never given a lot of thought to where they came from. In just a few days' time she'd come to understand that these vast forests, fields, and mountainsides were covered in wild plants just waiting to be turned into drugs for easing pain.

"Granny, did you say your mother taught you all about herbs and how to use them?"

Granny nodded. "I reckon we jist kinda handed it down from one generation to another. I got me those books that are on the table in the front room, and I studied them a lot too. You need to read 'em while you're here. They can tell you a lot."

"I will," said Anna.

Granny put her hands in the small of her back and stretched. "For hundreds of years people have been taking care of each other with the plants that grow all around them. God provides for His people in lots of ways, and He shore took care of the mountain folks when He put yarbs in these here hills."

"I want to learn everything you can teach me, Granny. I have so many questions you may get tired of answering."

"Naw, I won't. Glad to oblige."

Anna grabbed another handful of clover and tossed it into her basket. "For instance—can you gather your herbs anytime in the year, or is there a special time for harvesting?"

Granny shook her head but didn't look up from picking the blossoms. "Oh, no, child. You gotta be careful 'bout when you git yore roots. February and March be the best time, right 'fore the sap begins to rise. Most of 'em ain't no use after that. Some of 'em like sassafras and poke turn poisonous as they git bigger. Have to watch out for that."

"I'll remember that if I can figure out what they look like." Anna mulled over Granny's words for a few minutes while she continued to pick the clover. "Even if I ever did learn how to tell one plant from the other, there's the problem of knowing how much of one to use."

Granny nodded. "That's right. Rememberin' to use a pinch instead of a handful of a yarb can mean the diff'rence in life or death."

A shiver ran up Anna's back. "There's just so much to learn."

"And you won't know it all by the end of the summer. It takes a lifetime of practice. So jest take your time."

"I will, Granny."

"Good." Granny tossed another handful in her basket and picked it up. "I reckon we have 'bout enough to start with. Let's get on back to the house."

Anna followed Granny as they traipsed back toward the cabin, but she couldn't get their conversation out of her mind. Since arriving, she had listened carefully to all Granny's instructions and had written them in the journal she'd brought with her. But in one summer she could only hope to gain a tiny bit of knowledge about mountain remedies. Like Granny said, it would take a lifetime of practice. With a sigh Anna stepped through the back door of the cabin and set her basket of clover on the kitchen table.

An hour later they stood over a boiling pot of water set on top of the woodstove. Anna watched closely as Granny dumped the clover blossoms in the pan. "What do we do now?"

Granny handed her a spoon. "Stir all that while it boils. We want all the juice to seep out of them flowers. Then we gonna drain 'em, add honey to the water, and bottle it. Ain't nothing better for whoopin' cough. But we'll pray the good Lord will protect us this winter so we won't need this medicine."

It didn't take long for the flowers to boil. Just as Granny sealed the last bottle, a sound from the front yard caught her attention. Wiping the perspiration from her face, she headed toward the front door. "That sounded like a wagon pullin' to a stop outside. You finish cleanin' up here, and I'll go see who's come a-visitin' this time of day. Then we'll git us somethin' to eat."

Anna picked up the pan containing the drained clover blooms and headed to the back door. "If it's time to eat, then it must be Simon. He shows up a lot at mealtime."

Granny grinned at her. "He does seem to be findin' a reason to visit 'bout ev'ry day."

When Anna stepped back in the kitchen after dumping the pan outside, Granny rushed in, untied the apron she wore, and draped it over the back of a kitchen chair. "We got a baby a-comin'. Laura Ferguson done started havin' pains and looks like it ain't gonna be long 'fore that child gets here. Pete, her husband, is a-waitin' at the wagon for us."

"A baby?" Anna set the pan on the table and swallowed hard. It was about to happen, the moment she'd waited for while dreading its arrival. She was going to assist Granny with her first birthing.

Granny looked at her and her eyes softened. She stepped in front of Anna, placed her hands on her shoulders, and smiled. "Now remember what I told you. This first time you jist gonna be watchin'. I ain't gonna ask you to do nothing but try to keep Laura comfortable. I'll do all the work, but I want you to see how it's done."

Anna raised her chin and took a deep breath. "All right. I'm ready."

Granny released her. "Good. Then go git your things together and we'll head on out."

Anna hurried toward her room. But just before she entered she stopped and turned back to Granny. "What kind of things am I supposed to be getting together?"

Granny grabbed a basket from the peg on the wall and headed to the front room, where her medical supplies were stored. "Oh, some clothes for a few days."

Anna's eyes grew wide. "A few days? I thought you said the baby would be here before long."

Granny glanced over her shoulder. "Laura's sister is a-comin' to stay while she's confined, but it'll take Pete a few days to go git her and git back. I'm gonna leave you there to take care of Laura and her family till then. That's part of bein' a midwife. Your work's not done when the baby's born. The others have to be taken care of, and I reckon there's no time like the present for you to find out how to do it."

Anna's heart thudded in her chest, and she struggled to find breath. "But they don't know me. Will they feel all right with me staying there and taking care of their family?"

Granny stopped and turned to face her. "One thing you gonna have to learn, Anna, is what nursin' is all about. It's more than just takin' care of somebody's pain. It means givin' service to those who depend on you and forgettin' about what's convenient for you. You need to understand that, or you ain't never gonna make a nurse. So, do you think you can take care of Laura and her young'uns for a few days?"

Anna couldn't tear her gaze away from the challenge that blazed in Granny's eyes. She swallowed back her uncertainty and nodded. "I…I can."

A smile replaced the stern expression on Granny's face. "Good. Then I reckon we better git goin' if we gonna bring this baby into the world."

The warmth of Granny's smile melted the fear Anna had felt moments before. Excitement flowed through her at the thought of seeing her first birthing attended by Cades Cove's legendary granny woman.

"I reckon you're right."

Anna smothered the giggle rising in her throat. She'd been here less than a week, but these mountains were having an effect on her. She was even beginning to talk like a mountain woman! With a laugh she ran to get her clothes for however long the Ferguson family needed her.

~

Even with the window open the temperature in the room had been rising all afternoon. Anna grabbed the corner of her apron and wiped at the perspiration on her forehead. No matter how hot she was, though, her discomfort couldn't compare to what the woman on the bed was experiencing.

A soft moan escaped Laura Ferguson's mouth, and she turned her face into the pillow. Anna glanced at Granny, who stood at the foot of the bed. "Won't be long, Laura," Granny's voice crooned. "You a-doin' real good."

As she had done for the past four hours, Anna pressed a wet cloth to the woman's forehead. Laura opened her eyes and stared up at Anna. Gone was the suspicion Anna had seen on Laura's face when she first entered the room with Granny. Over the last few hours, it had been replaced with gratitude.

A weak smile pulled at Laura's lips. "Thank you kindly," she whispered.

Anna picked up the hand fan Granny had brought and swished it back and forth in front of Laura's face. "Just try to relax, Laura. Relax and breathe. Before long, you're going to be holding that sweet baby."

Laura started to respond, but her eyes darkened. She raised her head from the pillow, gritted her teeth and grabbed the side of the bed as a violent contraction seized her body. Anna gasped and looked at Granny. She motioned Anna to the foot of the bed. "The baby's comin'."

Anna swallowed hard and tried to put out of her mind the memory of watching the animals back at home give birth. "Granny needs me to help her. I'll be back in a minute."

With the contraction past, Laura collapsed back onto the pillow. "I…I'm fine."

Anna squeezed her arm before she joined Granny. She took a deep breath and directed her gaze to Granny's hands.

"It's almost over, Laura. You a-doin' real good," Granny said.

Granny glanced up at Anna and smiled. "Ain't nothing gives me more pleasure than watchin' a baby come into this world."

Anna leaned closer to get a better look, and the baby's head emerged facedown. Granny's hands probed around the tiny throat and down the chest and back. "What are you doing?" Anna asked.

"Checkin' to make sure the cord's not wrapped around the neck." Granny smiled. "It's not." She nodded toward Laura. "Now give me a push so's I can let you see this young'un."

Laura obeyed, and the baby slipped out into Granny's hands. A loud wail filled the room, and Granny chuckled. Tears filled Anna's eyes at the wonder of what she had just witnessed. She reached out and touched a tiny hand. "Laura, it's a beautiful boy."

"I got me another boy?" Laura whispered.

"You have, and he's perfect." She smiled at Granny. "I'll never forget this."

Granny grinned back, her eyes bright. "Help me cut the cord so's we can let Laura see her baby."

When the cord had been cut, Granny reached across the bed, grabbed a man's shirt, and wrapped the baby in it. Then she handed the bundle to Anna. "Let this boy's mama hold him. I know she's a-wantin' to."

Cradling the baby in her arms, Anna walked back to Laura and laid her newborn son in her arms. Laura pulled the shirt away from the child's face and smiled down at him. Then she looked up at Anna. "Thank you for helpin' me git this baby here."

Anna reached out and caressed the baby's head. The feel of him sent ripples of happiness through her. "He's the most beautiful baby I've ever seen."

She watched the mother with her child for a few moments more before she turned and rejoined Granny. She'd known since she was a little girl that she wanted to be a nurse, but today that desire had been forged into her soul. Now she was more determined than ever to get to New York.

~

An hour after the safe delivery of his son, Pete Ferguson helped Granny climb into the wagon for her trip home. When Granny had settled herself on the wagon seat, she glanced down at Anna on the ground.

"Now do you remember what I told you 'bout what needs to be done for Laura? We don't want her gittin' no infection."

Anna nodded. "I do. Don't worry. I'll make it fine with Laura."

Pete, a wiry little man who had spoken less than three words to her since she'd arrived at his house, glanced at his two older children sitting on the front porch. "Hope you have good luck with them two over there. They's a bit ornery at times."

Anna glanced over her shoulder at the boy and girl who eyed her with hostility. A lump of fear formed in her throat, but she managed a smile. "We'll make it fine, Mr. Ferguson."

He stepped around her and pointed his finger at the children. "Now you two mind what Miss Anna says while I's gone to git your aunt. If'n you don't act right, you gonna have to deal with me when I get home."

"Yes, Pa," the children said together.

Anna smiled at them, but her lips froze when Pete turned his back to climb in the wagon and the boy stuck his tongue out at her. Anna whirled to see if Pete had witnessed the exchange, but he was already guiding the horse out into the road. Granny smiled and waved to her as the wagon pulled from the yard.

Anna took a step toward the wagon and waved before she turned and faced the children. Ignoring their sullen expressions, she walked toward them and pointed to the door. "I have to go check on your mother. I want both of you to go inside and sit down until I get through. Then we'll see what we're going to have for supper."

Without speaking, the children followed her into the house. She cast a glance over her shoulder as she entered Laura's room, but they had sat down at the kitchen table and appeared to be deep in conversation. She only hoped they weren't dreaming up some horrible surprise for her, like a spider in her bed or a frog in the water bucket. If they were, she'd deal with them later—after she'd checked on Laura. With a sigh she directed her attention to the exhausted woman lying in the bed. Wispy brown hair plastered to Laura's pale forehead served as a reminder of the pain she'd endured a short time before. Now a contented smile lay on her lips.

Anna stopped beside Laura Ferguson's bed and watched the mother snuggle her newborn son close to her breast. The baby nuzzled her, then opened his mouth and began to nurse.

A feeling of awe and wonder flowed through Anna's body at the sight. She almost felt as if she were intruding on a reverent moment between mother and child. "Has your milk already come in, Laura?" she whispered.

Laura shook her head. "Naw, it'll be two or three days 'fore it does, but he don't know that. He's doin' what comes natural. For now, he's gittin' what he needs."

Tears formed in Anna's eyes, and she stared in amazement at the child she thought to be the biggest miracle she had ever experienced. A sense of wonder filled her at God's plan for bringing new life into the world and how He provided what was needed to sustain His creations.

Uncle Charles had been right when he said Granny could show her things the teachers in New York never could. Today she had helped a mother give birth to her child in a small cabin under primitive conditions in a remote mountain valley, and God had opened her eyes to the miracle of birth. She doubted if she would have experienced the same feeling in a city hospital with all its modern conveniences.

One thing she did know, however. No matter how many children she would see come into the world, this first one would always be special. "Granny said as soon as your milk comes in we are to wash the baby's eyes with some of it. If you'll let me know, I can help you with it."

Laura's tired eyes stared up at her. "I kin do it. I done it with the other two."

Anna patted her arm. "You were so brave, Laura. I don't think I could have done what you did today."

Laura hugged the baby tighter. "Most women think that 'fore it happens to them. But when the pains start, you gotta keep thinkin' about how good it's gonna be when it's over." The mother pulled the baby away from her and stared at him. A loud squall rang from the tiny mouth. "He's gonna be a loud one, but he shore is a purty baby."

"That he is. In fact he's the best-looking baby I've ever helped deliver."

"Is that right? And how many babies have you helped deliver?"

Anna giggled. "Just one, but he's still the prettiest I've ever seen."

A weak smile pulled at Laura's lips. "Oh, Miss Anna, you shore do make me feel good."

"I hope so. That's what I'm here for."

The baby squirmed in Laura's arms, and she snuggled him closer. "You was so good helpin' Granny, I thought you'd been doin' it for years. I reckon I was wrong about you."

"Wrong about me? What do you mean?"

"When I heared that Granny had a girl from outside the mountains comin' to help her, I was scared. I thought you might be real uppity, and I didn't want you to help me with my baby." Laura paused. "But I was wrong, Miss Anna. You done proved that to me today. I don't reckon nobody could have been kinder to me than you was. And I'm askin' you to forgive me for settin' my mind to something before I even met you. I hope you ain't mad at me for doin' it."

Anna shook her head and smiled. "There's no reason for me to be angry with you. After all, we hadn't met. Now that we have, I hope we're going to be great friends."

"I hope so too. We's lucky to have you here."

"No, I'm the lucky one to be here with Granny. I've never met anyone who knows so much about treating people's illnesses." Anna helped Laura settle the baby back into its nursing position and pulled the shirt tight around the baby. "Laura, I meant to ask Granny, but I forgot. Why did she wrap the baby in your husband's shirt?"

Laura ran her hand over the top of the baby's head. "It's jest a mountain way of doin' thangs. Been passed down for years. It's 'sposed to bring good luck."

A crash from the other room caught Anna's attention. "Uh-oh, that sounded like something hit the floor. I guess I'd better see about your other two children."

Laura reached out to Anna. "Watch out for them two. They can be a handful."

Anna felt a twinge of fear at the thought of the two surly-faced children. She tucked the cover around Laura and the baby. "They're such good-looking children. How old are they?"

"Lucy's seven and Ted's five."

Anna smiled and hoped it looked sincere. "I'm sure we'll be friends in no time," she said. She hoped she sounded convincing.

Laura gazed up at Anna. "Thank you for stayin' with us while Pete's off to git my sister. I thank you kindly for that."

"It's my pleasure. Your husband said for you not to worry. Some of the neighbors are going to check on your livestock while he's gone, and I'll take care of all of you here." She reached down and touched the baby's cheek. "Especially this little fellow."

Laura inclined her head toward the kitchen. "Well, you ain't tangled with them other two yet. Let me know if you need me to step in."

Anna glanced over her shoulder at the other room and swallowed. She wished for a moment that Granny hadn't left with Pete. Of course she needed to be at home in case someone else needed her, and Pete was going right by her house. With a sigh Anna squared her shoulders and headed to the kitchen.

Lucy and Ted sat at the kitchen table, their arms folded on its top. Anna stopped next to the table and stared at the two children. Their mouths were turned down in frowns. Her gaze drifted to the floor, where a pot lay on its side. She stooped, picked it up, and placed it back on the stove. Taking a deep breath, she turned to the children. "What's the matter?"

Lucy's eyes peered at her from underneath the auburn hair that hung across her forehead. Her lips protruded in a pout. "We're hungry. When's Mama gonna cook supper?"

Anna pasted a big smile on her face. "Your mother has to stay in bed with the new baby. I'll fix you something to eat."

They looked at each other and then back to her. Lucy crossed her arms and raised an eyebrow. "You know how to cook?"

Anna searched her mind for something to say. "Well, I'm sure I can't cook like your mama can, but I'll try."

Both of them sighed and sank down, their chins resting on their hands. Ted stared up at her, his freckled face drawn into a frown, and wiped the sleeve of his shirt across his nose. "What you know how to cook?"

Anna glanced around the kitchen and sighed. "We'll soon find out, but I think I'd better get a bucket of water first. We used most of what your Pa brought in from the well while your brother was being born."

Her statement triggered no reaction. She might as well have been talking to her uncle's horse Toby as these two. She waited a moment before she spoke again. "Would you like to help me draw the water?"

Neither child said anything. They stared at her without blinking.

Anna grabbed the oak bucket from the dry sink near the back door and stepped outside. The setting sun cast orange and red streaks across the sky, and Anna stopped for a moment to take in the beauty before she walked to the well behind the house.

A box-like wooden structure, perhaps two feet high and open at the top, rose out of the ground. A bucket dangled above it from a rope that looped around a crossbeam between two upright posts, and a handle for rotating the overhead beam lowered the bucket through a small opening to the water below. Anna wrapped her fingers around the handle and carefully lowered the bucket into the well. As she waited for it to fill, she thought about the two children in the kitchen. She had to think of some way to gain their friendship or her time at the Ferguson farm would prove unbearable.

Lost in thought, she pulled the bucket back to the surface and had just emptied it into the water pail she'd brought from the house when a man appeared at the entrance of the Fergusons' barn. She had often thought her brother was tall, but this person would tower over Robert's six feet. The man's height wasn't the only thing that caught her attention. The bulging muscles beneath his shirt gave evidence of great strength.

His unflinching gaze locked on her, and he plodded toward her. His eyes narrowing, he stopped a few feet away from the well and glanced at the water bucket, then back at her.

Anna tried to smile, but her lips wouldn't cooperate. She tightened her grip on the water bucket and took a step backward. "Hello. I'm Anna Prentiss." He didn't respond. After a moment she took a deep breath and inched back another step. "You may know my Uncle Charles. Doctor Prentiss. He brought me here to help Granny Lawson."

"I heared 'bout that." His expression didn't change, but he nodded. "The livestock's taken care of."

"Thank you, Mr.…." Anna paused, waiting for him to tell her his name.

"Davis." He glanced at the cabin and nodded in its direction. "You takin' care of Laura and her young'uns?"

"Y-yes."

His large hands hanging at his sides reminded Anna of the hams her father used to hang in the smokehouse. He flexed his fingers and took a step toward her. Her eyes grew wide at the vision of his long fingers clasped around her throat. With a sharp intake of breath she backed away.

The man stopped and tilted his head to the side. "I was just gonna tote the water to the cabin for you."

Anna cast a quick glance over her shoulder. Lucy and Ted huddled together next to the open kitchen door. Fear raced through her. She didn't know this man. If she let him in the house, she and the children might be at his mercy. She couldn't take that chance.

She gripped the handle of the water bucket tighter and backed away. "Thank you. I can manage on my own."

"Suit yourself." Without another word, he turned and walked into the field next to the Ferguson house.

Anna whirled around and ran awkwardly into the house, the full bucket of water clanking and splashing against her knee. Closing the door behind her, she ran to the window and watched the retreating figure head toward the woods. He strode into the distance without a backward glance.

When he'd disappeared, Anna looked down at the children. Lucy and Ted clung to her apron, their bodies pressed against her. Fear etched their faces. "Do you know that man?" she asked.

Lucy gazed up at her and nodded. "He lives on the next farm. His name is Cecil Davis. He doesn't smile like most folks. He scares me."

Ted huddled closer to Anna and pressed his head against her arm. "I don't like him either. You think he'll come back tonight?"

The question sent chills racing up Anna's spine. She set the water down and put one arm around Ted's shoulders and the other around Lucy's. She leaned over and smiled at them. "I think he's gone home. Don't worry. I'm here to take care of you."

The children's bodies relaxed, and for the first time since she'd come to the Ferguson cabin they smiled. Anna glanced out the window once more. She hoped she was right and the man wouldn't come again. There was something strange about him. She'd never felt that fear from anyone else, but Cecil Davis didn't look like anyone she'd ever known before. She certainly intended to keep a close lookout for him in the future.

Chapter 6

The sun had dipped below the horizon when Simon Martin, on his way home from visiting another family, tied his horse to the tree in Pete and Laura Ferguson's yard. He'd almost ridden on by without stopping. Every time he came, he hoped he wouldn't see Pete and Laura's children. There was something about those two that rankled him. They seemed to always be up to some mischief. When he had his own children, *if* he ever had his own children, he was going to see to it they did as he said.

He looked around for Pete but didn't see him anywhere. He stepped onto the front porch and was about to knock when he stopped in amazement. Laughter drifted through the walls of the house. He didn't remember ever hearing the Ferguson children laugh—not like they seemed to be doing now.

He knocked and the noise quieted. Slowly the door opened, and he caught his breath at the sight before him. Anna, a determined look on her face, clutched a rolling pin in her raised hand as if she was prepared for battle. Ted and Lucy peered at him from behind her.

Anna breathed what sounded like a sigh of relief before she lowered her arm and smiled. "Oh, Simon, it's you. What are you doing here?"

He frowned at the children who peeped at him from behind Anna. "Were you expecting someone else?"

Her cheeks flushed. "Of course not."

He stood there, drinking in the sight of her. Loose tendrils of hair hung over her forehead and smudges of flour dotted her cheeks and apron. Her hand went to her hair as she tucked a stray lock behind her ear.

His chest tightened as he tried to speak. "I…I didn't expect to find you here, Anna. I came by to check on Laura." He looked past her into the house. "Is she here?"

The children, flour spotting their clothes, suddenly seemed to come to life. They darted from behind Anna and grabbed at his hands. "Mama done had our baby brother this afternoon," Lucy informed him. "Miss Anna's helping us make a cake."

Anna laughed and held out her hand to him. "Come on in, Simon, and you can help us too."

He stopped just inside the door and inhaled. The sweet smell of something baking reminded him he hadn't eaten since morning. His stomach growled, and he grinned. "That cake smells mighty good, Anna!"

Anna grabbed a cloth and rubbed the white smudges from the children's faces. "I'm afraid I can't take credit for what you smell," she said. "Lucy and Ted have helped me make a molasses cake to welcome their baby brother into the world. It's for his birthday."

Simon looked down at the two children. Their faces beamed as they gazed up at Anna. He leaned forward and chucked each one under the chin. "It smells good. I hope you plan on letting the preacher have a piece."

The children's giggles brought a smile to Anna's lips. "Of course you can. In fact, why don't you stay for supper? Mr. Ferguson has gone to get Laura's sister. Granny left me here to take care of everybody until he gets home. We'd love the company."

The children clapped their hands and jumped up and down. "Stay, Preacher. You kin see our new brother," Lucy said.

"In that case, I'd love to."

Ted gave a whoop, and the two turned and ran back into the house. He leaned closer. "They really helped you bake a cake?"

She nodded. "It was the only way I could get them to settle down. They're really active children."

"I know what you mean. But they must have taken a liking to you."

"I don't know about that. I was just trying to keep them busy." A blush rose to Anna's cheeks as he looked at her, but he couldn't tear his gaze away. She put her hand to her face and brushed at it. "I must look a mess. But between taking care of Laura and the baby and trying to watch Ted and Lucy, I've had quite a day."

"You look fine to me." The fact was he'd never seen anyone lovelier, but he didn't dare speak those words. He swallowed and glanced past her. "Is it all right if I visit with Laura while you and your helpers are finishing supper?"

She turned and hurried toward the bedroom. "Let me see if she's awake. We'll call you when we get supper on the table." She peeked in the room and motioned for him to enter. "The preacher's here to see you, Laura."

As he stepped past her into the room his arm brushed against her, and his pulse raced. He glanced at her, but she was looking over at the children in the other room. "Ted, watch out. You're going to knock that lamp over," she called out before she dashed back toward them. Anna's footsteps tapped on the wooden floor, then her voice rang out again. "Lucy, put that hound dog back outside where he belongs, then come help me set another place at the table. Simon's going to eat with us."

He tore his thoughts away from Anna and turned his attention to Laura and the baby. "What a fine-looking boy you got there. Congratulations, Laura. You must be really happy."

Laura smiled up at him and cuddled the baby closer. "I am, Simon. The Lord's done blessed us agin."

A pot rattled in the kitchen and laughter rang out. He glanced over his shoulder in the direction of the noise. "It sounds like your young'uns are quite taken with Miss Prentiss."

Laura nodded. "They are. She's been powerful good to my family today." The children laughed again, and she smiled. "She's an angel, that's what she is."

Simon slipped his hand in his pocket and wrapped his fingers around Anna's handkerchief. He'd carried it with him since the first day he met her. A warm feeling flowed through his veins. "Yes, she is."

~

Supper with Anna and the Ferguson children provided the perfect ending for Simon's busy day. With the last bite eaten, he leaned back in his chair and patted his stomach. "I declare, Anna, where did you learn to cook? That's one of the best meals I've had in a long time."

Her cheeks flushed as she met his gaze. "My mama believes every woman needs to know how to cook. She taught me." She looked down at the empty dishes on the table and then at the children. "I reckon we did a good job with the ham your pa brought in from the smokehouse before he left. There's not a bite left."

Ted nodded. "And nary a one of my biscuits either."

Lucy propped her hands on her hips and frowned at her brother. "You ain't the one made them biscuits. Miss Anna did. She just let you help her knead 'em."

Ted, his fists raised for a fight, jumped from his chair and planted his feet in a wide stance. Anna sprang up in a flash beside him. Her arm circled his shoulders. "Now, Ted, remember what I said about not disturbing your mama. Lucy knows you helped make the biscuits. In fact, I don't think I've ever had a better helper."

He lowered his hands and stared up at her. "I 'spect I'm just about the best helper in these here parts, right?"

She squeezed his shoulders and smiled. "Oh, I wouldn't trade you for the best chef in Knoxville."

"Huh?" he said. Both children frowned, and Lucy cocked her head. "What's that?"

Anna laughed, and Simon remembered how she looked the first afternoon when she came to Cades Cove. Her laughter that day reminded him of bells. Tonight it touched his heart with a longing like he'd never known.

"That's a fancy cook," Anna said. "So from now on you two can tell everybody I said that's what you both are. Someday you may grow up to be the head chef in the swankiest restaurant in Knoxville."

"I asked Pa once if we could go to Knoxville," said Lucy. "He said we had 'bout as much chance of that as goin' to the moon, 'cause Knoxville's a far piece from here. Guess we'll just have to stay in these here hills."

"And it's a nice place to be." Anna began to gather up the dishes. "Tell you what, Simon and I will clean up the dishes while you two get ready for bed. Then I'll tell you a story."

With a whoop they ran from the room. Anna looked at Simon, a smile on her face. "Want to help?"

He pushed up from the table and stacked the remaining plates. "It didn't sound like I had a choice. I suppose it's the least I can do after such a good meal."

Her face flushed again, and she glanced down. "Thank you. I'm glad you liked it. How was the cake?"

A smile tugged at the corner of his mouth. "Better than the best chef in Knoxville's."

Anna laughed and turned toward the dry sink where the dishpan sat. Simon followed her and set the dishes in the sink. She reached across just as he was turning away, their hands touching for the briefest of instants. The momentary contact shot a thrill through him. He longed to grasp her fingers and lace them between his. But before he could, she caught her breath and drew back.

"On second thought, why don't we leave these for now? I'll do them after the children are in bed. Thank you for helping."

At that moment, Lucy burst into the room with Ted close on her heels. His fists flailed the air and he squealed at Lucy as she ran around the table. "I'm Chief Kade!"

"I'm a-gonna wallop you good if you don't leave me alone!" Lucy yelled back over her shoulder.

Anna grabbed Ted's arm as he ran by and brought him to a skidding halt. "What are you doing?"

Ted grinned up at her. "We's playin' Chief Kade."

"And who is that?"

Simon chuckled and tousled Ted's hair. "He's the Cherokee chief some say the Cove was named for. He was supposedly the leader of a hunting settlement here named Tsiya'hi."

"Tsiya'hi? What does that mean?" Ted squirmed in Anna's grasp and she tightened her grip.

Simon struggled to keep from laughing as Ted strained to escape Anna. "Otter Place. There aren't any otters left in the Cove now, though."

Lucy stuck out her tongue at her brother. "And there ain't no Cherokee here neither."

Ted wriggled from Anna's grasp and lunged for his sister. But before he'd taken a step Anna had put herself between the two of them. She propped her hands on her hips and stared from Ted to Lucy.

"Well, I'm sure the Cherokee saved all their energy for running outdoors. You can play Chief Kade tomorrow, but tonight we're going to settle down for a bedtime story."

Her words had an instant calming effect, and they allowed Anna to herd them toward the table. She pulled out a chair and sat down. Ted climbed up in her lap, and Lucy pulled her chair close to Anna. She reached up and patted Anna's face. "What story you gonna tell us, Miss Anna?"

Simon settled across from them and studied Anna's face as she positioned Ted until she had him where she wanted. "I think maybe a story about a boy and a slingshot."

Ted straightened. "I got me a slingshot. Pa made it for me. I'm gonna go a-huntin' with it."

Anna looked down at him. "Well, you must always be careful, because a slingshot can be dangerous. Let me tell you how a boy named David killed a giant with one."

Lucy wrinkled her forehead. "I think I heard this story at church. I like it. Tell it again."

"Yeah!" Ted said.

"A long time ago, in a place called Israel, there was a young boy named David." Anna began to tell the story of David and Goliath, and her soft voice had a soothing effect on the children. After a few minutes, Simon realized it wasn't only the children who couldn't take their eyes off her. Neither could he.

His breath caught in his throat at how beautiful she looked sitting there with the children's attention focused on her. Flickering patterns of light from the glow of the oil lamp on the table danced in her eyes. The gathering darkness, visible beyond the windows, cast shadows into the house, but her presence warmed the room as her voice transported them to a faraway land and a great battle.

Lucy's eyes grew wider as the story progressed. The quiet of the night settled in the room, and Ted's eyes drooped. He stilled in Anna's lap, and his yawns grew quieter. With the story completed, Anna shook him gently and smiled down into his sleepy eyes.

"Now it's bedtime. I need to check on your mama, and you can tell her goodnight."

Anna scooted Ted off her lap, grasped his hand, and reached for Lucy with the other. With both children in tow, she led them into the room where their mother and the new baby lay.

Simon's chest tightened. He couldn't get the sight of Anna and the children out of his mind. She'd looked so beautiful sitting there, teaching them about God's Word. It reminded him of other nights when he and his brother sat beside their mother, listening to the great stories from the Bible.

Simon stood and rubbed the back of his neck. For the first time he realized how lonely his life had been since he'd come back to the Cove. Now a beautiful woman had entered his life, but she would only be there for the summer. The way it looked for him, he would be in the Cove forever. His dream might have died, but Anna's hadn't.

Anna and the children slipped back into the room, and she shooed them into their bedroom. Her tiny hands fluttered about, tucking them into bed and smoothing the covers over them. After they were settled, she bent and kissed each of them on the forehead. Then she straightened and picked up the lamp that burned on a bedside table. She held it in one hand, the other cupping the top of the chimney. As she bent forward to blow out the flickering flame, she glanced up at Simon, and their eyes locked.

They stared at each other for a moment before she blew out the flame and walked toward him. He moved away to let her pass, closing his eyes at the pleasure of her presence.

Slowly she preceded him into the kitchen and stopped at the dry sink, her fingers grasping its edge. A smile struggled on her lips when she turned to face him. "There's no need for you to help me with the dishes. I can do them alone."

A knife-like pain stabbed at his heart. "In that case I'd better be getting on home. Tomorrow's Sunday, and I have to finish my sermon."

A look of surprise flashed across her face. "I've been so busy today I forgot tomorrow is church." She glanced toward Laura's bedroom. "I won't be able to make it, but I hope I get to hear you preach next Sunday."

He swallowed. "I do too. Anyway, thanks for supper."

"Anytime."

He walked to the front door and grabbed his hat from a wall peg. He looked back at her. "Goodnight, Anna."

"Goodnight, Simon."

A blast of cool night air calmed the heat rising in his cheeks when he opened the door and stepped onto the porch. His horse raised its head and nickered as he drew close. Simon stopped, his hand on the saddle, and looked up into the sky.

Movement at the front window caught his eye, and he turned to look back at the house. A lamp on a table glowed, and he saw Anna bend over and blow it out. His heart constricted at the sight of her. "God," he groaned, "why did You bring her here? Just to let me know what I'm missing?"

No answer came. Wearily, he climbed onto the mare and began his long journey to the honeymoon cabin where he lived alone.

~

Anna listened to the hoofbeats of Simon's horse die away in the distance before she walked back to the sink and the dishes that waited there. For some reason Simon's presence tonight had been disturbing. There was something about the way he looked at her that flustered her. Maybe, if she was honest, it wasn't the way he looked at her that concerned her, but the way it made her feel.

She'd had men look at her before, but none had ever affected her like Simon did. Not even Paul Sparks, who'd made no secret of his intentions toward her. But she'd never had any interest in Paul other than as a friend. Of course Mama and Robert had wanted her to marry Paul so their two farms would be joined someday, but that hadn't been her plan.

Sighing, she rolled up the sleeves of her dress and began to scrub the dishes left from supper. Hard work would take her mind off Simon and the way her heart fluttered when he smiled at her.

Twenty minutes later, with the dishes put away and her pallet of quilts spread on the floor, she still couldn't drag her thoughts away from the way Simon's dark eyes set her heart to pounding. Groaning, she lay down on the hard floor and wiggled in search of a comfortable position. She thought of her soft bed at home and almost laughed. Six months ago she would never have believed the time would come when she would sleep on the hard floor of a mountain cabin. But here she was, and it felt right. In the next room a new baby she'd helped bring into the world slept in his mother's arms. Nothing would ever compare with that experience.

Her eyelids drooped, and she was about to drift off when a voice next to her startled her awake. "Miss Anna, you asleep?"

Anna sat up and stared at Lucy kneeling beside her. "Lucy, what are you doing out of bed?"

"I cain't sleep."

"Are you sick?"

Lucy shook her head. "No'm. Sometimes, I jist get scared, and Mama comes and sleeps with me."

Anna cupped Lucy's chin with her hand and leaned close to her. "Since your mama has the baby in bed with her, she can't sleep with you tonight."

A soft sob escaped Lucy's mouth. "I know."

"But I'll tell you what." Anna scooted over on the pallet. "How about sleeping with me? I'm a little lonely in here by myself."

Lucy dropped down next to Anna. "You are? Then I'll stay and keep you comp'ny."

"Good. I can't think of anything I'd like better." They settled down on the pallet, and Anna drew the cover over both of them. Then she leaned over and kissed Lucy's cheek. "I hope you sleep well."

A contented sigh drifted from Lucy's mouth. "I like you, Miss Anna. I'm glad you came to our Cove."

Anna blinked back the tears that sprang unbidden to her eyes. "I am too, Lucy."

She stretched out on the floor, and for some reason it didn't seem as hard as it had before. Within minutes Lucy's breathing became steady. Anna reached over and tucked the covers around the sleeping child once more.

She lay there in the darkness listening to the sounds of the night. In the distance an owl hooted, and a hound dog's bay drifted on the night air. In the next room the baby cried. Laura's soft whispers floated through the cabin.

Anna closed her eyes and let the sounds wash over her. Next to her Lucy stirred, and Anna smiled at the thought of a birthday cake and Simon's presence at supper. Today had started with a lesson in mountain remedies and ended in the stillness of a remote cabin. Though she was tired, it had been one of the best days of her life.

For the first time she felt as if she was on her way to proving Robert wrong. *Maybe,* she thought as sleep overtook her, *maybe I have the grit to be a nurse after all.*

Chapter 7

The following Tuesday, Simon, a fishing pole in his hand, sat on the bank of Abram's Creek. The weight on his line bobbed up and down in the water as a fish nibbled at the baited hook.

"Come on, little fellow," Simon coaxed. "Take a bite."

His brother, John, seated beside him, chuckled. "You think that there fish is gonna listen to you?"

Simon grinned. "Don't know. Just trying to help him make a commitment."

"Yeah, to end up in the fryin' pan."

The weight disappeared under the water and Simon jerked the line out of the creek. Giving a whoop, he pulled the fish to shore and grinned at his brother. He unhooked the fish, dropped it in his basket, and peered over the edge of his brother's straw basket. "How many you got?"

John shrugged and cast his line into the water. "About four, I guess. Enough for me and Martha's supper. How many you trying for today?"

"Oh, I don't know. I thought I'd take some by to Granny."

A quiet breeze ruffled the leaves on the trees for a moment before John chuckled. "Well, I guess that fish done made his commitment to Granny's frying pan."

Simon joined in the laughter. "Yeah, guess so."

John scooted back a little from the water's edge and repositioned his hook in the water. "Speaking of commitment, when you gonna do that?"

The question surprised Simon, and his eyes grew wide. "What're you talking about?"

John wrinkled his brow and stared up at the sky. "Oh, I was just a-thinkin'. There's a few women in the Cove that'd like to put an end to your bachelor days. When you gonna choose one and put 'em out of their misery?"

"I don't know where you get some of your ideas. There aren't any women who have their sights set on me."

"How about Linda Mae Simmons? She seems real interested."

A shock rippled through Simon at the mention of Linda Mae, and he sat up straight. "Now, hold on there, John. She's the daughter of one of my deacons. I have never done anything to encourage a relationship with her."

John snorted. "Simon, you 'bout as dumb 'bout women as you can be. They don't need no encouragement. They just naturally interested in any eligible man. You could do a lot worse than Linda Mae."

Simon scowled at his brother. "I'm not dumb. I just haven't found the right woman yet." He reached for the bait jar, pulled a worm out, and threaded it on his hook before he continued. "One thing's for sure, Linda Mae's about the prettiest girl in the Cove—with the exception of Martha, I should say. But I don't know. I don't think I could ever be interested in her."

John pushed his straw hat back on his head and sighed. "Martha was right, I guess."

"About what?"

John drew back his hook and cast again. "She said you must have it real bad for that girl over at Granny's. Martha says you're over there all the time, and she feels like she already knows Anna from all you done told her."

His fingers tightened around the fishing pole at his brother's words. He didn't realize his attraction to Anna was so obvious, but he'd never been able to hide anything from his brother. He pulled the fishing line from the water and pushed himself to his feet. "Martha's wrong.

Anna's only here for the summer. She doesn't have any interest in staying in Cades Cove."

John's face mirrored the pain squeezing Simon's heart. After a moment, he rose and dropped his pole on the bank. He grasped Simon's shoulder. "I'm sorry, brother. How you making it with that?"

Simon shrugged. "Not much I can do but accept it." Then he smiled. "Maybe God just intends for me to be alone. There aren't many like your Martha around."

Or Anna, he thought as he picked up his catch and walked toward his horse.

~

"So you enjoyed your two days at the Fergusons?"

Granny shifted in her chair. The shade tree in the backyard provided welcome relief from the afternoon sun beating down on their heads. Anna tilted her head to the side and dropped the hulls of the peas she'd just shelled to the ground. "I don't know if *enjoy* is the right word. Ted and Lucy were a handful. If they weren't fighting with each other, they were dreaming up some joke to play on me."

"Like what?"

"Well, once they put a frog in the water bucket. And another time they caught a snake and threw it at me when I came out the back door."

Granny chuckled. "What did you do 'bout it?"

"I guess they didn't know I grew up on a farm and had been around frogs and snakes all my life. I think they were disappointed that their tricks didn't scare me. But I have to say I was glad to see Mr. Ferguson pull up to the house yesterday. Those were the longest two days of my life." She picked up another handful of peas. "But you know what? I think Ted and Lucy were sad to see me leave."

"They prob'ly were. But two days ain't long to stay. You're lucky they didn't need you longer. It can git mighty tirin' takin' care of a family."

Granny's wrinkled face displayed the same serene gentleness Anna had observed since the first day. Not a hint of sorrow or regret lined her features. Yet Anna didn't think she'd ever heard Granny speak of her family.

"You've spoken of your mother several times but never about a husband or children. I don't mean to pry, but I've wondered if you had a family, Granny?"

Granny's lips pursed for a moment, but her hands never hesitated in the rhythm of stripping the peas from their pods. "I married right young. Me and my husband settled here on this farm. Life was hard, but we had all we needed." She threw a handful of hulls to the ground. "And we was happy."

Anna hesitated at the thought of bringing up unpleasant memories. Her heart warned against asking questions that might bring Granny grief, but her tongue itched to speak. "What happened to your husband?"

Granny's hands stilled, and she stared out across the fields. "He took sick one winter. Real bad, he was. 'Course that was 'fore Doc come to the mountains. I done ev'rything I knowed to do, but he jest got worse. Pneumonia—bad thing to happen when you ain't got nothing to treat it with." She was a silent for a moment. "Anyhow, after he died, me and my daughter jest stayed on here."

Anna's hands stilled, and she sucked in her breath. "You have a daughter?"

Granny shook her head. "She died in childbirth when she was a little younger than you. The baby died too." Moisture sparkled in Granny's eyes, and she sniffed. "Deborah was my daughter's name. I picked it out of the Bible 'cause I thought it was the purtiest name I'd ever heard. I don't talk about her much. It hurts too bad."

Anna reached over and covered Granny's hand with hers. "I'm sorry, Granny. I didn't mean to bring up sad memories for you."

A sad smile pulled at Granny's mouth. "That's all right, child. I reckon I got some memories that ain't never gonna leave me no matter what I do."

"Did you ever think about leaving the Cove after you lost your family?"

Granny's gaze drifted to the mountains in the distance. "There warn't nowhere else for me to go. And besides, this is my home. So I stayed on here, and the good Lord's taken care of me."

They shelled the peas in silence for a few minutes. It seemed strange that neither Uncle Charles or Simon had mentioned Granny had a daughter who died. Was there more to the story than Granny had told her? One glance at the sadness lining Granny's face told her there had to be. Whatever it was, it brought great pain to Granny, and she wouldn't question her about it again.

There were other things she wanted to know, though, and one of them concerned Simon. She picked up several pea pods and broke one open. "I've wanted to ask you something else, Granny."

Granny glanced up, but her hands didn't still. "What's that?"

"It's about Simon." Anna cleared her throat. "It's plain to see he's a very educated man. I wondered why he came back here to preach instead of going somewhere else. Maybe a big city, like Knoxville."

A wary expression flashed across Granny's face, and she stopped shelling peas. "Has he said somethin' to you?"

Anna straightened and shook her head. "Oh, no. And it's really none of my business. I just wondered, that's all."

Granny stared off into the distance for a moment before she spoke. "Simon always said he wanted to be a preacher, and his ma was determined for him to go to school. She believed God had great things planned for her boy. So Simon went to Milligan College over to Eliza bethton, and he was a-makin' it fine. Until three years ago, that is. We had us a bad epidemic of influenza in the Cove, and Simon's ma and pa both took down with it. John, Simon's brother, wrote him and told him they was sick. Well, Simon, he come a-runnin' home fast as he could, but it didn't do no good. Both of 'em died."

"I know that part. He told me. But why didn't he go back to school?"

"We had lots of sick folks in the Cove, and me and Doc Prentiss were pert near worn out from takin' care of everybody. Simon stayed on to help. By the time the worst had passed, it was too late for him to finish the school year. He thought he'd go back in the fall, but he didn't."

"Why not?"

"'Cause the church here didn't have no preacher, and the folks asked Simon to stay on 'til they found somebody. He's been the preacher ever since."

"And the church members still haven't found a replacement after three years?"

Granny nodded. "That's right. I reckon as time passed folks decided they wanted Simon for the preacher and didn't bother lookin' nowhere else for one."

Anna sank back in her chair and thought about what Granny had told her. She wondered how Simon felt about what had happened to him. "Granny, does Simon regret not getting to finish school?"

A sad smile pulled at Granny's mouth. "I 'spect that's somethin' you'll have to ask him yourself. He won't give me a straight answer 'bout it, but maybe he'll tell you."

Anna shook her head and directed her attention back to the peas in her lap. "I doubt that. Like I said, it's really not my business. I shouldn't have asked."

Before Granny could say anything, a voice called from the front yard. "Anybody home?"

Granny glanced in the direction of the sound, and a broad smiled deepened the creases on her face. "It's Simon. That boy sure is a-comin' round here a lot."

Anna busied herself shelling the peas as Simon walked around the house. She hoped her face didn't give away the fact they'd been discussing him a few moments before.

Simon stopped beside Granny's chair and held out a string of fish. "Here you are. I been over to Abram's Creek and thought you might like to have these."

Granny's eyes widened. "Rainbow trout! You shore do know how to make yourself welcome. We'll have 'em for dinner. I 'spect you ain't got no plans, so you can eat with us too."

He laughed. "Thanks, Granny. I'll clean these for you."

She motioned to the house. "There's a pan on the table inside you can put 'em in when you git through. Then I got another job for you."

"What's that?"

"Me and Anna been a-peelin' more of them June apples, and we got a big bucketful. I need you to climb up on the roof and spread 'em out to dry for me."

Simon nodded. "Just as soon as I get the fish cleaned." He glanced at Anna. "Afternoon, Anna. How did you make it with the Ferguson children?"

She looked up and smiled. "Fine, Simon. At least I survived."

He whistled a tune as he turned and headed to the house. Granny watched him go. "That boy shore do seem happy lately. Wonder what's gotten into 'im?"

Anna picked up a handful of peas. "I'm sure I don't know."

Granny chuckled and resumed shelling. By the time they'd completed their task, Simon had the fish ready. Granny stood up and started scooping the pea hulls from the ground and dumping them in a basket. "Anna, you take them fish and the peas inside. I'm gonna toss these hulls in the field past the chicken coop. I'll be back in just a minute."

Anna took the fish from Simon and grinned. "I'll take these inside then come back to help you. I want to make sure you do it right."

His mouth curled into a smile, and he cocked an eyebrow. "I tell you what. If you have any doubts about my ability to do the job, maybe you should be the one to climb to the roof. I'll hand the bucket of apples up to you."

She sniffed and straightened her shoulders. "No thanks. I'll just watch."

"Then the least you can do is hold the ladder for me while I climb up."

"Oh, I don't know. Maybe I'll remove it while you're on the roof and strand you up there." She grinned and backed away.

He wagged a finger at her. "You have a wicked streak in you, Anna Prentiss."

She turned toward the house and looked over her shoulder. "Just wait until you get to know me better. Remember, I grew up with an older brother."

His laughter followed her as she stepped into the house. There was something about Simon that made her feel good when she was with him. It was so easy to laugh and joke with him. She'd never felt that way with any other man she'd known, not even Paul, who had practically grown up at their house. Even though he'd been her friend, she had known she could never fall in love with the serious-natured young man. When she fell in love, it would be someone who made her laugh and someone she respected because he was good and kind and made her happy. Somebody like Simon.

Her eyes widened at the thought, and her face grew warm. She set the pan of peas on the kitchen table and pressed her palms to her hot cheeks. The pulse in her neck pounded. What was the matter with her? She couldn't think about falling in love. Nothing was going to distract her from Bellevue.

She rushed to the water bucket by the back door, scooped some water in the dipper, and drank it down. After a few moments her pulse slowed and her face grew cooler. She licked her lips, tugged at the waist of her dress, and smoothed a stray lock of hair into place before she walked toward the back door.

Just as she reentered the backyard, Simon emerged from the smokehouse with a ladder that looked as if it had seen better days. He propped it against the side of the house. "I think this'll hold me."

Anna stopped beside the rickety ladder and let her gaze wander over it. It looked as if it hadn't been used in years. Concerned about its sturdiness, she wrapped her fingers around one of the rungs and pressed on it. "I don't know, Simon. It looks like some of the wood is rotten. Maybe you shouldn't use this."

He chuckled, put his foot on the first rung, and shifted his weight onto it. He bounced on the step several times before he nodded. "This will be fine. Don't worry."

Anna studied the ladder once more. "I think you should find something else to use."

Simon sighed and shook his head. "I'm telling you it's okay."

She looked up at the roof and frowned. "But that's a long way up."

Simon shook his head and laughed. "It's not as bad as it looks from the ground. Granny's roof has the lowest pitch of any cabin around here, and I'm only going to the edge. I won't be more than eight feet off the ground. I've climbed trees higher than that. Quit acting like a mother hen."

"Well, if you're sure, but be careful."

He put both feet on the first rung and inched up to the next. When he got to the third one, he smiled down at her. "It's all right. If you'll hand me the bucket of apples, I'll go on up."

She did as he asked and watched as he reached the roof and climbed out onto it. "Those wooden shingles look slick, Simon. Be careful."

He peered at her over the edge. "I've done this a hundred times, Anna. I'm not going to fall."

Just as the words slid from his mouth his foot caught on a piece of loose roofing and he lurched sideways. Simon struggled to regain his footing, but he only succeeded in knocking the ladder away from the roof.

Anna jumped out of the way as the ladder fell away and crashed down at her feet. A few of the rungs had broken in half. Apples showered down on her head, and she threw her arms over her head to protect herself from the falling bucket. When it hit the ground, she looked up in fear. Simon, his fingers grasping the edge of the roof, dangled over the side of the house.

A scream tore from Anna's throat. "Hang on, Simon!"

She grabbed the ladder and tried to push it upright. But before she could scoot it underneath him, Simon lost his grip on the roof and plummeted downward. He hit the hard-packed dirt with a thud.

Anna rushed to where he lay and dropped to her knees. "Granny!" she screamed.

He lay unmoving on his back, his eyes closed. As Anna stared down into Simon's pale face, fear swept through her. What if Simon was dead? Or what if he had suffered injuries that would affect him for the rest of his life? She took a deep breath and placed her hand on his chest. He coughed, and his chest rose.

"Can you hear me, Simon?" He didn't move, and she glanced over her shoulder. Where was Granny? Had she not heard her call for help? She took a deep breath and yelled again. "Granny, I need you!"

Anna pressed her fingers to the pulse in his wrist and breathed a sigh of relief at the throbbing beat. Even after she was convinced that his pulse was steady, she didn't let go but covered his hand with her free one.

His eyelids fluttered open, and his eyes glazed as he stared up into the sky. He gasped a deep breath and shook his head as if to clear it.

Anna leaned closer to him and squeezed his hand. "Simon, are you all right?"

He stared up at her. "I-I think so." He lay still for a moment. Then a slow smile curled his lips, and his dark eyes stared up at her. "I do believe, Miss Prentiss, you are trying to hold hands with me."

Anna's mouth gaped open, and she stared down at their intertwined fingers before she squeezed his hand and laughed with relief. "Of all the impertinent remarks! And to think I was worried you'd killed yourself."

At that moment Granny hurried around the side of the smokehouse and charged across the yard toward them. The rooster and hen who'd been pecking at the ground squawked and scuttled out of her path. "I was way out yonder in the field when I heared all the ruckus. I came as fast as these legs would take me. What in tarnation's happened?"

"Simon fell off the roof."

Granny ran to him and dropped to her knees. Simon struggled to sit up, but she pushed him back down. "Be still, boy. I gotta see if you broke any bones."

For several moments her hands pressed and probed, her sharp eyes looking for signs of pain on Simon's face. Finally she sat back on her heels and smiled. "I reckon you ain't broke nothin'. How you feel?"

Simon inched into a sitting position and rubbed his head. "Like I just fell off a roof."

Anna struggled to control the grin that tugged at her mouth, but Granny convulsed in laughter. Granny shook her finger in his face. "Boy, you gotta be more careful."

"It just knocked the breath out of me. I'll be okay."

With a hand on either elbow Granny and Anna helped Simon to

his feet. He stood between them for a few moments, his body swaying back and forth.

"Here, boy," Granny said, putting his arm around her shoulder. "Lean on me and Anna. We'll git you inside."

He looped his other arm across Anna's shoulders and together they limped their way into the house. When they got inside they sat him in a chair at the kitchen table. His face turned crimson at their stares. "Now don't fuss over me. Just let me sit here for a few minutes."

Anna slid into the chair next to him. "You're lucky you didn't kill yourself. I thought you were either dead or crippled."

A slow smile spread across his face. "Are you sure you didn't move that ladder and make me fall?"

Her eyes grew wide. "What?"

His lips twitched, and he glanced at Granny. "Well, you did threaten me. I'm just wonderin' if I need to watch out for you from now on."

Her face grew warm. "Of all the…"

He gazed up at Granny. "You'd better sleep with one eye open, Granny. This woman can't be trusted."

Anna took a deep breath, leaned over, and arched an eyebrow. "I know what you're trying to do, Mr. Martin, and it won't work."

He scooted his chair backward. "And just what is that, Miss Prentiss?"

"Ever since I came here you've taken a lot of pleasure in teasing me. You like to see me get flustered, but it's not going to happen today."

"And why's that?"

The memory of the fear she'd felt when she knelt over Simon sent a chill up her spine, and she swallowed hard. "Because I was so scared when you fell." She tried to blink back the tears flooding her eyes, but she couldn't. "I was afraid you'd been killed. I'm so glad you weren't hurt."

Simon's Adam's apple bobbed, and he nodded. "That means a lot to me, Anna."

Granny put her arm around Anna's shoulders and smiled. "Well, we've all been blessed today. Simon's not hurt, and I'm blessed to have you two here. It's been a long time since my cabin had this much life in it." She hugged Anna closer. "I shore am glad you come to the Cove, darlin'."

Simon's eyes softened. "Me too. I think you're just what we've needed around here."

Anna looked into his eyes, and for a moment she forgot New York and the letter she had to earn from Granny before the summer ended. All she wanted was to enjoy being with this man whose smile made her heart race.

Chapter 8

Granny's buggy bounced along the road that wound through the Cove, but Anna ignored the bumps and concentrated on the warm Sunday morning sunshine. The crisp mountain air filled her lungs as she breathed in the scent of honeysuckle and pine that drifted on the breeze. She turned her face up to the sun and closed her eyes. A sense of peace rippled through her body at the beauty of God's handiwork.

Beside her, Granny kept her eyes focused on the horse that pulled the buggy. She had spoken little since they left the cabin. As if she could read Anna's thoughts, Granny turned to her. "It's a purty day, ain't it?"

Anna sighed. "Oh, yes. I've never seen a more beautiful day."

Granny's hands tightened on the reins. "You nervous 'bout meetin' folks today?"

The familiar churning in her stomach reminded Anna of what lay ahead of her at church that morning. She forced a smile to her lips and turned to face Granny. "A little. After all, I've only met Simon and the Fergusons." Her face warmed, and she bit down on her lip. "And Luke Jackson, of course."

Granny snorted and straightened in her seat. "No need to worry 'bout seein' Luke today. He don't never darken the door of the church."

Anna opened her mouth to respond, but at that moment she

caught a glimpse of a barn behind the cabin they were passing. She craned her neck to get a better view of the strange structure before she turned to Granny.

"The barns in the Cove aren't like the ones we have at home."

Granny didn't take her eyes off the road. "What do the barns look like over at Strawberry Plains?"

Anna thought a moment. "Well, they look like…like…well, they look like a barn. But the ones here look like somebody built two little houses side by side and then set a bigger house on top of them."

Granny chuckled. "I s'pose they do look strange to you, but it's what works best in the Cove. It's called a cantilever barn."

Anna opened her mouth to ask another question about the strange-looking structures she'd seen ever since coming to the Cove, but the church where Simon preached was coming into view. The small house of worship almost seemed to glow in the Sunday morning sunlight. Granny guided the horse into the yard and pulled to a stop.

Anna clasped her hands in her lap and glanced around at the assembled wagons and buggies scattered across the yard surrounding the church. A young man and woman stepped onto the church porch. As he reached to open the door, the woman turned, her gaze raking Anna. The simple homespun dress and sunbonnet with its ribbons tied under her chin offered a stark contrast to Anna's blue-and-white cotton dress with its leg-of-mutton sleeves and full skirt gathered tightly at the waist.

Her mother had spent hours sewing the dress made from the material Robert had bought at the general store in Strawberry Plains. Now as Anna looked down at the full skirt that billowed about her legs, she felt out of place. Next Sunday she would wear a plainer dress, but there was nothing to do about it at the present.

She took a deep breath and squared her shoulders. It was time to meet the people of Cades Cove, and all she could do was be herself and hope they liked her. Simon had assured her they would be friendly, and she hoped he was right.

A wagon stopped beside them and the young driver pulled back on the reins, set the brake, and jumped down. He tipped his hat to

Granny and smiled. "Wait a minute, Granny. Let me tie these here horses to this tree, and I'll git yours next."

Granny nodded in his direction. "Thank ye kindly, Andrew." She leaned over to Anna and whispered in her ear. "Now, don't go a-thinkin' I can't handle my own horse, but when a friend offers help, you need to let 'em have the blessin'."

Anna smiled. Her Poppa had often said the same thing. "I'll remember that, Granny."

Granny leaned over and whispered to Anna. "Andrew's wife, Gracie, is just about ready to give birth. You'll git to meet her 'fore too long."

After Andrew had tied Granny's horse to a tree, he helped Granny from the buggy. When he reached out to Anna, she grabbed his hand and hopped to the ground. "Thank you."

He tipped his hat again. "My pleasure, Miss."

Granny glanced at Anna. "Anna, this be Andrew Long." She inclined her head toward Anna. "This here is Anna Prentiss, Andrew. She's helpin' me for the summer. She'll be a-comin' with me when it's Gracie's time."

Andrew's lips tightened, and he stared at her as if he was trying to decide if this stranger standing in front of him could be trusted to help his wife when the time came for their child to be born. He gave a slight nod, but his somber expression didn't change. "Pleased to meet you, Miss Anna."

"I'm happy to be here. I can't wait to meet your wife. Is she here today?"

"No, ma'am. She ain't feelin' too good. Maybe next Sunday."

Granny chuckled and took Anna by the arm. "We better git inside, or Simon's gonna start without us."

They stepped into the church and halted as Anna let her gaze rove over the interior. A table with a cross on it sat in front of the pulpit. Rough-hewn benches, very different from the pews in her church at home, lined the sanctuary on either side of the center aisle.

As if a silent signal had been given, the people sitting in the church pews turned and looked toward the rear of the church. Granny nodded to those on the back benches and, with Anna in tow, walked down the aisle.

Anna's skin warmed at the perusal of the congregation. Every eye was trained on her, and she felt like she was a prisoner walking the last steps to her execution. She tried to smile, but no one returned the gesture or spoke as she and Granny made their way to the front of the church. When they reached the second pew from the front, Granny pointed to the seat. "This here is where I sit."

Anna sank onto the bench, straightened her shoulders, and turned to Granny. "There seems to be a good crowd here today."

Granny leaned close and whispered, "There is. Sunday is the time we git to visit with each other." She patted Anna's hand. "And you gonna git to know ev'rybody too. They may be strangers now, but 'fore long they'll be friends."

Anna glanced across the aisle and smiled at a young woman who stared at her. Without acknowledging the friendly gesture, the woman ducked her head and stared at her hands. Anna sighed and glanced back at the cross at the front of the church. Suddenly a sweet peace filled her soul. Even if she was among strangers this was a place where God was worshipped, and she wanted to be a part of it.

A door at the front of the church opened and Simon entered to the left of the pulpit. He smiled when he spotted her—was that smile just for her?—and her heart thudded. He showed no signs of having fallen off a roof a few days earlier. If anything, he was more handsome than ever. He laid his Bible on the pulpit and stepped down to speak to a man who sat on the front pew across the aisle.

Anna leaned close to Granny. "I'm looking forward to hearing Simon preach."

"Oh, he's a good preacher," Granny said. "Good singer too. He'll lead us in a few hymns 'fore he gits down to preachin', though."

A rustling movement sounded behind them. "Mornin', Granny," a deep male voice said.

Anna glanced over her shoulder at the couple who sat behind them. "John, Martha," Granny said. "Good to see you."

"We's glad to be here." The soft female voice differed from the man's.

The young woman's eyes glowed from an inner happiness probably produced by the fact that she was expecting a baby. Wisps of blonde hair stuck out from the bonnet, framing a face that almost took Anna's breath because of its beauty. The corners of her hazel eyes crinkled as she smiled at Anna.

"And you must be Miss Anna?"

Before Anna could answer, Granny spoke up. "Yup, this here's Anna Prentiss. She's the one helpin' me this summer. She may even be here when it's your time, Martha." She glanced at Anna. "Anna, meet John and Martha Martin."

Anna nodded in recognition of the names. "Oh, I'm so glad to meet you. Simon's told me about you." She looked at John. A little taller than Simon, he had the same broad shoulders and dark hair. "I can see the resemblance between you and Simon."

John and Martha exchanged a quick glance. "He's told us a right smart bit 'bout you too," John said.

Granny chuckled. "That Simon's been a reg'lar vis'tor ever since Anna came."

Suddenly the air seemed stuffy in the church. Anna picked up a paper fan—it had an advertisement for a funeral home in Knoxville on the back of it—and waved it in front of her face. "I'm looking forward to getting to know you better, Martha."

Martha leaned forward and pressed Anna's shoulder. "Me too, Anna."

Granny straightened. "It looks like Simon's 'bout ready to git the singin' started."

Anna turned to look at Simon and spied the pump organ sitting to the side of the congregation. It reminded her of the one Poppa had brought home when she was a little girl. Ornate carving swirled across the tall upright instrument, and little shelves on either side of the music rack held some old hymnals. She couldn't see the keyboard, but from where she sat the organ appeared to be in good condition.

Simon picked up a hymnal and announced the page number. As the people turned to it, Anna looked around to see who would play the organ, but no one stepped forward. She leaned over to Granny.

"Who plays the organ?"

"We ain't had nobody to play since Miriam died 'bout a year back."

Anna glanced back at the instrument. "That's a shame. It looks like such a nice organ. Almost like the one I had."

Granny stopped trying to find the page in the hymnal. "Child, can you play that thang?"

Anna smothered a giggle. "I suppose so. I played the one at home."

From the front of the church Simon's voice caught their attention. "Now let's raise our voices in song to the Lord this beautiful morning."

Granny jumped up and pointed a bony finger at the organ. "Hold on there, Simon. I jest found out that Anna here can play the organ. Why don't we let her help us out with our singin' this mornin'?"

Simon stared at her. "Why, Miss Prentiss, we'd be honored to have you accompany us. Come on down."

Every head in the church turned in her direction, and Anna's face felt as if it was on fire. Embarrassment at her forward attitude made her want to beg off, but then she looked back at the organ. The urge to play it overcame everything else, and she stood up and walked to the front of the church.

Simon stepped from the pulpit to the organ and leaned down to whisper in her ear. "These hymnals are from a singing school we had here a few years ago. The folks know nearly every song by its page number. When we finish one hymn, somebody will call out a number, and we'll sing that one."

She nodded. "All right. Which one is first?"

He flipped through the pages. "How about number fifteen?"

She turned to the page and propped the book on the music rack. "'Old Time Religion.' I like that one."

She seated herself on the bench, studied the stops, and pulled the ones she thought would produce the best sound. Slowly she began to pump the pedals, filling the bellows with air, and placed her hands on the keyboard. The first touch of the keys released a sweet sound as she played an introduction to the song.

She glanced up at Simon, smiled, and nodded for him to begin. His tenor voice rang out and the congregation joined in. The people jumped to their feet and sang, their voices reaching to the rafters of the church. When they finished, a voice in the back rang out. "Number twenty-four!"

Anna turned to "Amazing Grace" and played an introduction. One after another, requests were shouted from the congregation, and before she knew it they had spent at least twenty minutes in singing.

Finally Simon brought the singing to a halt and turned to her. "Thank you, Miss Prentiss, for blessing us with your playing today. It's been a long time since we've been able to sing with our organ. We're thankful the Lord sent you, and we hope you'll play as long as you're here."

She nodded, slipped from the bench, and stared at the floor as she walked back to the pew where Granny sat.

As Simon opened his Bible, Anna was struck with how handsome and confident he looked in the pulpit. He looked as if he had been born to stand before the people and preach God's Word. That became even more evident to her as his sermon unfolded.

He preached that day on Psalm 100 and how thankful the children of God should be for all the Lord had done for them. Throughout the sermon, *Amens!* rose from every corner of the church. The more the men agreed with Simon's words, the harder he preached. At one point he stopped and took off his jacket. Dark circles dampened his white shirt, but it seemed to inspire him to expound even more on the God he loved.

At the end of the sermon he asked Anna to come play again. Anna was touched by the number of people who came from the back of the church to kneel at the front and offer up prayers before they shook Simon's hand and returned to their seats. It had been a long time since she had been in a service where the Spirit of God seemed to hover over the congregation. The thought made her heart lighter as she played the final chords of the final hymn.

After the closing prayer, two young girls wedged their way through the congregation and stood by the front pew. Anna smiled at them. "Hello. How are you today?"

They stepped a little closer. The taller of the two smiled. "That shore was purty. I liked hearing you play."

"Thank you. My name is Anna. Who are you?"

The girl who had spoken inched a little closer. "My name's Myrtice, and this here is my sister Hope. We like to sing, but there ain't been nobody to play for us lately."

Anna motioned to the girls. "Would you like to see how the organ works?"

The girls smiled and crowded next to her. Myrtice pointed to the pedals. "What's them for?"

"You have to pump these to force air inside so it'll make a sound. See? Like this."

She began to play again, and Myrtice's mouth fell open in a gap-toothed grin. "Look at that, Hope. Reckon we could ever learn to do that?"

Hope shook her head. "Don't think so, sister. But it shore does sound good."

"Whatcha doin'?" A new voice sounded behind them.

Anna glanced around at two freckle-faced boys who'd just joined the group. Hope turned to the newcomer. "Miss Anna's showing us how she plays."

One of the boys moved closer. "Show me."

Within minutes all the children in the church were crowding around the organ and singing as Anna played. At the end of each song, another child would yell for them to do one more.

After several minutes Anna glanced over her shoulder. Except for the children, the church was empty. She closed the hymnal and smiled. "Oh, it's time to go home. I don't want your parents to be upset because I've kept you so long."

Hope shook her head. "Naw, they won't care. They be outside visitin'."

Anna stood up from the bench. "Well, we'd better join them. I'll see you next Sunday, and then we'll sing some more."

When they stepped onto the porch the children clustered around her. Myrtice pulled on her dress. "You promise we can sing agin, Miss Anna?"

She leaned down and tugged one of the girl's braids playfully. "I promise, Myrtice." She straightened and glanced around at all the children. "I enjoyed getting to know all of you. I hope I'll see you again next Sunday."

With a whoop the children rushed down the church steps and scattered across the yard. Anna hesitated at the top of the steps and gazed at the adults standing in groups across the yard. Simon and Granny were standing beside her buggy.

Anna eased down the steps and glanced around at the congregation scattered across the church grounds. Several groups of men appeared deep in discussion and didn't seem to notice her exit the church. At the foot of the steps, two women stared at her for a moment before they turned and walked away.

She swallowed back her disappointment that no one had come forward to speak to her when she noticed John and Martha standing at the other side of the steps. A frown wrinkled Martha's forehead. "Sadie, Louise," Martha called out. "Don't go."

The two women stopped and turned to face Martha. "What is it?" the older lady asked.

Martha motioned Anna to join them. "I want you to meet Anna. She's new to our valley and don't know everybody yet."

Anna stepped down from the porch and flashed a smile of gratitude at Martha before she turned to the two women who eased up beside her. She held out her hand. "I'm Anna Prentiss. I'm spending the summer with Granny Lawson, and I'm looking forward to getting to know all of you. I've never been anywhere as beautiful as your valley, and I received a great blessing from your church service today."

The older woman studied her as if she was trying to decide if there was a hint of untruth in Anna's words. After a moment she held out her hand. "I'm Sadie Carter. I enjoyed havin' the organ to sing with today. You did a right good job."

Anna smiled. "Thank you, Mrs. Carter. I consider that a great compliment."

The other woman, who appeared to be in her twenties, held out her hand. "And I's Louise Adams."

"I'm so glad to meet you, Mrs. Adams. I hope to see both of you again soon."

Mrs. Carter nodded. "We 'spect we'll see you at church next Sunday." She turned and headed toward a buggy parked at the side of the yard.

A shy smile pulled at Louise's face. "Goodbye, Miss Anna. It was nice meetin' you."

Anna watched the two women hurry away before she turned back to Martha. "Thank you for introducing me."

Martha grabbed her hands and smiled. "I know it's gonna be hard gettin' to know everybody, but you will. In the meantime you got Simon and Granny and me and John to help you. I want to git to know you better while you're here."

Anna smiled and squeezed the woman's hand. "I want that too, Martha. I think we'll be great friends. Maybe we'll see each other soon."

Martha looked at her husband, and he winked at her. They glanced toward Granny's buggy where Simon stood talking to her. "I 'spect we'll be a-seein' you. Sooner than you think."

They walked toward their wagon, and Anna hurried to where Granny waited beside the buggy. "Go on and climb in," Granny said. "I'll jest check on Jim 'fore we head home."

Simon hustled to take the reins from her. "Let me do that, Granny."

She waved him away with a flutter of her hands. "Nonsense. You talk to Anna. This ole horse and I won't be half a minute."

Simon turned to her, and Anna's breath caught in her throat. His gaze drifted over her face. "So what did you think of our church?"

"I enjoyed the service very much, Simon. Your message was one I'll think about for a long time."

His face flushed, and he cleared his throat. "Thanks. I appreciate that."

"I liked your brother and sister-in-law too. They're a lovely couple."

He smiled. "I'm glad. They mean a lot to me."

He reached for her hand and helped her into the buggy, his fingers holding hers a bit longer than necessary. When she was settled in the seat, he leaned against the side of the buggy and stared up at her. "You made quite an impression on the folks here today, Anna."

Her eyes grew wide and she shook her head. "How can you say that? Hardly anyone even spoke to me—except the children, I suppose."

Simon propped his foot on the buggy step and leaned closer. "The Cove people appear reserved, and you have to prove yourself to them before they will accept you. I could see how they appreciated you playing the organ for them to sing, and then there was something more."

Puzzled, she looked at him. "What?"

"It was how you treated their children. I saw it in the way you tamed the Ferguson children, and I saw it in the faces of the mothers who stood at the back of the church and watched their children singing with you after services. You were patient and kind, and everybody appreciated that. I think you've won the hearts of the Cove people."

"But I don't understand. What am I to do when no one speaks to me or seems to want to talk to me?"

"Just remember, they're as afraid of not being accepted by you as you are of them. Don't be afraid to make the first move toward friendship, and they'll respond."

In that moment Anna realized she had entered the church expecting the people to distrust her, and that's what she had seen. She had misjudged them just as she had misjudged Ted and Lucy at first. From now on, she decided, she would make every effort to get to know the people who inhabited this beautiful valley.

She glanced at Simon, and her faced warmed as it so often seemed to do when Simon was around. "I've liked everyone I've met. I hope I can become a part of this community while I'm here."

His gaze flitted across her face before he glanced back at the church. "Well, I guess I'd better close the church up. I'll see you later."

Granny stepped back to the side of the buggy, and Simon helped her climb in before he turned and walked back toward the church. Anna studied his retreating figure and thought of how handsome he'd looked standing in the pulpit earlier. She'd only known Simon for a few weeks, but for some reason she felt as if she'd known him all her life. There was kindness in his heart and concern for everyone he met.

Anna suddenly realized Granny was talking, and she pulled her attention back to the present. "I'm sorry—What did you say?"

"I said I need to git home and git dinner ready. Simon and John and Martha are a-comin' to eat with us."

"I'm glad you invited them. It'll give me a chance to get to know Martha better."

Anna closed her eyes and thought about Simon's words today and the voices of the people as they sang. Her fears about fitting into life in the Cove dissolved as she recalled the friendly manner of John and Martha and Simon's reassuring words. She might still be considered an outsider by some in the Cove, but something she didn't understand was drawing her to the people and their way of life here. She smiled as she realized the thought made her happy.

Chapter 9

Sunday dinner at Granny's house proved to be very different from the meals Anna's family had shared together. Her parents had insisted that Sunday was a time for reflection about the blessings God had provided the week before, and conversation at the dinner table was discouraged. Not so around Granny's kitchen table.

Simon and John talked and laughed throughout the meal. She didn't think she'd ever seen two brothers who were closer, and it made Anna wish she'd had the same kind of relationship with her brother. Now too much had passed between them, and it was too late to forget the angry words that had been spoken, or the heartbreak they'd produced.

She glanced at Granny, who was shaking with laughter over something Simon had just said. Contentment welled up in her. It had been a long time since she felt such peace. Coming to Cades Cove had been one of the best decisions she'd ever made.

Anna swallowed her last bite of the apple pie Granny had baked before leaving for church and sighed contentedly. Across the table Simon grinned. "I hope you like your pie, Anna. I almost lost my life trying to provide you with the apples."

Anna laid her fork on her plate and laughed. "I'm sure Granny will think of you every time she bakes an apple pie from now on."

Martha giggled and wagged a finger at her brother-in-law. "It's a good thing you weren't killed. Granny might never have wanted to bake an apple pie again."

A little shiver raced up Anna's spine at the memory of how scared she'd been that day. She clasped her hands in her lap. "Simon tried to make out like it was nothing more than falling down and skinning his knee. But when he was lying on the ground, I thought he was dead. I don't think I'll ever forget how he looked."

Simon smiled. "I do have to say your face was rather pale."

"I'm just glad it ended well." She picked up the bowl of potatoes and spooned some into her plate. "Even if I have finished, I need another bite of these potatoes. They're the best I've ever eaten. What did you put in them, Granny?"

Granny chuckled and glanced at the others seated at the table. "Think we need to let Anna in on our mountain secret?"

John and Simon put their forks down and leaned forward, frowns pulling at their brows. Simon propped his elbows on the table and tented his fingers. "I don't know, Granny. You think we can trust Anna to guard the secret of the hills?"

Anna sat back in her chair and sighed. "Martha, I believe Simon takes great delight in teasing me. If I encourage him, he'll only tease me more about the big secret of the hills. If John's as bad as his brother, I don't know how you stand being around these two all the time."

Martha laughed. "It can git mighty rough at times, but I guess I'm used to it." She put her fork down and pushed her plate away. "But don't pay no mind to them, Anna. I'll tell you what the secret is. It's ramps."

"What's ramps?"

"Kinda like an onion," Granny said. "Better get used to the taste, Anna. We use 'em in ev'rything in the hills—taters, eggs, seasonin' for peas and beans. We like our ramps."

Martha twisted to face Anna. "I wish you was gonna be here next spring. You could go with us to the ramp patch." She directed a scowl at John. "Maybe you won't make me sit out and miss all the fun like you did this year."

Anna looked from Martha to Granny. "What happens at the ramp patch?"

Across the table Simon laughed. "It's a big day for us. All the families go to the place in the Cove where our little delicacy grows. We take a shovel and a flour sack, and we dig ramps to put in our root cellars. After we've dug all we can use, the women put out all the food they've brought, and we eat 'til we're about to bust."

Anna winked at Martha before she faced Simon. "Considering the way you eat every time you come to Granny's, I can't imagine you getting enough to make you bust."

Martha laughed and grasped Anna's arm. "Good for you, Anna. Don't let him git away with nothing." She glanced down at the last bite of pie on her plate. "Granny, that was good, but I'm full. You make the best apple pie of anybody in the Cove."

Granny hopped up from the table and grabbed the coffeepot from the stove. She held it aloft. "Go on, now. It's the coffee what makes it so good. Anybody want more?"

Martha held up her cup for a refill. "Have you noticed, Anna, that Granny don't like to be complimented?"

Anna nodded. "Like it or not, I'm sure it's the truth. But I suppose Simon could be a good judge of who makes the best pie in the Cove. If he eats everywhere else like he does here, he should be able to tell us."

Simon shoveled the last bite in his mouth and grinned. "I have to say Granny and Martha are tied for the winner."

John shook his head. "Maybe you shoulda been a politician 'stead of a preacher."

Granny set the coffeepot back on the stove and surveyed the group. "Can I git anythang else for you?"

From across the table Simon grinned and gazed at Anna in a way that made her heart flutter. She'd never met anyone like Simon. One minute she could be laughing at his teasing, and the next her pulse would race at the way he stared at her. The fork dropped from her hand and clattered against the plate.

Granny looked up, surprise on her face. "What's the matter, Anna?"

"Just clumsy," she said, blushing. She pushed her chair back from the table and reached across to stack Simon's plate on top of hers. He grabbed her hand just before she pulled it away. "Wait, Anna. I want some more of Granny's apple pie."

"More? But you've already had two pieces."

John slapped Simon on the back. "Well, brother, I'd say this little gal has you pegged." He pointed to Anna. "Let 'im have it, Anna. Ma never could teach him any manners. Maybe you can."

Simon glanced at his brother. "Now that's an idea. Maybe I need to take lessons in how to act in company." He looked up at Anna. "You willing to teach me?"

She opened her mouth to make a retort, but the words wouldn't come. She felt as if they were the only two people in the room. Her heart pounded in her ears as she broke into a grin. "Anytime, Simon," she smiled.

The muscle in the side of his jaw twitched. "I guess you're right. Two pieces is enough for anybody." He cleared his throat, and a crooked smile pulled at his lips. "I don't want to make it hard on my poor old horse."

John scooted his plate from in front of him. "Yeah, me neither. I better quit."

Martha reached over and grabbed John's plate. "Good. Granny won't invite us back if you and Simon eat up all her food." She shook her finger at her husband and brother-in-law. "And you two leave Anna alone. She's not used to your shenanigans." She patted Anna's arm. "Don't let 'em bother you. They do this to me all the time. You just gotta ignore 'em."

Granny chuckled and stood up. "This here's been 'bout the best Sunday I've had in years. It's good to have friends to share the day with. Now why don't you young folks go on outside and set under the tree? Enjoy this beautiful Lord's day in the mountains. I'll come out after a while."

Martha stood and headed to the dry sink. "I'll help you clean up."

Granny put her hand on Martha's arm. "Naw, I kin do it. Go on and enjoy the sunshine."

Martha put her hand to her abdomen and grasped the back of her chair. "If'n you don't mind then, Granny, I think we best go home. I need to rest some this afternoon."

Fear prickled up Anna's spine. "Are you all right? Do we need to do anything?"

"No, I'll be fine."

A worried expression clouded Granny's features, and she stepped next to Martha. "You havin' any pains, Martha?"

"No, nothing like that. Just tired after the long morning." She darted a glance at Simon. "And the long sermon."

Anna burst out laughing and put her arm around Martha's shoulder. "I couldn't have said it better myself."

John, who'd suddenly gone mute, came around the table. His dark eyes that had laughed just minutes ago now appeared veiled. Anna wondered if Martha had been having problems they hadn't shared. He put his arms around his wife's shoulders. "Come on, Martha. Let me get you home."

As John propelled her toward the door, Martha turned back to Anna. "Come visit me, Anna."

"I will."

She and Granny walked to the front porch and watched as Simon escorted John and Martha to the wagon. When John had lifted her up, he climbed beside her. Simon stood in the yard until they disappeared down the road.

When he returned to the porch, all the good humor of earlier had disappeared. A frown wrinkled his forehead. "Granny, you think Martha's all right?"

Granny waved her hand in dismissal and held the door for them to reenter the house. "Women go through all kinds of thangs when they waiting for a baby. Now don't fret about Martha. We gonna take good care of her."

Simon stopped by the fireplace in the sitting room and bit his lip. "I don't know what John would do if something happened to her. Or to the baby."

Granny patted his shoulder. "Now don't go lookin' for trouble. You two go on outside and enjoy the day like I told you."

Despite her words, a troubled frown creased her face as Granny turned back to the kitchen. Anna longed to return the afternoon to the lighthearted chatter of minutes before. She couldn't bear to see Simon so concerned. She stepped up beside him.

"Well, sir, if you've finally filled your belly, why don't we take a walk around the yard?"

A transformation took place at her words, and the Simon she knew reappeared. He chuckled, grabbed her hand, and pulled her toward the back door. With a bow he opened the door and motioned outside. He cleared his throat and spoke in a deep voice. "After you, Miss Prentiss."

Anna lifted her chin and walked past him. "Thank you, Reverend Martin."

In the sunshine she lifted her face toward the sky and closed her eyes. "Oh, that feels good. It is a beautiful day."

"It is," he murmured.

Thoughts of her mother and brother back home flickered in her mind, and she wondered if the day was as gorgeous there as it was in the mountains. She doubted it. The clover blossoms in the field behind the house waved in the afternoon breeze. "Did I tell you about Granny teaching me to make whooping cough syrup?"

"I knew Granny made some each year when the clover's blooming."

Anna walked to the edge of the field, plucked a bloom, and sniffed it. "It's amazing that this sweet flower can be used for medicine."

The teasing smile she'd come to know pulled at Simon's mouth. "Say, that clover sure does look inviting."

Her eyebrows arched. "What do you mean?"

"Well, it looks like it's just waiting for two people to have a race through it."

Her eyes grew wide. "Simon Martin, have you lost your mind?"

He grinned at her. "You may think so when I tell you I like to run barefoot."

She crossed her arms and regarded him with a skeptical look. "Are you suggesting that I take off my shoes and run a footrace with you?"

Simon plopped down on the ground and pulled off one of his shoes. He sat there holding the shoe, his sock still on. "Come on, Anna. It's a lot of fun."

Anna remembered how she and her brother had raced through the meadows back home when they were children. Suddenly she was filled with a longing for days gone by. Days when the innocence of childhood had not yet turned to the disappointments in adulthood. Back then her father always told her she could hold her own with any boy. Maybe she could recapture a bit of those moments with Simon.

His toes twitched, and his grin grew larger. "Afraid to race me?"

She shook her head. "No, but I don't think I want to run barefoot. I think I'll just keep my shoes on." She whirled and dashed toward the field. "Catch me if you can…just as soon as you get your shoes off!"

"What? No fair!" Simon yelled as she sped away.

She glanced over her shoulder and giggled at the sight of him struggling to get his other shoe off. Then he was on his feet and flying after her. She squealed and ran faster, but she knew he was gaining on her. Just as she reached the far edge of the field, she felt him grab her arm.

He spun her around, and before she knew it his arms were wrapped around her. She collapsed in giggles against him.

Simon gripped her arms tighter, and she fell against his chest. "Aren't you a tricky one? Thought you could pull one over on me while I was taking my shoes off."

She laughed and twisted in his arms. Suddenly he was very still, and she looked up into his face. The laughter died in her throat at his intense expression. She shivered, but she couldn't pull away from him. His arms tightened, and he groaned. "Oh, Anna, you're so beautiful."

Her heart pounded in her chest as his lips pressed against hers. Even though her mind cried out a warning, she brought her arms up, circled his neck, and reveled in the thrill of the moment. Never had anything felt so right as it did to be in Simon's arms. Suddenly the thought of her brother flashed into her mind and she pulled away. She wiggled from his embrace and took a step to distance herself from him.

"Anna, what's wrong?" His husky voice was barely more than a whisper.

"We can't do this, Simon."

He swallowed, and his Adam's apple bobbed. Anguish lined his features, and he hesitated as if debating whether or not to speak. He let out a long breath. "Why not? I feel drawn to you, Anna. I can't help it. I find myself thinking about you all the time. When I'm with you, I can't make myself quit looking at you. I wanted to kiss you, and I know you wanted it too."

She couldn't meet his gaze. "It doesn't matter if I wanted it or not. I feel guilty because it happened."

He frowned at her. "Why?"

"Because I got caught up in the moment and forgot about why I'm here."

Simon's shoulders slumped. "And you're going to leave."

"Yes. I was honest with you about that from the first day I arrived."

Anna turned away and walked toward the big tree at the other end of the field where she and Simon had first peeled apples together. Simon followed. When she reached the chairs still sitting under the tree, she sank down on one. Simon dropped down in the other and put his shoes back on.

She struggled to keep the tears from flooding her eyes. "I want to be fair to you. I've told you ever since I came here that I'm going to New York."

"I know that's what you thought. But things change. What if there's something better for you here, Anna? Have you thought about that?"

She wanted to make him understand. "I can't change what was set in motion before I came. My brother is the reason I'm here. He'll only give me the money for school if I get a good report from Granny." She doubled her fists. "I'm not going to let him win."

He stood and stared at the clover for a few moments before he faced her. "I see. Then the way I feel is of no importance to you?"

She jumped up and grabbed his arm. "Of course you're important to me, and of course I have feelings for you like I've never had for anyone before. But falling in love is something I want to do in the future… after I've finished school."

A muscle in his jaw twitched, and his lips trembled. He took a deep breath and cleared his throat. "It seems like you have your life planned out. Thank you for speaking so frankly with me, Anna. I hope everything works out, and you get to New York."

The hurt in his eyes pricked her heart, and a tear trickled down her cheek. She took a deep breath. "And what about you?"

"What do you mean?"

"Granny told me you came back when your parents were sick and that you didn't get to return to school. Don't you ever wish you hadn't stayed here? You're such a good preacher I'm sure you could have pastored a big church in a city."

His face drained of color, and his lips trembled. "How did you know?"

She frowned. "Know what?"

"That I wanted to do just that, but God didn't give it to me. I thought He wanted me to preach to large congregations and win lots of souls for Him, but He kept me here in the Cove."

"And you've regretted that?"

He tilted his head to the side. "Maybe not regretted. I don't understand why God left me here. My teachers at Milligan said I was the best student of the Bible they'd seen. They thought I would do great things. Instead I'm still here in the Cove where most of the people are Christians. Now I doubt I'll ever leave."

She grasped his hand. "Then why not come to New York with me? I'm sure your former teachers could help you find a church there. We could see each other all the time, and it would give us time to figure out this…whatever it is we feel for each other."

He didn't speak for a moment, but then shook his head. "Somehow I don't think God wants me in New York. If He wants me to leave the Cove, He'll work it out for me. Until then I'll stay right here."

She took a deep breath. "When I'm an old woman, I don't want to question God about why He didn't let me become a nurse. I intend to go to New York in the fall. If that means putting my personal feelings aside, I'll do it. Do you understand?"

Simon blinked and backed away from her. "Yes. I didn't mean to upset you. Forgive me, Anna. It won't happen again."

She struggled to speak. "There's nothing to forgive."

He straightened his shoulders. "I think I'd better be gettin' on home. I hope to see you soon."

Anna watched him leave, her heart aching at the slump of his shoulders. In a few minutes she heard the clip-clop of his horse's hooves on the road in front of the house. She wanted to run around the house and watch him leave, but she steeled herself to walk back inside.

When she entered the kitchen, Granny, an astonished look on her face, put out her hand to stop Anna, but she rushed past into her bedroom. She threw herself across the bed and began to sob.

A gentle hand touched her back and she sat up. Granny sat down beside her, concern on her face. "Child, what happened? Simon come in and left in a hurry, then you run in here a-cryin'. What is it?"

Anna threw herself into Granny's arms. "Oh, Granny. I don't understand what it is about Simon that makes me forget everything I've dreamed about for years. Is my brother right? Am I so spoiled that I want everything I see?"

Granny caressed her head. "Hush, now," she crooned. "You ain't spoiled. Jest maybe mixed up 'bout your feelin's. That ain't uncommon for a young woman."

She pulled back and stared into Granny's eyes. "Why do I feel like I've always known Simon? When he looks at me, I forget all about New York."

"What does Simon say?"

Anna wiped away the tears. "He said he feels drawn to me—that he thinks about me all the time."

Granny smiled. "Sounds like there's somethin' a-brewin' 'twixt the two of you. Don't worry, child. Jest pray about it, and God will lead you in the right way."

Anna nodded. "I'll pray, Granny, but I'm going to pray that God will take these feelings away."

~

As much as he wanted to, Simon didn't look back as he rode away from Granny's. He was afraid he would see Anna standing in the yard. But then, why would she? She'd made it very plain that she was committed to attending school in New York, and there was nothing he could do to change her mind.

There was no reason for him to even think about her anymore, and yet he felt their hearts had bonded the moment she stepped out of that buggy on her first day in the Cove. How else could she have realized the depth of his despair over having to stay here instead of preaching in the city? Only a woman who could see into his heart would know how his lost dream haunted him.

He shook his head in resignation. He had to forget her. But how could he after the kiss they'd shared this afternoon? When she'd responded, his heart had jumped for joy. But it had taken only a moment for his hopes to crash down around them.

He doubled his fist and gritted his teeth. Anna was only in the Cove for a short time, and he needed to stay away from her until she left. It was just for the summer. There were other young women who'd grown up in the mountains and intended to stay. Maybe he hadn't looked at them in the right way. He'd seen them as his congregation members, not as potential candidates for marriage. Marriage— the thought made his heart sink even lower. He'd always known what his wife would be like. No one had even come close to fulfilling his dreams until Anna arrived.

One of his friends at seminary had told him about falling in love, and how he'd known the first time he laid eyes on the girl he would marry. Simon wanted that same experience and thought it happened when he first saw Anna. But she'd dashed all those hopes today.

He looked up toward the sky. "God, give me the strength to stay away from her."

At that moment Horace Simmons's buggy approached from the other direction. Simon pulled his horse to a halt. The family was probably out for an afternoon ride enjoying the warm sunshine.

Horace pulled the buggy to a stop beside him. "Afternoon, Simon. Beautiful day, ain't it?"

"It is indeed." He raised himself up in the stirrups and tipped his hat to Horace's wife. "Afternoon, Mrs. Simmons."

The woman, who Simon had always thought seemed shy, ducked her head and smiled. "Hello."

Their daughter, Linda Mae, sat in the back seat of the buggy. A smile lit her face, and her eyelashes flickered. "Where you goin' this afternoon, Simon?"

Her sultry voice reminded him of John's words about Linda Mae's interest in him. He propped his arm on the horn of the saddle and returned her smile. "On my way home from visiting, Linda Mae."

She scooted to the side of the buggy and leaned out toward him. "Me and Mama been sayin' we sure wish you'd come by for supper one night. Haven't we, Mama?"

Mrs. Simmons nodded. "You's welcome anytime, Preacher."

"That sounds good. I'll try to make it by there real soon."

Horace flicked the reins over the horses. "We's always glad to have you, Simon."

Simon tipped his hat to Linda Mae as the buggy rolled past him. She turned around and waved to him. He raised his hand to return the wave, and then lowered it. Guilt raced through him. Had his exchange with Anna made him overly friendly with Linda Mae? He had to be careful. He'd never given any encouragement to a young woman in his congregation before, and he didn't need to start now.

With a heavy heart he headed toward home, but his head was filled with thoughts of a beautiful girl running through a field of clover. He didn't think he'd ever forget that sight.

Chapter 10

Later that afternoon Anna wandered out the back door and stood in the yard, gazing at the field beyond. She closed her eyes and relived her race through the clover with Simon.

She wrapped her arms around her waist in an effort to calm the quiver she felt each time she remembered the afternoon. For an instant they'd laughed and shrieked in delight, and then they had shared the moment she couldn't forget. Her fingertips brushed her lips, and she closed her eyes at the memory of Simon's lips touching hers. It had been so wonderful until the shadow of New York and nursing school rose between them.

Anna gazed into the distance at the towering trees clustered together at the far edge of the field and wondered what lay beyond. She shaded her eyes with her hand and squinted at the forest.

The scene reminded her of home and how as a child she had waited patiently at the end of the rows while her father and brother hoed the weeds that threatened their crops. She always had a dirt cake or pie waiting for them when they worked their way toward her, and they would make a big pretense of eating what she'd cooked.

Suddenly a homesick feeling welled up inside her. She wanted to see her mother and even Robert. She wanted to lie down on her bed and pull the familiar patchwork quilt around her. She wanted to chase Lucifer the rooster across the backyard and sit on the porch with her dog Fluff at her feet.

Although the people at church appeared to welcome her, only Martha had seemed truly hospitable. But after this afternoon she probably wouldn't be seeing Simon much…which meant she wouldn't get to know John and Martha either. A tear squeezed from the corner of her eye and trickled down her face.

A gentle breeze blew down from the surrounding mountains. The branches on the trees in the distance waved as if beckoning to her. Granny had mentioned there were blackberry bushes at the edge of the woods. Her mouth watered at the thought of plopping a juicy berry into her mouth. Picking a few would, at least, take her mind off her own problems for a few minutes. With a determined stride, she set off through the clover field for the tree line in the distance.

The clover brushed her legs as she trudged through its thick carpet at her feet, but her gaze didn't stray from the line of trees. As she approached, she slowed and peered at the low-hanging branches. Thick vegetation blocked the sunlight beyond, and an eerie gloom covered the area beneath the trees until it dissolved into blackness.

To her right she spied a tall clump of blackberry brambles, heavy with fruit. She plucked a berry and popped it into her mouth. She smiled as the sweet juice trickled down her throat. Berry picking with Mama had always been one of her favorite times of the year.

As she reached for another, her hand froze in midair at a rustling from the other side of the bush. Her eyes grew wide. The brambles moved again, this time to the accompaniment of a low animal sound. Fear rose in her throat. She willed her trembling legs to move, but they seemed anchored to the earth. A loud snort ripped through the silent forest, and the bush shook again.

Only one thing could make a sound like that and be tall enough to reach the top of a blackberry bramble—a bear. She hesitated, uncertain whether to run or try to scare the animal away.

Suddenly a black paw snaked through the thorny plant and pulled at a clump of berries in front of her nose. The branches parted, revealing the form of a large black bear, separated from her by the thorny growth that dipped with the weight of the berries. Fear like she'd never known coursed through her. The bear, intent on feeding, stilled for a moment. Anna held her breath, expecting him to crash through the brambles at any minute, claws raised and teeth bared.

Careful not to step on a twig in the process, she slowly inched backward until she felt the clover lapping at her ankles again. With one last glance toward the berries, she spun around and ran for the safety of the house. If she'd run that fast earlier Simon never would have caught her.

She dashed through the field, checking with every other step to confirm the bear wasn't following. Relief washed over her as she reached the edge of Granny's yard. Winded, she fell on her knees and leaned forward, gasping for breath.

The back door burst open. Granny, wiping her hands on her long apron, charged out of the house. She dropped to her knees beside Anna and grasped her shoulders. "What happened?"

Anna struggled to respond, but she could only pant in short spurts. Pointing a shaking finger in the direction of the trees, she gulped air and tried to form the word. "B-b-bear."

Granny's face paled and her eyes grew wide. She shot a startled glance across the field. "Where?"

"Over there." Anna pointed to the tree line again.

Granny increased her grip on Anna and pulled her to her feet. "Let me git you inside, then you tell me what in the tarnation you talkin' 'bout."

Leaning against Granny, Anna allowed herself to be led into the kitchen. Once inside Granny deposited her into a chair and reached for the hollowed-out gourd hanging on the wall. When she'd dipped it into the water bucket, she slipped it into Anna's hands. "Drink this."

The cool water soothed the burning in Anna's throat. When she finished, she handed the dipper back to Granny. "Thank you."

Granny returned the gourd to its place and sat down next to Anna. "Now, darlin', tell me 'bout this here bear. Where'd you see it?"

Granny's eyes narrowed as Anna told her of the decision to walk to the far side of the field. By the time Anna finished, Granny's mouth had formed a grim line across her face. She leaned back in her chair and raised her eyebrows. "Seems like I recollect havin' a talk with you 'bout the wild critters round here. What'd I say?"

Anna, unable to look into Granny's eye, clasped her hands in her lap and stared at them. "You said there are wild animals everywhere in the Cove, and I wasn't to go off by myself. No telling what I might run into." Her soft words quavered with remorse.

Granny bit her lip and nodded. "You jest gotta be careful. They's all kinds of varmints out there that don't mean no harm. They jest livin' the way the good Lord made 'em, but they'll attack if'n they think there's danger."

Anna still couldn't look Granny in the eye. She picked a blade of grass from her skirt and rolled it between her fingers. "I know. It's my fault. I should never have gone over there."

"This be the time of year when our bears are feedin', and blackberries be some of their favorites. In the Cove, we don't go berry pickin' alone." She put her finger under Anna's chin and tilted her face up. "And you don't go off on your own no more, you hear?"

The concern in Granny's eyes fueled the guilt Anna felt over the mishap. "Yes, Granny."

Granny smiled and wrapped her in a big hug. "Don't know what I'd tell Doc if somethin' happened to you. And Simon—land's sakes, he'd never speak to me again."

Tears flooded Anna's eyes again at the mention of Simon, but she managed to shake her head. "I don't think Simon would care so much, but thank you for being concerned."

Granny stood up and stared down at her. "You only been here a few weeks, Anna, but I declare you already seem like a daughter to me. Now don't you go scarin' me agin."

Anna jumped up and kissed Granny on the cheek like she'd seen Simon do before. "I won't. From now on I'm not leaving your side."

Granny put her arm around Anna's shoulders. "In that case, why don't we git in a little studyin' on my yarbs 'fore bedtime?"

Granny's suggestion stirred a resolve in Anna. After all, she'd come to the Cove to learn from Granny, and that's what she was going to do. No more thinking about Simon Martin. She had more important matters to address.

Anna smiled up at her. "I can't think of anything I'd rather do."

～

Two weeks later Anna sat under the tree behind Granny's house as the sun climbed higher in the morning sky. The sunrise had been one of the most beautiful she'd ever experienced, and she'd enjoyed it from the safety of Granny's yard.

She'd thought her family had risen early on the farm, but the Cove residents came to life the minute the new day crept over the top of the mountains. Granny's house was no exception.

Anna felt as if she'd already put in a day's work. The peas she'd picked right after breakfast had to be shelled, and she had volunteered for the task. The time alone gave her some undisturbed moments to think, and her mind wandered, her fingers moving in the rhythm she'd learned years ago as a child.

At times like this she was surprised at how her thoughts always returned to Simon. He hadn't visited since the day they raced through the field. Every time she thought of that afternoon she felt a prick in her heart. She sighed and threw a fistful of hulls to the ground. If she was lonely, there was nothing to be done about it now.

The rattle of a wagon on the bumpy road in front of the house caught her attention, and she paused in her task. Anticipation swept over her. Could it be Simon coming? She sat back in the chair and shook her head. He always rode his horse. It was probably one of the farmers.

"Anna," Granny's voice called from the back door. "Come on in, child. Andrew Long's here. We gotta go and tend to Gracie. She's a-needin' us right away."

Anna jumped up and grabbed the pan. "Coming, Granny."

She ran toward the house, apprehension mingled with excitement filling her at the thought of another baby. Within minutes she and

Granny climbed into the wagon and began the two-mile journey to Andrew and Gracie's farm.

Andrew looped the reins around his shaking hands and urged the horses forward. "Gracie never told me she was a-havin' pains when we got up this mornin'. I would've come for you 'fore now, but she waited 'til I got through milkin' and tendin' the livestock to tell me."

Granny reached over and patted his arm. "Now don't you fret none, Andrew. We gonna be in plenty of time. First babies take a long time gittin' here."

Andrew looked up at the sun. "I shore did hate to leave her alone, but I knowed I had to git you. What if somethin' happens whilst I'm gone?"

Granny smiled. "Now, now, don't go a-lookin' for trouble where there ain't none. We gonna have a long wait 'fore that child comes into the world."

Andrew shook his head. "I don't know. I jest cain't git the look on her face outta my mind." He turned to Granny, and Anna could see fear in his eyes. "She was skeered, Granny, and I didn't know what to do."

Anna leaned around Granny. "You did the right thing, Mr. Long. You knew your wife needed help, and you rushed to get it. Even though she's in pain right now, her heart is happy because she has a husband who wants to take care of her and his child."

For the first time Andrew smiled. "Yep. I reckon you're right."

Granny patted his arm again. "Now you just make these horses git us there as quick as you can, Andrew."

He popped the reins across the horses' backs, and the wagon surged forward. "We's on our way, Granny."

An hour after their arrival at the Long farm, Anna didn't think she'd ever been so hot. Even with the window open, the stifling air hung like a heavy blanket over the bedroom. Anna sat by Gracie Long and fanned the perspiring woman. Gracie bit down on her lip, and her body strained with another painful contraction. Anna could only imagine Gracie's suffering, but not a sound escaped the young woman's lips. With the calculation of the time Andrew said the pains began, Gracie had now been in labor for nearly twelve hours.

"Anna." Granny's voice interrupted her thoughts.

Anna jumped up. "Yes, Granny."

"I think we need to dose Gracie with some raspberry tea." She motioned toward one of the baskets she'd brought. "Can you make some for her?"

Anna leaned over and mopped Gracie's forehead. "Gracie, I'm going to make you some tea. I'll be back in a minute."

Gracie reached out and grabbed her hand. "Thank you, Miss Anna."

Anna wrapped her fingers around Gracie's and caressed them. "I'm just Anna, Gracie. After this baby gets here and you feel better, I know we're going to be great friends."

"I reckon we…" Gracie's voice trailed off with the onset of another contraction.

Anna turned and hurried from the room. When she stepped into the kitchen, Andrew jumped up from the table where he sat. Tired eyes stared out of his haggard face.

"Is the baby here yet?"

Anna shook her head. "No. Granny wants me to make Gracie some raspberry tea."

He eyes widened, and he glanced at the closed door behind Anna. "Is she hungry?"

Anna repressed a smile and stepped to the stove. "No. Raspberry tea will relax the muscles and make them work more efficiently. Maybe this will speed up the birth of your child."

Andrew raked his hand through his hair and paced back and forth across the floor. "I never thought about it bein' this hard on Gracie." Andrew stopped and faced Anna. "She shouldn't have waited so long to tell me. I'd've been to get Granny sooner had I knowed."

Anna opened the container holding Granny's tea leaves and dropped some in a pot. "You did fine, but Granny told her not to wait so long the next time."

Andrew shoved his hands in his pockets and began to pace again. "No need to worry about that. I reckon we won't be havin' no more young'uns after this."

Anna poured water from the kettle over the leaves. "That's what you say now, but after a while you'll want another."

Andrew shook his head. "No, ma'am. This gonna be it."

"We'll see." Anna filled a cup with the tea, picked it up, and headed back to the bedroom.

As she opened the door, Granny looked up from bending over Gracie. "Thank you, Anna. Now help me set 'er up so's she can drink."

Together they propped Gracie up and held her until she drained the cup. Exhausted, Gracie lay back on the bed.

Granny rubbed her arm and smiled down at her. "It's not gonna be long now, Gracie. You been a mighty brave girl, and the Lord's 'bout to reward you with your own little baby. Jest he'p me out a little more, and it'll be all over."

Gracie smiled, her lips trembling. "I'm makin' it fine, Granny."

Anna began to fan Gracie again. "I've never seen anybody braver, Gracie. Now just relax, and let's get this baby into the world."

For the next hour Anna continued to apply cool cloths to Gracie's head and wave the fan in front of her face. With the onset of each contraction Gracie bit her lip, but she couldn't hold back the soft moan that rumbled in her throat.

Suddenly Gracie's eyes grew wide, and her mouth gaped open. Her body convulsed, and she grabbed Anna's hand and squeezed it tight. "Hold onto me, Gracie. I'm right here with you."

For the first time fear flashed in Gracie's eyes. "Wh-what happened?"

Anna glanced toward the foot of the bed at Granny. Her eyebrows were pulled down over her nose in a frown, and she motioned for Anna to join her. Anna eased her hand out of Gracie's grasp. "I'll be right back." She moved toward Granny and stopped next to her. "What is it?"

"She's tearing. It happens a lot, especially with first babies."

Anna scooted closer to Granny. "What are you going to do?"

"Nothing yet. That'll come later, but I wanted you to see what happens."

Within minutes the baby's head emerged and then the body. As she had done with the Ferguson baby, Anna helped Granny cut the cord and placed the baby in Gracie's arms. Then she again joined Granny, who had picked up the basket she brought from home. She pulled out a jar filled with leaves and handed it to Anna.

"Now, I've got some things to do here to take care of Gracie. While I'm finishing up, I want you to take these leaves into the kitchen and steep them in some boilin' water. They's wild comfrey leaves, and I need 'em made into a tea."

Anna nodded. "Is this for Gracie to drink?"

Granny shook her head. "No, child. We's gonna use it on that tear Gracie had. After Gracie's cleaned up, I'm gonna soak a cloth in that comfrey tea and put it on the tear, sorta like I would a poultice. Then she's gonna have to sit in a pan of that tea a few times every day to start the healin'."

"Is that all you'll do?"

Granny shook her head. "I'm also gonna tie her legs together so she won't move around and reopen that place while it's healing. It's mighty uncomfortable for a woman, but that and comfrey tea is the only thing I got to help her. Now run along and get that tea a-seepin'."

"Do you want Mr. Long to come in yet?"

"Not yet. Tell him to give me a few more minutes."

Anna hurried to do as Granny said. As expected, Andrew jumped up from sitting at the kitchen table. "Is the baby here? Can I go in?"

Anna smiled and shook her head. "Not yet, Mr. Long. Give Granny a few more minutes, then I'll come get you. In the meantime, you can be happy that you have a healthy baby boy."

Andrew dropped down in the chair, his eyes wide. "A boy? How's Gracie?"

"She's fine, but I have to make some wild comfrey tea. I'm afraid she's going to have some healing to do."

"Just tell me what to do, and it'll git done."

"Granny will explain it to you before she leaves." Anna turned to the stove and dipped some water into a pan from the big pot they'd kept hot throughout the delivery. Ten minutes later she returned to the bedroom with a pan of comfrey tea. Granny dipped a cloth in the mixture and applied it to Gracie's wound. She glanced up at Gracie and smiled. "There now, Gracie," she crooned. "This is gonna soothe you some, but I'm afraid you ain't gonna like it when I have to tie your legs together. I want you to know it's for your own good."

Gracie opened her eyes and hugged her son tighter. "I know, Granny. I been a-hearin' the other women talkin' 'bout having to do it. I reckon if they can, I can too."

"You sure right about that. You're as brave as any woman I ever helped birth a baby, and I'm right proud of the way you did it."

Anna let her gaze travel over Granny as she worked to make Gracie more comfortable. She thought of all the things about childbirth she'd learned since coming to the mountains. But most of all, she'd learned about the attitude a nurse should have when ministering to a patient. Granny did it with a calm composure that hid any agitation or uncertainty she might have. Her ability to keep the mother relaxed during the birthing process even when a problem occurred was something Anna hoped she could master in time to come. If she could be half the nurse Granny was, she would be happy.

An hour later Anna opened the bedroom door again and stepped into the kitchen. Her heart plummeted to her stomach and she drew back in surprise. Simon sat at the table with Andrew.

Before she could say anything, Andrew jumped up and ran toward her.

"Can I go see Gracie and my boy now?"

Anna tore her gaze away from Simon and smiled at Andrew. "Go on in."

The lines in Andrew's tired face dissolved into a big smile. He grabbed Simon's hand and pumped it up and down. "Thanks for coming." With a whoop, Andrew disappeared into the bedroom. His voice drifted into the kitchen. "I been 'bout to go outta my mind, Gracie. You all right?"

Granny stepped out of the room and smiled at the sight of Simon. "Well, if it ain't the preacher come to see the new baby. Why don't you give the family a few minutes 'fore you go in?" She glanced from Simon to Anna. "I think I'm gonna git me some fresh air."

She walked out the back door and left Anna and Simon alone in the kitchen. Simon turned away from her and sat back down at the table. The silence beat on Anna's ear, piercing her heart.

With hesitant steps Anna moved to the table and slipped into a chair next to Simon. "It's good to see you. You haven't been to Granny's lately. We've missed you."

The muscle in his jaw twitched. He folded his hands on top of the table and stared at them. "I've been busy. I've had lots of visiting to do."

"Granny's been wondering what happened. She said you'd never stayed away from her house for this long before."

He fidgeted in his chair. "I'll make it up to her."

"How's Martha doing?"

"Fine." His fingers rubbed at a spot on the table, but he didn't look up.

Anna frowned. "Simon, are you angry with me?"

He shook his head. "What makes you think that?"

"Because you haven't been back to Granny's since...since the day we raced. I've missed you."

Simon let out a long breath and stood up. He pulled his watch out and glanced at it. "I've just been trying to pay more attention to the rest of my congregation. I don't want anyone to think I have favorites."

Anna blinked back the tears that were already threatening to fill her eyes. "Oh."

"In fact I have another visit to make before I go home. Tell Andrew and Gracie I'll come back and visit later. I don't want to disturb them now."

He picked up his hat and strode to the door, but Anna jumped up and ran after him. "Wait. Don't go."

His hand reached out to open the door. "What is it, Anna?"

She stopped beside him. "I'm going to cook supper for everyone in just a bit. Why don't you stay?"

He shook his head. "I can't. I'm sorry."

She took a little step away from him. "Are you eating with someone else?"

"No. I just need to get home."

Her chest tightened as if a heavy weight sat on it, and she struggled to keep from groaning with the hurt his cold attitude inflicted.

"Then please stay. I've hardly gotten to speak to you at church, and we can catch up on what's been going on with each other in the past two weeks."

"I've told you I can't stay. Now I have to go." His expressionless face gave no indication that the Simon she'd known lived within the man facing her.

He reached for the door, but she grabbed his arm. He recoiled and shook free of her. Confused, Anna stared up at him. "Simon, what's wrong?"

His eyes bored into her. "I think it's best if we stay away from each other."

She wiped at the tears that were starting to spill from her eyes. "You don't want to be my friend anymore?"

His lips trembled. "I can't be your friend."

He jerked the door open and walked out, leaving her alone. An emptiness consumed her, and she covered her face with her hands. She didn't think she'd ever hurt so much in her life.

~

Simon mounted his horse and galloped away from the Long farm. He fought the urge to wheel his mount about and dash back to Anna— to tell her he wanted to be more than her friend—but he couldn't. Since he'd met her, he'd yearned to share with her what Andrew and Gracie and John and Martha had, but that would never be.

If she only knew how hard it had been for him to stay away from Granny's these past few weeks. Seeing her at church had been agony for him, and today had even been worse. When she'd walked out of Gracie's bedroom his heart nearly burst with joy, but he couldn't let her know.

Lost in thought, he raced down the familiar road through the late afternoon shadows. As the Simmons' farm came into view an idea crossed his mind. Why not stop? They'd invited him to supper whenever he was passing, and today was as good a day as any. Maybe spending some time with them would take his mind off Anna.

The minute he tied his horse to the tree in the front yard of the farmhouse, the door opened and Linda Mae emerged on the porch. She waited on the top step as he walked toward her. "Ev'ning, Simon. You decide to take us up on our invite?" Her brown eyes flashed from underneath long lashes, and a bun at the back of her head held her long brown hair in place.

There was no doubt about it, he thought. Linda Mae was an attractive woman. She was taller than Anna, and her complexion was darker than Anna's creamy one. He shook his head to clear it. There was no need to compare Linda Mae to Anna. No one would ever measure up to Anna. But if Linda Mae's manner toward him was any indication, she was definitely open to a friendship with him.

A voice inside urged him to get on his horse and leave, but he ignored it. "I hope I'm not imposing on your mother stopping by like this."

She looped her arm through his and leaned against him for a moment before she drew him toward the door. "You's always welcome at our table, Preacher. C'mon in and talk to Pa whilst I help Mama git supper on the table. I done made an apple pie this afternoon, and I'm jest dyin' to show you what a good cook I am." She squeezed his arm as she guided him inside.

Suddenly his visit didn't seem like such a good idea. He felt like a victim being pulled into a web, and Linda Mae was the spider dragging him with her. His stomach churned. What was he doing here?

Chapter 11

For the next few days after arriving home from the Long farm, Anna immersed herself in Granny's teaching. She wrote so much in her journal she wondered if she was going to have to send to Gatlinburg for a new one. Every day Granny told her something new to add to her growing knowledge.

Anna was happy to have her mind occupied so that she wouldn't dwell on Simon and how much she missed him. In her heart, though, she understood his reasons for not visiting at Granny's anymore. If he wanted more from her than friendship, perhaps it was best they stay away from each other. After all, she would see him at church on Sundays. That would have to be enough.

On the third afternoon after being back at home, Anna prepared for another long session of study with Granny. They'd worked in the garden all morning, and this was the first time they'd taken a break from their everyday chores. Anna sat at the table where the herbs hung on the wall. Her open journal lay before her, and her pencil skimmed across the page as she tried to record everything Granny said.

Straightening from leaning over the table, Granny propped her hands on her hips and stretched her back. "So, how you feelin' 'bout them yarbs? Think you're a-larnin' 'em?"

Anna looked up from writing in her journal and nodded. "I feel much more at ease than I did the first day I came, but I'm more comfortable just watching you use them on a patient. I still worry I might make a mistake. How long did it take before you felt like you knew what you were doing?"

Granny walked over to the chairs in front of the fireplace and pulled one to the table. She eased down beside Anna. "I don't know if'n I feel that way even after all these years. But I larnt a long time ago that the Lord's in control. I jest turn ev'ry birthin' over to Him. I'm there to let 'im work through me."

"I want to be the same way, Granny. I pray every night that I'll be more like you, but I still have a long way to go in gaining confidence. I know a lot can go wrong when a woman's having a baby. I wonder how I can handle that when it happens."

The pencil slipped from Anna's fingers to the journal. Hoping Granny would dismiss her greatest fear with some witty words, Anna gazed up at her. Granny's somber expression frightened her even more.

"It's always pos'ble somethin's gonna go wrong during childbirth," she said. "That's why I thought we'd jest set a spell, 'cause there's some thangs I need to tell you and you'll prob'bly want to be a-sittin' when I talk about it."

Anna's eyes grew wide. "Have I done something wrong, Granny?"

Granny laughed and patted her arm. "Lands, no, child. You done a good job. 'Specially takin' care of the mother after the baby comes. That's a mighty important time."

"I know."

"That's why I try to keep thangs clean. Always remember to wash your hands a lot and put clean bedding on after the birth. We gotta be real careful with the mother 'cause we don't want no infection to set up. Most women what die in childbirth act'ly die from puerperal fever."

Reminding herself to check with Uncle Charles about the correct spelling later, Anna grabbed the pencil and wrote down the word. "What's that?"

"The first month after birth they's all kinds of germs kin git in the mother's womb then jest go all through her body. Ain't much I can do if that happens, so's I try to head if off at the beginnin' by keepin' the birth room clean as I can. And like I said, you been doin' a good job of that."

Anna's skin warmed with pleasure at the compliment. "Thank you, Granny."

Granny straightened in her chair. "But they's lots more you need to know. So far the birthin's you've seen been real easy ones."

Anna tilted her head and thought about the babies she'd seen born. "Easy? I thought Gracie never would have her baby."

Granny shook her head. "That ain't what I'm a-talkin' about. Gracie's time warn't near as long as you thought it was. Sometimes it's hours and hours. Don't know why. Some women jest take longer. But sometimes there's real problems, and I want you prepared if'n we have one."

Anna swallowed back the fear that rose inside her. "What kind of problems?"

Granny hesitated a moment. "Well, most times everythin' works out—maybe nine times outta ten you got no problems. Then along comes one you wish hadn't happened. Those are the time I'm a-talkin' 'bout."

Anna tightened her fingers on the pencil, poised her hand over the journal, and took a deep breath. "All right. I'm ready."

"Ev'ry once in a while you gonna have a breech birth. Now they's diff'rent kinds, and you need to know what to do." Granny hesitated. "Fact is most times there ain't much you can do. If the baby is a-comin' faceup or crosswise, it's real bad."

Anna frowned and wrote the terms in her journal. "Faceup I understand, but how will I know if the baby's crosswise?"

"You'll see the arms or the feet a-comin' first. If this happens, the first thing you try to do with a faceup or crosswise birth is to turn the baby. I'll show you later how you can try on the mother's stomach by a-pressin', but if'n the baby's settled, it prob'ly ain't gonna work."

"What do you do then?"

"Then you gotta try to turn 'im in the birth canal. You understand?"

"Yes. I've seen my father do it with our animals on the farm."

"Good. But it's a diff'rent feelin' when you gotta do it for a woman.

You jest pray the good Lord's gonna guide your hands." Granny thought for a moment before she went on. "If'n you cain't turn the baby, there's one more thang I've tried, but it don't always work."

"What's that?"

Granny pointed to the bedroom. "I sewed me a stuffed baby doll one time so's I could practice. When we git through, I'll go git it and teach you. But before I do, there's somethin' else you need to know about breech births."

Granny knelt beside her chair and reached underneath the table. When she stood, she held a long box in her hands. She placed it on the table and stared at it for a moment.

In Granny's eyes Anna detected a deep sorrow. Whatever was in the box was not something Granny wanted to show her. She didn't want to see it, either, but she knew she must. Anna leaned forward and touched Granny's hand. "What is that?"

Granny lifted the top of the box. Anna recoiled at the horrible instrument lying inside. Never in her life had she seen anything like the long iron rod with the curved hook at the end. Granny pulled it from the box and held it up.

Her lips trembled, and Anna realized Granny held death in her hands. "When nothing works to deliver the baby, you hafta save the mother's life."

Anna's mouth gaped open. "What do you do with it?"

Granny's creased face turned white. Anna wondered if she was remembering past experiences with the horrible instrument. Granny tried to speak and cleared her throat. "You gotta pull the baby's body apart so's the mother can git rid of it." The droning words cut a swath through Anna's heart, leaving a hollowed-out feeling in its wake.

A queasy feeling washed over Anna, and she jammed her fist into her mouth to keep from losing everything she'd eaten all day. When the wave of nausea passed, she shook her head and recoiled. "Oh, Granny. I could never do that. It's sickening." Her shrill voice echoed in the room.

Granny, anger flashing in her eyes, turned back to Anna. "You said you wanted to larn about helpin' mothers during childbirth. Well, sometimes you hafta help 'em by savin' their lives. When you see a woman in agony and know she's a-gonna die if you don't do somethin', you do what you hafta do. Now I know they ain't gonna use this here instrument in New York, but you ain't there yet. When you in the mountains all alone with a woman who's about to die, you hafta do what you can to save her life. Do you understand?"

Shame replaced the queasy feeling. Granny was right. Uncle Charles once told her the hardest part of being a doctor was having to watch a patient die. He said when he was losing a patient, he tried everything he knew to keep the person alive. Now she would be expected to do the same thing.

Anna gulped a deep breath and nodded. "All right, Granny."

Granny stared at the hook as if it held her in its spell. "I'm jest an ole mountain woman. Don't know much 'cept what my ma taught me. But I did tell Doc one time about having to do this with a baby. He told me I performed a craniotomy. I practiced on saying that word for a long time so's I'd remember it. Jest seemed like if I was gonna hafta do it, I oughter know what it was called."

Anna took the hook from Granny's hand and laid it back in the box with a shudder. "Well, maybe you've used it for the last time." She slipped the box back under the table and smiled at Granny. "Now, how about getting that baby doll? I'd sure like to know what the alternative is to using that thing."

Granny pulled her apron up and wiped at her eyes. "Be back in a minute." She stopped at the door and faced Anna. "The first time you went with me to Laura's for her baby, I knowed you was a-gonna be a good nurse to women in childbirth. Maybe the Lord's gonna lead you to stay in the Cove and work with our women."

When Anna said nothing, Granny left the room.

Within moments Granny returned with a rag doll dressed in a yellow calico dress. Small pieces of brown yarn had been sewn onto the head for hair. Embroidered wide blue eyes, small nostrils, and a smiling mouth decorated the face.

Granny laid the doll on the table. "I made this here doll myself, and I've used it a lot of times to practice on."

Anna studied the doll that looked as if it would appeal to any little girl. "How has this helped you with a breech baby?"

"I'll show you." Granny placed one hand at the bottom of the doll's abdomen and the other at the top. She pushed upwards with the lower hand while rotating the top hand to the side and downward. "You git your left hand positioned around the baby's head at the top and twist downward counterclockwise while your right hand pushes up from the bottom of the mother's belly. The first thing you gotta do is lift the baby's bottom out from where it's a-sittin' and try to move him crosswise. After a few minutes if he's moved to that position, let the mother rest a bit 'fore you start again. Then put your hands back in the same position and turn again to try and git the head to move down."

Anna nodded. "Does this usually work?"

Granny sighed. "I wish it did, but sometimes it just ain't meant to happen. Could be something's blocking the way, or just that the baby don't want to move." Granny stepped back from the table. "Now you try."

Anna placed her hands where Granny's had been moments before and tried to perform the movements the way Granny had done. After a few minutes she glanced up, and her hands froze in position. Tears sparkled in Granny's eyes. "What's the matter? Did I do something wrong?"

Granny wiped at a tear that trickled down her cheek. "You ain't done nothing, darlin'. I was just rememberin' something I try not to think about."

Anna released the doll and reached for Granny's hand. "I'm sorry. Is there anything I can do to help you?"

Granny turned away from the table and sank down in one of the chairs by the fireplace. Anna eased down next to her and waited for Granny to speak, but she appeared to be lost in thought. After a moment she took a deep breath.

"You remember I told you I had a daughter that died?"

"Yes."

"Well, since you been here, I cain't help thinkin' 'bout her all the time. She never did like livin' in the Cove. Wanted to see the world, she said. This feller come to our valley one summer, and he promised her all kinds of things if 'n she'd go with him over to Gatlinburg to live. I didn't want her to go, but she run off and married him. Just left me a note tellin' me maybe she'd see me agin someday."

Anna's heart constricted and tears filled her eyes. "Oh, Granny. I'm so sorry. Did you ever see her again?"

"She come home 'bout a year later. Her husband turned out to be a right bad feller just like I thought. He stayed drunk a lot, and he'd beat her for no reason. When she got here, she was sick and expectin' a baby. She'd saved enough money from takin' in washin' to pay a man to bring her home. When she got here, she didn't do nothin' but sleep for two days."

Anna reached over and laced her fingers with Granny's. "I know you were glad to have her back."

"I was." Granny sighed. "Then came the night she started havin' the baby. He was a breech baby, and I tried everything I knowed to turn him, but he wouldn't move."

"What happened?" Anna could barely whisper the words.

Granny's eyes narrowed, and she stared into space as if she had traveled back in time to that horrible night. "I told her I had to use the hook and git the baby out of her. She begged and pleaded for me not to. She wanted her baby to have a chance to live. She told me if I killed her baby she'd hate me for the rest of her life."

Tears ran down Anna's face, and she tightened her grip on Granny's hand. "How terrible."

Granny tilted her head to one side. "I knowed what I needed to do, but I couldn't. Not with Deborah a-beggin' me to save her child." She shook her head. "I shouldn't have listened to her. By morning they was both dead, and I knowed I had killed them."

Anna dropped to her knees beside Granny and threw her arms around her. "You can't think like that. No, you didn't."

"Yes, I did. I could have saved Deborah. Even if she had hated me for it, at least she'd be alive." She reached down, put her finger under Anna's chin, and tilted her face up. "I wanted to tell you this 'cause someday you may have to make a decision like that. Do what you have to do so that at least the mother or the child will live. Promise me, Anna."

Anna stared at Granny through her tears. "I promise," she whispered. Then she laid her head in Granny's lap and cried for the anguish Granny had suffered for the decision she'd made years ago, for Deborah who gave her life in hopes her child would live, and for a baby who never had the chance to know what his life could have been.

The afternoon lesson had left Anna shaken. She'd attended each birth as if nothing could go wrong. Thankfully nothing had yet, but she'd never make the mistake of not recognizing the dangers again.

Her mother told her there was nothing greater she could do than help women at the most dangerous time of their life—when they were giving birth. Now Granny had opened her eyes to what could happen. She prayed she was strong enough to cope with what might lie in the future.

～

The next afternoon Anna stood at the kitchen table and scooped the last of the cooled jam from inside the pan. With quick movements she ladled it into the jar on the table.

"That's the last one fer today," Granny said as she screwed on the top. "Mmm. This jam's gonna taste mighty good when winter comes."

Since coming to the Cove, Anna had worked alongside Granny each day to prepare for the coming winter. Although the days were warm and food was plentiful, the cold days weren't far off. Then Granny, as well as all the Cove residents, would rely on what they'd laid by in the summer. Rows of canned beans and peas lined the walls of the root cellar along with the sacks of ramps and buckets of dried apples. The sweet jam would be next.

Anna pushed a strand of hair out of her face and propped her hands on her hips. "Well, Granny, it looks like you're gonna be eating well this winter."

Granny ran a spoon around the inside of the pan to collect a scoop of jam. She popped the tasty morsel in her mouth and smiled. "That's good. I shore do thank the good Lord fer providin' my needs. I larnt a long time ago that if'n you do a little bit ev'ry day, by the end of the summer, you'll be surprised at what you done."

Anna nodded. "That's wise. Gather all the vegetables from the garden every morning, cook what you need for the day, and preserve the rest. I'll remember that."

Granny dropped the spoon into the empty pot. "That's jest the way the mountain women do. Guess your ma did the same."

"She did, but she had a larger garden. We would put up a bushel of peas or beans at one time. And we had hogs and cattle. So we always had lots of meat to get us through. I've noticed the Cove people don't raise cattle."

Granny shook her head. "Naw, but ev'ry farm has a milk cow or two. Most jest raise hogs and chickens. We got all kinds of wild game here, so that's 'bout all the meat we get. 'Cept of course hams and bacon. Ev'ry farmer tries to raise a hog to kill." She chuckled to herself. "Hog killin' time be real excitin'. Ev'rybody helps each other. I don't raise no hogs, so folks give me hams and bacon for he'pin' with a birth."

Anna set the jam pan in the dry sink and poured some water into it. "I wondered where the meat in your smokehouse came from. I knew you didn't have hogs."

"If'n you were here in fall, you could go with me to all the hog killin's and have a great time."

"It sounds like fun."

Granny pulled a basket from the pegs by the back door and began to set the jars in it. "Well, we gonna dig taters in a few weeks. The ground where they's planted is beginnin' to bust open. So them hills are 'bout ready to be dug. And then the corn be ready after that."

Anna took the basket from Granny. "Lots to look forward to. I'll put this in the root cellar for you."

A frown pulled at Granny's brows as she rubbed her hip. "Thanks, darlin'. It's getting' harder for me to git down there. You shore have been a big he'p to me."

Anna studied the woman who'd been so kind to her since she arrived in the Cove. "Not nearly as much as you've helped me, Granny. Thank you for everything."

Granny waved her hand in dismissal. "Go on and get that to the root cellar. Then we gonna eat a bite before we head out."

Surprise rippled through Anna. "Head out for where?"

"We jest been talkin' 'bout how the Cove people have to get ready for winter. Well, Laura Ferguson still ain't a-feelin' well. I thought we might go over and see how we can he'p her out this afternoon."

The thought of Ted and Lucy brought a smile to Anna's face. "Oh, good. I've been wanting to see the children."

Granny chuckled and shook her head. "I reckon you 'bout the only one ever been able to make them young'uns behave. They shore did take a likin' to you."

Anna called over her shoulder as she pushed the back door open. "I liked them too."

Outside Anna hurried to the root cellar and deposited the jam, then turned back to the house. In the backyard she paused and let her gaze wander. Granny's rooster Jasper strutted across the yard, his head cocked to the side. Anna looked around for Jewel, the setting hen, but she was nowhere in sight.

Anna stuck her head in the henhouse and stared into the dim interior. A clucking sound, almost like a growl, came from the direction of Jewel's nest. "Just checking, Jewel. Didn't mean to bother you." Anna backed from the building.

Granny looked up from pouring hot water into the dishpan as Anna walked in. "What you smilin' 'bout?"

Anna hung the basket on the peg. "I looked in on Jewel. She didn't seem to want any company."

Granny leaned over the dry sink and concentrated on scrubbing the jam pot. "A settin' hen shore don't want to be disturbed. Cain't blame her much. She's a-doin' her job so's we'll have some chickens. I shore hope I can get me another broody hen outta this batch. I been tryin' for a long time to git me a big flock of chickens. I used to have more, but the foxes around here jest kept raidin' my henhouse. Purty soon all I had left was Jasper and Jewel." She thought for a moment before she chuckled. "Yeah, that Jewel shore is doin' her job."

Granny's words reminded her of how different this world was than the one she'd come from. Her mother's large flock had provided their table with many chicken dishes—fried, baked, in stews, and with dumplings. She'd always taken those things for granted, but she knew she never would again. She was just beginning to understand how difficult survival in the Cove really was.

~

Granny climbed from the buggy and tied the horse to the lowest branch on a scrubby tree in the corner of the Fergusons' yard. Anna scanned the yard for the children but didn't see them anywhere. She hopped from the buggy and waited until Granny stepped up beside her.

"I don't see anybody. You think they could be gone somewhere?"

Granny shook her head. "Not likely, with a baby. They's around somewhere."

At that moment a squeal of pleasure pierced the air. "Miss Anna!" Lucy and Ted, their arms outstretched, ran toward Anna.

Lucy's auburn hair sparkled in the sun, and Ted's face appeared to have sprouted a new batch of freckles since she'd last seen them. Dried mud spots stained both of the children's clothes.

Anna braced herself for the children charging toward her across the yard. When they plowed into her, she grabbed both of them in a tight embrace. "Lucy, Ted, I'm so glad to see you." She held them at arm's length and studied their faces. Dirt streaked their faces. "What have you two been doing?"

Ted grinned up at her. "We been a-makin' mud pies. We's the best chefs in the Cove."

Anna laughed and hugged them close.

Granny tapped her on the shoulder. "What these young'uns talkin' 'bout?"

Anna glanced at her. "Just something we talked about when I was here before." Her heart constricted with the words. She'd almost added "and Simon came by." She swallowed and turned back to the children. "How have you been?"

Ted frowned at her. "We been a-wantin' you to come agin. What took so long?"

"It hasn't been that long. Granny and I have lots of women to take care of just like with your mama. Which reminds me, how's your baby brother doin'?"

"He's fine. Mama says he's growin' like a weed." Lucy's grin revealed a missing front tooth.

Anna's eyebrows arched. "Lucy, you've lost a tooth since I was here."

Lucy opened her mouth and pointed to the gap. "Yes'm. It got loose, and Poppa put a string around it and jerked it. That ole tooth jest popped right out."

Anna leaned over and examined the space in the front row of Lucy's teeth. She shuddered. "Oh, that sounds painful. You must have been a very brave girl."

Ted shook his head. "Naw, she cried somethin' fierce."

Lucy, her fists doubled, turned on Ted. "That ain't true."

Ted clenched his fists and backed away. "Is so."

The squabbling between the two children reminded her of the childhood spats she'd had with Robert. A quarrel could be sparked over the least thing, but anger quickly cooled when they were presented with something to distract them. Anna reached back in the buggy for a bag she'd brought. "All right, you two. I brought something for you, but you only get it if you behave yourselves."

Their anger instantly forgotten, the children clustered closer to her. Ted's freckled face beamed in anticipation. "What you brung us, Miss Anna?"

She reached inside the bag and pulled out two small bundles wrapped in homespun scraps from Granny's sewing basket and tied with a piece of yarn. She handed each of the children one. "Before I came to the Cove, my brother rode to Sevierville and bought me some shoes, but he brought me something else—stick candy. He knew how

I liked it and wanted me to bring some with me. So I thought you two might like to have some."

The children's eyes grew wide with awe as they unwrapped their gifts—three pieces of candy for each. At that moment Laura, with the baby in her arms, walked around the side of the house.

"Granny, Anna, good to see you," she called.

Their mother's voice brought the children back to reality, and they bolted toward her. "Mama, look what Miss Anna brung us," Lucy squealed.

Ted stopped in front of his mother and jumped up and down. He cupped the present in his hand. "Candy, Mama," he screamed. "Jest like the time Pa went to Gatlinburg and brung us back some."

Laura smiled down at her children. "Where's your manners? You thanked Miss Anna yet?"

The children whirled, raced back to Anna, and grabbed her in a tight hug. "Thank you, thank you," they yelled in unison.

When they released her, Anna bent down and pointed to the candy. "Now you each have three pieces. Try not to eat it all at once. Eat a little every day so you can enjoy it longer."

Lucy nodded. "Yes'm. I'll remember that."

Ted glanced down at the candy, a skeptical look in his eyes. "Don't know if I kin do that, but I'll try."

Anna patted him on the head. "Good. Now you two go play. Granny and I are here to help your mama."

The children giggled and ran toward the backyard. Laura tilted her head to one side. "You's come to help me?"

"That's right," Granny said. "Thought you could use some extra hands now that you got a baby to tend."

Laura brushed her hair out of her eyes, and Anna frowned inwardly at Laura's tired eyes. Tiny wrinkles lined her face. She stepped closer. "How're you feeling, Laura? You look tired."

Laura straightened her shoulders. "I'm all right. Just tired. Pete needed help hoein' the corn this morning."

Anna gasped. "You worked in the field today?"

A crimson flush spread across Laura's face. "Yeah, and yesterday too."

"But, Laura, your baby is just a few weeks old. You shouldn't be doing that kind of work."

Granny touched Anna's arm. "Darlin', Pete cain't do the work by hisself. And Laura's the only one to help. If'n they don't git a good crop, then the fam'ly is in for a hard time this winter."

Anna wished she had bitten her tongue before blurting out the words she'd just spoken. She swallowed and faced Laura. "Well, just take it easy, Laura. Try not to strain yourself, and stop when you get tired."

Laura smiled. "I will."

Anna reached out toward the baby. "Well, how about letting me hold this big boy while we go inside and see what we can do to help you out today?"

Laura handed the baby over but shook her head. "No need for that. Let's just visit."

Granny shook her head and chuckled. "No ma'am. We come to work, and that's what we mean to do. Now, what you got waitin' in the house for you?"

Laura grinned. "Well, I picked some blackberries this morning."

Anna juggled the baby in her arms and nodded toward the house. "Well, you're in luck. We're two of the best berry pickers and jam makers in the Cove. Let's go get started."

"Oh, Anna," Laura said as they headed toward the house, "you shore give my soul a lift. I never figured you for a girl that liked to pick berries."

Anna stopped before entering the front door. "Really? Well, let me tell you about the time I picked blackberries with a bear."

Laura's eyebrows shot up. "A bear?"

Granny grabbed Laura's arm and propelled her into the house. "Don't know if I can listen to this story agin."

Anna laughed, hugged the baby close, and followed Laura into the house. She looked around at the familiar surroundings and remembered the molasses cake and Simon sitting at the kitchen table listening to her Bible story.

She hadn't seen Simon in days, and she missed him so much. Every time she heard a horse on the road in front of Granny's cabin, she hoped it was Simon and waited for him to call out to them.

She hadn't realized how much his friendship meant to her until it wasn't there anymore. Thoughts of how to mend their differences poured through her mind all the time, but so far she hadn't come up with a solution. If only he'd come back, she was sure they could work it out. All she could hope was that he would come to Granny's for a visit soon.

Chapter 12

That night Anna sat at the small table in her bedroom and reread the letter she'd written to her mother. She could imagine her mother's excitement at receiving the message and could almost envision the happiness on her face as she read it. She wondered how her mother would react to her stories about life in the Cove. The births of the Ferguson and Long children, the endless food preservation, the beauty of the scenery—all her experiences were there. She'd closed by telling how much she enjoyed the work and looked forward to going to New York in September.

Yawning, she rose from the table and leaned over the oil lamp. She was about to blow out the flame when a shotgun blast from the backyard startled her.

She jerked upright and hurried into the kitchen. The back door stood open, and Anna dashed into the backyard. Her nightgown billowed about her legs in the mountain breeze as she stared out into the dark night.

Fear tightened her throat. "Granny? Are you all right?"

"Yeah, darlin', I'm fine." Granny's soft voice drifted from the shadows.

Anna strained to see Granny in the night. "What happened?"

Granny appeared in the circle of light that shone through the back door. A shotgun dangled from her hand. "A fox got in the henhouse. I was jest scarin' him off."

Anna's gaze darted toward the shed that served as Granny's henhouse. "Are Jasper and Jewel all right?"

Granny shook her head. "He got Jewel. I could see 'er in his mouth when he run off."

Without speaking, Anna followed Granny into the house and watched her put the gun in the cabinet in the corner of the kitchen. Tears stung her eyes.

Granny turned to face her, and for the first time since coming to the Cove, Anna saw something akin to defeat on Granny's face. "Seems like somethin' always happens to my chickens." She took a big breath. "But that's jest how life is in the Cove. We have setbacks, but we know the good Lord's still a-lookin' after us."

Tears poured from Anna's eyes and streamed down her face. "But Granny, what about the eggs Jewel was hatching?"

Granny shook her head. "They won't be no use no more. I'll jest put this in the Lord's hands. That's all I kin do." Granny trudged from the room, her shoulders drooping.

Anna slipped back into her room and dropped to her knees beside the bed. She clasped her hands and leaned over until her face touched the patchwork quilt. "Dear God, I've come to see how difficult life is for women like Laura and others in the Cove. Be with the people I'm coming to love, and comfort Granny tonight. I thank You for her example of faith, and I pray to be more like her. Amen."

Anna raised her head and eased onto the bed. She couldn't shake the image of Granny's face from her mind. Tonight a fox had dined on Granny's only laying hen, and because of that their food supply had been affected.

The Cove was a strange world to try to survive in, and she wondered if she would ever understand it. As the words drifted through her mind, another thought welled up. On the table next to her lay the letter she'd written to her mother. The one thing she hadn't confessed and the thought she was only beginning to recognize was how a love for Cades Cove had begun to take root in her heart. She dreaded the day when she would have to leave.

~

The next morning Anna wiped the last plate from breakfast dry and set it on the shelf. She hung the dishtowel on a peg and turned to Granny. Still upset over Jewel's death, neither she nor Granny had spoken much during the meal.

Granny crumbled a leftover biscuit into a pan and stared at it. "Jasper'll be wond'rin' where his breakfast is. Guess I better git this to 'im. Seems strange not to give Jewel one."

"Granny, I…" Anna stopped at the sound of a knock on the front door. Granny glanced up, but Anna touched her arm. "I'll get it."

Anna dried her hands on her apron and hurried through the house. When she pulled the door open, she gasped in surprise. The man who'd frightened her at the Fergusons' home stood on the porch. Dark hair stuck out from under his sweat-stained hat and dirt streaked the front of his overalls. To Anna he looked like a giant towering over her, and the old fear returned.

He gave no sign of recognition but stared past her into the house. "Granny here?"

Anna backed away from the door. "I'll get her."

"Tell 'er Cecil Davis be here." The words rolled from his mouth like a growl.

All Anna wanted was to put some distance between herself and the hulking frame of this man. Granny set the empty pan on the table as Anna reentered the kitchen. "Who's here?"

"Cecil Davis."

Granny's body tensed. She stood still, her thumb touching one finger after another as if she was counting. When she finished, she frowned. "Land's sakes, I shore hope Pearl ain't started havin' that young'un. It ain't due for two months."

Granny rushed from the kitchen, her heavy stride thumping against the wood floor. Anna strained to hear the conversation in the next room. Who was Pearl? Could she be Cecil's wife? The thought of going to his house filled her with dread. Maybe she was jumping to conclusions. For all she knew, Pearl could be his neighbor. In an attempt to distract her thoughts, she sat down at the table and began to shell the peas she'd picked earlier.

Granny hurried into the kitchen, pulled her apron off, and hung it on a peg. "We gotta go, Anna. Pearl Davis done started havin' pains. I tol' Cecil to go on home, that we'd come in my buggy." She pointed to the pan of unshelled peas. "Let's take these here peas to Pearl's. We can cook 'em there. Hurry up, child, and get your thangs. I'll git my yarbs and medicine."

Anna pushed up from her chair and grabbed the edge of the table. Her knees shook so that she thought she could hear them knocking together. She could barely voice the question that filled her with dread. "Will I be staying at the Davis's, Granny?"

Granny halted and thought for a moment. "Maybe we'll both stay tonight. Pearl lost her last baby. If she loses this one she may need us, but Cecil'll go git his brother's wife. They live on t'other side of the Cove. Won't take him long to git back."

Relief flooded over her. She'd been ready to tell Granny she wouldn't stay alone at the Davis's cabin. Anna nodded and rushed to her bedroom. She pulled a dress from the peg on the wall and put it in her valise before she hurried from the room.

Thirty minutes later Granny was guiding the horse and buggy into the yard of the Davis cabin. It sat almost hidden in a grove of trees off the main road of the Cove and was much smaller than the other houses Anna had seen. A barn sat several hundred feet back of the cabin, but no cows or horses inhabited the pasture where lush grass grew. A few chickens pecked at the ground around the cabin, and Anna wondered if the foxes had also visited the Davis farm.

Cecil Davis opened the door when Granny knocked. With a nod he stepped aside for Anna and Granny to enter. Anna followed

Granny into a sparsely furnished room. Two chairs sat before a fireplace. A quilt hung over the back of one of the chairs.

Granny headed toward the door beside the fireplace where she stopped and stared into the next room. "Hello, Josie."

Anna peered over Granny's shoulder into the kitchen and spied a little girl, perhaps two years old, in a chair at the table. Her dark hair hung in tangled curls down her back. Her unkempt appearance told Anna no one had taken time to comb the child's hair all day. Food stains spotted the wrinkled dress she wore. Anna eased forward and smiled at the child.

Josie's mouth curved in a smile, and she squirmed to get down. Her father walked into the room at that moment. His sharp voice sliced through the silent cabin. "Sit."

The smile on Josie's face faded, and she stilled.

Granny nodded toward a closed door at one side of the kitchen. "Pearl in there?"

Cecil nodded and headed for the back door. He took the hat he'd worn to Granny's from a peg and set it on his head. "I got work to do. Be back in a while."

Anna, unable to believe he wasn't staying, turned to Granny. "He's not going to take care of Josie?"

Granny smiled. "It 'pears like that. Guess you'll hafta be the one. I'll check on Pearl and call if'n I need you."

Granny patted the child on the head and walked to the bedroom. When she'd closed the door, Anna looked down at the little girl still sitting at the table. She scooted another chair close to the child and held out her arms. "Hello, Josie. Want to come to me?"

For a moment Josie wavered, her bottom lip quivering. She pointed toward the closed door. "Mama."

Anna nodded. "Yes, Mama's in the other room."

Josie stuck her finger in her mouth and chewed on it for a moment while she studied Anna. Anna wiggled her fingers and smiled. "Come on. Let me hold you."

Josie hesitated before she leaned forward and held out her arms.

Anna pulled her close. "Poor baby. Granny's going to take care of your mama, and I'll fix you something to eat." She held the child against her body and looked around the kitchen. Only an iron cook-stove and the table and chairs occupied the space. There was no food in sight.

No heat came from the stove. The first thing she had to do was light a fire and boil some water. Granny would need it any minute. She glanced around for something to occupy Josie. A wooden horse lay on the floor. She picked it up and handed it to Josie, who smiled and grabbed the toy.

"Horsie!"

Anna eased her back into the chair. "Play with your horse until I can fix you something to eat."

Granny opened the bedroom door at that moment. "The water boilin' yet, Anna?"

"Not yet. I've got to get the fire started."

Granny propped her hands on her hips. "You mean Cecil let that fire go out? I'm gonna hafta talk to him about that."

Anna pulled the stove eye up and stirred at the embers inside. "Shouldn't take long. I see some kindling in the wood box."

"Good. I 'spect I'm gonna need that water real quick."

"How's Pearl?"

A shadow crossed Granny's face. "Don't look good. Her pains are a-coming close together, and they ain't gonna slow down at this point. I 'spect she'll be having that baby purty soon."

Anna stuck the kindling in the stove and blew on the embers. A flame flickered up and ignited the wood. "And she's two months early?"

"Yeah, and she needs that time real bad, but she ain't gonna git it. If Cecil comes in, don't say nothin' to him, though."

Anna shivered. "Don't worry. I won't be saying anything to him. He scares me."

Granny gave a little snort. "Reckon he does look kinda fierce, but he's a good man."

Anna picked up a piece of wood and stuck it in the flame inside the stove. "If you say so."

"Granny!" Anna and Granny whirled at the scream from the bedroom. Granny ran toward the bedroom, and Anna started to follow.

"Mama." Anna stopped at Josie's whimper. She had her job to do, and Granny would take care of Pearl.

She caressed the child's tangled, silken curls. She'd have to find a comb somewhere and a clean dress for Josie. She grabbed a poker from the wood box and stoked the fire. Within minutes she had a pot of water sitting on top. With the fire heating up, it wouldn't take long for the water to boil. Now for food for Josie.

A sack of cornmeal sat on a shelf. Mush appeared to be the only choice right now since she could use some of the boiling water to make it. Josie whimpered, and Anna reached for her.

Helping Granny differed at times from what she thought it would be. Today her task was to watch a two-year-old. All she could do at this point for Pearl was say a prayer for her and the baby that was about to be born.

An hour later Anna wiped the last remains of Josie's cornmeal mush from her mouth. Granny had come from the bedroom several times and looked more troubled each time she entered the kitchen.

For the last few minutes, however, it had been extremely quiet behind the closed door. Josie reached up and patted Anna's face. Anna glanced down and laughed at Josie sitting there, her mouth open as she tried to reach the spoonful of mush Annie held in midair.

Anna slipped the spoon into Josie's mouth. "Sorry, little one. I guess my mind wandered."

Josie swallowed the mouthful and pointed to the door. "Mama."

Anna hugged the child closer. "Yes, darling, Mama's gonna be all right."

The back door opened and Cecil stepped into the room. He stopped just inside the door and stared at Anna holding his daughter. His cold gaze made her skin prickle, but she didn't want him to know how much he frightened her.

Anna stood up and hoisted Josie to her hip. "Mr. Davis, would you like something to eat?"

He stared at her for a moment, then glanced down at the child.

Josie smiled and held out her arms. "Poppa."

He didn't move but turned toward the bedroom door as it opened. The look on Granny's face told them she didn't have good news.

She closed the door behind her and stepped next to Cecil. Her hands fluttered to her side before she clasped them in front of her. Her eyes sparkled with unshed tears. "I done everythin' I could, Cecil, but I couldn't keep the baby from comin'. Pearl's fine, but the baby was jest too little. He never took a breath."

Cecil's expression didn't change. "A boy, you say?"

Granny nodded. "Tiny little feller. You want to see 'im?"

Cecil shook his head.

"What 'bout Pearl? She'd like you to come in."

Cecil backed toward the door. "In a bit. I got work at the barn."

He opened the door and stepped outside, but before he could close the door Josie reached out to him. "Poppa."

Without acknowledging Josie, he pulled the door shut. His reaction presented a contrast to what Anna had seen from Andrew Long and Pete Ferguson. Both had been so concerned for their wives. Anna couldn't understand a man who would refuse to see his dead son and would ignore his wife when she needed his comfort. And what about Josie? He barely noticed her.

Josie wriggled in her arms and began to cry. Anna stroked the dark curls that tumbled to Josie's shoulders. "She's getting tired."

Granny reached out and patted Josie on the back. "She's a sweet little thang. I got Pearl all fixed up right now, but I'll go back in and set with 'er. Why don't you see if you can get Josie to sleep?"

Anna nodded. "I'll put a pallet in the front room and lay down with her. But if you need me, call me."

"I will." Granny turned and reentered the bedroom.

Anna remembered seeing a quilt hanging on the back of a straight chair when they'd entered the house. After she'd spread it on the floor, she gathered Josie in her arms and lay down with her.

Josie grew still right away, but Anna found it hard to get settled. Since coming to the Cove, she'd discovered that sleeping on a pallet didn't seem as much fun as it had when she was a child. If she and

Granny stayed at the Davis cabin tonight, she would probably sleep where she and Josie now lay.

As far as she could tell, the house only had three rooms—the one where she and Josie lay, the kitchen, and the bedroom where Granny tended Pearl. Since there wasn't a bed in either of the rooms she'd seen, she decided Josie must sleep in her parents' room.

The absence of food in the house bothered Anna too. With Pearl not feeling well, she must not have worked in her garden. She wondered why Cecil hadn't brought food into the house.

This home seemed very different from the others she'd visited in the Cove. Even though most of the people in Cades Cove could be considered poor by the standards of the farm families in Strawberry Plains, she thought Cecil and Pearl Davis must be among the poorest.

Josie's quiet nature also disturbed Anna. She wasn't at all like other active two-year-olds she'd been around. Perhaps the uncaring attitude displayed by her father had caused Josie to be so withdrawn. Of course she hadn't seen Pearl with her yet. She hugged the child tighter and hoped Josie's mother showed her more love than what her father had demonstrated.

Anna awoke sometime later to the sound of soft voices coming from the kitchen. She sat up and listened but wasn't sure who was speaking. Beside her Josie, her thumb in her mouth, slept soundly. Anna pushed up from the pallet, tiptoed to the door, and listened.

Her eyes grew wide, and she clamped her hand over her mouth to silence the gasp from her throat. Reaching up, she tucked a stray strand of hair behind her ear, took a deep breath, and stepped into the kitchen.

"Hello, Simon."

He stood with his back to her. At the sound of her voice, he stiffened. After what seemed an eternity, he turned and stared at her. "Hello, Anna. How are you?"

A smile spread across her face. She'd only seen him at church in the last few weeks, and he'd barely spoken to her then. He still hadn't returned to Granny's.

"Did you come to visit Pearl?"

His gaze wandered over her face, but his eyes narrowed. There was no smile on his face. "I was passing by and saw Granny's buggy. I was afraid something might be wrong."

Anna glanced at Granny. "How is Pearl?"

"She's 'bout the same. Poor thang cries ev'ry few minutes. She shore did want this baby."

Anna swallowed. "Do you need me to do anything for you?"

Granny shook her head. "I gotta git back in there. You jest keep a watch over Josie and see what you kin find for supper. Don't forgit we brought them peas from home." She smiled at Simon. "It's good to see you, preacher boy. Don't stay away so long agin."

Simon smiled at Granny. "Take care of yourself, Granny."

She walked to the bedroom and closed the door behind her.

The silence in the room hung heavy between them, and Anna wished for the easy banter they'd once shared. She stepped closer to Simon. "Want to stay for supper?"

He suddenly seemed engrossed in the hat he held and stared at it as he turned it around in his hands. "I can't. I promised a family from the congregation I'd eat with them."

Anna swallowed back her disappointment and smiled. "Well, maybe another night."

"Maybe."

She glanced over her shoulder toward the room where Josie still slept. "I haven't gotten to help Granny today with Pearl. I've taken care of Josie."

Simon nodded and looked up at the ceiling. "She's a pretty little girl."

Anna eased a step farther into the room. "She is pretty. I just wish her father cared for her more."

A startled look entered Simon's eyes. "What're you talking about?"

"He hardly pays her any attention. Doesn't even speak to her. And he wouldn't even go in to see Pearl after the baby died. He must be a hard-hearted man."

Simon regarded her through narrowed eyes. "So now you're judging the folks in the Cove? Think you know what makes them tick?"

His words and the tone of his voice sliced through her. The first time she'd met Simon, she'd felt a bond with him—like they were already close friends. Suddenly, though, he seemed like a stranger. There had to be some way they could return to the friendship they'd had in the beginning.

"Simon, what's the matter? I've never heard you speak with anger before."

He grimaced, but he couldn't meet her eyes. "I guess I should've known it wouldn't take you long to decide we were all too different from you. But I didn't think you were so unkind that you would judge a man without knowing a single thing about him."

The wound inflicted by his words a few moments earlier deepened as she stared at him. His veiled eyes gave no indication they'd ever been friends. She had to make him understand what she'd seen since arriving at the Davis home. "I'm not judging Cecil. But I've seen how he's treated Josie ever since I got here. He ignores her even when she calls out to him. He doesn't act like she's even alive."

Simon chuckled, not with the happiness of earlier days but with contempt. Anna flinched as he shook his head. "You still don't understand about life here, Anna. You don't know how it can beat down a proud man like Cecil who works from sunup 'til sundown on some of the rockiest soil in the Cove trying to make a living. Only a man who loves his family does that. You don't know how he's tried to do everything by himself so Pearl can stay in bed because they wanted this baby so much. Only a man who cherishes his wife does that. You don't know how he sits up at night after Josie's gone to sleep and carves toys for her. Only a man who loves his daughter does that."

Anna remembered the wooden horse Josie had played with while she was cooking the mush. "I...I didn't know."

"And you don't know that this is the third son Pearl's lost and the last she'll be able to have, according to Granny."

Tears pooled in her eyes. "I'm sorry, Simon. I didn't know any of that."

His eyes bored into her. "Life here is hard, Anna. Nothing like the fairy tale you've lived. It can chew you up and spit you out and leave you dying surrounded by some of God's most beautiful creation. Don't judge us, Anna. Not until you know what it's like for us and what makes us try to survive here."

He turned and walked out the door, but Anna ran after him. "Simon, please don't go. I didn't mean…"

He didn't look back but strode toward the barn. Anna watched him go, the tears she'd held back finally spilling from her eyes.

Granny's strong arms encircled Anna and pulled her close. "I heard loud voices in here. What's goin' on? What's the matter, child?"

Anna stared after Simon. "Oh, Granny, I've lost the best friend I ever had."

～

Simon heard Anna calling after him, but his willpower prevented him from answering. How he wanted to run to her and dry the tears he'd seen in her eyes, but he couldn't. Not anymore. Maybe a few weeks ago, but he couldn't stand to be around her knowing his love couldn't compete with her dream. It would be better for her to think him indifferent to her.

He rubbed his hands across his tired eyes. He hadn't slept in days. Every time he lay down her face drifted into his mind. Even when he did manage to drift off to sleep, she haunted his dreams. He didn't know how much longer the war within could go on—his heart telling him to go to her and his mind telling him to stay away.

The frustrations of the last few weeks had built up until he unleashed them on her today. He shouldn't have been so hard on her. Anna wasn't alone in thinking that Cecil Davis was a cold, hard man, but nothing could be farther from the truth. He wanted Anna to see beyond the reserved nature of many of the Cove residents. But most of all he wanted her to understand them and come to love them. If he couldn't make her stay, maybe they could.

Chapter 13

*A*nna picked the last ripe tomato and dropped it in the basket. A soft breeze stirred the leaves on the trees, but the morning sun promised a hot day for the Fourth of July celebration. The tomatoes she'd just picked would taste good at the church picnic.

She put her hands in the small of her back and stretched. The memory of Simon hurrying away from her at the Davis farm two days earlier flashed into her mind. Her heart still ached every time she thought of his words.

She hoped he wouldn't be at the picnic today, but she knew he would. After all, the preacher was expected to be at all the church functions. But she didn't know if she could face him after their last meeting. Their relationship would never be the same again, but one thing she knew—she missed his presence at Granny's. Mealtimes hadn't been the same since he quit coming.

With a sigh she picked up the basket of tomatoes and juggled the load on her hip with one hand. At the back door she slipped her shoes off and padded across the wooden floor. "Granny, here are the tomatoes you wanted."

"Thanks. Jest drop 'em in with everythin' else. I'll slice 'em at the picnic." Granny picked up a bowl of green beans and placed it in the basket. "I think that's everythin'."

Anna headed to her room to change clothes but stopped at the door. Without turning she spoke. "Granny, how can I face Simon today?"

A serious expression covered Granny's face. "You gonna act like you don't care whether he talks to you or not. After all, he ain't the only young man in the Cove. No telling who you'll meet today. You jest make up your mind you gonna have a good time and enjoy the folks there." She pulled off her apron and hung it on a wall peg. "But if Simon acts as ornery as he's been lately, I 'spect I'm gonna need to have a talk with that boy. Now I'm goin' out to hitch up the horse. You finish dressin' and bring the basket out. We need to git goin', or we gonna miss all the fun."

Anna nodded and entered her bedroom. She closed the door and leaned against it, her head pounding at the thought of seeing Simon today.

Her heart raced at the memory of their last conversation. He'd said some hateful things to her—hardly what she'd expect from a preacher. His words made her seem like a snobbish brat who looked down on people who didn't meet her standards. He'd said she judged people and accused her of living a fairy-tale life compared to what the people of the Cove had.

How could he have been so cruel? She clenched her fists and gritted her teeth. She had to quit thinking about him. He'd made it very clear he had no interest in continuing their friendship.

Anna pulled her dress off and grabbed the one she was wearing to the picnic. "Well, if that's the way he wants it, that's the way it'll be. I can get along fine without Simon Martin."

She dressed quickly and hurried back to the kitchen where the basket of food sat. For a minute she stared at it and thought about staying home. Then she straightened her shoulders and grabbed the basket from the table. Simon Martin wasn't going to ruin a day of fun for her. She didn't need him to have a good time. Granny was right. There were plenty of other people in the Cove to visit with. She'd just seek them out and ignore him.

"Anna, let's go." Granny called from outside.

"Coming." She grabbed the basket, rushed out the door, and climbed into the buggy for the short ride to the church.

They rode in silence through the summer day, the buggy stirring up clouds of dust behind them. The mountains, lit by the backdrop of the blue sky, gleamed in the sunshine. Even on this warm day a misty haze hung over them.

The horse slowed. Anna drew her attention away from the hills and spied a wagon ahead of them turning off the main road. Granny followed close behind to the picnic grove beside the creek which ran gently behind the church.

As the horse came to a stop, a young man hopped out of the buggy in front of them. "Morning, Granny. Beautiful day, ain't it?"

Granny nodded. "That it is, William."

William reached for Granny's reins. "Let me git this for you."

Granny smiled. "That's right kind of you, William." She leaned over and whispered to Anna. "That there's Sadie Carter's son William. You remember meeting Sadie at church?"

"Yes."

William walked back to the side of the buggy and extended his hand. "Let me help you down, Granny." When Granny stood beside him, he smiled up at Anna. "And now you, Miss Anna."

Anna clasped his outstretched hand and jumped to the ground. "Thank you so much, Mr. Carter."

His face flushed. "You know my name?"

Anna tilted her head to one side. "I've seen you with your mother at church. She was one of the first ladies to introduce herself to me."

A big smile curled his lips. "That's right nice to hear, Miss Anna." He reached for the basket in the back of the buggy. "Let me carry this for you."

Granny's eyebrows arched. "You see? Guess I was right."

William's forehead wrinkled. "Huh?"

Anna pasted a smile on her face and tilted her head to stare up at William. "Granny said I would meet a lot of nice people today. I'm glad you were the first."

"So am I, Miss Anna. Maybe we can eat together."

"I would like that very much, Mr. Carter."

Granny shook her head and chuckled. She turned to walk toward the tables where the women were setting the food but stopped. "William, did you think to bring your silver dollars?"

William patted his pants pocket. "Have 'em right here."

"Silver dollars? What for?" Anna turned a questioning glance to Granny.

Granny waved her hands in dismissal and chuckled. "Oh, it's one of them man things. It's kind 'uv a Fourth of July tradition."

"Yeah, we wouldn't want to miss that." A shy grin wrinkled William's mouth. "Maybe you'll cheer for me."

"I would be honored, Mr. Carter."

They didn't speak again until William had set the basket beside one of the tables underneath the trees next to the church. He tipped his hat and backed away. "I'll see you later, Miss Anna."

"Thank you for your help."

Anna tried to concentrate on following William's departure, but all she wanted was to find Simon in the crowd. After a moment, she spied Martha waving at her from the end of the table .

Anna hurried over. "With your time so near, I didn't know if you'd be here."

Martha reached out and hugged her. "Wouldn't have missed it. Good to see you, Anna."

Anna drew back and mentally calculated how much longer Martha had before the baby would arrive. "How're you doing?"

Martha, a grimace on her face, placed her hand in the small of her back. "It won't be much longer. I cain't hardly wait, Anna."

"Maybe I'll still be here to help you through it."

"That would be a great comfort to me." She glanced behind her and grabbed Anna by the hand. "But come say hello to the other women."

Sadie Carter and several other women stepped away from the table and hurried toward her. "Anna, we's glad you come today."

"Thank you, Mrs. Carter. It's good to see you."

"I seen William a-totin' your basket."

The women facing her exchanged glances before they smiled at Anna. Her face warmed, and she looked around for Granny. She had stepped to the other end of the table and didn't notice the exchange.

Anna's face warmed. "Uh, yes, he did. He's very courteous…which I'm sure is a tribute to his mother."

Sadie cast a pleased smile at all her friends. "Thank you kindly, Miss Anna. Now we'd better get this here food ready."

She and the other women turned back to the table. Anna glanced at Martha, who was grinning. "You sure got a way with words, Anna."

Anna shook her head and frowned. "I meant it. William seemed very nice."

"Oh, he is. Fact is, there's lots of girls in the Cove got their eyes on him. You best not make any of them mad."

"Quit teasing, Martha."

"I'm just sayin'…Oh, look who just turned up."

Anna turned in the direction Martha stared. A woman with a small child in her arms and the young boy who had come to Granny's cabin on her second day in the Cove walked toward the assembled group. Her brown hair was pulled back in a tight bun at the back of her neck, and her tanned skin told of long hours of working in the sun. Dark circles ringed her eyes, and the dress she wore appeared frayed.

She stopped a few feet away from the table, but Martha drew Anna toward the woman. "Anna, I don't think you've met Naomi Jackson. Naomi, this is Anna Prentiss. She's livin' at Granny's and helpin' her out this summer."

"Hello, Naomi. I'm so glad to meet you. And Matthew—we've already met." She smiled at the boy and stuck out her hand to Naomi.

Naomi stared at Anna's hand for a moment before she grasped it. "You the one helped Granny with my man Luke when he got hurt." Naomi's smile revealed several rotten teeth.

Anna struggled to keep her face from revealing the revulsion she felt at the mention of his name. "I wasn't much help to Granny that night, I'm afraid. I hope I've improved since then."

"I thank you for it."

"There's no need to thank me. I really didn't do anything." She shifted her attention to the child Naomi held and reached out to stroke his blond hair. "And you have another little boy. What's his name?"

"We call 'im Eli."

"Oh, that's a beautiful name." She bent down and looked in the child's face. "And you're a handsome little fellow too, Eli."

Naomi turned to Matthew, who had been standing silently by her side. "Why don't you go on and play with the other boys? I'll git along all right."

He glanced at a group of boys who were running races in the field beside the church. "You sure you can handle Eli by yourself?"

She prodded his shoulder with her hand. "Go on now."

He glanced at the boys but hesitated. Anna gestured toward the group. "Go on, Matthew. I'll help your mother with Eli. It's the Fourth of July, and you need to have a good time." A smile flitted across his face before he turned and ran across the field toward the boys. Anna wondered what kind of life Naomi and her sons must endure with Luke. "You have two mighty fine sons, Naomi. I was quite taken with Matthew the morning he came to Granny's house."

Naomi smiled again. "I heared some of the women say you was nice. I reckon they was right."

Anna laughed. "I think that would probably depend on who you ask." She glanced back at the table and took Naomi by the arm. "But what are you doing standing over here? Let's get up here so we can help with the food."

She drew Naomi along with her as she and Martha walked back to the table where Granny stood slicing the tomatoes she'd brought. "Granny, look who's here!"

Granny looked up and smiled, then stepped away from her tomatoes, wiped her hands on her dress, and enveloped Naomi and her child in a warm embrace. "You're a sight for sore eyes, Naomi. It's shore good to see you here today. And you brought that sweet Eli with you! One of the easiest babies I ever delivered."

Anna laughed. "I don't suppose there's a baby in the Cove Granny didn't deliver."

Naomi nodded. "Reckon not."

Warm laughter rippled across the grounds. Anna let her gaze wander over the groups of men lounging under the trees. She tried to concentrate on talking with Martha and Naomi instead of looking for Simon, but she couldn't help casting her eyes about for a glimpse of him.

Then she saw him. He stood at the end of the table, a tall young woman by his side. Anna's heart plummeted to the pit of her stomach as the girl raked her long brown hair back from her eyes and smiled up at Simon. He smiled at her, then turned when Mrs. Carter said something to him.

He nodded and faced the people gathered around the table. "May I have your attention everyone?" He waited as the laughter and eager chatter died down and all eyes turned to him. "The ladies tell me we're ready to eat. Before we do, I'm gonna voice our thanks for this food and God's blessings on us." The crowd stilled as everyone bowed their heads. "Our Father," prayed Simon, "we come to You on this day thanking You for the blessings You've given us. Today we celebrate the birth of our nation, and we thank You for this great land. We thank You for placing us here in the mountains You made and in the land You provided for us. Now we gather to eat, and we give thanks for the abundance of our harvests and the food You provided. And we pray for guidance to serve You in all areas of our lives. Amen."

Amens echoed from the crowd. Simon opened his eyes and stared straight at Anna. For a moment they stood still, as if daring the other to break the contact. She smiled and raised her hand to wave, but the young woman beside him touched his arm and he glanced away.

Martha's mouth pulled down into a frown, and she shot a quick look in Anna's direction. Shaking off the rebuff, Anna turned to Naomi and reached out to pat Eli's head.

Simon picked up a plate and progressed through the food line. When he moved close to Anna, she took a deep breath and prepared to speak to him. But the young woman, still at his side, stepped between them and pointed to a dish on the table.

"Simon, would you like to have some of these here fried green tomatoes I fixed?"

"Why thank you, Linda Mae. They look real good."

Anna forced a smile to her face and reached for Eli. "Let me hold him while you fix your plate, Naomi."

Naomi smiled and handed her child to Anna. "That shore is nice of you, Anna."

Anna glanced back at Simon and the young woman as they headed away from the table. Her throat constricted, and she hugged Naomi's son tighter. "Thank you for being so kind to me, Naomi."

Naomi walked to the table, leaving Anna alone with the child. Martha touched her arm. "That's nice of you to hold Eli so's Naomi can eat. Most of the women don't have much to do with her."

Anna turned to Martha in surprise. "Why not?"

"Her husband drinks a lot, and she has a right hard time livin' with 'im. She works right hard." Martha snorted. "More than Luke does."

Anna heard what Martha was saying, but she was unable to take her eyes off Simon. "Martha, who's that girl Simon's sitting with?"

Martha gave a little grunt of disgust. "That's Linda Mae Simmons. She's had her eye on Simon for quite a spell now. For a while I thought she'd given up on him and set her sights on William Carter, but I guess I was wrong."

Anna's chest tightened, and she laid her cheek against Eli's soft hair. "She's very pretty," she whispered.

"Excuse me, Miss Anna."

Anna and Martha turned at the deep voice. William Carter, holding a plate loaded with food, stood on the other side of the table. He shifted from foot to foot.

"Yes, William?"

"I wondered if I might have the pleasure of your company whilst we're eating?"

Anna glanced down at Eli. "I'm sorry, Mr. Carter. I told Mrs. Jackson I'd hold her son."

Martha reached over and pulled Eli from Anna's arms. "No need to miss out on gettin' to know William better. I'll hold Eli. You go fix your plate and eat with him."

Anna started to refuse, but at that moment she caught a glimpse of Simon and Linda Mae sitting together. Anger boiled up inside her and she clenched her fists. She took a deep breath and smiled at William.

"All right. Let me get my plate and I'll join you…on one condition."

"What's that?"

"If you'll call me Anna and allow me to call you William. Is that all right with you?"

He smiled. "I'll wait right here for you, Anna."

She mouthed a thank-you to Martha and strode toward the table. If Simon Martin had decided that their friendship was over, there was nothing she could do about it. From now on she wouldn't think about him again. She would concentrate on helping Granny and getting to know the people in the Cove. Then when September came, she would be off to New York and away from Simon forever.

Before she left, though, she was going to show him she wasn't sitting around worrying over him and their lost friendship. William Carter appeared to be a likeable young man, and he wanted her company.

She finished filling her plate, walked back to where William waited, and tilted her head to one side. "I hope you've picked out a quiet spot for us to sit, William. I can hardly wait to get to know you better."

His face flushed and his Adam's apple bobbed. He nodded toward a tree near the creek bank. "How 'bout right over yonder?"

She glanced past William to where Simon sat with Linda Mae. Her heart lurched, but she lifted her chin and smiled at William. "That's a wonderful spot." She fought the urge to look at Simon again. Instead, she trudged after William toward the tree by the creek.

Chapter 14

What was I thinking? Simon asked himself. He should never have stopped for supper at the Simmons' farm. Now he had Linda Mae thinking he was interested in her and he didn't know how to get out of the situation. In the past when he'd had a problem Granny had been the one he'd go to, but not anymore—not with the root of his problem living under Granny's roof.

Linda Mae's relentless chatter drummed in his ears. He'd never intended to spend the picnic visiting with her. But when he saw Anna approaching the picnic area with William Carter holding her basket, he decided he would show her how two could play that game.

While Linda Mae talked, he kept glancing to where Anna and William sat together. From time to time she would laugh, and he thought she'd never looked more beautiful. If he had any sense, he could be the one sitting with her. Then he remembered her words the day they raced through the clover, and his heart shriveled. He jumped to his feet and brushed off his pants.

"It's been good talking to you, Linda Mae. I think I'll go on over and get ready to pitch silver dollars."

She looked up at him, her lips curling in a coy smile. "Would you help me up, Simon?"

"Sure, give me your hand."

He grabbed her arm and pulled her up. She wobbled on her feet and swayed towards him. "I saw how good you was at pitchin' silver dollars last Fourth of July. I think I'll jest go on over and watch."

He glanced around and saw the men all assembling. He didn't want to miss the beginning of the game. "Well, I need to hurry."

She looped her arm through his and pulled him closer to her side. "I'm right with you, Simon."

The men who'd gathered for the contest laughed and punched each other in the ribs as he and Linda Mae walked toward them. Simon felt a warmth slowly spread from the base of his neck to the top of his head. What had he gotten himself into?

~

Anna set her plate on the table and turned to Granny and Martha, who were busy stacking dirty dishes. "Let me help."

Granny shook her head. "No need for that. Me and Martha got this under control. We thought you was still busy talkin' to William."

"No, he went over to pitch silver dollars. He wants me…" Her throat constricted at the sight of Simon with Linda Mae hanging onto his arm and walking toward the assembled men where the contest was to take place. "Well, of all the…"

Granny glanced in the direction she stared. A gasp escaped her lips, and she frowned. "What's got into that boy? I'm gonna have to have me a talk with him."

Anger flared on Martha's face and she banged a pan down on the table. "I 'spect I'll git to him first, Granny."

Anna grabbed Martha's arm. "No, it's all right. Simon can be friends with whomever he wants."

Martha frowned. "But he ain't actin' like hisself."

Anna picked up her plate and stacked it on top of the others. "Why don't we go over and watch the silver dollar games?"

Martha glared in Simon's direction once more before she glanced back at Anna. "Are you sure you all right? If'n you want me to, I'll take him down a peg or two."

"Really it's all right." Anna took Martha's hand and pulled her forward. "Let's go. We're going to miss the game."

They made their way slowly across the picnic grove to the area where everyone was gathering. Anna came to a stop next to Linda Mae and watched as Simon, a penknife in his hand, knelt on the ground. He scratched away the dirt with the knife until he had a shallow hole. He laid down a silver dollar, and the coin fit perfectly in the bottom of it.

When he'd finished, he stood, faced in the opposite direction, and counted as he stepped away from the hole. He halted, looked over his shoulder, and addressed the gathered men. "Think that's about twenty-one feet?"

"That's good," William called out.

Simon dropped to his knees again and dug another hole, the same size as the first one. When he completed the task, he rose and headed back.

"All right, Ed, you partner with me, and we'll show William and Charlie here how to pitch silver dollars."

John, who'd just joined the group, stopped next to Martha and cupped his hands around his mouth. "Come on, Simon. Show these fellers how the Martin boys can pitch."

Simon grinned and nodded toward his brother.

"You ain't pitched against me yet." William glanced over his shoulder and smiled at Anna before he took his place next to Simon. Charlie and Ed walked to the far hole and faced Simon and William.

From behind, Granny bent over and spoke into Anna's ear. "The partners pitch from opp'site holes."

"I wondered about that." Out of the corner of her eye, Anna studied the girl beside her, then leaned closer. "You're Linda Mae Simmons, aren't you? I'm Anna Prentiss. I don't think we've met."

Linda Mae twisted from the waist and settled a contemptuous glare on Anna. In all her life, Anna had never encountered such open hostility, and her breath caught in her throat. "I know who you be. I seen you at church playin' the organ." Linda Mae muttered something under her breath before she turned back to gaze at Simon.

Anna inched back to stand next to Granny. "What are the rules for this game?"

Granny studied the men for a moment before she replied. "It looks like Simon's gonna pitch his three silver dollars first. Then William pitches. They see who came closer to the hole to get a point 'fore the ones at the other end take a turn. The first team to score twenty-one points wins the match. I'll tell you more after the first pitch."

Simon drew his arm back and threw his first dollar. It landed to the left of the hole. The next two landed even closer.

John gave another whoop. "Good job, brother."

Granny pointed to their positions and spoke slowly. "Now you see them two closest to the hole. Simon's a-hopin' William don't do better."

Anna pursed her lips and frowned. "I see. So if William throws one that lands closer, his will score, and Simon's will be disqualified."

"That's right."

"Let's see you beat that, William." John's voice echoed across the crowd.

Anna cast a quick glance in John's direction, cupped her hands around her mouth, and called out, "Come on, William. Put that dollar in the hole."

Simon whirled, a shocked expression on his face, and stared at Anna in disbelief. Beside him, William nodded in Anna's direction.

Martha elbowed Anna in the ribs. "Good girl." She straightened her shoulders and yelled out, "You heared her, William. Let's see you do it."

John's mouth dropped open as he gaped at his wife. "Martha, William's pitching against Simon."

She smiled. "I know."

William faced the hole, concentrated on his target, and swung his arm backward, then forward. The coin sailed through the air and landed inside the hole with its surface resting against the side. He pitched the next one, and it settled to the right of the hole. The last one rolled outside the six-inch scoring circle.

The crowd cheered, and Anna turned a questioning look to Granny. "What's the score?"

She pointed to the holes in the distance. "The one what landed inside is called a leaner, and it scores three points. So, it's three for William and zero for Simon."

"Good job, William," she yelled.

As the game progressed the crowd became livelier. Some cheered for Simon's team, while others shouted encouragement to William. Dollar after dollar flew through the suspense-filled air as the minutes ticked by.

With the game tied sixteen points each, Simon jingled his three silver dollars in his hand and prepared for his next turn. With great precision he lobbed the first two through the air and watched them land next to the hole. Slowly he drew the third one back and pitched it forward. The dollar landed flat in the hole. Cheers rose from the crowd.

Simon's lips curled into a smile, and he patted William on the back. "That's five points and the game unless you can do better."

"You can do it, William!" Anna screamed and jumped up and down.

"Show Simon what you can do," Martha called out.

John looked at both of them like they'd lost their minds. "I don't know what's come over you two."

William didn't look around. He stepped to the line and concentrated on his throw. The first one landed to the left and the second to the right of the hole.

A low groan rumbled through the crowd.

He took a deep breath, drew back, and gently lobbed the third silver dollar forward. The arcing coin swished through the air and plopped in the hole on top of Simon's dollar.

William's arm shot into the air in a victory wave, and he turned to Simon. "Hey, Preacher, I believe my holer cancels out yours, and the five points are mine. I think that's the game."

Applause exploded from the crowd. The men rushed forward to congratulate William. Anna glanced around at Granny. "That was very exciting."

She grinned. "You acted like it was."

At that moment Simon turned toward her, and her heart lurched at the anger in his eyes. William held out his hand and Simon dropped the coins in it. He mumbled his congratulations to William before he turned and walked away.

Martha stepped up beside her and grasped her hands. "Oh, Anna, I don't know when I've ever had so much fun."

"Me too, Martha, but I think I've really upset Simon." Her voice trembled as she spoke.

Martha laughed as she took her husband's arm. "Don't fret over him. The way he's acted for the last few weeks, I's glad to see 'im git his comeuppance."

Remorse filled Anna at how she must have embarrassed Simon in front of everyone. She should have controlled her emotions better, but Simon had made her so angry with his attention to Linda Mae. She watched him go, but a voice inside begged him to come back.

"Miss Anna." A voice behind her interrupted her thoughts. Anna turned to see Naomi staring at her. "It's 'bout time for me and my young'uns to be a-goin'. It was real nice a-meetin' you."

Her anger at Simon dissolved as she gazed at the woman. She couldn't have been more than twenty-five, but the weariness in her eyes made her look twice that. Anna reached out and grasped Naomi's hand. "I'm so glad I got to meet you and Eli today. You've got two fine sons, Naomi, and that's a great credit to the kind of mother you are."

Love for her sons sparkled in her eyes. "That's right kind of you to say so. I hope we get to meet agin."

"Me too."

Matthew, a somber expression on his face, appeared beside his mother. "Ma, we best be a-gittin' on. It's a long walk home, and Pa may be back from over to Wear's Valley."

A brief flicker of fear flashed across Naomi's face, but she extinguished it and smiled at her son. "I reckon you're right, Matthew. It be a long walk home."

Concern washed over Anna. If Luke had gone to Wear's Valley, that meant he would probably be drunk when he arrived home. She put her arms around Naomi and hugged her. "If you ever need me, Naomi, send Matthew."

Naomi's body trembled underneath the embrace. "I will, and thank you, Anna."

When Anna released her, she turned to Matthew and brushed at the tears in her eyes. "You take good care of your mother, Matthew. And come for me if you need me."

He nodded. "I will, Miss Anna."

"Take care of yourselves."

They turned and walked back toward the tables, where the women were busy gathering up their dishes and leftover food. They had almost reached them when the sound of a wagon rumbling along the road caused everyone to turn in surprise.

A wagon, drawn by two horses, rolled into the churchyard and slid to a stop at the entrance to the church. The man driving the team lurched from the wagon seat and fell to the ground.

Naomi grabbed Anna's arm and gasped. "Oh, dear Lord, no."

Before Anna could ask her what had happened, Granny rushed up. "Matthew, run in the church and git Simon. Tell him to hurry."

Matthew glanced at his mother and then dashed toward the church. His feet skimmed the ground before he leaped onto the porch and disappeared inside.

"What is it?" Anna asked.

Granny nodded in the direction of the man who was trying to get up from the ground. "That there's Luke. Looks like he's in one of his mean moods."

Naomi's body shook so hard Anna thought she would drop Eli. She reached for the boy and pulled him from Naomi's arms. "Let me hold him for you."

Luke pushed to his feet. He spread his legs in a wide stance and weaved back and forth for a moment. "Naomi!" he yelled. "Git yore-self over here right now. You hear me, woman. Don't make me come find you."

Naomi took a step forward, but Granny grabbed her arm. "Wait a minute. Let's see if Simon can calm him down."

Simon ran from the church and down the steps to where Luke stood. He said something to him, but Luke shook his head. Several of the men inched past Anna and joined Simon next to Luke's wagon.

Anna couldn't hear what was being said, but she could tell Luke was having none of their suggestions. His voice bellowed from the group. "I don't want my fam'ly havin' nothin' to do with no hypocrites. You tell 'um that we's got to go home."

The men talked several more minutes, and gradually Luke became quieter. The minutes dragged by, and everyone waited in silence. Finally, Simon stepped away from the group and walked to Naomi. "Luke's over his mad spell. He says he just wants you and the children to go home with him. What do you want to do?"

Naomi glanced at Matthew, who'd followed Simon over. "What you say, son?"

Matthew shrugged. "I 'spect we better do as he says. I'll help you put him to bed, Ma."

Anna reached out and touched Naomi's arm. "No. You can't go with him. What if he hurts you or the children?"

Naomi's lips quivered. "He be my husband, Anna. Me and my young'uns got nowhere else to go." She patted Anna's hand. "Don't worry. I been takin' care of Luke for a long time now."

Anna faced Simon. "Don't let her do this, Simon. Make her stay here."

He shook his head. "There's nothing I can do if she wants to go home."

Naomi took Eli from Anna and nodded to Matthew. "Let's go."

"No!" Anna cried. She cast a wild glance in Granny's direction. "Don't let her go with him."

Granny shook her head. "Child, there's nothing I can do."

Anna watched Naomi and her children walk toward Luke, and fear for them rose in her throat. They looked as if they walked toward their execution. Tears gushed from her eyes, and she pressed her fists to her temples. "Matthew, don't forget what I told you," she called out.

The boy turned, and for the first time she saw a smile on his face. He gave a slight nod before he turned away.

Matthew took Eli when they reached the wagon. Naomi stepped onto the wheel, pulled herself into the seat, and reached for Eli. Luke stumbled forward and Matthew guided him to the rear of the wagon and helped him to lie down in the wagon bed. Then Matthew clambered up to the seat, planted himself beside his mother, and took the reins from her hands. With Matthew guiding the horses, the wagon rumbled from the churchyard and turned into the road. Anna watched until they disappeared in the distance.

The churchyard suddenly seemed quiet, and Anna glanced around. Only she and Simon still stood there. The rest of the people had returned to the picnic area where they continued their preparations to leave.

Simon stepped closer to her. "Anna, I'm sorry."

Sorrow lined his face, but Anna refused to believe he cared about Naomi and her children. She backed away from him. "Don't say that."

"You don't understand…"

"You must think I'm an ignorant woman, Simon. You've been quick to point out everything about your precious valley that I don't understand ever since I arrived. Maybe I don't know the people here, but I know Naomi and her children don't deserve to live with a man like Luke Jackson."

"Anna, please, let me explain."

"Explain what? Are you talking about Luke and Naomi or your own actions?"

He frowned. "What actions of mine are you talking about?"

She crossed her arms and glared at him. "Let's start with how you wanted to be my friend and showed up at Granny's every time we sat down to eat. Then all of a sudden you ignore me and say awful things to me. Then you act like a schoolboy with Linda Mae Simmons at the picnic today."

His eyebrows drew down over his nose, and he sneered. "Oh, so that's what you're mad about. It's not Naomi at all. It's the fact that I ate with Linda Mae instead of you."

"Don't be ridiculous. I couldn't care less who you ate with. But the way you behaved was shameful."

"And I suppose you weren't acting the same way with William Carter. How could you cheer for him and embarrass me in front of my entire congregation? And besides, what difference does it make to you who I show attention to?"

She advanced on him until they stood so close she could almost feel his breath. "I don't care who you carry on with, Reverend Martin."

"Well, it sounds like you do. What's going on with you? You don't want any kind of relationship with me, but you don't want me to have one with anybody else." He glared at her for a moment. "You're the most selfish woman I've ever known, Anna. You want to be the center of attention, and you don't care who gets hurt in the process."

Anna sucked in her breath at his words. She narrowed her eyes and leaned toward him. "How dare you talk to me that way! I'd never expect to hear anything like that coming from a man who's supposed to be a preacher. I think you'd better go back and read your Bible. See if you can find a way to get rid of the mean streak I see in you."

He backed away from her, his eyes wide. He stared at her for a minute, and then turned away. His shoulders slumped, and he looked back at her. "I may be a preacher, Anna, but I'm also a man."

The hurt she saw in his eyes crushed her anger and left her heart pounding against her chest. She struggled to hold back her tears, but one slipped from the corner of her eye and trickled down her cheek. She had to get away from him before she dissolved in tears.

Turning, she ran toward Granny's buggy and climbed in. She wondered if Simon had returned to the picnic, but she wouldn't let herself glance back toward the church. It didn't matter where he was or who he was with or what he was thinking. After their argument today, she doubted if he would ever speak to her again.

For the first time she wished she had never come to Cades Cove. The heartache over not getting to go to nursing school couldn't be any worse than what she was feeling right now. At the moment all she wanted was for her mother to wrap her arms around her and tell her everything was going to be all right. Somehow she didn't see how it ever could be again.

Chapter 15

Simon took a step to run after Anna, but he clenched his fists at his side and forced himself to stand his ground. He hadn't had a peaceful day since Anna came to the Cove, and he was tired. He had to conquer the unrest in his soul some way. He raked his hand through his hair and shook his head. "Women," he muttered.

He took a deep breath and turned to rejoin his congregation at the picnic area, but his eyes widened at the sight of Linda Mae standing a few feet away. From the expression on her face he knew she must have heard his entire exchange with Anna.

He swallowed back the remorse rising in his throat and took a step toward her. "Linda Mae, I didn't know you were here."

Her dark eyes gazed past him, and he knew she was watching Anna's retreating figure. "I reckon you didn't."

An awkward silence hung between them for a few seconds before he forced himself to speak. "I was having a conversation with Anna."

She nodded. "More like an argument, I'd say." She glanced once more in the direction of Anna's retreat before she straightened her shoulders and took a deep breath. "The folks all been sayin' how you're right taken with Miss Anna, but I didn't want to believe it. Now I guess I will."

Simon searched his mind for the right words. "Linda Mae, I'm sorry if I gave you the wrong impression. I've known you since we were children, and I wouldn't hurt you for anything in the world."

"I know. You jest can't help how you feel."

"That's right. Please understand and forgive me if I've caused you any pain."

A gradual transformation took place as Simon stared into Linda Mae's face. The hurt look that had flickered in her dark eyes when he first turned around vanished, and the seductive smile he'd witnessed before twisted her lips. She tilted her head to one side and laughed. "Why, Simon Martin, I didn't take you for a silly man, but I guess you are. What makes you think yer so special that I'd think of you as anything but the preacher at my church? I'm sorry if you thought I had my sights set on hookin' up with you."

"Linda Mae, please..."

She held up a hand and backed away. "I guess you don't know me and William Carter been keepin' comp'ny for some time now."

Her words surprised him, and he shook his head. "I didn't know about you and William."

"I thought ev'rybody in the Cove done found out 'bout William and me. The bad thing is we had a fuss a few weeks ago, and he ain't been around since. But I can tell by the way he looks at me that he ain't over me. I guess we tried to make each other jealous today."

Simon forced a smile to his face. "If you love each other, I hope it works out."

"I do too." She glanced over her shoulder. "I see William helpin' his mama get ready to leave. Maybe I better go talk to him and ask him to come to supper one night this week."

Simon nodded. "Maybe you should."

With a whirl of her skirts, Linda Mae strode toward the church members still at the picnic grounds. Simon watched as she approached William. They talked for a moment before he took her arm and guided her away from the group.

Simon wanted to go back to the picnic grounds, but he couldn't make his feet move. He sank down on the front steps of the church and thought about the events of the day. The memory of tears in Anna's eyes and the hurt on Linda Mae's face made him wince.

In his years of being a pastor he had helped many people resolve problems they had with friends or family members, but when it came to his own relationships he had no idea where to begin or even what to do. In the course of one day he had hurt both Anna and Linda Mae, and now guilt gnawed at his heart.

Thoughts of the conversation he and John had the day they fished at Abram's Creek flashed into his mind, and he groaned. His brother was right. When it came to women, he was about as dumb as he could be.

~

Thirty minutes later Simon waved goodbye as the last buggy pulled away from the picnic grove. After it disappeared, he walked to the spot where they'd pitched silver dollars earlier. He thrust his hands deep into his pockets and kicked at the grass with the toe of his shoe.

His gaze drifted to the spot where Granny's buggy had parked. The argument with Anna still blazed like a wildfire in his heart, and he clenched his fists in anger. She'd accused him of being mean. If that's what she thought of him, then he'd made the right decision in staying away from her.

But he'd also been right when he said she was selfish. She didn't care about him or his feelings. She'd proven that today with the way she carried on with William Carter. All she wanted was to go to New York. She thought of him—and William, for that matter—as someone to help her pass the time until she boarded the train. Then she would probably never think of either of them again. The time for her to leave couldn't come soon enough for him.

He turned and strode toward the church. He had better things to do than to stand around reliving the events of the day.

As he stepped onto the porch of the church, he spied a basket of apples by the door and remembered Sadie Carter telling him she had brought some from their tree for him. He picked one from the basket and groaned. The memory of peeling apples with Anna and her wrapping a handkerchief around his cut finger the first day she came to Granny's flashed in his mind.

His shoulders drooped with the weight of defeat. Why was he trying to fool himself into believing something that wasn't true? He knew he'd fallen in love with Anna the day he met her. Maybe if they'd had more time she could have come to love him, but circumstances he couldn't control had put that to an end.

Staying away from her had seemed a good idea at first, but now he wished he'd gone back again and again until he'd worn her resistance down. It was too late now. From the look in her eyes this afternoon, it was clear she hated him.

Something pulled at him to enter the church where he had preached for the last three years. He stepped inside and let his gaze drift over the interior. The old remorse rose in him, and he realized it wasn't only Anna that troubled him so. It was also the secret he harbored and only spoke of with God.

The small cross on the table at the front drew him forward. He moved to stand in front of it. The Bible next to it lay open, and he picked it up and sat down on the step leading to the pulpit.

The late afternoon sun shone through the windows, illuminating the pages. He began to flip through the Bible, then stopped, closed his eyes, and stared upward for a moment.

"God, I hope You don't get tired of me asking You the same thing over and over. It's just that I need to understand what it is You want from me. I've tried to be your man here, but the people of the Cove don't need me. Most of them are Christians and show it in their lives. I haven't been able to figure out why You keep me here. My teachers at Milligan said I was going to pastor big churches and lead lots of souls to You. Instead You brought me back here, and it's beginning to look like I'm not going anywhere. The only thing I can figure out is that You're keeping me here so I can reach Luke. If that's Your plan, help me. His heart gets harder every day. I've tried everything with him, but he won't listen. Show me what to do, Lord."

Simon sat still and waited, but no answer came to mind. He sighed. That's the way it usually was when he had this conversation with God. Perhaps in time God would reveal what he needed to do to reach Luke. But with every passing day, Luke drank more and grew more hard-hearted toward his wife and children.

Today had been the worst Simon had seen, and he wondered what had happened when the Jacksons reached their farm. Probably the same as always. Naomi and Matthew would put Luke to bed, where he would sleep off his intoxication. Then tomorrow he would rise, kiss Naomi, and play with Eli. He might even take Matthew hunting. And for a few days life at the Jackson farm would be happy until the urge for a drink took Luke back to Wear's Valley.

He was sorry Anna had to see Luke drunk again, but she had no way of knowing how penitent he could be when he sobered up. That was what made Naomi go home with him. She lived for the good days, and tomorrow would be one.

Simon sighed and glanced upward again. "Then there's Anna, God. I have to confess ever since Anna came to the Cove I've had my mind on her, and I haven't paid attention to the rest of the congregation like I should have. I'm sorry about that. Help me to get her out of my mind, Lord. I can't stand thinking about her any longer. It's about to drive me crazy."

He jumped up from where he sat and paced back and forth across the front of the church, one hand clutching the Bible and the other gesturing back and forth. "I just want to forget about her. Erase her from my head like she never existed. That's what I need."

Simon dropped back down on the step and glanced at the page where his fingers rested. He pulled the Bible closer and began to read from Proverbs 31. The words at verse ten jumped off the page at him. *Who can find a virtuous woman? For her price is far above rubies.*

The words sliced through his soul. Guilt washed over him. Ever since she'd come to the Cove, Anna had worked hard to learn everything Granny taught her. All she wanted was to help other people, and he'd accused her of being selfish. There was nothing farther from the truth. She was a virtuous woman.

He turned the pages of the Bible until he found the chapter he'd preached from last Sunday, Romans 14. He glanced down the page, his eyes coming to rest on verse nineteen. *Let us therefore follow after the things which make for peace, and things wherewith one may edify another.*

He'd preached on those words in hopes they would touch the lives of his congregation, but he had failed to apply that truth in his own life. Anna had approached him several times to try and mend their broken friendship, and he had refused. Maybe she was right to accuse him of having a mean streak.

His eyes closed, and he fell on his knees before the altar of his church. "Oh, God, forgive me," he cried. "I've been the selfish one. I've been angry because I didn't get what I wanted, and I've hurt everyone around me. Help me to make peace with Anna and be her friend. Give me the strength to help her while she's here…and then to let her go when the time comes."

Simon stayed that way for a long time and thought about Anna and his actions of the past few weeks. Anna had been honest with him from the first day they met, and he'd ignored her words. He owed her an apology. And in his self-pity, he'd ignored Granny, who treated him like a son. He needed to make that right too. And then there were John and Martha. They'd loved him even when he wasn't lovable.

He rose from his knees, looked upward, and swallowed hard. "Well, God, I don't know how You plan to help me reach Luke, but You've given me the answer to what I need to do about Anna. I have a lot to make up for, and I guess there's no time like the present to get started."

~

Granny pulled the buggy to a stop at the back of the house and glanced over at Anna. "Want to git out here, child? After I git this here horse settled I'll come on in, and you can talk to me if you want."

Anna smiled at her. "Thanks, Granny. I'll take the basket inside."

Anna climbed out of the buggy, grabbed the basket, and trudged to the back door. The excitement she'd felt earlier when she left for the picnic was gone, and in its place one of the greatest heartaches she'd ever experienced.

In the kitchen the basket slipped from her fingers and clattered to the floor. With a sigh she looked at the spilled contents, dropped to her knees, and scooped up the scattered dishes.

It seemed everything today had ended in disaster, but the leftover food lying on the kitchen floor was hardly as bad as what happened at the picnic. With both of them still upset over their last meeting, today she and Simon had managed to destroy a friendship she thought meant a lot to both of them.

With the angry exchange still ringing in her ears, she wiped the floor and sank down in a chair at the table. Her stomach churned when she remembered accusing him of having a mean streak. She knew that wasn't true. In the weeks since she'd known him he'd never been anything but a gentleman.

But then he'd said she was selfish. Was she? Had she encouraged him when she knew she would leave at the end of the summer? Her head hurt from pondering the questions, and she rubbed her fingers across her forehead.

"You all right, Anna?" Granny wrapped her arm around Anna's shoulders.

Anna sobbed and pressed her body next to Granny. "Oh, Granny, I didn't mean to make Simon angry with me. I don't know what's wrong with him."

Granny patted her shoulders as she cried. When Anna finally pulled away, Granny sat down and reached across to hold her hand. "Darlin', I seen you and Simon together since you been here, and I reckon he's right taken with you. I 'spect he's mighty upset 'cause you don't return his feelin's."

"But I told him the first day about going to New York. He knew we could only be friends."

Granny nodded. "I know you told 'im that, but you ain't acted like you meant it."

Anna sucked in her breath. "You mean I've given him encouragement without realizing it?"

Granny smiled. "Now, child, be honest with yourself and with me. If'n you was so set on going to nursing school in New York, you wouldn't care about a silly ole argument with Simon."

Anna dissolved into tears again. "But, Granny, I have to go. My father wanted me to be a nurse. He would have been so disappointed if I let him down. I can't let Robert win. I am going to become a nurse, and no one's going to stop me."

Granny's eyebrows wrinkled. "But, child, what if you love Simon?"

Anna squeezed Granny's hand. "I love him like a friend. That's all he can ever be."

Granny stood up and patted her shoulder. "Then there ought not to be a problem. Don't go a-worryin' 'bout Simon. He'll be fine."

The memory of Linda Mae hanging on Simon's arm crossed her mind, and she frowned. "I guess you're right. He already has somebody taking care of him."

Granny laughed and picked up the basket that still sat by Anna's feet. "I'll jest wash up these dishes, and then I'll see what we's gonna have fer supper."

Anna rose to help her just as a knock sounded at the front door. "Who could that be? Is anybody expecting a baby right away?"

She thought for a moment. "We ain't got nobody ready until Martha's time comes due."

Anna headed to the front of the house. "I'll get it."

She hurried through the sitting room and jerked the front door open. And then she had to clutch the side of the door to keep from sinking to her knees. Simon stood in front of her, his hat in his hand and a worried expression on his face.

He took a step forward. "Hello, Anna."

Anna's breath caught in her throat. "S-Simon, what are you doing here?"

He gazed down at his feet before he looked up into her eyes. "I couldn't let what happened this afternoon go without trying to fix it. Can I come in?"

She moved to the side of the door and opened it wider. "Of course you can. You know you're always welcome here."

He walked to the fireplace and stood with his back to her for a moment before he turned to face her. His fingers tightened on the brim of his hat. "I didn't know if you would want to see me again."

"Who is it, Anna?" Granny called out as she entered. She stopped, her eyes wide, and stared at Simon. "Hello there, preacher boy. Come a-callin' on us?"

Simon nodded. "I thought I'd better come by and make some apologies to both of you."

Granny chuckled. "You don't owe me nothin', but I 'spect you and Anna have lots to talk 'bout. I'll jest take that pan of green beans in the kitchen and go set under that there tree out back to string 'em whilst the two of you talk." She paused at the door. "And Simon, you's welcome to stay fer supper with us."

"Thank you, Granny."

Anna clasped her hands in front of her and waited until Granny disappeared. She wondered if Simon could hear her heart pounding. "I'm glad you came by, Simon. I've been very upset about the events of the day."

"Me too."

Anna took a deep breath. "Let me begin by saying I'm truly sorry for my behavior today. I admit I wanted to make you angry when I cheered for William, and that was childish. I'm sorry if I humiliated you." The words tumbled from her mouth.

Simon stepped nearer. "No, I'm sorry, Anna. I'm the one who behaved like a child. What I said about you being selfish is about as far from the truth as anything. I don't think there's a selfish bone in your body. Please forgive those words."

Anna's throat constricted. "I will if you'll forgive me for saying you have a mean streak. You remind me so much of my father, and there never was a finer man. Please forget I said that."

He nodded. "I will." He stood there for a moment as if there was something else he wanted to say. "And one more thing."

"Yes?"

His hat brim crumpled in his hands, and his Adam's apple bobbed up and down. "About Linda Mae. I had a talk with her after the picnic. It seems William Carter has been calling on her for some time, but they had a misunderstanding a few weeks ago. I think they both used us today to make the other one jealous."

Anna tried to ignore her relief, but she couldn't. "Are you sure?"

"That's what she indicated to me. The last time I saw them they were talking to each other, and I could see a big smile on William's face. So I doubt if he'll be stopping by to see you now."

Anna chuckled. "I must say that's a relief. I didn't want to hurt him. But I didn't mean to hurt you either, Simon."

He inched closer to her. "I know. It's just that ever since you've been here I've felt like we could have something special, but you won't let it happen. I've been in such turmoil that I think I wanted to make you unhappy."

"I see."

"But what you said about me being a preacher brought me down to earth. I went back to the church, and I prayed. God's shown me that He'll work everything out for me. So I'm going to put aside my feelings for you, Anna, and replace them with my love for God. I'm going to take care of my congregation, and that includes you. So please, can we start again? With me as your preacher and you as a member of the congregation?"

Tears filled her eyes. "I'd like that, Simon. I want us to be friends."

He let out a long breath. "Friends. Yes, I guess that's what we'll have to be."

He held out his hand to her, and she shook it. His fingers tightened on hers for a moment, and a tingle of pleasure raced up her arm.

She smiled at him. "Want to stay for supper, friend?"

His dark eyes softened, and he nodded. "There's nothing I'd like better."

Chapter 16

*A*nna bolted upright in bed. She rubbed her hand across her forehead and struggled to shake the sleep from her body. Was it time to get up? A glance toward the window told her that it was still night outside.

She sat there a moment gathering her wits. When she'd gone to bed her heart had felt lighter than it had in weeks, but now something was terribly wrong. She could sense it.

She listened for sounds of Granny stirring in the house, and then she heard it—the sound that had awakened her. The distant pealing of a bell pierced the nighttime quiet of the Cove.

She jumped out of the bed and stumbled from her bedroom into the kitchen. A lit oil lamp sat on the kitchen table and the back door stood ajar. She tiptoed to the door and peered out into the night. Granny stood in the backyard.

The grass, wet with dew, tickled her bare feet as Anna joined her. "Granny, what's wrong?"

Granny cocked her head to one side. "Listen, you hear that?"

"Yes, the bell woke me. What does it mean?"

"That's a call for help. Somethin's wrong in the Cove."

A chill rippled down Anna's back. "What do you think it is?"

"Could be anythin'. Somebody could be sick or dead, or…" She stopped speaking and pointed to the distant sky. "Or it could be a fire."

Anna looked in the direction Granny pointed and sucked in her breath at the orange glow spreading across the night sky. She inched closer to Granny. "Where do you think it is?"

Granny studied the direction for a moment. "'Peers like it might be over to Cecil Davis's farm."

Anna shivered at the thought of Pearl or Josie being in danger. "Do we need to go?"

Granny shook her head. "The men'll go. If'n they need me, somebody'll come." She let out a long breath. "I 'spose we better git some sleep. We may have work to do in the morning."

Anna followed Granny back into the house. In the kitchen Granny picked up the oil lamp and headed to her room. "Say a prayer for those folks, Anna. We don't know what's a-happ'nin' over there, but the good Lord does. All we kin do is put it in His hands."

"I will, Granny."

Anna entered her bedroom and crawled back into bed. She lay there a long time thinking about the Davis family and fire at their farm. She prayed none of them would suffer any kind of injury. She drifted off to sleep with the image of Josie's long curls bobbing up and down as she played with the wooden horse in the kitchen.

By sunup Anna was out of bed and dressed. When she entered the kitchen, Granny had breakfast ready. A platter of ham sat on the table. It looked strange sitting there without a big bowl of eggs, but with Jewel gone, there would be no more of Granny's scrambled eggs flavored with ramps from the root cellar

"You cut the last ham in the smokehouse." Anna hoped her voice didn't reveal the anxiety rippling through her. With all the meat gone from the smokehouse, she wondered what they'd do. It would be months before hog killing, and even then Granny would be at the mercy of the Cove people's generosity.

Granny nodded. "Figured we might as well eat it."

Anna swallowed. "What will we do when that one's gone?"

Granny took a pan of biscuits from the oven and set them beside the ham. "Jest what I al'ays do—trust the Lord to provide. If'n I didn't, don't know how I could live."

Anna felt ashamed of her lapse of faith and gave Granny a quick hug. "I'm learning a lot more from you than just how to be a nurse. You teach me something about overcoming doubt every day."

Granny waved her hand in dismissal. "Go on now. You sure got a way with makin' an ole woman feel good." She wiped her hands on her apron and motioned for Anna to sit. "Now set down and eat. Somebody's bound to come by in a while to tell us 'bout last night."

Anna slipped into her chair. "I was hoping you would have already heard."

Granny shook her head. "Not yet."

They bowed their heads and asked the Lord to bless the food. When they opened their eyes, Granny picked up the platter but paused as a knock sounded at the front door. They both jumped up and hurried toward the sitting room. Anna got to the door first, pulled it open, and gasped.

Simon, his face and clothes streaked with soot, stood on the front porch. His tired eyes stared out from under the brim of his hat.

Anna's eyes grew wide, and she clutched at her throat. "Simon, what happened?"

He took his hat off and backed away. He slapped the hat against his leg and soot flew from his clothes. "I been up all night over at Cecil and Pearl's. Their barn burned."

Anna, her gaze roving over Simon, stood rooted in the doorway, and Granny stepped around her. "Anybody hurt?"

Simon shook his head. "Thank the Lord, no. Cecil got his cow and mule out, but he lost the hay and feed he had in there."

Granny pursed her lips. "That's bad, but we kin be thankful they's all right." She turned back to Anna and smiled. "Well, I reckon you gonna git to see a big party."

Anna glanced between her and Simon. "Party?"

Granny chuckled. "We's gonna have us a barn raisin'. When somethin' happens to one of our folks, we all pitch in and help. That's the onliest way we kin all make it."

A tingle of excitement bubbled up in Anna. "When will it be?"

"Probably next week sometime," Simon said. "Some of the men

are going to start clearing away the remains when everything cools off. Then some of the others will come over to cut the trees and make the logs. They'll work real fast so we can get the barn up in time for Cecil to have a place to store his corn and wheat when the harvest comes."

"Anna," Granny said, "you ain't never seen nothin' like it. That barn'll be built in a day, and we'll be right there a-feeding 'em so they work faster."

Simon laughed. "It is a sight to see." He glanced down at his dirty clothes. "Well, I'd better get on home and get cleaned up."

Granny took him by the arm. "You ain't a-goin' nowhere 'til you eat some breakfast."

Simon tried to back away. "I'm too dirty, Granny. I don't want to get this soot all over your house."

Granny shook her finger at him. "Preacher boy, when'd you ever know me to worry 'bout a little dirt? Now you go on round to the back and wash up at the well, then come on in. You've been up all night, and I intend to feed you 'fore you leave here."

Anna laughed. "You'd better do as she says, Simon. She wants you to stay." She hesitated. "And I do too."

His soot-streaked face broke into a big grin, and he nodded. "Well, in that case, I sure have been missing Granny's cooking. I'll just go wash up, then come inside."

Anna watched Simon disappear around the corner of the house before she reentered. Granny was already in the kitchen setting an extra plate at the table. "It shore is good to have Simon back, ain't it?"

Anna smiled. "It sure is."

It was near noon when Granny pulled back on the horse's reins and brought the buggy to a stop in the same spot they'd occupied when they came to the Davis farm for the baby's birth. Today the scene across the property bore a difference to what it had been that day.

Now only a mangled pile of debris lay in the spot where the barn once stood. Men wielded shovels and other tools as they sifted through the ashes and loaded the debris onto the waiting wagons.

She remembered how the barn looked the day Simon had lashed

out at her. He'd accused her of judging those she didn't understand. Now as she gazed at the men united in their group effort, she saw only commitment to help a neighbor who had suffered a disaster.

"You gonna set there all day?" Granny's voice caught her attention.

Startled, Anna realized Granny had climbed from the buggy and was waiting for her to join her. Anna jumped down and brushed at the dirt on her dress. "If it doesn't rain soon, this dust is going to choke us to death."

Granny chuckled and headed for the house. "This ain't nothin' like I seen in years past. In fact, we's had a right mild summer so far."

Anna glanced at the men once more before stepping to the front door. "I guess Cecil and Pearl wish it had been raining last night. They might have saved something."

"I reckon so, but they didn't. And we jest gotta deal with what's left."

The door opened as soon as Granny rapped on it. Cecil's sister-in-law stood in the doorway. The corners of her eyes crinkled as she smiled. "Granny and Anna, come in, come in. I was a-wond'ring if'n you two was gonna come by."

Granny chuckled. "Wild horses couldn't've kept me away, Lavinia."

"Me neither," Anna said. "I had to see how my little friend Josie is doing."

They stepped into the small sitting room where Anna and Josie had napped the day of the baby's birth. Lavinia motioned for them to follow her into the kitchen. "Pearl's takin' a nap, pore thang. Don't think she slept a wink last night. I been a-feedin' Josie, and she's set-tin' at the table."

Anna chuckled to herself at her first impression of Lavinia Davis the day Cecil arrived after bringing her to care for Pearl. When the tall, slender woman walked into the house, her take-charge attitude disturbed Anna. Within minutes of arriving she made it clear she needed no help with Pearl, Josie, or the household chores. She had, she announced, come to stay two weeks for Pearl's confinement, and Granny and Anna were free to go.

After checking Pearl one last time, she and Granny had headed home. With the two weeks not up yet, Lavinia was still in charge.

"Josie," Lavinia called out as they walked into the kitchen, "look who's come to see you. Granny and Anna."

When Josie saw Anna, she dropped the biscuit she was eating onto the table and held out her arms.

Lavinia laughed and picked her up. "That's Anna. Kin you say Anna?"

A big smile creased Josie's face and her brown curls, neatly combed today, bobbed up and down. "An-na."

Lavinia hugged the child. "I been a-tellin' her 'bout Granny and Anna, and she's been larnin' yore names. She's a sweet little thang, and smart too."

Anna regarded the pinafore Josie wore. "What a beautiful dress. Is it new?"

Lavinia nodded. "I sewed it t'other night outta some scraps I found in Pearl's sewin' box."

Anna's eyes grew wide as she ran her fingers over the ruffles at Josie's shoulder. "Oh, Lavinia, you are a wonderful seamstress. My mother tried to teach me, but I never could learn. Maybe you can show me how you do it."

Lavinia beamed. "Ain't nothin' to it. I've larnt a bunch of Cove girls how to sew, and I reckon I could larn you too. Maybe while you're here you and Granny kin come stay a few days at my house, and we'll sew."

"Thank you. I'd like that." Anna stepped closer and held out her arms to Josie. "Want to come to me?"

The child giggled and Lavinia passed her to Anna. Lavinia pointed to a chair. "Set yourselves down and I'll fix us somethin' to eat."

Anna glanced around at the kitchen, which had been so bare of food when they were here before. Today bowls of food sat on the table and pots simmered on the stove. Granny set the basket she'd brought on the floor and began to unload it.

"I brung some vittles, Lavinia. Ain't much. Jest some ham and a blackberry cobbler. And a few tomatoes, and oh, yeah, there's a bowl of peas too."

Lavinia shook her head. "Land's sakes, ev'rybody been so kind to

Cecil and Pearl. I think ev'ry fam'ly in the Cove done brought some-thin'." She darted a glance at the bedroom as if she didn't want Pearl to hear and spoke in a soft voice. "It's a good thang they did. Food's been mighty scarce 'round this place lately. The foxes done got all their chickens 'cept a rooster and two laying hens, and they's down to two hams and a side of bacon in the smokehouse."

Granny nodded. "Them foxes been bad this year."

"Shore have. So's I was glad to see all this here food. And the men, they's worked so hard helpin' Cecil. I declare, I don't want to live nowhere else but in the Cove. Folks cain't be as good anywhere else."

Josie clapped her hands as Anna juggled her on her knee. "I think you're right, Lavinia. I've never met kinder people."

Lavinia turned to her. "Then maybe we can talk you into stayin'. How long you gonna be with us, Anna?"

"I'll be leaving the first of September. I'm going to New York to enroll in nursing school."

Lavinia frowned. "Why you want to go there? We need you here in the Cove. All the women are talkin' 'bout how you doing such a good job with Granny. Pearl's raved 'bout how you took care of Josie. We need you, Anna."

Granny set the last bowl on the table and placed the basket on the floor. "That's what I been tellin' Anna, but sometimes I think I'm jest a-wastin' my breath. This child got the gift of healin', and I shore would like to see her take my place when I cain't do it no more."

Before Anna could say anything, Pearl's voice called from the bed-room. "Lavinia? Do we have comp'ny?"

"We do, Pearl. Granny and Anna come by."

"They gonna come in here?"

"We's coming, Pearl," Granny said as she headed toward the bedroom.

Anna got up, shifted Josie onto her hip, and followed Granny and Lavinia into the bedroom. Pearl lay in the bed with her long brown hair fanned out across the two pillows beneath her head. Her hazel eyes lit up, and she smiled.

Pearl's face didn't look quite as gaunt as it had when Anna had last

seen her, probably a testimony to the good care Lavinia had been giving her. Pearl held out her hand and Granny grasped it. "Granny, I's
so glad to see you."

Granny leaned over and kissed Pearl on the forehead. "You look
mighty good, Pearl. I knowed Lavinia would have you back to normal in no time."

A shadow crossed Pearl's face. "Normal? I ain't never gonna be
normal agin, Granny. Not after what you said 'bout me not havin' no
more babies."

Granny sat down on the edge of the bed and rubbed Pearl's hand.
"I jest tole you what I think's for your own good. Your little body cain't
handle no more, Pearl. Don't kill yourself tryin' to have another child."

Josie squirmed and tried to get down, but Anna tightened her grip
on her. Anna stepped forward, Josie still hanging on her hip. "Listen
to Granny, Pearl. You've got the sweetest little girl I ever did see, and
she needs her mama around until she's grown."

Tears shimmered in Pearl's eyes. "You right, Miss Anna. She's the
best thing ever happened to me."

Josie whimpered and held out her arms to her mother. "Mama."

Anna leaned over and held Josie down to her mother for a kiss.
"She loves you a lot, Pearl. When Granny was helping you and I was
taking care of Josie, she kept crying for you. I don't know what she'd
do if you left her."

Pearl hugged the child before Anna stood and held Josie to her side
again. Pearl smiled up at Anna. "You shore got a way of makin' me see
thangs the right way, Anna. I got me a child the Lord done given me. I
cain't go a-grievin' over what He took away. The Good Book says the
Lord gives and the Lord takes away. Blessed be the name of the Lord.
I guess I jest gotta remember that."

Josie squirmed again and rubbed her eyes. Anna glanced down at
Josie's mouth, which she'd pulled down into a frown. "I think Josie's
tired."

Lavinia nodded. "She didn't sleep much last night neither. With
all the comin' and a-goin' round here, I don't know if'n she'll go to
sleep or not."

Anna drew the child's head down to her shoulder and Josie snuggled against her. "She did real well with me the other day. Why don't I lie down with her in the sitting room and see if I can get her to sleep?"

Pearl smiled up at Anna. "I ain't never gonna forget how good you been to my little girl."

Anna hugged Josie. "It's easy to be kind to a child as sweet as she is." She glanced at Granny. "You and Lavinia can stay and visit with Pearl, and I'll see if I can get Josie down."

Granny nodded. "Thank you, child."

Anna turned and walked from the bedroom. As she entered the kitchen, she stopped at the sight before her. Cecil Davis, his arms braced on the kitchen table, leaned forward, his head bowed and his shoulders drooping. He glanced up as Anna walked into the room.

"Hello, Mr. Davis. I'm so sorry about your barn."

He pushed himself up to his full height and straightened his shoulders. His red eyes stared out of a soot-streaked face crisscrossed with lines of fatigue. He glanced at Josie and Anna clasped her tighter. Without a word, he nodded and walked out the back door.

Anna stood in the kitchen a moment, her legs shaking and her heart pounding. Simon might think Cecil Davis was a good man, but so far he'd given her no indication of that. His aloof attitude frightened her, and she resolved she would never place herself in a situation where she was alone with him.

She stepped to the back door and watched Cecil rejoin the men at the barn before she entered the sitting room. The patchwork quilt still hung on the chair, and she spread it on the floor.

Within minutes of lying down Josie drifted off to sleep. Anna lay there, wide awake, listening to the soft, rhythmic breathing of the child. Anna's back ached from lying on the wooden floor and her head hurt from lack of sleep, but she wouldn't allow herself to doze. Even with Granny, Lavinia, and Pearl in the house, she didn't trust Cecil, and she intended to keep guard against him.

Chapter 17

In the few days since Simon had appeared to tell them about Cecil's barn he had become a frequent visitor again, and his appetite hadn't decreased during the time he'd been away. Anna watched him shovel the last bite into his mouth and swallow.

"Simon, you git 'nough to eat?" Granny propped her hands on her hips and stared at his empty plate.

Simon glanced at Granny. "What'd you say, Granny?"

She raised her voice. "I said, did you git 'nough to eat?"

Simon laid his fork down and glanced up at Anna. "I don't know. Did I, Anna?"

His words startled Anna, and she frowned. "How should I know?"

Simon grinned at Granny and leaned forward. "Well, you're the one usually tellin' me to quit eatin' up all Granny's food. I wanted to check with you before I asked for another helping of those fried apples."

A retort sprang to her lips, but the teasing glint in his eyes made her smile instead. She settled back in her chair and crossed her arms. "I know what you're up to, Simon Martin, and it's not going to work."

His eyebrows arched. "Whatever do you mean, ma'am?"

"You're baiting me into fussing at you so you can keep on teasing until I lose my temper." She leaned forward and wagged her finger at him. "Well, it's not going to work this time." She picked up the ladle in the bowl and spooned a mound of apples onto his plate. "How's that, sir?"

Simon looked down at his plate and frowned. "Is that all I get?"

Anna giggled and wagged a finger at him. "There you go again. Trying to make me mad."

He laughed and took a bite of apples. "Am I succeeding?"

Granny, who'd stood listening to the exchange, burst out laughing. "I declare. Thangs are a-gittin' back to normal 'round here. You two sure can go at it worse than any I ever seen." She shook her head and turned toward the stove, then glanced over her shoulder. "I'd say you right taken with each other."

Anna didn't answer but scooped up the remaining dishes on the table and carried them to the dry sink. Simon might eat a lot, but she had to admit he never came without bringing a string of fish or some kind of wild game for their table.

She had to admit too, that having him back had brought life into the house again, and she could endure the teasing just to have him here. In fact she was beginning to think that he added a missing ingredient to her life, and she didn't want to think about the time when she would no longer be able to see him. She took a deep breath before turning back. It would probably be wise to change the subject. "How's it going with the barn raising?" she asked. "Is everything ready for tomorrow?"

Simon nodded and handed his now-empty plate to Granny. "All the logs have been cut and hewn to the size and shape for the different parts of the barn. We'll get started early in the morning. You two coming?"

"'Course we comin'. I 'spect ev'rybody in the Cove's gonna be there," Granny said.

Simon sighed and slumped down in his chair. "I don't know about that, Granny. I hope Luke Jackson's able to come. I hate to think what the men are gonna say if he doesn't show up. You know they helped him out when he needed a new barn."

Granny eased into the chair beside Anna, shook her head, and grunted. "Has he been drinkin' agin since the church picnic? I feel so sorry for Naomi and what she puts up with. I pray for her ev'ry night."

Simon smiled at Granny. "You need to keep doing that."

Anna reached over and patted Granny's hand. "I've been praying for her too. The Lord has really put her and her children on my heart."

Simon's gaze raked over her. "I'm glad to hear that. You do care about the people here, don't you?"

"I do, Simon." She tried to swallow the lump in her throat, but it refused to budge.

They stared at each other for a moment before Granny coughed. "Now back to the barn raisin'. We'll be there early in the mornin' with lots of food. When those men get to workin', Anna, they can eat enough to feed a big army."

Anna laughed at the thought of what tomorrow would bring. "Will they build one of those cantilever barns like I've seen all over the Cove?"

Simon nodded. "Yes. It's what works best for us."

"I'd never seen anything like them before I came to the Cove."

"I guess the way they're built does look kind of strange to folks who haven't seen them before. I could explain how they're built if I could draw it for you," Simon said.

"Let me get my journal. You can use that." Anna jumped up and ran to the bedroom.

She grabbed the book and her pencil and hurried back into the kitchen. She pulled her chair around next to Simon and plopped the journal down in front of him. "There's a blank page in the back."

Simon opened the book and picked up the pencil. "This is how we start." He drew two box-like figures side by side with a space between them. "First of all we build two long cribs about eighteen feet long, but we place them about fourteen or fifteen feet apart."

"Those are the parts you said looked like little houses," added Granny.

"Right," Simon laughed. "Actually they serve as animal pens. The space between them is left so the farmer can pull into the barn to unload his wagon. Understand so far?"

Anna stared at the drawing. "Yes."

"Next we place two long logs across the top of both cribs. We want them to extend, oh, about eight feet out from the top on either end of the cribs. Those are the primary supports, but then we place some timbers, purlins they're called, on top of them from front to back across the full length of the barn. These with the bottom timbers are the supports for the whole second floor where hay and corn can be stored." He glanced up from his drawing. "Still following me?"

Anna nodded.

He continued to draw as he spoke. "We put a heavy timber frame on top of these supports and line it up with the corners of the cribs. This frame supports the eaves and horizontal timbers in the loft. After we get the gabled room on, the loft runs out about six or eight feet on either side of the cribs. So we have a top-heavy barn with a wide space in the middle where equipment can be stored and wagons can pull in for unloading."

Anna studied the drawing and understanding began to dawn. "And with the loft sticking out on both ends of the barn, the rain drips off there and doesn't go down into the cribs. So the animals and any grain stored there is protected."

Simon smiled. "That's right. And the animals outside the barn can stand underneath the extended ends to get out of the rain."

Anna leaned closer to Simon and stared down at the drawing. "So the strange-looking barns have a real purpose behind their design. That's amazing." She glanced up at Simon, and the look in his eyes took her breath away. She gazed at him for a moment before she closed the journal and stood up. "Thank you for explaining it to me, Simon."

He scooted his chair back from the table. "Anytime, Anna."

~

Simon slumped in his saddle as he rode home from Granny's house. Every time he went he argued with himself about the wisdom of being so close to Anna. He couldn't hide how he felt, and he suspected she saw it in his eyes every time he looked at her. No matter how much he debated the matter, he knew he couldn't stay away.

Tonight, when she'd studied his drawing of the barn, she'd been so close his heart ached. He wanted to reach out and touch her hair as she bent over the drawing, but he didn't dare. One false move on his part could undo all the repairs they'd made to their relationship, and he didn't want that.

Time—that's what he needed. The Cove had a way of putting a lock on your heart and ruining you for life anywhere else. If he could just be patient, that would happen to her. And she would come to see it wasn't just the Cove that had her under its spell, but it was a mountain preacher named Simon Martin.

From now on he had to guard his actions more closely than ever. He'd almost lost his chance with her once, and he wasn't about to let it happen again.

~

The next morning the men were already hard at work when Granny pulled her horse to a stop at the Davis farm. As Granny tied her horse beside another buggy, Anna glanced around for Simon. Within seconds he emerged from the center of activity and ran toward them. His clothes were already sodden with perspiration and he wiped his arm across his forehead.

"Good morning. I wondered when you were going to get here."

Granny closed one eye and peered up into the sky. "We's not that late, Simon."

He laughed. "I guess not. It's such an exciting day. I didn't want Anna to miss a moment of it."

Anna reached in the buggy for Granny's basket. "I'm sure we'll get to see plenty. And I expect to astound everybody with my knowledge about a cantilever barn."

Simon reached for the basket. "Let me take that over to where the women have the tables set up. Then I have to get back to work."

Anna and Granny followed him over to a spot behind the house where the women had gathered. All kinds of food covered the table, and Simon set Granny's basket down. Granny patted his arm. "Thanks, preacher boy, now you run on. I 'spect I can handle thangs from here on out."

Simon glanced at Anna and nodded. "See you later."

Anna watched him go before she turned back to the women. Martha Martin stood behind her, a half-smile on her face. "Hello, Anna. How you been?"

Anna grasped Martha's hand. "Fine, but how about you?"

"I'm fine." She let her gaze move to Simon's retreating figure. "How are things between you and Simon now?"

Anna's heart seemed to skip a beat. "Wh-what do you mean?"

"He mooned around for weeks after that Sunday we ate dinner at Granny's. Wouldn't tell me and John what was the matter, but I thought the poor boy was gonna up and die. Couldn't eat hardly a bite. Then after the Fourth of July picnic, he perked right up."

Anna looked over her shoulder to see if any of the other women had overheard before she pulled Martha aside. "That day at Granny's after you left, Simon and I had a misunderstanding. He came to Granny's the night after the picnic and apologized for his behavior and asked me to be his friend again. So things are fine between us now."

Martha stared at her with wide eyes. "Anna, are you crazy or somethin'? It ain't never gonna be fine between you and Simon until you admit your feelin's for him."

Anna shook her head. "You're wrong. Simon is just a friend. I'm going to New York and he's staying here."

Martha glanced out to the barn, and Anna followed her gaze. At that moment John turned and looked her way. He smiled and waved. Martha's eyes glistened in the sunlight. "Has any man ever made your heart hurt with love so much that sometimes you think you're gonna bust?"

Anna frowned. "I don't understand what you mean."

Martha reached out and grasped her arms. "If'n you don't ache with the need to see a man and be with him, then you don't have love like you should. I've seen you and Simon together. I know you got that kinda love in you. It's for Simon. But you're the one who's gotta see it."

Anna pulled away from Martha. "Don't say that. I can't love Simon. I'm going to New York."

A sad look flashed in Martha's eyes. "Don't turn your back on what God's placed in your path, Anna. Let Him give you the blessing He's got waitin' for you."

Anna turned away. "I don't want to talk about this anymore. Come on. Let's join the other women."

Martha sighed and fell into step beside Anna as they rejoined the group at the table. Pearl sat in a chair under a tree while Josie played at her feet. Anna walked over and knelt down beside Josie. "Hello, dar-lin'. How're you today?"

Josie looked up from digging in the dirt and smiled. She looked up at her mother and pointed. "An-na."

Pearl laughed. "She ain't forgot you, Anna."

Anna stood up. "I hope not. But how are you feeling?"

"Fine. Lavinia won't let me do nothin' yet, though. She tole me to set down in this here chair and not move." Pearl leaned closer and whispered. "I love her like a sister, but to tell the truth, it's time fer her to go home."

Anna chuckled and glanced over at Lavinia, who was dispensing orders to all the women present. "I see what you mean. But you're really lucky to have someone who loves you so much."

Pearl nodded. "I know. Not like some people." Pearl stared past Anna, and she turned to see who was approaching.

Naomi Jackson was coming toward them, Eli held tight in her arms. Matthew walked beside her carrying a basket.

Pearl started to get out of her chair. "I need to welcome her."

Anna restrained her. "You stay right where you are," she insisted. "I'll do it for you and bring her over here." She hurried across the yard toward the three of them. "Naomi!" she called. "I'm so glad you came today." She stopped in front of them and bent to stroke Eli's head before she acknowledged the boy beside his mother. "How are you, little fellow? Hello, Matthew. It's good to see you again."

The boy glanced up at his mother, then back to Anna. "Good to see you too, Miss Anna."

She pointed to Lavinia. "Why don't you take that basket to the tall woman at the end of the table? She'll tell you what to do with it, and, Naomi, you come with me to say hello to Pearl."

Naomi allowed herself to be led to where Pearl sat. When they got there, Pearl held out her hand. "I'm so glad you could come today. I would get up, but…" She cast a look in her sister-in-law's direction, "I have strict orders to stay put."

Naomi grasped Pearl's hand. "We's glad to be here. My husband is powerful sorry he couldn't come, but he's not feelin' good today."

Pearl nodded. "I know how men be. They act like babies sometimes. Now women, we jest go on and don't say nothin' bout how we feel unless our sister-in-law comes to visit."

Anna chuckled and leaned close to Naomi. "Lavinia takes over when she visits, but she has a heart of gold."

Pearl laughed. "That she does."

At that moment Lavinia's voice boomed out above all the noise. "All right, ladies, they jest sent word from the barn that the men'll be ready to eat in a half hour. We gotta git this here food ready."

Anna sighed and pulled Naomi toward the table. "Sorry, Pearl, we've got our orders. We'll see you later."

Anna could hardly believe it as one dish after another appeared on the table until it was covered in a feast fit for royalty. She surveyed the display and had reached over to rearrange some dishes when a voice behind her spoke into her ear.

"Will you sit with me while we eat?"

She smiled at the familiar voice and turned to see Simon standing behind her. His face was red from the heat and the sun, but the gentleness in his eyes made her smile. "Of course. I'll help serve, then find you as soon as I get my plate fixed."

He nodded and turned toward the assembled group. "Cecil has asked me to bless this food and the efforts of all our friends and neighbors gathered today. Shall we pray?"

A thrill raced through Anna as Simon began to pray. "Lord, we thank You for the folks who've come together today with nothing on their minds but to help a friend in need. We thank You for their efforts this morning and for watching over us as we worked. For the blessing of this food You've provided and for the good women of this community who've prepared it, I thank You. Now guide us as we continue to live and work in harmony so we can live in Your will. Amen."

Anna didn't open her eyes as soon as the prayer was over but stood there thinking about Simon's last words. Live in God's will. She wanted to do that, but how could she know the difference? She'd always thought it God's will she should go to nursing school, but her talk with Martha made her wonder.

Finally, she opened her eyes and glanced up. From across the table Simon stared at her, a questioning look on his face. She smiled and began to help Lavinia pass out plates to the men.

When all the men had filled their plates and found places to sit, she joined the other women as they began to choose their food. With her plate piled high, she looked around for Simon and saw him sitting under a tree near the house. She walked over and eased down onto the ground next to him.

He arched his eyebrows and glanced over his shoulder. "Have you seen who can't seem to stay away from each other today?"

"No. Who?"

"Linda Mae and William. From what her father tells me, William's become a steady visitor at their house. He thinks I may be asked to perform a wedding before too long."

She stared in the direction Simon had indicated and spied the couple. They appeared to be involved in deep conversation. Anna smiled. "I hope things work out for them."

"Me too. But enough about them. I want to enjoy this beautiful day and all the good food." He picked up a large piece of cornbread from his plate and arched his eyebrows. "And I'm happy you're here to share it with me."

Before she could say a word, she felt movement and glanced around to see Lucy and Ted Ferguson dropping down next to her.

"Hi, Miss Anna," Lucy said. "We seen you settin' down over here and decided we wanted to eat with you."

Anna looked at Simon and laughed at the frown on his face. She turned back to the children. "We're glad you did, aren't we, Simon?"

"Sure." Simon grimaced before he stuffed a bite of cornbread in his mouth.

Anna suppressed the giggle she felt welling up. "Where have you two been all morning? I haven't seen you at all."

Ted took a big bite of ham and chewed. "We been playin' hide-and-seek with the other young'uns. I 'spect I found the best hidin' places on this here farm."

Lucy snorted. "Naw, you ain't. I done found the best ones."

Ted doubled up his fists. "I done found 'em."

Anna reached out and touched Ted's arm. "It doesn't matter who found the best spots. I just want to enjoy eating with you two. Don't you, Simon?"

He sighed. "Sure."

At that moment Pearl walked around the corner of the house and stopped beside them. "Have you seen Josie?"

The worry on Pearl's face frightened Anna, and she stood. "No, can't you find her?"

Pearl shook her head. "She was right beside me digging in the dirt. Then the next time I looked she was gone."

Simon set his plate aside and rose to his feet. "Don't worry, Pearl. She's around here somewhere. We'll help you look."

Anna nodded and glanced at the children. "Lucy, Ted, you can help too." She pointed toward the back of the house. "You go that way and Simon and I will go the other."

Lucy and Ted jumped up. "We'll find her," Lucy said. "Come on, Ted. Let's go."

Simon grasped Pearl's hand. "Now you go back and sit down, Pearl. Anna and I will find Josie and bring her back to you."

A tear trickled from Pearl's eye and rolled down her face. "Thank you. I jest ain't hardly let 'er outta my sight since I lost the baby. So I'm gittin' scared."

Anna hugged her. "Don't worry. We'll be right back."

Before they could take a step, Ted ran around the edge of the house.

A look of horror masked his features. "Miss Anna, come quick. We found Josie."

Anna and Simon bolted at Ted's words and ran after him. He raced across the field back of the house to where Lucy stood at the edge of the pond.

Oh, dear God, no, Anna prayed. *Don't let her be in the pond.*

She halted at the pond's edge but Simon waded in, thrashing his way toward the little body floating facedown in the murky water.

Chapter 18

"Josie!" Pearl's wail, more piercing than any Anna had ever heard, ripped through the air.

Anna glanced over her shoulder at everyone running toward the pond. As Pearl neared the water, she stopped several feet from the edge and sank to her knees. She clasped her hands to her chest and stared upward. Another scream tore from her throat. "Oh, God, don't take my baby. Please, please, please, jest leave me one baby, Lord!"

Lavinia knelt beside Pearl and put her arm around her shaking shoulders. Cecil, unmoving, stood next to his wife.

Simon waded from the pond, the limp body in his arms. His anguished eyes stared down at Josie and then back to Anna. His lips moved, but Anna didn't want to believe the words he spoke. "I think she's dead."

The verse her father had marked in her Bible flashed into Anna's mind. *I will trust, and not be afraid: for the Lord Jehovah is my strength and my song.*

Lavinia pushed in front of her and reached for Josie. "Give her to me."

Anna reached out and grasped Lavinia's arm. "No."

Lavinia whirled around, a surprised look on her face. "What'd you say?"

Anna pointed to a grassy spot a few feet from the bank. "Put Josie down there, Simon."

Lavinia gasped. "Anna, she's my niece. I'll take care of her."

Anna whirled and faced Lavinia. "I said no. Now let me see about this child."

Granny appeared at that moment and pulled Lavinia away. "Fer once in your life, listen to somebody else, Lavinia. Git outta Anna's way."

Lavinia, her mouth gaping, stared at Granny, but Anna didn't have time to worry if she'd hurt the woman's feelings. A child's life was at stake.

Give me strength, Lord, Anna prayed. *Help me remember what Uncle Charles told me about the time he revived a boy.*

She dropped to her knees beside Josie, grasped her shoulders, and turned her on her side. With one hand on her back and the other positioned right below Josie's rib cage, Anna pushed. A stream of water trickled from the child's mouth. She pushed again, and more water streamed out.

Anna leaned over Josie, pried her mouth open, and ran her fingers around the inside to rake away any lingering water. Then she rolled Josie on her back and grasped the child's nose, squeezing the nostrils shut with her fingers.

Taking a deep breath, Anna knelt over Josie and breathed into her mouth. Anna straightened and looked at Josie's chest, but there was no movement. She repeated the breath, then checked again.

Behind her in the crowd she heard someone murmur. "It's too late. That child's done passed."

Anna closed her ears to the voices around her and bent over Josie again. She breathed into the child's mouth again, and this time the chest moved. Once more she repeated the process, and the little girl's lungs expanded. Her eyes opened, and she coughed as if she were choking.

Anna sat back on her heels and watched Josie gulp air into her little body. After a moment her chest began to move up and down in a regular rhythm. Josie stared up into Anna's face. "Mama."

Simon grabbed Anna's hand. "Thank God."

Granny's voice drifted to her. "Thank you, Jesus."

Cheers rose from the crowd, and Pearl rushed forward and grabbed Josie. Sobs wracked her body. "Josie, Josie."

She clutched the child to her, her fingers stroking the wet curls, and repeated the name over and over as if it were the sweetest sound in the world. Tears streamed down her face. She reached out, grasped Anna's hand, and pulled it to her lips. Kissing Anna's fingers over and over, she mumbled her gratitude. "Thank you, thank you, Miss Anna. You done saved my child."

Anna shook her head. "It wasn't me, Pearl. God did it."

Lavinia, her back straight and tears streaming down her face, leaned over and squeezed Anna's shoulder. "Thank you, Anna."

Holding Josie, Pearl struggled to rise. Simon grasped her arms and helped her get to her feet. "Do you want me to carry her inside for you?"

"No, I jest gotta hold onto her." Pearl hugged the child tighter.

Anna reached out and rubbed Josie's back one more time. The pinafore dress she'd thought so pretty now clung to Josie's skin. "Watch her for a few days, Pearl. I heard my uncle say one time a person who almost drowns runs the risk of pneumonia afterwards, so be careful."

Tears glistened in Pearl's eyes. "I will, Anna, and God bless you fer comin' to the Cove."

Granny put her arm around Pearl. "Let's git this child inside and put some dry clothes on her, then wrap her up good."

Anna watched Granny propel Pearl and Lavinia toward the house. When they reached the spot where Cecil stood, Pearl stopped and glanced up at him. She smiled, and he reached out and patted Josie's head. He watched his wife and sister-in-law walk with Granny toward the house. When they disappeared inside, he turned to the crowd still gathered behind him.

"Well, folks, I guess we got a lot of work to do. Let's finish our dinner, then get back to work."

The crowd, smiles on their faces, stared at Anna for a moment before they began to clap and cheer. Anna wiped at her eyes in an effort to stop the flow of tears before she smiled and nodded in acknowledgment of their praise. Near the front Naomi Jackson studied Anna with wide eyes and clutched Eli closer to her.

One by one they turned and headed back toward their waiting meal until the only ones left were Naomi and Cecil. After a moment Naomi joined the crowd, but Cecil didn't move. When he glanced around and realized he was now alone, he walked forward and stopped in front of Anna. He pulled the sweat-stained hat from his head and swallowed before he spoke. "Thank you, Miss Anna."

"You're welcome, Mr. Davis."

He nodded to Simon, then replaced his hat and, without looking toward the food tables, walked off in the direction of the barn.

Anna glanced at Simon, who still stood beside her. "He's a strange man."

"He's a very private man, Anna. He asks nothing from his neighbors but is always there when they need him. That's why everybody was so willing to help him today. I wish you could see the goodness in him I've known for years."

"Maybe I'll see it someday." She turned to Simon. "He seemed so unconcerned when you pulled Josie from the pond. Most fathers would have been in that pond before you could have reached her."

Simon nodded. "Maybe so, but Cecil isn't like that. He doesn't show his feelings. That doesn't mean he's uncaring. Sometimes I think he feels things more deeply than anyone I've ever known. I think he was so scared he had lost Josie he couldn't move." He pointed toward the construction area where Cecil had gone. "Did you notice how he couldn't join the group and go back to laughing and talking? He went off to be alone to deal with his feelings—just like he did the day the baby died."

"I know you keep telling me this, and I hope I'll understand someday. In the meantime you need to get out of those wet clothes."

He shook his head. "They'll dry soon enough when I get back to work. But what about you? That experience must have left you feeling drained."

"It did. As soon as everyone's finished eating, I hope we can go. I'll come back and see the finished barn another day."

Simon stared at her for a moment. "I need to say one more thing before you leave."

"What's that?"

He swallowed before he began to speak. "The way you took over and saved Josie's life today was wonderful. Granny's right. You do have the gift of healing in your hands. You've touched the lives of so many people already, not to mention the effect you know you've had on me. And I want to repeat what Pearl said. God bless you for coming to the Cove."

"Thank you, Simon."

The words Simon spoke sounded sweet to her ears. She hoped she'd had a good effect on the people she'd worked with, but today had been very special. With God helping them, today she and Simon had saved a child's life. That was a bond they would always share. For a moment she wanted to throw her arms around Simon and tell him she didn't ever want to leave, but then the image of her brother popped into her head. If she stayed in the Cove Robert would win, and she wasn't going to let that happen.

～

The next morning Anna sat under the tree in Granny's backyard shucking some corn while Granny hoed around the plants still producing food in the garden. She remembered other days back at home when she and her mother gathered corn. Shucking and silking the ears had always been among her least favorite tasks, but in the peaceful surroundings at Granny's cabin she enjoyed the quiet and the time it afforded her to view the mountains.

She dropped an ear of corn into the pan next to her and reached for another. She'd just stripped off the first layer of the husk when a voice called out. "Granny, you home?"

Granny looked up from her work, leaned on her hoe, and called out. "We's in the back."

Cecil Davis walked around the house, a burlap bag in each hand. "I knocked on the front door. I's beginnin' to think you warn't here."

Anna rose to her feet and smiled. "Good morning, Mr. Davis. How's Josie today?"

"Fine, doin' fine."

"Did they get the barn built?" Granny walked out of the garden and propped her hoe against the side of the house.

"All done, and bigger'n before." One of the sacks he held moved, and he looked down at it.

Granny chuckled. "Cecil, what you got in that sack? It 'pears to be somethin' alive."

Anna wasn't sure, but she thought she saw a little smile crook the corners of Cecil's mouth. He set the other sack on the ground and carefully opened the one that had moved.

"I's jest a-thinkin', Granny, that I got no use for two settin' hens and thought you might be a-needin' one." He pulled the top of the sack open enough so that the head of a hen could be seen inside.

Anna's heart raced. A setting hen! Just what Granny needed.

Granny's face broke into a big smile, and she looked from the hen to Cecil. "That's mighty neighborly of you, Cecil. I don't know when I had a better gift."

He rose to his feet and pointed to the other sack. "And this here is a ham. I 'spect I better put the hen in the henhouse so she gets used to the place, and I'll hang the ham in the smokehouse."

When Cecil disappeared into the henhouse, Anna ran to Granny and grasped her arm. "Oh, Granny, I can't believe it. I saw what was in Cecil and Pearl's smokehouse when I was at their house, and he's given you half of what he had. That's a very generous gift."

Granny patted Anna's arm and smiled at her. "Darlin', I done tole you the Lord was a-gonna take care of us, and He done it. I jest never figured he'd use you saving a child's life to do it."

Cecil walked out of the henhouse and walked toward the smokehouse. When he reappeared, he pointed to the henhouse. "Better make sure this here place is closed up good at night. Them foxes been bad this year."

Granny nodded. "They sure have."

Cecil glanced up at the sun and back at them. "Well, I guess I better be a-goin'. Got lots of work to do. But I jest wanted to thank you agin for savin' my little Josie yestid'y."

Anna could see the difficulty Cecil was having in speaking, and she hastened to make him feel comfortable. "I'm so glad I was there and that the Lord showed me what to do."

His chiseled features cracked a bit, and for the first time Anna saw in the man's eyes what Simon had been trying to tell her. He did care.

"It's jest that me and Pearl set a big store in that child, and I wanted to tell you in person. I couldn't talk in front of all those folks at the barn raisin'."

Anna smiled. "I understand. Josie is a precious little girl, and I can see why she's the apple of her daddy's eye. Only a daddy who loves a little girl so much would take the time to carve her toys like you do."

For the first time since she'd met Cecil Davis, a smile lit his face. "Well, thanks agin, Miss Anna, and I hope to see you and Granny a lot more at our house."

Granny slapped him on the back. "You can count on us, Cecil. And thank you kindly for what you done shared with us today. I won't be forgettin' it."

Cecil nodded and pulled the brim of his hat lower over his eyes. He walked across the yard toward the side of the house but stopped and turned back to them before he left. A frown wrinkled his brow. "There's jest one bad thing come outta this whole mess."

Granny took a step toward him, concern etched on her face. "What's that?"

"Lavinia's gonna stay another week." Smiling, he disappeared around the side of the house.

Granny and Anna stared at each other for a moment and then collapsed against each other in laughter.

~

Right after breakfast the next morning Simon knocked on the back door. "Granny, I got a string of fish for you."

Anna opened the back door and motioned for him to enter. "Come on in. There are still some biscuits left."

Simon shook his head. "My shoes are muddy. I've been fishin' this morning and I wanted to leave these."

Anna stepped outside and eyed the catch. "Those are big. Where did you catch them?"

"Over to Abram's Creek." He laid the fish on the ground, and Anna thought she detected a faraway look in his eyes. "It's one of the prettiest spots in the Cove. Has all kinds of rock formations along the creek bank. I'd love to show it to you sometime."

Granny stepped out of the house at that time. "What's this yore a-wantin' to show Anna?"

"Abram's Creek."

Granny picked up the string of fish. "Oh, my, yes. No place in the Cove like Abram's Creek." A smile creased her face. "Say, preacher boy, why don't you take Anna and me fishin' over there soon? You catch it, and I'll cook it right there on the creek bank."

"That sounds like a lot of fun. When can we go, Simon?"

Simon's eyes softened as he stared at Anna. "Anytime you want."

"How about…" Anna hesitated and tilted her head to listen. "Did you hear something?"

Granny glanced back toward the house. "Like what?"

Anna stood still a moment. "There it goes again. Somebody's knocking on the front door."

"Well, let's go see who's come so early in the mornin'." Granny strode across the yard and around the house with Simon and Anna on her heels.

Anna's breath caught in her throat at the sight of Matthew Jackson standing at the door. Without a word he stepped off the front porch and walked toward them. His dark eyes stared at Anna from underneath the brim of a straw hat.

"Matthew, you comin' to see me this mornin'?" Granny called.

He shook his head. "No'm. I come to fetch Miss Anna."

Anna's reminder to Matthew to come for her if his mother needed help flashed into her mind. His presence could only mean something was terribly wrong. Anna stepped around Granny. "Did your mother send you?"

"Yes'm."

Anna heard Simon suck in his breath, and then he walked over to the boy. "You've come a long way to do what your mother asked. What does she need?"

Matthew took a deep breath and blinked at the tears he was trying to control. In that movement Anna saw what Simon had been telling her about the reserve she'd seen in Cecil Davis and others. The impulse to cry warred with the unspoken Cove principle. Mountain people were proud, and they'd rather hide their emotions than share them.

Matthew straightened his shoulders and Anna knew pride had won out. "The sheriff came this morning and brought my pa home. My ma wants you to come."

Anna smiled at Matthew and squeezed his shoulder. "Of course I'll come. Is your pa hurt? Does Granny need to bring her medicine bag?"

Matthew shook his head. "Won't do no good now. They brought my pa home dead."

"Dead?" Anna and Simon spoke at the same time.

Simon grasped Matthew by the shoulders. "What happened to your father?"

The boy wiped his sleeve across his nose. The tears had now disappeared from his eyes. "Pa went off to that there tavern over to Wear's Valley. Ma begged him not to, but he wouldn't lis'en. The sheriff said Pa got drunk and was gonna shoot a man, but he kilt Pa first. Said it was self-defense."

Anna could hardly believe the nonchalant manner in which the boy related the news of his father's death. A stab of pain pierced her heart for Naomi and her two children, and she put her arm around the boy's shoulders. "Matthew, I'm so sorry. How's your mother doing?"

Matthew stared up at her, his face now impassive. "She been cryin' a lot, but I told her to never mind. Leastways he won't be hittin' her no more."

Tears filled Granny's eyes, and she pointed toward the house. "Tell you what, Matthew, you come on in whilst Anna and I git ready to go. You kin eat some breakfast, then we'll all leave." She turned to Simon. "You a-goin', preacher boy?"

He nodded. "I'll go home and get cleaned up and meet you there."

Granny put her arm around Matthew's shoulders and drew him toward the house. "And, Simon, git those fish and take 'em to Naomi's. I 'spect we kin cook 'em up over there."

Simon's mouth hardened into a grim line. Without answering, he headed to the back of Granny's house where he'd left the fish.

Anna waited, but he didn't reappear. When several minutes had passed, she frowned and went to search for him.

~

Simon stooped over and picked up the fish, but he couldn't make his feet move. Rooted to the spot, he stared across the field toward the mountains. Defeat consumed him and he closed his eyes.

"Oh, Lord, I don't understand why You let this happen."

"Simon." Anna's voice startled him, and he clutched the string of fish tighter. He turned slowly and faced her. Her questioning eyes stared at him. "What's the matter?"

Ever since he'd been forced to return from seminary, he'd prayed for someone to share the struggles of his ministry—someone who could understand his desire to pastor a large church. Someone who could understand his belief that God had brought him back here to reach Luke Jackson. Someone like Anna. Standing with her now, he longed for her to wrap her arms around him and tell him everything would be all right. He wanted her to whisper in his ear that no matter what disappointments came to him in his work, she would be by his side helping to ease the burden. But he knew that was impossible.

He'd failed to convince her of how much he needed her, how much the people here needed her. His efforts with her had been as futile as his desire for Luke Jackson to come to know God. Every time he tried to reach her, she'd rebuffed him—just as Luke had. He had failed with her, and now he had failed with Luke. He was tired of being a failure.

After all, he was a product of the Cove and shared the characteristics of his proud neighbors. Sometimes it was better to bury your emotions deep inside instead of exposing them and risking more heartbreak.

He shifted the string of fish to the other hand. "Nothing. I'll see you at Naomi's. Tell her I'll bring John. We can build a coffin for Luke."

She nodded. "I'm glad you thought of that. You're such a help to the people in the Cove."

Her words, meant to compliment him, had the opposite effect. His shoulders slumped, and he pushed his hat farther down over his eyes. "Yeah, that's what they tell me. I just wish I could have helped Luke more."

He strode past her without waiting for a response. There were things to be done for the Jackson family. Maybe afterwards he would find a way to live with how he'd failed Luke, but he doubted if it would ever happen. He would probably live with his guilt for the rest of his life.

Chapter 19

Granny guided the buggy over the rough road leading to the Jackson cabin. Anna braced her feet against the floor to keep from bumping against Granny or Matthew, who were sitting on either side of her. Wedged between the two, she darted a glance from time to time at Matthew, but the boy appeared to be lost in thought. She wondered what he was thinking.

Her two encounters with Luke Jackson had left her with memories that still sent chill bumps up her arm each time she thought of them. She could only imagine how much worse Matthew had fared living with his drunken father every day.

She clasped her hands in her lap and said a quick prayer for the right words before she spoke. "Matthew, I'm so sorry about your father's death."

His long lashes blinked, and he inhaled before he turned to stare at her. The dispassionate look in his eyes almost took her breath. It was as if she were staring into the face of an old man who'd waged battles no other human could understand and had emerged with no visible scars. But this boy had wounds that cut deep into his soul, and Anna knew none of Granny's herbs could ever heal what he'd endured.

"Bound to happen sooner or later," he said.

Those few words told her the mountain pride had taken over again. Whatever he was thinking, he wouldn't share it with her.

Granny guided the horse down a lane and into the front yard of the most ramshackle cabin Anna had seen since coming to the Cove. Anna's gaze drifted over the sagging roof with its missing shingles, and she wondered how the family managed during a rainstorm.

The sheriff rose from sitting on a stump in the front yard when they pulled to a stop. He stuck a pocketknife and the piece of wood he'd been whittling into his pocket, walked to the buggy, and grasped the horse's halter. With one hand he tipped his hat in their direction. "Mornin', Granny. Good to see you."

"Good to see you too, Jim," Granny said as she climbed down from the buggy. "Me and Anna came as soon as we could."

He tied the horse to a small tree and nodded. "I knew you would. That's why I waited. Didn't want to go off and leave Naomi alone 'fore you got here."

"That was right nice of you." Granny pulled a basket out of the buggy and pointed to Anna. "This here is Anna Prentiss. She's a-helpin' me this summer. Anna, this be Sheriff Jim Wade."

The man pulled his hat off and held it in front of him. "Glad to meet you, Miss Prentiss. Doc told me you was over to Granny's."

Anna smiled. "Oh, you know my uncle?"

"Yes, ma'am. I reckon everybody in these here mountains know Doc." He glanced back toward the house. "I'm just sorry we had to meet this way. Naomi's inside."

Granny pursed her lips. "We'll go tend to her and see 'bout gettin' Luke ready for the burial. Simon and John are comin' to build the coffin. They should be here 'fore long."

"Then I'll stay around so's I can help them." He pushed his hat back on his head. "If you ladies need anything, you jest let me know."

"Thanks, Jim." Granny squared her shoulders and headed for the house.

Anna took a step to follow, but she stopped when she realized Matthew had disappeared. "Where's Matthew?"

Sheriff Wade pointed toward the back of the house. "He took off when he got out of the buggy. Guess he wanted to be by hisself for a while."

"I guess so. Maybe I'll see him later."

Right now she had to concentrate on Naomi. She inhaled and followed Granny into the cabin. Naomi sat at the kitchen table and stared at a tin can filled with mountain laurel blooms in front of her. Eli lay sleeping on a pallet at her feet.

She looked up and smiled when they stopped beside her. "Thank you for comin'. I didn't know who else to send Matthew for."

Granny put her arms around Naomi's shoulders and gave her a hug. "You done the right thing, Naomi. We's glad to help you out. This is a mighty bad thing that done happened."

Anna knelt beside Naomi's chair and grasped her hand. "I'm sorry about your husband. I can't imagine the pain you're feeling right now."

Naomi's shoulders slumped and her tormented eyes stared into Anna's. "What am I gonna do? How am I gonna feed Matthew and Eli?"

Anna blinked back tears and tightened her grip on Naomi's hand. "We'll think of something. For now, though, we need to take care of Luke. Where's his body?"

She nodded toward a door off the kitchen. "The sheriff put him in there when he brung him home." She glanced down at Eli. "Pore little feller. He fretted most of the night. I's glad he finally dropped off to sleep." A frown puckered her forehead, and she stared past Anna. "Where's Matthew?"

"Sheriff Wade said he ran around back of the cabin when we were getting out of the buggy. I'll look for him later if he doesn't come in."

"Won't need to go far," Naomi said. "I reckon he's a-sittin' out back by that big mountain laurel bush. It's one of his fav'rite thinkin' places."

Anna glanced back at the flowers in the center of the table. "Did these come from that bush?"

A tear trickled out of the corner of Naomi's eye. "Yeah. When me and Luke was first married, he knew how I loved mountain laurel. One day he come home with a little plant he'd dug up in the woods. He planted it for me and told me ev'ry time I looked at that bush he wanted me to think about him and how much he loved me." She stared into Anna's eyes. "He was diff'rent then. Didn't drink. A few years of failed crops made him change, though."

Anna glanced up at Granny, whose mouth was set in a grim line.

Her heart ached for Naomi and how her life had gone so differently from the way she'd dreamed and planned it as a young bride. "I'm so sorry, Naomi."

She tilted her head and a sad smile curled her lips. "I wish you'd knowed Luke then, Miss Anna. You only got to see what the drink did to him. Most folks saw that, but they didn't see the Luke I knew. He'd be real sorry after he got drunk, and then he'd hire on somewhere for a few days. We'd have a little money, and things would be good for a little while. Until the itch for the bottle took over agin." She reached out and touched the blooms in the tin can. "But he always brung me mountain laurel when they was a-bloomin'."

Eli stirred and cried out in his sleep, and Granny bent down and picked him up. She cuddled him a moment before she handed him to Naomi. "You take care of Eli whilst me and Anna get to work. We'll get Luke cleaned up and ready for the buryin'. Simon and John will be here soon, and I reckon other folks will come when they hear about what happened."

Naomi hugged her son close and smiled. "Thank you agin for a-bein' here."

Anna gave Naomi another quick hug before she followed Granny. She came to a halt at the door of the room where Luke's body lay. Naomi had spoken of a person very different from the man Anna had encountered since coming to the Cove. She couldn't reconcile the two images in her mind.

"What's wrong?" Granny asked.

"I'm thinking about what Naomi said about Luke. How could the man she described be so different from the one I saw?"

Granny placed her hand on Anna's shoulder and squeezed it. "It's like I been a-tellin' you ever since you got here, Anna. Life's hard here. It'll break a man. A woman too. When Luke's crops failed, he lost all hope of takin' care of his family. When that happens to some men, like Cecil Davis for instance, they buckle down and do ev'rything they can to put food on the table. Luke didn't. He was weak, and he turned to the bottle and lost hisself in liquor. I 'spect we never will know all Naomi done to keep this family goin'."

"I think she's a very special woman."

Granny nodded. "She is, and she loves her family. It pained her a lot 'cause Luke didn't want Matthew to get no book learnin'. He said Matthew was needed to help with the farm." A disgusted grunt rumbled from her throat. "He just wanted Matthew to do all the chores he didn't do 'cause he was a-layin' in bed drunk."

"I feel so sorry for them. They must have had a terrible life."

Granny sighed. "Yeah, but I guess it's a-gonna git worse now. I don't know what they'll do to git by. Matthew's a good boy, but he's too young to take over responsibility of a family. I reckon the Lord will just have to show us how to help them." She glanced into the room. "But right now we's got work to do. Ready?"

"Yes."

Anna took a deep breath and followed Granny into the little room. She dreaded what the next few hours would bring. Maybe if she kept her mind focused on how she could help Naomi and her children she'd be able to get through the preparations for Luke's burial. There had to be something she could do for them.

~

Simon backed away from the finished coffin and placed his hammer in John's toolbox. Only a few rays of sunshine penetrated the walls of the dilapidated shed where he and John, along with Sheriff Wade, had been working for the past few hours. The shadows that filled the gloomy interior matched the desolate feeling he couldn't banish from his heart.

He closed his eyes for a moment and tried to blot out the image of Luke's lifeless body lying in the house. He couldn't remember what he'd said to Naomi when he arrived. Maybe he'd offered a little comfort. Nothing had brought him any yet.

John looked up from pounding the last nail into the end of the box and frowned. "What's the matter?"

"I need a drink of water. I'll be back in a minute."

He strode from the shed into the light of mid-afternoon. He headed toward the house, but he didn't stop at the well. A mountain laurel bush with its blooms beckoned him, and he dropped down beside it and buried his face in his hands. All he could think about was how many times he'd talked to Luke about God's love. There would be no more conversations now. Soon they would carry the coffin inside and place Luke in it.

A coffin should be more than a few boards nailed together, Simon had always thought. In the city, there were undertakers who sold all kinds of burial caskets with insignia and carving on them. They also had hearses and carriages available for use at the funeral. In the Cove, however, they had none of those things. Luke's simple wooden coffin only hinted at a poor man who'd lived out his life in the rugged Smokies. Nothing more.

Luke Jackson would be buried in the wooden box he, John, and Sheriff Wade had hammered together. Instead of a carriage, it would be transported to the church on the back of a farm wagon, and the people of the Cove would gather around the grave to offer sympathy to Naomi and her children.

Few would probably give Luke a second thought in the months and years to come. If they did, they would remember his angry rant at the Fourth of July picnic or his drunken horseback rides through the Cove. If only he had reached Luke, folks would have good things to talk about when Luke's name was mentioned. But he hadn't succeeded.

"You okay, Preacher?"

Simon jerked his hands away from his face and stared at Matthew, who sat a few feet away. How had he missed the boy when he'd dropped to the ground?

He wiped at his eyes and tried to smile. "Matthew. I didn't see you there. What are you doing?"

"Just thinkin'. It's my best place for doin' that." He glanced past Simon. "I came over a little while ago and seen the coffin you and your brother was makin'. It looked real nice. Ma will be proud to have such a nice one. Thank you for a-doin' that for her."

"We were glad to help out."

Matthew took a big breath and nodded. "I been a-thinkin' 'bout how I can repay you. I figured I can go over to Mr. John's place and help him with his chores for a few days. That ought to pay for the wood and his time, and I reckon I can come clean the church up for you and do anything else you need."

Simon frowned and shook his head. "We don't need you to repay us, Matthew. We helped out because we wanted to."

Matthew nodded. "I know you did. But since I be the head of the family now, I want to do things different than my pa. I got to be a man, and a man takes care of his debts."

Simon rose, and Matthew stood to face him. Determination lined the boy's face, and his dark eyes didn't flinch from Simon's stare. "Matthew, how old are you?"

He straightened his back and lifted his chin. "I'm gonna be ten real soon."

Simon placed his hand on Matthew's shoulder and squeezed. "You don't have to be a man yet. You need to be a boy."

Matthew glanced at the cabin. "I reckon I ain't got no time to be a boy, Preacher. My pa done seen to that."

He wriggled free of Simon's grasp and walked toward the house. The despair that had consumed Simon since Luke's death welled up in him again, but this time it threatened to suck the breath from him. His failure with Luke didn't end with his lifeless body. It lived on in the impact it had had on Luke's son.

~

Two days later dark clouds drifted across the sky as the crowd of mourners gathered next to Luke's grave. The threat of rain was increasing by the minute. Eli squirmed in Anna's arms, and she jiggled him up and down in an effort to quiet him. Beside her Naomi and Matthew stared at the wooden box resting on the ground. The women of the congregation held jars of wildflowers and mountain ferns they'd brought to decorate the grave.

Simon, his Bible open, stood in front of the coffin and read from Psalm twenty-three. "The Lord is my shepherd," he began. "I shall not want."

Anna glanced at Naomi's face and tried to determine what she was feeling, but her expression divulged nothing. Anna wondered what thoughts were running through the woman's mind. A little over forty-eight hours earlier she'd found out her husband had been killed, and now she faced the task of burying a husband and trying to provide for her children alone.

Simon concluded reading the chapter. "Let us pray." The Cove residents, gathered in the small cemetery beside the church, bowed their heads as Simon began to pray. "Lord, we don't understand when tragedies like this happen, but we do know You're still in control. We come to You today in this sad hour to ask Your blessings on Naomi, Matthew, and Eli. We ask You to be with them and help them through the hard days ahead. Help them to draw on the promises found in Your Word and keep them in Your safekeeping. Their friends and neighbors place them in Your hands. Amen."

Naomi, who hadn't shed a tear at the service, opened her eyes and stared at Matthew standing next to her. He reached up and took her arm. "You ready to go now, Ma?"

She smiled down at her son. "I reckon I am."

Naomi held out her arms for Eli and Anna handed the child to her. "Thank you kindly, Anna, for all you done for us since they brought Luke home." She glanced at Granny, who stood behind Anna. "And thank you, Granny. You two been better to me than anybody ever. I won't be fergettin' it."

Granny touched Anna's shoulder. "Darlin', the men want to git the grave filled in. Doc's gonna drive Naomi home, and then he'll come back by my house."

Together they walked from the cemetery toward the front of the church. Uncle Charles, who'd arrived a few hours before the burial, moved along in the midst of the mourners leaving the grave. Anna grasped Naomi's arm. "You will think about what Uncle Charles and I told you?"

Naomi's expression didn't change, but she nodded. "I been a-thinkin' all through the fun'ral. I reckon a woman with two young'uns gotta do what she kin to take care of 'em. You and your uncle are good friends to be lookin' out for me and mine. I al'ays knowed he was, and when I met you, I said to myself you was jest like 'im. I reckon I was right."

"Thank you, Naomi. When will you be leaving?"

"Doc said he'd send a wagon fer us in 'bout two weeks."

Anna smiled. "Good. That'll give me time to visit with you before you go."

They stopped beside the buggy Anna had ridden in when she came to the Cove. Toby whinnied as distant thunder rolled across the valley. Naomi glanced down at her son. "All right, Matthew, let's go home. We's got lots to do."

The boy's dark eyes stared back at his mother, and he nodded. "I reckon I gotta get on the chores. Then we'll talk about leavin'." He helped his mother climb into the buggy, his protective manner with his mother proclaiming his position as head of the family now. He might only be a boy, but he was a boy who'd grown up overnight. He took off the straw hat he wore and held it in front of him. "Thank you, Miss Anna and Granny. I won't never forgit your kindness to my ma."

Uncle Charles stopped beside Matthew and grasped his shoulder. "You're a credit to your mother, Matthew. She's lucky to have a son like you."

The boy didn't smile but gave a small nod in acknowledgment of the compliment. Uncle Charles turned to Anna. "I'll drive Naomi and her sons home. Then I'll be back by Granny's in just a bit."

Uncle Charles climbed in the buggy and flicked the reins across Toby's back. Anna watched him ride away from the church, the little family huddled beside him. A few drops of rain splattered against the dry earth. Dust whirled across the dirt yard.

One after another the families left until only Anna, Granny, and the men filling the grave were left. Granny looked up at the sky. "Looks like we're in for a downpour. We oughta wait a while 'fore drivin' home. I'll jest go in the church and clean up some for Sunday service. You coming?"

Anna looked around for Simon, but he was nowhere to be seen. She took a step toward the cemetery. "I'll be there in a minute. I want to find Simon first."

She walked back to the cemetery and stopped at the grave. John, working with the men to fill the grave, paused and leaned on his shovel as she approached. "Anna, I thought you'd gone home."

Her gaze drifted over the tombstones scattered across the small hill next to the church. "I was looking for Simon. Have you seen him?"

John pointed to a field behind the cemetery. "I saw him walk out that way a little while ago."

Anna hurried to the back of the cemetery and let her gaze drift across the area. At the far edge of the field she spotted a dilapidated cantilever barn that looked as if it had been abandoned years ago. She squinted and caught a glimpse of Simon sitting underneath the barn's overhang, his arms resting on his bent knees and his head bowed. Another drop of rain hit her head. She looked up at the dark sky and hurried across the field toward the barn.

"Simon, what are you doing?"

He didn't look up as she approached. "I needed to be alone."

"But it's about to become a downpour. You need to come back to the church."

He shook his head. "I'll be all right. You go on before you get wet."

Anna dropped to her knees. Raindrops leaked through the rotting wood overhead and dripped onto her face. "Tell me what's troubling you."

He glanced up, and she gasped at the tortured look in his eyes. She'd seen it once before, the day he'd learned of Luke's death. "Leave me alone, Anna."

His raspy voice shocked her, and she grasped his hand. "Simon, you're scaring me. Please tell me what's the matter. I want to help you."

He stared at her for a moment as if debating whether or not to allow her to see into his soul. He reached up with his free hand and brushed away a raindrop that had landed on her cheek. "I wonder if God is crying today."

Surprised, Anna sat back on her heels. "What do you mean?"

He tilted his head to one side and narrowed his eyes. "God wants everyone to accept Him, and I'm supposed to be doing His work. But I failed with Luke. I told him time after time about how much God loved him, but he wouldn't listen. He got to where he wouldn't even talk to me when I went by his house."

Anna rubbed his hand. "That wasn't your fault. You tried."

He sat up straighter and glared at her. "Oh, I tried all right, but I won't anymore. I've failed again."

"You haven't failed anybody, Simon. Everybody loves you."

A sarcastic chuckle escaped his mouth. "Oh, sure, they love me. Everybody in the Cove loves me so much they made me feel guilty about going back to school. They needed me here, they said, and I believed them."

"But it's true. They do need you."

He shook his head. "No, I was supposed to do God's work. I was supposed to lead lots of people to Christ. After I told them I'd stay here, I realized they were nearly all Christians. All except Luke."

Understanding dawned on Anna. "And you thought it was your mission to bring him to Christ?"

"Yes. That's why God brought me back. Now I've failed in what He wanted me to do."

The agony Anna saw in his face scared her. The Simon she knew had a joy for life and loved to tease and laugh. The brooding man before her didn't resemble that person at all. There had to be something she could do to ease his pain.

Before she realized what she was doing, Anna lifted Simon's hand to her mouth and kissed it. "Simon, you're one of the best men I've ever known. You take your calling seriously, and you try to follow God's will. But you can't take responsibility for other people's actions."

He swallowed. "What do you mean?"

"God expects us to tell the people around us about His love, but He's also given everybody the choice to either accept Him or not. Luke chose to ignore what you told him of his own free will. That's not your fault. You did what was expected of you."

He glanced down at his hand she still held. "I would like to believe you."

She smiled. "Simon, you're a man of faith. You have to understand you can't take the sins of the world on your shoulders. Jesus has already done that. He just wants you to tell the people around you about Him and let them make their own choices. It doesn't matter if you do that in Cades Cove or in a big city somewhere."

"But on top of the tragedy of Luke, there's Naomi and the boys," said Simon. "I don't know how she'll make it without a husband. Luke may not have been the best one in the world, but at least he kept some food on their table."

Anna smiled. "You don't have to worry about that either." She shifted from her heels to sit on the ground. "Before Sheriff Wade left Naomi's house the day before yesterday, I asked him to take a note back to Uncle Charles for me."

"What did it say?"

She settled her skirts around her. "When Uncle Charles was bringing me to the Cove we stopped at Mrs. Johnson's inn over at Pigeon Forge. She kept complaining about not having anybody to help her do the work. I asked Uncle Charles if he would talk to Mrs. Johnson about the possibility of Naomi coming to work for her."

Simon sat up straight, his eyes wide. "You what?"

"Well, it seemed like a good idea. Mrs. Johnson needs a worker, and Naomi needs a place to go. She and Matthew can't work that farm. I really didn't expect Uncle Charles to get over there right away, but he made a quick trip to Pigeon Forge and then came on over here for the funeral."

"Well, don't keep me in suspense. What did she say?"

Anna smiled. "She thought it was a wonderful idea. She has a little cabin out behind the inn where Naomi and the children can live, and Naomi will help her with the cleaning and cooking. Matthew will do odd jobs like chopping wood and drawing water, but the best part is he'll also get to go to school."

Simon stared at her for a moment before he leaned forward and kissed Anna on the cheek. "Thank you, Anna. You're wonderful. Not only have you helped Naomi, but you've given *me* a lot to think about too." Her skin tingled with pleasure where his lips had grazed her face.

From the edge of the field John's voice rang out. "Simon, Anna, it's 'bout to become a downpour. You're gonna drown if you don't git inside."

For a moment Anna felt as if their souls had connected, but John's words brought her back to the reality of rain pouring from the sky. They laughed and jumped to their feet. Simon grabbed her hand and pulled her out from underneath the barn's overhang into the drenching rain. In surprise she looked down at her wet dress and Simon's shirt clinging to his body.

Anna turned her face up to the rain and let the water trickle down her face. Simon smiled at her, and the look in his eyes sent a thrill through her. "Want to race me back to the church?" she asked.

He shook his head. "No. You might beat me again, and I don't want anything to spoil this moment with you."

Chapter 20

Simon latched the tailgate on the wagon and studied the items Naomi was taking to Pigeon Forge. Anna's uncle had returned as he promised, and now they were about to send the family to a new life outside the Cove.

Anna walked from the house. She'd never looked lovelier than she did today. The gingham dress she wore rustled against her legs as she hurried toward him. "Simon, is there room for this box? I found it in the kitchen."

He leaned against the back of the wagon and watched her move toward him, her slight figure swaying as she walked. Her hair sparkled in the sun, but it was the happiness on her face that ignited his spirit. It was the joy he often saw on the face of someone who'd given of their time to help someone.

"I think it'll fit in the space beside the cedar chest." He pushed a quilt aside and took the box from her hands. Their fingers touched, and he felt a tingle all the way to his elbow. Her expression didn't change and he wondered if she felt anything.

Anna closed her eyes and took a deep breath. "The world smells so good today, doesn't it?"

Simon chuckled. "I guess I never thought about that."

She laughed. "It's such a beautiful day in the Cove." She cocked her head to one side. "Say, when are you going to take Granny and me fishing? You promised, but you haven't done it yet."

"We'll do it soon."

She grinned and wagged a finger at him. "I'm not going to let you forget."

Her uncle stepped to the door at that moment. "Anna, Granny needs you in here for a moment."

She spun around and ran for the door. "Coming, Uncle Charles."

Simon watched her go and sighed before he turned back to securing Naomi's belongings in the wagon.

Anna's uncle walked from the house and stopped beside him. He studied the furniture and clothes piled in the wagon. "How's it goin', Simon?"

Simon tugged on the rope holding the tailgate in place. "Fine. I think it's about ready to go. Everything loaded?"

Doc Prentiss nodded. "Granny wanted Anna to help her check the rooms one more time before we left. Naomi seems to be having some last-minute problems. She's gone out back to be by herself."

Simon nodded. "I can understand. She's starting a new life, and no one can promise her it's going to be easy."

Doc Prentiss glanced back at the house and then to Simon. "And how about you, Simon? How are you doing?"

Simon felt his eyebrows arch. "I'm fine. Why—have you heard otherwise?"

Doc Prentiss put his hand on Simon's shoulder. "Anna is my niece, and I love her like a daughter. Granny tells me there seems to be a problem between the two of you. Is there anything I can do to help?"

Simon shook his head. "Only God can take care of that situation." Suddenly the day seemed hot, and he pulled his hat from his head. Wiping his shirtsleeve across his forehead, he managed a weak smile. "I guess I fell in love with Anna the day she jumped out of your buggy at Granny's. A lot of folks would say that doesn't make sense, but I knew she was the one I'd been waiting for." He paused a moment, then gritted his teeth. "I knew, Doc. Can you understand that?"

Doc Prentiss nodded. "I can. But how does Anna feel?"

"I don't know. Sometimes I feel like she loves me, but she won't give up on going to New York." He paused and slapped his hat across his leg. "And I'd be doing wrong if I encouraged her to forget her dream. I lost mine, and I don't want that to happen to her."

Sadness flickered in Doc Prentiss's eyes. "It'll be hard for her to put the dream of nursing school aside. She's wanted it since she was a little girl."

"Are you telling me to give up? That it's hopeless?" The old fear of failure reared its head inside him.

Doc Prentiss stared at the house. "I don't know. I think you and the Cove have had a big influence on Anna, but I don't know if it's enough to make her change her mind."

Simon sagged against the back of the wagon. "I thought she might stay here, but I'm beginning to have my doubts."

"All I want is for both of you to be happy. I'll pray for you."

The door of the house opened and Anna, holding Eli, walked outside. Granny followed her and Matthew and Naomi brought up the rear. A mountain laurel bloom stuck up above the rim of a tin can in Naomi's hand. Simon and Doc Prentiss met them as they approached the wagon.

Simon held out his hand. "Let me help you up, Naomi."

Matthew stepped in front of him. "I kin do it."

He took the tin can from his mother and set it on the ground, then grasped her arm and helped her climb into the wagon. When she was seated he picked up the can, handed it back to her, and glanced at Simon. "Ma cut a twig offa that bush out back. Maybe it'll grow in the ground over to Miz Johnson's place," he said.

A sad smile pulled at Anna's lips. "I know it will grow, Matthew."

He nodded and reached for his brother. When he had handed Eli to his mother, Matthew turned to face them. He took off the hat he wore and held it in his hands. "I want to thank you kindly for yer help with my fam'ly. We won't never forgit what you done for us." He glanced at Anna and Granny. "Specia'ly the two of you. You been right at my ma's side a-takin' kere of her. Miss Anna, I reckon you bin our special angel."

Anna dabbed at her eyes. "Thank you, Matthew."

He turned to Simon. "And, Preacher, I won't never forgit you neither. You were the only man in the Cove who tried to help my pa. It warn't your fault he wouldn't listen. Me and ma thank you for tryin'."

Simon cleared his throat. "I'm sorry I didn't succeed, Matthew."

"Don't make no diff'rence now, I 'spect." The boy's gaze traveled over the house. "This always gonna be home to me. I ain't never gonna forgit it."

A sob escaped Naomi's mouth, and she buried her face in Eli's curls. Anna stepped forward, reached up, and grasped her hand. "Take care of yourself. I hope to see you soon." She turned back to Matthew and held out her hand. "You're a good boy, Matthew. I'm glad your mother has you to watch out for her."

Matthew glanced down at her outstretched hand. The muscle in his jaw twitched, and then he stepped forward and wrapped his arms around Anna. After a moment he loosened his grip and took a step away from her. His steady gaze didn't waver from her face. "Don't know when, but I'll be back someday."

He glanced at the house once more, stepped onto the wagon's wheel, and hoisted himself into the back of the wagon. Doc Prentiss shook Simon's hand, hugged Granny, and kissed Anna's cheek before he climbed onto the seat. "Simon, Granny, I'll leave you today with the same words I said the day Anna came to the Cove. Take care of my girl."

The wagon pulled out onto the road, and Anna waved as it drove away. Simon gazed at her and wished with all his might she would let him take care of her forever.

~

A week after Naomi left the Cove Granny pulled the buggy to a halt at John and Martha's house. Anna glanced around the yard but didn't see anyone.

Granny jumped from the buggy, tied the horse to a tree at the edge of the yard, and called out. "Anybody home?"

"Granny! Anna! Come in and set awhile." Martha Martin, wiping her hands on her apron, walked around the house from the direction of the backyard.

"We wondered if'n you were gone."

Martha placed her hands in the small of her back and stretched. "Not like this, Granny. I 'spect I won't be goin' nowhere 'til this baby gets here."

Anna grabbed Granny's bag and hopped from the buggy. "We wanted to check on you. How have you been feeling, Martha?"

Martha rubbed her hands over her abdomen and frowned. "I know I've got another month, but I declare I do believe this little one is 'bout ready to come." Her hands stilled, and she winced. "He's a kicker. You think he'll come early, Granny?"

Granny chuckled. "Land's sakes, Martha, the good Lord don't tell me that. I jest show up when the time comes." She put her arm around Martha's shoulders. "But why don't we go inside and check you over? I'd like to know how the little feller is doin'."

As Anna followed Granny and Martha into the house, a sweet aroma of something baking tickled her nose. Martha turned before they entered the bedroom. "Anna, I have a blackberry pie bakin'. Will you keep an eye on it while Granny's a-checkin' me over? Then we can eat some of it."

Anna handed the bag to Granny. "I'll do it. Come into the kitchen when you get through."

Anna stopped at the kitchen door and inhaled. Blackberry pie—it had become one of her favorites since coming to the Cove. She wondered how many blackberries she'd picked in the time since she'd been here. Every one of them had either found their way into one of Granny's cobblers or were canned and sitting in the root cellar waiting for the coming winter.

Anna grabbed a dishcloth and opened the oven door a crack, then closed it to allow more baking time. She sank down in a chair at the table to wait and found her gaze drifting around the room.

This was her first time in John and Martha's home—the house where Simon had grown up. She rubbed her fingers across the smooth wood of the table. Perhaps he'd sat in one of the chairs to eat with his family. How she wished she could peer into the past and see what his parents were like, how he and his brother had played together.

His face flashed into her mind and she smiled. What did he look like when he was a little boy? Did his hair tumble over his forehead like it did now? Did his dark eyes sparkle with the laughter that sent a thrill through her?

Simon occupied her thoughts more and more. Sometimes it was difficult to believe that he hadn't been a part of her life forever. Her face warmed and she pressed her fingers to her cheeks. Being in the house where Simon grew up had triggered some emotions better left undisturbed. She glanced around for a distraction and thought of the pie.

Jumping up from her chair she hurried to the oven and peered inside. Dark juice bubbled at the edges of the brown crust covering the top. Anna eased the pan out of the oven and set it on the table.

A cow mooed in the distance and she moved to the back door. A smile tugged at her lips as she surveyed the cantilever barn—a structure she once thought so strange. But she had come to understand that life in the Cove, just like the barns, followed an orderly tradition set years before.

The longer she stayed, the harder it was going to be to leave.

⁓

Simon pushed his way through the dried cornstalks in the field beside John's house. "You behind me, John?"

Brittle leaves rustled behind him. "I'm a-comin', Simon. Jest checking some of the corn."

At the end of the row Simon stepped from the field. A horse nickered, and he glanced toward John's front yard and spied Granny's buggy. If Granny was here, then Anna must be with her. He scanned the yard but didn't see them. They had to be inside the house.

"Hey, John. Granny and Anna are here."

John stopped beside him and chuckled. "Brother, don't go actin' like you're surprised. You told me this mornin' Anna said they was comin' by for Granny to check Martha today. I figured that's why you been ridin' my coattails all day."

Simon laughed. "I still can't put anything over on you, can I?"

John shook his head. "Not where that pretty girl is concerned. Why don't you go on in and see her?"

There was nothing he'd like better, but he'd told John he'd help with feeding the livestock. "Well, maybe after we're through at the barn."

John slapped him on the back. "Oh, go on. I reckon I can feed my own cows. Do it most of the time by myself anyhow."

Simon hesitated, then grinned at his brother. "Well, if you're sure."

John laughed, shook his head, and walked off toward the barn. Simon glanced down at his pants. Dust from the cornfield covered his legs. He bent over and brushed his trousers. No time to wash up, though.

He strode toward the house and entered the front door. Stopping inside the sitting room he listened for voices. He didn't hear anything but the growl of his stomach. Martha was baking one of her pies again, and he headed toward the kitchen.

At the door he stopped. Anna stood looking out the back toward the barn. She didn't move, and he enjoyed a moment of being able to study her without her knowing it. He wished he could step behind her and wrap his arms around her, but his better judgment told him that wouldn't be wise.

He leaned against the side of the door. "What are you looking at?"

Anna whirled around, her hand going to her throat. "Simon, you scared me half to death."

Her cheeks had a rosy tint, and he wondered if it was the result of embarrassment or the heat from the oven. He chuckled and walked into the kitchen. "I hope I didn't make you so angry that you won't let me have any of that pie."

With downcast eyes she moved toward the table. "Granny and Martha are in the bedroom, but I'm sure Martha wouldn't mind you having a piece."

The forced words sounded strange to him. He cocked his head

to one side and studied her as she approached the table. Her glance darted around the room but passed over him as if he weren't there. She pulled a plate from the shelf, set it on the table, and backed away, her hands clasped behind her back. "Help yourself."

Something was wrong and he had no idea what it was. He'd followed John all day, helping him with his chores in hopes of seeing her, and now she acted like he was a stranger she was inviting to eat his fill.

"What's the matter, Anna?"

She turned back toward the shelf and grabbed three more plates. "Nothing. I guess you just caught me daydreaming."

He touched her arm as she set the dishes on the table. "And what could you be thinking about on such a lovely day? My niece or nephew who's going to make an appearance before long?"

She shook her head. "No."

He put his finger under her chin and tilted her face up. "What's the matter? You can tell me anything."

Tears pooled in her eyes, and she wiped at them. "I was thinking about how much I love living here and how sorry I'll be when I have to leave."

Simon fought the urge to yell out the relief that coursed through him. The Cove had affected her, and she was having second thoughts. If she was willing to admit it, then maybe there was hope she was also thinking about him in a different light—as more than just a friend. Swallowing, he smiled and nodded. "I understand. If anyone stays here long, they never forget it."

She smiled at him and glanced around the kitchen. "I like being in the house where you grew up, Simon. What was it like here?"

He'd never talked about his parents much to anyone, but he wanted Anna to understand them. "My father worked hard to make a livin' here, and my mother worked right beside him. John and I had a wonderful childhood. We worked in the fields with them, but there was always time to go fishin' or huntin'. Most of our social activities involved our church friends and our neighbors. Seems like there was always a get-together at somebody's cabin. Nothing fancy, just neighbors being friendly."

She nodded. "And it's still the same. Just like when Cecil's barn burned and when Naomi had to leave, everybody pitched in and helped. And then there was the Fourth of July picnic."

Simon cleared his throat and arched his eyebrows. "I'd prefer it if we didn't talk about that day. It brings back painful memories."

She reached out and swatted his arm. "You're teasing again. We're way past that incident."

His eyes narrowed, and he stared at her. He was far past their argument, and he wished he could tell her how far. Her comments, however, had raised new hope in his heart. "Yes, we are."

She stared at him a moment before she glanced down at the table again. "I don't know what's keeping Granny. Martha wanted us to have some pie."

Afraid he might reach out and pull her toward him, Simon shoved his hands into his pocket. "They'll be out in a minute. But while we're waiting, come outside with me."

"Why?"

"You were asking about my family. I want to show you something very special to me."

~

Anna followed Simon into the yard and toward two maple trees in the field at the right of the house.

"Over there," he said.

Something stuck up from the ground beneath the trees, and Anna squinted to see what it was. Her breath caught in her throat as she drew nearer. Two tombstones rested beneath the trees.

Simon stopped and knelt at the foot of one of the graves. "This is where we buried our parents. Ma always loved these trees because John and I used to climb them when we were little boys. She always said she wanted to be buried under them. Said she wanted their leaves to decorate her grave in the fall."

Anna knelt next to Simon and studied the stones. "What a beautiful thought."

He nodded. "It was a hard winter in the Cove, and they both took sick and died when the influenza epidemic hit. Granny did everything she could, but nothing helped."

Anna glanced up at the overhanging trees and smiled. The name Simon stood out on the trunk of one and John on the other. "When did you and John carve your names there?"

Simon chuckled. "We were little. Maybe eight and ten. Ma always touched those places on the trees when she was out here. She came here a lot to read her Bible and be by herself."

Anna sank down on the ground. "Tell me about her, Simon."

He settled beside her. "My father grew up in the Cove, but my mother came here with her father. He was a teacher at a college and wanted to learn more about the Cherokee who sold the Cove land to the first settlers. My father fell in love with her that summer and didn't want her to leave. Her father, of course, thought she was throwing her life away, but she was determined. She stayed and never left my father's side until the day she died."

"What a beautiful story, Simon. They must have loved each other very much."

He nodded. "They did. They were alike in so many ways and yet different too. Pa didn't see any reason for me to go away to school, but Ma was determined I would. She said she chose to give up her chance at an education, but she wasn't going to make her son give up his dreams. And I guess I have part of both of them in me. I inherited my love of learning from Ma and my commitment to the traditions of the Cove from Pa."

Anna reached over and covered his hand with hers. "Thank you for showing me your parents' graves, Simon. I'm sorry I never got to meet them, but I feel like I know them because I see them in you."

He stared at her for a moment before he leaned closer, his gaze riveted to her face. "Anna, I want you to know..."

Before he could finish his sentence, Granny's voice called from the direction of the house. "Anna, where are you?"

Anna jumped to her feet. "Granny may need me. I have to go."

Simon rose and stood beside her. "I'll walk back with you."

Anna smiled. "Thank you for bringing me here, Simon. I'm glad you told me about your parents."

And without speaking, without touching, they walked back toward the house.

~

"Granny, what's the matter?" Granny hadn't spoken since they left Martha's house, and the silence hung heavy in the buggy.

Granny didn't take her eyes off the horse. "I'm a mite worried 'bout Martha."

"Why?"

Granny shook her head. "The baby hasn't settled in the birth canal yet."

The thought of anything happening to Simon's sister-in-law or her baby made Anna's stomach roil. "But I thought you said sometimes the baby may not settle until right at the end."

Granny nodded. "That's right. But with Martha I don't know for sure when this here baby is a-comin'. I'm afeared it might be any time, and I'd jest feel better if'n that young'un would get ready."

Anna looped her arm through Granny's and laid her head on her shoulder. "You worry too much. But then that's what makes you the best granny woman in the mountains."

Granny reached up and patted her head. "Don't go a-butterin' me up. You know lots of the women been askin' me if'n you was goin' to be 'round when their time comes next winter."

Anna laughed. "Did you tell them I'm leaving in September?"

Granny glanced down at her. "No, 'cause I keep a-hopin' you won't go. I seen you and Simon out there where his folks is buried. I reckon a man don't take a woman to his folks' graves unless he's right smitten with 'er."

Anna laughed. "Oh, Granny, you don't miss anything. He said he wanted me to know more about his family, and he told me how his mother gave up her chance at an education to stay in the Cove with the man she loved."

"You think Simon might been a-tryin' to tell you somethin'?"

Anna's eyes widened. "Like what?"

"Well, child, if'n you cain't fig'er that one out, you ain't as smart as I thought you was." Granny popped the reins across the horse's back. "Git up there, Jim. Git us on home."

Chapter 21

*A*nna sat on the edge of her bed and let her mind wander as she pulled the brush through her hair. Her friendship with Simon had changed in the weeks since the Fourth of July. They had finally been able to return to the easy relationship they'd had when she first came, and it felt good. She felt happier than she had since she'd come to the Cove.

But it was already the first week in August. In three short weeks she would leave the Cove and everyone she'd come to know. The thought of not seeing Simon again brought tears to her eyes.

From her bedroom window she could see the mountains her soul had connected with in the two months since she'd lived in the Cove. Granny said there was no way to describe the colors God painted across the Cove when fall arrived. She wouldn't be here to see it, though. She'd be in New York studying at Bellevue Hospital.

Anna sighed and turned away from the window. There was nothing to be done about it now. She pulled the brush through her hair one more time and stepped into the kitchen.

"Is this dress all right to wear today?"

Granny glanced up from the pot she was stirring. "Anna, we goin' fishin' at the creek. Ain't gonna see nobody. Jest be sure you wear somethin' you don't mind gettin' caught on the thornbushes 'long the way."

Anna laughed. "Then I think this is the right one." She glanced toward the front room. "Simon's not here yet?"

Granny chuckled. "No, he ain't, but he'll be on purty soon. That boy's gotten to be reg'lar as clockwork 'round here agin. I ain't seen him so happy in a long time."

Anna smoothed the front of her dress. "It is good to have the old Simon back."

Granny turned back to the pot. "He don't seem like the old Simon to me. That boy's changed a lot since you came along."

The nicker of a horse sounded from the front yard. "That must be him. I'll go tell him to hitch the horse to the buggy."

Granny looked up and smiled. "You do that, child. I'll jest be here in the kitchen."

Anna ran through the house and out the front door. Simon, who was tying his horse to the tree, glanced over at her and waved. "Morning, Anna. Ready for the big fishing trip?"

She ran outside and stopped beside him. "Oh, Simon, I'm so excited! I haven't been fishing in so long. I can hardly wait to see what's in the mountain streams around here."

He glanced up at the sun. "Are you and Granny ready? We'd better get going. It's a good distance to Abram's Creek."

Anna nodded. "Granny's stirring something on the stove, but I think she's about through with that. Why don't you hitch her horse up, and we'll be ready when you're done."

"Fine." He headed around the side of the house, and Anna ran back inside.

Ten minutes later Anna and Granny waited on the front porch while Simon drove the buggy around the house. Anna ran to the buggy, shoved the basket Granny had packed for the day in the back, and helped Granny climb in beside Simon.

He smiled at the two of them. "Ready?"

Granny nodded. "Let's git a-goin'. Those fish are a-waitin' to git caught."

With a laugh he slapped the reins across the horse's back and they headed toward Abram's Creek.

"I wondered if you were ever going to take us to the creek," Anna said.

Simon turned to her, a smile on his face. "I hate to tell you this, Miss Prentiss, but I do have other congregation members I have to take care of. I can't drop everything the minute you get a whim about wanting to do something like go fishing."

Anna jabbed her elbow into his rib cage. "Don't you start teasing me today. It's too beautiful, and I intend to enjoy every minute of it."

She leaned back against the seat, closed her eyes, and listened for the sounds of the Cove—the clip-clop of the horse, the birds, and the breeze ruffling the tree leaves. How she loved it here. But how much more she loved the sound of the two people on either side of her chatting back and forth.

"You think we gonna have a hard winter, Simon?" Granny asked.

"Don't know, Granny. I did hear Andrew Long say the shucks on his corn were a lot thicker than last year. Could mean some cold days in store for us."

Granny chuckled. "That Andrew always says that. But I cut a persimmon seed open t'other day."

"You did?" Simon asked. "What did it look like?"

"Jest like a little shovel."

"Then sounds like we may be in for a worse winter than last year."

Anna smiled to herself as she listened to the twang of the mountain speech. It was becoming more familiar to her every day, and she had even begun to follow some of the patterns herself.

Anna opened her eyes and sat up straight as Simon guided the horse off the main road onto a dirt path that ran past a farmhouse. She had never been to this part of the Cove before. She pointed to the house. "Who lives there?"

Simon gripped the reins a little tighter as the horse made the turn. "That's the old John Oliver place. He was the first settler in the Cove. Some of his descendants live there now."

Granny nodded. "We goin' on past here to where Mills Creek and Abram's Creek come together. It's a right good place to fish."

They rode for a few more minutes until Simon pulled the horse to a stop. He hopped out, tied the horse to a tree, and reached back to help Granny and Anna out. "This is as close as we can get in the buggy. We'll have to walk the rest of the way."

Anna jumped to the ground and looked around. The longer she stayed in Cades Cove the more she was struck by the scenery. The trees formed a towering canopy above them. "The Cove must be the most beautiful place on God's earth," she said.

Simon stood beside her, his gaze taking in the landscape. "Yes, it is. This area is even more lovely in May and June when the rhododendron arc in full bloom. We're a little late for it this year, but maybe I can bring you back here sometime to see it."

Her face warmed as she reached for Granny's basket in the buggy. "Maybe."

She and Simon followed Granny as she headed through the thick growth toward the water's edge. Granny forged ahead, clearing the way for Anna and Simon. In a few minutes they emerged onto the bank of the clearest stream Anna thought she'd ever seen.

Granny motioned to them. "Jest set those things down here, and you two go git to fishin'. I'll get a fire goin' so's we can cook them fish."

Simon handed Anna one of the poles he'd brought and pointed to the water. "Come on, Anna. Let's see who can catch the most."

Granny raised her eyebrows and stared at Simon heading toward the water. "Enjoy your day, Anna. Simon's been real excited to bring you here."

Anna laughed. "I know. He acts like it's a real special place."

Granny frowned at her. "It is to him."

A tingle rippled through her at the look in Granny's eyes. "What do you mean?"

At the water's edge, Simon turned and yelled. "Anna, are you comin'?"

Without waiting for an answer from Granny, she smiled and ran toward where he waited.

~

Three hours later Simon set his plate aside and pulled his watch from his pocket. The afternoon sun was beginning to make its way across the sky, bringing an end to the day's fishing trip. He didn't know when he'd ever enjoyed anything so much. Standing beside Anna and hearing her squeal as she pulled fish from the creek had thrilled him more than he could have imagined.

And the meal. He didn't remember ever eating as much as he had today. The mountain air and the fish fresh from the stream had combined to increase his appetite. Anna and Granny had teased him as he ate, but he knew it had all been in fun. They seemed to have enjoyed the day as much as he had.

With a shove he pushed himself up from the ground. "I think I ate too much."

Anna widened her eyes and looked at Granny. "Granny, what do you think?"

Granny chuckled and stood up. "I reckon I ain't never cooked so much since the last time I went to that corn shuckin' over to Andrew Long's place. 'Course that day I only cooked for twenty men. That ain't nothing when it comes to tryin' to feed Simon."

He laughed and reached out to hug Granny. "And you love cooking for me, don't you?"

Her eyes softened. "I shore do, preacher boy."

Anna stood up and picked up the plates scattered about. "Granny, I'll take these down to the creek and wash them off."

Granny grabbed at the dishes. "You'll do no such thang. Simon's gonna show you the rocks up the creek a ways. It's jest a short walk up the trail." She waved her hands to shoo them off. "Now git goin' so's we can git home before dark."

He motioned for Anna. "Follow me."

They walked a short distance up the creek bank until they came to a spot where the limestone formations branched out into the water. The trail climbed at this point across the rocks, and Anna viewed the path with uncertainty.

Simon reached his hand out toward Anna. "Come on. There's a great view of the creek from up here."

Anna hesitated. "It's too steep. I don't think I can make it."

He continued to hold his hand out to her. "I'll pull you up, but be careful. The moss on the rocks makes it slippery."

She grabbed his hand, and he gripped her fingers. With careful steps he guided her to the top of the outcropping until they stood looking down to the water eight feet below. He released her as she looked around, her eyes wide.

"It feels like we're alone in the world, doesn't it?"

He stared at her, unable to make himself look away. "I wanted to bring you here to see this, Anna." She tilted her head and looked into his eyes. He swallowed. "I told you about my parents the day you were at John and Martha's, how my grandfather didn't want my mother to stay in the Cove. She wanted to stay, but she hated to defy her father. My father brought her here to see Abram's Creek. He thought if she fell in love with the beauty of the Cove, she'd never leave him."

Anna let her gaze drift over the rocks and the tumbling water below them. "It worked because you and John are still here."

"Yes, we're still here."

She turned to him. "Thank you for bringing me to see a place so special to your parents. I think this is my favorite place in the Cove too. I'll never forget it."

He'd failed again. He thought maybe the magic that Abram's Creek had worked on his mother would also work on Anna, but it hadn't. His chest tightened at the thought that he probably would never be here with her again. He had nothing left to convince her to stay.

"We'd better go," he said.

She nodded and turned to leave. Without warning her foot slipped on the wet rock and she lurched forward. He grabbed her and jerked her back before she toppled over the edge to the creek below.

He pulled her close and wrapped his arms around her shaking body. His heart pounded in his chest and he tightened the embrace. Her cheek lay next to his mouth, and he whispered in her ear. "You scared me."

Her shaking arms went up to encircle his neck. "Thank you, Simon. I would have gone over if you hadn't caught me."

He pulled back from her and gazed down into her face. She returned his stare with unblinking eyes. Suddenly he didn't care if she was leaving or not. This was the woman he loved, and he wanted her to return his love.

"Anna, I've tried to just be your friend, but I don't think I can."

Her lips trembled. "Simon…"

He tightened his arms around her. "Anna, you belong here in Cades Cove with me. I can't believe God brought you here without there being a purpose in it."

Tears stood in her eyes. "Simon…"

He clenched his teeth. "You don't want to go to New York, and you know it. You're committed to something you decided when you were a child. Well, you're a woman now. You can make your own decisions, Anna."

She closed her eyes and a tear trickled out of the side. Then she took a deep breath and stared up at him. Her arms tightened around his neck.

His eyes went to her mouth, and his lips descended toward hers. She lifted her head, welcoming his kiss. But just before their lips met, he hesitated and pulled back. A frown creased his forehead.

"Did you hear that?"

She stared up at him. "What?"

"I thought I heard someone."

They stood still for a moment, still wrapped in each other's arms. "I don't hear anything," Anna said.

He stared back at the way they had come. "There it goes again. It sounds like Granny."

Anna stiffened and released him. "Granny? Oh, Simon, what if something's happened to her? We have to go back right away."

He grabbed her hand and began to descend the rocky ledge. "Be careful. Hold onto me until we get down."

Once they reached the level trail below the rocks, they ran along the creek until they arrived at the spot where they'd fished and eaten earlier. Granny sat on the bank, her hands rubbing her ankle.

Anna dropped down beside her. "Granny, what happened?"

Granny looked up at them, her face flushed. "I guess I's jest gittin' old. I never seen that big rock 'til I stepped on it. My foot turned, and I reckon I got me a bad sprain."

Anna ran her hands over the injury. "Are you sure it's not broken?"

"Naw, it ain't broke, but I guess I cain't walk. Think you two can he'p this old lady back to the buggy?"

Simon dropped to his knees beside Granny. "Now you just take it easy for a few minutes. Anna and I will gather up everything and I'll put it in the buggy. Then we'll get you. I expect you need to get home and in bed."

Anna looked up at him. "Simon, do you think you need to go for Uncle Charles?"

Granny sat up straight. "Land's sakes, no. I treated worse than this for years, and I 'spect I can take care of my own ankle without botherin' Doc. Now you two get everything loaded, and I'll jest set here 'til you do."

Simon and Anna ran back and forth to the buggy until everything was loaded. As Simon laid the fishing poles in the back his hand brushed against Anna's. They both stood still as if frozen in place. His thoughts returned to how close he'd come earlier to kissing her. He wondered if she was thinking about it. At the time she had pulled him closer, but now he wondered if she regretted what had almost happened between them.

She swallowed, glanced down at the ground, and turned to run back to Granny. He stood there a moment, remembering how she'd looked up at him on the ledge. He knew she loved him. What was he going to have to do to make her admit it?

Then he remembered Granny, and he ran to help her to the buggy.

Chapter 22

$\mathcal{A}$nna bent over Granny and tied the poultice around her ankle. She straightened and stared out the bedroom window, surprised at how dark it had gotten. It seemed like it hadn't been that long since she and Simon helped Granny into the house from the picnic, but it must have been several hours ago.

Ever since they got home, she'd been busy getting Granny settled and following her instructions about what to do for her sprained ankle. Anna had mentioned sending for her uncle again, but Granny had refused. Even though Anna was concerned over Granny's injury, she had learned a lot about treating such a sprain.

"There now," Anna said as she straightened up. "How does that feel?"

Granny smiled. "Cain't say as how I could've done better. You gonna make a good nurse, darlin'."

Anna smiled. "Thank you, but I don't like practicing on you." She stepped back and propped her hands on her hips. "Now, what can I get you to eat?"

Granny shook her head. "Nary a thing. I 'spect a good night's sleep is gonna he'p a lot."

Anna leaned over and kissed Granny on the forehead. "If you need anything, call out for me. I'll come right away."

"I'll do it. Now you go on and fix yourself somethin' to eat. I'll prob'ly be able to walk some in the mornin'."

"Goodnight." Anna slipped out of the room and closed the door.

She trudged to the kitchen table and sank down in one of the chairs. For the first time she let herself think back to what had occurred on the rocky ledge. Her heart sank as she remembered the feeling she'd had when Simon's arms held her and how she'd pulled his head down to receive his kiss.

Tears flowed down her cheeks and she wiped at them with her fingers. Ever since she'd come to Cades Cove she'd enjoyed being with Simon, and today she had wanted him to kiss her. The truth hit her, and she almost doubled over in shock. She loved Simon. The thought made her heart sing and brought a smile to her face. Her lips might say one thing, but she knew the truth—never in her life would she feel for any man what she felt for Simon.

Of course that made no difference. She was committed to going to school in New York. That had been her plan for years, and she wasn't going to change it now.

Tears welled in her eyes. Was beating Robert worth giving up Simon? She sank back into the chair and buried her face in her hands. What was she going to do?

A pounding knock at the front door interrupted her thoughts, and she jumped up from the chair. Could it be Simon returning? She couldn't face him again tonight. She was afraid she might lose control and tell him the secret of her heart.

Slowly she made her way to the door and opened it. Her eyes widened at the sight of John Martin standing on the front porch.

"John, what is it?"

He pushed his way into the house, his eyes filled with fear. "Martha's havin' the baby. Granny needs to come right away."

Anna glanced back to the room where Granny lay and swallowed. She took a deep breath and turned back to John. "Granny's been hurt and can't walk. I reckon I'm the one who's gonna have to deliver this baby."

John's face turned pale. "Miss Anna, I know you been a-helpin' Granny, but do you think you can do it by yoreself?"

She reached out and touched his arm. "Don't you worry about a thing, John. I'll get my things, and we'll leave in a few minutes."

He nodded and sat down in one of the chairs in front of the fireplace. Anna ran from the room, grabbed an oil lamp off the kitchen table, and stopped at Granny's bedroom. She inched the door open a little and whispered into the room. "Granny, are you awake?"

The bed creaked. "What is it, Anna?" The glow from the lamp lit the room, and Anna saw Granny wince in pain as she sat up in bed. "You all right?"

Anna set the lamp on the table next to the bed and knelt beside it. "John is here. Martha's having her baby. What should I do?"

Granny sighed and tried to push out of bed, but she fell back in pain. "I cain't do it, Anna. You gonna have to take care of this 'un yourself. Jest remember ever'thing I tole you and you'll be fine."

A fear nagged at Anna's mind. "But you told me when you examined Martha, her baby hadn't turned. What will I do if it still hasn't?"

Granny patted her hand. "We talked 'bout this. You know what you gotta do. I'll be here prayin' for you, child."

Anna leaned closer. "Are you sure I can do this?"

"You can."

"But, Granny, this is Simon's family. What if something goes wrong?"

Granny raised up on her elbows. "Don't go a-borrowin' trouble 'fore you even got some. Now go on. Martha's a-needin' you, and I'll keep a-prayin' for you."

Anna got up and headed for the door. "Anna…"

She stopped and turned back to Granny. "Yes."

Her eyes held a sad look. "Don't forget to take the hook."

Anna's stomach roiled, and her arms crossed over her abdomen at the reminder. She didn't think she would ever be able to use that horrible instrument. And certainly not on a member of Simon's family.

She stared upward. "Oh, God," she whispered, "give me the strength to deal with this birth."

As soon as John pulled the wagon to a stop in front of his home, he jumped down and helped Anna out. He grabbed her arm and pulled her toward the house. "Hurry. Martha's been alone too long."

The frightened look he'd had on his face back at Granny's was still present. Anna reached back into the wagon for the baskets she'd brought. "Help me with these, John. I'm going to need all this later."

He picked up the box containing the hook and turned questioning eyes to her. "What's in here?"

She reached out and took it from him. "Oh, just something else Granny carries with her. If you'll get the other basket, I'll take this."

Anna turned toward the house and hurried to the front porch. It would never do for John to see what was in the box. He was already so scared she wondered if he would last through the long night.

John opened the door and followed her inside the house, then led her to the bedroom. He rushed into the room and dropped down beside the bed. "Martha, Granny cain't come. She got hurt today, but Anna's here."

Martha's face glistened with perspiration. She looked up at Anna and smiled. "Thank you for coming, Anna."

Anna set her instruments down and turned back to John. "Now I want you to do two things for me while I'm getting started here."

John jumped to his feet. "Give me anything you want done, and I'll take care of it."

"First, I want you to put a big pot of water on to boil. Then I want you to go get Simon."

John frowned at her. "Why you want Simon here?"

Anna smiled. "Because you're going to need somebody to keep you company through the night, and your brother is the one to do that."

John nodded. "I 'spect yer right." He leaned back over Martha. "I'm gonna git that water to boilin', then I'm gonna go after Simon. You mind me leavin', Martha?"

She reached up and stroked his cheek. "I think Anna's right. You're gonna need him tonight. Now don't worry 'bout me. Anna will take care of me. You go get Simon."

John kissed his wife on the forehead and rushed from the room. Anna pulled an apron from one of the baskets and tied it around her waist. "Is there any hot water in the kettle, Martha?"

Martha groaned as another pain hit her. She waited for it to pass before she answered. "There should be some left."

"Then I'm going to the kitchen to wash my hands. I'll be back in just a minute—I promise."

In the kitchen John finished putting the water in the pot and turned to Anna. "I'm a-leavin' now. You need anything else 'fore I go?"

She shook her head. "No, I'm just going to wash my hands before I examine Martha. Now you go on."

John rushed out of the house before Anna had finished pouring water from the kettle into the wash pan. She picked up the home-made soap that lay beside the pan and began to scrub her hands. She wished she could prolong the moment of examining Martha, but she knew she could not.

She dried her hands and carried the wash pan to the back door. After throwing the water into the yard, she turned back to the stove and poured clean water in the pan before she walked back toward the bedroom. Martha smiled and held out her hand as she walked in. "Anna?"

"What is it?"

She grabbed the side of the bed as another pain hit her. "I'm glad you're the one here with me."

Anna forced a smile to her face as she set the pan on a table across the room from the bed. She walked back to the bed, reached for Martha's hand, and covered it with both of hers. "I'm sorry Granny couldn't be here, but I don't want you to worry. We're going to work together to bring this baby into the world."

"I ain't worried. I feel like I have family with me."

Anna felt her heart constrict. "What do you mean?"

"I already think of you as family 'cause Simon loves you, and I know you'll do everythin' possible for his brother's child."

Anna's lips trembled. She patted Martha's hand and pressed her arm back down to the bed. "I promise you I'll do the best I can. Now don't you worry. God's gonna help us get through this together."

Martha nodded and closed her eyes. "Thank you, Anna."

Anna reached down and grasped the hem of Martha's gown. "I have to raise your gown so I can examine you, Martha. I don't mean to hurt you, so just relax. And don't worry about being embarrassed. Before tonight's over, I'm going to know your body very well."

Martha's chest rose with heavy spurts of breathing. "I know. You do whatever you need."

Anna pulled the gown up until Martha's abdomen was completely exposed. Gently, she began to press her fingers across the surface in an effort to determine where the baby's head was. It only took a moment before she knew. She forced a smile to her lips and looked up at Martha.

"Now that wasn't so bad, was it?"

Martha shook her head.

How could she tell her? She leaned over Martha and pressed a cool hand to her forehead. "Now you rest for a minute," she said.

Martha looked up at her, fear in her eyes. "Something's wrong. I kin tell. What is it?"

Anna remembered what Granny had told her. "Always be honest with a woman, child. Tell her what's what." Still, she dreaded what she must say. She sat down beside the bed and took Martha's hand in hers. "The baby is in a breech position, Martha. That means he's not in the head-down position to be born. I'm going to put one hand on the top of your stomach and one underneath. I'll try to rotate him into the head-down position, but I'm afraid he's settled and this won't work. Still, we need to try."

"All right."

God, help me, Anna prayed as she began.

~

Simon followed as John opened the door to his house and rushed in. He'd never seen his brother so upset, and he was glad Anna had suggested John come for him. John stopped at the closed door to the bedroom and turned back to Simon. "Anna's in there with her. You think I need to let 'er know we're back?"

Simon put his hand on his brother's shoulder. "Don't interrupt Anna. She'll come out and let you know when there's any news. We just need to settle down and wait. That's gonna be the hard part."

John nodded and sank down in one of the kitchen chairs. His hands shook as he laced his fingers together and rested them on top of the table. He turned frightened eyes to Simon. "I just got this real bad feelin', Simon. I don't know why, but I do."

Simon walked over and gripped his brother's shoulder. "We'll pray through this night, John. Martha and the baby will be all right."

At that moment the door to the bedroom opened, and Anna emerged. John was out of his seat in a flash and ran toward Anna. "Miss Anna, how's Martha? Can I see her?"

Anna grabbed his arm and steered him back toward the kitchen. "Let her rest a minute, John."

She glanced up, and Simon's heart constricted at the look in her eyes. There *was* something wrong. He could see it in her face, and he could hear it in her trembling voice. John was too wrapped up in his concern for Martha to notice, but to Simon there was no mistaking the fact this wasn't going to be a normal birth.

Simon cleared his throat. "John, did you get a chance to tend to the livestock before you went to get Anna?"

A look of surprise crossed his face. "When Martha started havin' pains, I stayed with her and didn't go to the barn. Then when I got back from Granny's, I forgot."

Simon put his hand on his brother's back and steered him to the back door. "Why don't you go check on things now? It'll take your mind off Martha for a few minutes."

John glanced back at the bedroom door. "Yeah, I guess I'd better go to the barn. But you'll call me, won't you, Miss Anna, if you need me?"

Anna smiled. "I will, John."

Simon stood at the back door and watched his brother walk

toward the barn. Then he whirled around and faced Anna. "All right, tell me what's wrong."

She sucked in her breath. "How do you know something's wrong?"

He took a step closer. "It's obvious to me, but I don't want John upset. That's why I sent him to the barn. Now tell me."

Anna's lips trembled as she looked at him. "The baby's in a breech position, and I haven't been able to turn him from the outside."

Simon frowned. "Is this dangerous?"

"Yes."

He swallowed. "For Martha or the baby?"

She closed her eyes for a moment, then opened them. "If it comes down to the two, I would try to save Martha first."

Simon exhaled in surprise. "It's that serious?"

She bit her lip and nodded.

Simon walked back to the door and looked outside. He rubbed the back of his neck with his hand, then turned back to face Anna. "Do you want me to go for your uncle?"

"I thought of that, but it's miles there and back. Besides, he might not even be there. He could be anywhere in the mountains taking care of a patient."

Simon came back to her and gripped her arms. "Then what are we to do?"

She looked up at him, and his heart sank at the fear he saw in her eyes. "John is too upset already to be any help to me. I want you to stay with me and help until this ordeal's over."

He nodded. "I'll be here as long as you need me."

~

Simon sat beside Martha's bed, his watch in his hand as he timed the contractions. He blinked his eyes in an effort to stay awake and peered at the time. Four o'clock in the morning. He and Anna had been at this for hours, and Martha had progressed little since he first entered the room. According to Anna, Martha must be approaching her fifteenth hour in this ordeal.

The door opened and Anna tiptoed back inside. She bent over and whispered in his ear. "John's fallen asleep at the kitchen table. I didn't disturb him. It's better if he doesn't realize how long this is taking."

Simon nodded and stood up. "I think I'll stretch my legs for a few minutes. The pains are now about seven minutes apart."

Anna frowned. "They're getting closer."

Simon stretched his arms over his head and yawned before he walked to the far end of the bed. He glanced down at Anna's instruments laid out on the table. His foot hit a box on the floor, and it rattled. Anna, bent over Martha, seemed not to notice. He reached down and lifted the top. What he saw caused him to recoil in horror, and he dropped the lid back in place.

Anna turned at the sound and walked toward him. "What are you doing?" she hissed.

His teeth clenched as he glanced back down at the box. "What is that thing?"

Anna held her fingers up to her mouth to silence him. "Shh! She might hear you."

He grabbed her arms. "Tell me what it is."

She glanced back at Martha, took his hand, and pulled him from the room. They passed John, who was still sleeping, and stepped outside the house. Then she turned back to him. "Simon, you shouldn't have looked in the box."

"Tell me what it is!"

Her trembling hand went to her head, and she smoothed her hair back from her face. "I don't even want to think about it, but I'm so scared. If Martha's not able to deliver the baby, I may have to use that horrible thing."

Fear rose up in Simon. "How?"

She began to cry. "You have to dismember the baby with it so the mother can expel the body."

"No!" he gasped. "You can't do that to Martha and John's baby."

"I don't want to. But what if it means saving Martha's life?"

Her body convulsed with sobs, and Simon, feeling completely helpless, stared at her. Slowly he reached out and wrapped her in his arms. She clutched at his shirt and cried into his chest. He pressed his mouth to the top of her head and kissed the golden hair he'd thought so beautiful the first time he'd seen her.

He stroked her hair and held her close. "Anna, don't cry. We're going to get through this. I'm going to be there with you every minute. And I'll help you with anything you have to do."

She grasped his shirt tighter. "Oh, Simon, thank you. I couldn't stand it if I were alone tonight."

He reached in his pocket and pulled out the handkerchief she'd wrapped around his finger that first afternoon and began to dry her tears. "Calm down. We've still got a long road ahead of us."

They walked back into the house, tiptoeing past John. As Anna opened the door to Martha's room, she glanced down at the handkerchief in Simon's hand. She looked up at him. "You still have my handkerchief?"

He smiled at her. "I told you I would tell everybody you were a good nurse. Martha was the first one I told. Now let's go see about bringing my brother's child into this world."

A groan came from the bed as Anna and Simon reentered the room. Remorse at leaving Martha alone washed over Anna, and she rushed to bend over her. "Did you think we'd deserted you, Martha?"

She smiled up. "I think I drifted off to sleep between pains. When I woke up you were gone, but I knew you'd be back."

Simon patted his sister-in-law on the arm. "We just stretched our legs for a minute and checked on John. But we're back to stay for the duration now, Martha."

She tried to push herself up in bed, but Anna restrained her. "What do you want?"

She glanced toward the door. "How's John doing?"

Simon chuckled. "He's doin' fine. Better than any of us. He's drifted off to sleep at the kitchen table."

Martha smiled and lay back against the pillow. "Good. He worries so about me. It's best he sleep through all this."

Another contraction hit her at that moment, and she gasped with the pain of it. After it had passed, she relaxed and looked up at Anna. "How much longer you think this is gonna go on, Anna?"

Anna bent over and brushed Martha's hair back from her eyes. "This baby still hasn't let me know. As soon as I get the message, I'll tell you."

Martha closed her eyes, a weak laugh coming from her throat. "You're so sweet, Anna. I cain't wait for us to be sisters."

Anna's eyes widened, and she glanced up at Simon. He studied her with serious eyes. How she wished it were possible to be a part of this family.

Suddenly Martha's eyelids shot upward and she cried out. Anna rushed to the far end of the bed and her heart plummeted to the bottom of her stomach at what she saw.

Chapter 23

Simon heard the gasp from Anna's mouth and turned to see what had caused it. She stood at the far end of the bed, her face white. Martha struggled to raise her head from the pillow but fell back. He rearranged the pillow under Martha's head and turned to face Anna.

For a moment she stood there as if frozen in fear. Then, slowly, her eyes narrowed and her head tilted. As he watched, a transformation began to take place. Her teeth bit down on her lower lip and she took a deep breath. She squared her shoulders and straightened, her body language now giving the impression of someone who was in control of her emotions.

"Martha," she crooned, almost as if she was singing a lullaby, "the baby's bottom is coming first. Now this is a problem, but Simon and I are going to get you through this."

Martha gasped as another pain convulsed her body. "I…I know."

Anna raised cool eyes to Simon. "Be ready to do whatever I say, Simon."

He nodded and swallowed, in awe of the strength he now saw in Anna. She moved so that he couldn't see what her hands were doing, but she appeared completely absorbed in the mission before her.

Martha groaned. "Anna?"

"Yes, darling, take it easy. I need you to bear down with your contractions now."

Martha writhed on the bed as another pain hit.

"That's good, Martha. I have her legs out now."

Martha's eyes lit up. "Is it a girl?"

"It's a girl." The muscle in Anna's jaw twitched and she took a deep breath. "All right, we have another little problem. Her arms are over her head and aren't going to deliver on their own. I'm going to give her body a half turn to try to deliver the first one."

She worked in silence for a few moments, then nodded her head. "And now a half turn to get the other one. I don't mean to hurt you, Martha, but we have to do this as quickly as possible."

Martha gripped the side of the bed. "D-don't w-worry 'bout m-me."

Anna worked silently for a moment longer before she looked up. "Now Simon, I need you to help me with the head."

He moved closer to Anna, his eyes growing wide at the sight of the baby's lower body lying with its stomach resting on Anna's upturned left arm, its head still enclosed. Her right hand rested on the baby's shoulders.

"What do you want me to do?" he asked.

She glanced up. "I have two fingers of my left hand in the baby's mouth. I'm going to apply some downward pressure on the jaw. I want you to press on the lower part of Martha's abdomen to help me deliver the head."

Simon placed his hands where she directed and began to press down as Anna's right hand fingers gently flexed the back of the head toward its chest. Slowly the hairline of the head appeared. Simon's heart pounded as Anna raised her arm when the mouth and nose emerged. She looked up at him, a huge smile beaming on her face as a loud wail filled the room.

She nodded toward John's shirt, which hung on a chair next to the wall. "Put that on the bed for me."

Simon rushed to do as she said and watched as she laid the child in it. Before he realized what was happening, she had clamped the cord and wrapped the baby in the tradition of the mountains.

From the other end of the bed came Martha's soft whisper. "Give her to me."

Anna handed the baby to Simon. "I can take care of Martha from here on out."

His arms tightened around the baby as he gazed down into the face of his brother's child. With a smile he placed the bundle in Martha's arms and watched her wrap the baby next to her body.

Anna was still busy, but he couldn't watch anymore. He knew there were other things to be done, but he was unable to help her. Her hands worked quickly, intent now on aiding his sister-in-law's body to begin the healing process from her great travail.

Sharing this experience with Anna and Martha had left him in awe of the miracle of childbirth. He couldn't count the number of animals he'd assisted through the years on the farm, but now he had been privileged to be a part of bringing a human life into the world. He gazed upward, a silent offering of thanks ascending to the Creator of the universe.

"Simon." Anna's voice startled him.

"What?"

"Get that pot of blackberry tea I brought in a little while ago. Give Martha a big cupful and see that she drinks every drop. We don't want her to hemorrhage at this point."

He turned to the table where the pot sat and did as she asked. By the time he had gotten Martha to drink all the tea Anna had completed her work. She bundled up the bedding and placed a clean covering over Martha.

Then she stepped back beside Martha and smiled down at the two. She turned shimmering eyes toward Simon. "Why don't you invite your brother in to meet his new daughter?"

Simon threw the door open and laughed at the sight of John standing just outside, his head turned as if his ear had been pressed against the wood. Simon grabbed him by the arm and drew him inside. "Come see the baby."

John rushed to the bed and fell to his knees beside Martha. He buried his face in the cover and began to cry great gulping sobs. "I been so scared, Martha. I never been that scared in my life."

Martha patted his head. "John, I'm all right now, thanks to Anna and Simon." She pushed his head up. "Don't you want to see our daughter?"

Slowly John raised his head and stared at the baby in Martha's arms. "A girl? We got a little girl?"

He stared at her a minute and then turned to look at Anna, his eyes wet. "Thank you for takin' care of my wife and little girl. I ain't never gonna forgit you for this."

Anna hugged him. "I'm glad I could be here to help."

John looked at Simon. "Brother, she's a fine woman."

Simon smiled. "I know."

Anna's face flushed, and she looked down at the floor. Simon stepped to the bed and bent over to look at the baby again. The red-faced infant clenched her fists and screamed out.

John smiled and touched her tiny fist. "I reckon I got me two beautiful women now."

Simon nodded and turned back to Anna, but she wasn't there.

~

Anna backed slowly from the room as John and Simon bent to gaze at the infant lying in Martha's arms. Even though the window remained open all during the time she'd been there, the air in the room closed in, threatening to suffocate her. She had to get away from the fear that had consumed her since she first entered Martha's room.

In the kitchen she ran through the back door and into the yard. Her feet skimmed across the grass, wet with dew, until she reached the smokehouse. With a cry she ran behind the building and fell to her knees. She clasped her hands to her chest and stared across the fields just becoming visible in the early morning light. A new day was dawning, and new life had come into the world.

Her body began to shake at the memory of the fear that overwhelmed her during the long night. When she'd first examined Martha she had been sure the birth would end in tragedy, but it had not.

The thought of what she might have been required to do washed over her, and she cried out. Could she have done it if it meant saving Martha? And what about the next time she encountered the same circumstances?

She clenched her fists, raised her hands over her head, and shook them. "No. I can't do this again."

She bent forward until her forehead pressed against the ground. She lay there, sobbing. And then someone knelt beside her. Gentle hands touched her shoulders. The voice she'd come to love whispered in her ear. "Anna, what's wrong?"

She straightened and looked into his eyes, then threw her arms around him and pressed her face against his chest. His arms came around her in a protective embrace.

"Oh, Simon. I was so afraid."

He laid his cheek on the top of her head. "I was too, but you were wonderful. Martha was fortunate to have you here with her. We can never thank you enough for what you did for her."

She pulled away and shook her head. "I was foolish to think I could ever work in Bellevue's maternity ward. I don't have what it takes to be a nurse."

He frowned at her. "What are you talking about? You did what you were supposed to do, and because of you Martha and her baby are alive."

"But I was afraid." She began to cry again.

He smiled and wiped the tears from her eyes. "I was too, but you stepped right in and did your job like you'd been doing it for years. You looked like you'd delivered dozens of breech babies. Your uncle couldn't have done it better."

Her body jerked in a hiccup. "Really?"

"Yes. How did you know what to do?"

The hours she and Granny had spent practicing on the rag doll popped into her mind, and she suddenly realized God had prepared her for the moment when Martha would need her. "Granny taught me."

His fingers under her chin tilted her face up. "Granny was right.

God has given you a gift for this work. I saw it today. Don't ever doubt yourself."

She swallowed and looked into his eyes. "I don't know what I would have done if you hadn't been there. Thank you, Simon."

His arms tightened around her, and he drew her closer. "I want to be there with you all the time."

Her heart pounded so she thought it would burst. "Simon…"

"I love you, Anna. God brought you to the Cove for me. I'd prayed He would send me someone to share my life. The minute I saw you I knew you were the one He'd chosen for me."

"But…"

He shook his head. "There's no use arguing about it. I love you, and I know you love me too, whether you want to admit it or not."

How she longed to voice the words he wanted to hear, but she couldn't bring herself to do it. She reached up and stroked his cheek.

He closed his eyes at her touch. "Anna, be my love."

As if of their own accord, her arms encircled his neck and drew his face toward her. With a little gasp he crushed her against him, his lips covering hers. Her heart soared as she welcomed his sweet embrace.

They clung together for a few moments until she pulled away. "We can't do this."

She stood up and he rose to face her. He placed his hands on her shoulders and stared into her eyes. "Anna, I know you want to go to New York. But you can be a nurse right here in Cades Cove. The people here need you. I need you. Please don't leave me."

She pressed her hands to her face and shook her head. "I can't think about this right now. I need to get back to Martha."

He nodded. "All right, but this is not the end. We'll talk later."

"Later." She whirled and ran toward the house.

Once inside they entered the bedroom where John still sat beside Martha. John looked up and grinned. "We wondered where you two been."

Anna tucked the stray locks of hair that had come loose from their pins back into place. "We had to get a breath of air. Sorry to be gone so long."

Martha motioned for them to step closer. "We've decided on a name."

Simon smiled down at her. "And what am I to call my niece?"

John and Martha smiled at each other before Martha spoke. "Anna."

Surprise shot through Anna. "You want to name her after me?"

Martha reached out to grasp Anna's hand. "If it hadn't been for you, me and little Anna might both be dead now. We cain't ever thank you enough for what you done today."

Tears blinded her. "Thank you. I consider it an honor to have your child share my name."

She glanced at Simon, and her heart quaked at the love she saw shining there. How could she ever deny that she loved him?

Her head hurt and her body screamed for sleep. Maybe when she'd rested the answer would come to her.

~

In the week since the baby's birth Anna had washed more clothes than she thought possible. Since John and Martha had no family members other than Simon in the Cove, she had stayed on to take care of the new mother and baby. Her days spent cooking, cleaning, and watching Martha and the baby had helped her develop a new understanding of what her mother's life had been on the farm.

The work never seemed to let up. She straightened from bending over the washtub in the backyard, stretched her back, and squinted at the sun. She wiped her sleeve across the strands of hair plastered to her forehead and heaved a big sigh. But she really didn't mind all she'd done in the past few days, because John and Martha now seemed more like family.

When she began her work with Granny she hadn't thought she would become attached to those she worked with, but now she knew that wasn't true. There were new babies in the Cove who were alive partly because of her help. They would always be special to her because she'd been there at their births…but none would ever compare with little Anna Martin.

Every time she looked at that baby girl she was reminded of what a miracle she was. Anna also knew she would never be the same again after witnessing Martha's long ordeal. She would never again take for granted the birth of any child. But most of all she would always remember Simon's calming presence throughout the time.

In the days since the birth Simon had been a constant visitor. He was there for every meal, his eyes never wavering from Anna's. A bond had been established that night at Martha's bedside, and their souls had merged into one as together they faced the shadows of death. He told her he loved her, and those spoken words had changed everything between them. Up to then she could pretend they were friends, but that wasn't possible anymore. A line had been crossed, and she had to decide what to do. Maybe she could decide when she got back to Granny's.

Granny, now able to walk with a cane, had come to visit three days after the birth. Her face beamed her pleasure at Anna's care of Martha and the baby. She'd hugged Anna and announced for everyone to hear, "I don't 'spect I could've done a bit better if'n I'd been here myself. Anna, you got the gift in your hands."

Those words of praise coming from the legendary granny woman of the mountains thrilled Anna's heart. She smiled and wrung the water from the gown she had scrubbed. As she spread it on the line to dry, she heard a shout and turned toward the field. She shaded her eyes with her hands and glimpsed Simon and John coming back from hunting.

"Any luck?" she called out.

John held up two rabbits. "There's gonna be good eatin' today."

She propped her hands on her hips. "Well, you know the rules. You skin it and clean it, and I'll cook it."

Simon was grinning at her. "Sounds good to me."

John headed toward the smokehouse where he kept his tools, but Simon stopped beside her. "Want me to pour the water out of your washtub?"

She smiled up at him. "That would be a real help, kind sir."

He moved closer to her. "Anything for you."

His words thrilled her, and she turned her face away to keep him from seeing how red her cheeks had grown. "I'll go check on Martha and the baby, and then I'll get dinner started. Tell John to bring me the rabbits when he gets them cleaned."

Simon hefted the washtub and headed across the yard. "I'll do it."

Anna stepped back into the house and peeked into the bedroom. Martha and little Anna both seemed to be sleeping, and she tiptoed back to the kitchen. For several minutes she busied herself with chopping vegetables and dunking them into a big pot of water to cook. The addition of the rabbit was going to make this a meal fit for a king...or the best chef in Knoxville.

The sound of a horse stopping in the front yard caught her attention, and she frowned. Who could be dropping by? She wiped her hands on her apron and stepped to the front door. Her face broke into a big smile at the sight of her uncle climbing from his buggy.

She ran to meet him. "Uncle Charles, what are you doing here?"

He grabbed her in a hug. "I came by Granny's, and she told me about Martha. Just thought I'd stop and check on you." He held her at arm's length. "I hear you had quite a time with the birth."

She nodded. "I did, but everything's all right now."

He smiled. "That's what Granny said. I'm right proud of you, Anna. You showed what you were made of."

Anna waved her hand in dismissal. "I think God did all the work. I was just there to assist Him."

Her uncle's eyes held hers in a steady gaze. "Always remember that, darling. There's only so much we humans can do. It's all in God's hands."

She swallowed back the tears she felt stinging her eyes and grabbed his hand. "Come on into the house. John and Simon have just gotten back from hunting, and we're having rabbit for dinner. You have to eat with us."

Anna started toward the house, but he pulled her back. "Anna, wait."

She turned questioning eyes toward him. "What?"

He reached in his pocket and pulled out an envelope. "This came to Granny's yesterday. She asked if I would bring it to you."

Her name was written on the envelope in a hand she knew all too well. She licked her lips and glanced up at him. "It's from Robert."

He nodded and pressed the letter into her hand. "I've had one from him too, and I want to talk to you about it."

Her hand shook as she reached for the envelope. If Robert had finally agreed for her to go to New York, it would mean the first step in fulfilling her dream. On the other hand, if he was determined to stand by his original decision she could stay in the Cove with Simon. Anna's fingers curled around the letter.

New York. Cades Cove. Bellevue Hospital. Simon. Which did she want? At the moment she had no idea. This was one letter she didn't want to read.

Chapter 24

"*A*nna?"

Anna spun around at the sound of Simon's voice. "I'm in the front yard!" she called back. She stuffed the letter in the pocket of her apron and grabbed Uncle Charles's hand. "Don't say anything to Simon. I'll read it later."

He nodded as Simon came out the front door. Simon's eyes lit up in welcome when he saw Doc Prentiss standing beside Anna. "Didn't expect to see you today, Doc."

Uncle Charles put his arm around Anna. "Just wanted to check on my girl. I hear she did a mighty good job with Martha."

Simon smiled at her. "I don't expect a doctor in the best hospital in the country could have done any better. I don't know what would have happened if she hadn't been here."

Anna took her uncle's hand and smiled up at him. "He's exaggerating, Uncle Charles. He was right beside me the whole time and was a big help with the delivery."

Uncle Charles nodded. "That's what Granny said. I sure would like to see the new baby. Is she awake?"

A cry rang out from inside the house, and Simon jerked his thumb in the direction of the sound. "Just follow the wails. I never would have thought anyone as tiny as little Anna could have such a set of lungs."

Her uncle's eyebrows arched. "Little Anna?"

"Yeah." Simon's eyes softened. "John and Martha named her after the woman who brought her into the world."

Anna followed the two onto the porch and into the house. With each step she took the letter in her pocket grew heavier. Apprehension at its contents made her legs tremble and her stomach roil with sudden nausea. She wiped at the perspiration that had popped out on her head and slipped past Simon and her uncle as they entered the parlor. "Simon, take Uncle Charles in to see Martha. I have to get something from my room."

Her uncle cast a quick glance in her direction. "Anna, are you…"

She shook her head quickly to cut off his words, and he nodded. Simon didn't appear to notice the brief exchange as he headed toward Martha's bedroom. He knocked on the door. "Martha, Doc Prentiss is here to see the baby."

"Come in," Martha called out.

Anna waited until they'd entered the bedroom before she hurried to the room where she'd been sleeping. She closed the door and leaned with her back against it for a few moments. Her shaking fingers drew the letter from her pocket as she sank down on the patchwork quilt that covered the bed. Her heart pounded in her chest and her fingers shook. Slowly she ran her finger under the seal and pulled the sheets from within. Her eyes glistened with tears, and she blinked them away to focus on the words.

> *My Dearest Anna,*
>
> *When we arranged for you to spend the summer working with Matilda Lawson, Uncle Charles assured me she would be honest in whatever she told me about you. I have received a letter with a report of your work with her, and I must say I am very pleased with what she says.*
>
> *She writes that your work as her assistant since arriving in the Cove has been outstanding, and she states you have the gift of healing in your hands like few she's ever seen. She also mentions she would like for you to stay in Cades Cove and*

take over her work, but you have your mind set on going to Bellevue School of Nursing.

I have always tried to be a man of my word like our father taught me to be, and I will keep the promise I made to you when you left home. I will arrive in Cades Cove on August 10 to bring you home. That will give you and Mother time to get all your needs taken care of before you depart for New York on September 1.

I hope you know it was never my intent to cause you any pain. I saw the uncertainty you had about what you might encounter in New York, and I wanted you to be sure you could stand up to the pressures you would face as a student in a big hospital. Mrs. Lawson assures me you have the grit to face whatever comes your way. I am very proud of you, Anna.

Your loving brother,

Robert

Proud of her? She had never thought she would hear those words from him. And he was sending her to New York with his blessings.

She crushed the letter into a ball, wrapped her fingers around it, and walked to the window. In the distance the mountains she'd come to love rose toward the sky, their peaks shrouded in thick, smoky mists. She didn't want to live in New York. She wanted Cades Cove and the people she'd come to know and love. But most of all she wanted Simon.

But you've won. The thought niggled at the back of her mind. Wanting to beat Robert was what had gotten her through everything she'd experienced this summer. Could she just throw away the opportunity that had fallen in her lap?

The paper crackled in her hand and she began to unroll the ball, smoothing out the page with her fingers. Something tugged at her mind, and with a frown she reread the message, her eyes growing wider at the date Robert said he would arrive. August 10.

Tomorrow.

She rushed from the room in search of her uncle. He and Simon were still admiring the new baby. He turned as she entered the room, and the look on his face told Anna the letter he'd received from Robert said the same thing as hers. He stepped away from Martha's bed and walked toward her. "Anna, Granny sent some things over. Want to help me get them from the buggy?"

Simon glanced over his shoulder. "No need for you to do that, Doc. I'll get them."

Simon started toward the door, but her uncle's hand on his arm restrained him. "You stay with Martha. Granny had some special instructions for Anna I need to give her."

Simon nodded and turned back to the baby. "Martha, you think she might want her uncle to rock her awhile?"

Martha chuckled and handed the baby to him. "I 'spect she would."

Uncle Charles took Anna's arm and steered her out the front door toward the buggy. When they were well out of earshot, he turned to her. "Well, what do you think?"

Anna shook her head in bewilderment. "I don't know yet. I don't know what to think."

Her uncle stepped in front of her. His big hands wrapped around her smaller ones. "But isn't this what you wanted?"

"Yes. Yes. But it's happened so quickly. I need time to think about it."

Uncle Charles cocked his head to one side. "Think about what?"

Tears leaked from the corners of her eyes, and she wiped at them with the hem of her apron. "I don't know. It's just that I didn't expect Robert to give in, and I've had such a wonderful summer with Granny."

"And with Simon?"

She took a deep breath. "How did you know?"

"It's not hard to see what's going on between the two of you. Granny told me how you and Simon hit it off the first day you arrived, and Simon told me how he felt about you the day Naomi moved to Pigeon Forge."

"He did?"

Uncle Charles reached out, grasped her shoulders, and stared into her eyes. "He loves you a great deal, Anna. Do you love him?"

She shook free of him. "It doesn't matter. I'm supposed to go to Bellevue. I can help people there."

Uncle Charles leaned against his buggy and pulled a handkerchief from his pocket. Wiping his forehead, he gazed at the mountains in the distance. After a moment he straightened. "People need help no matter where they live. What about the people of the Cove? Don't they deserve a good nurse too? Granny's getting older, and she needs somebody she trusts to turn her work over to. She believes you're the person for the job, and she thinks God sent you here for that purpose."

"I've suspected that's what she wanted."

Anna let her gaze drift to the mountains that ringed the valley she'd come to love. In her heart she knew she would never find another place that could compare with the Cove, and she would never feel the kinship she'd come to share with the folks who struggled to survive here. But most of all she knew she would never love another man the way she loved Simon.

She shook her head and gritted her teeth. No, she wouldn't be distracted from what she'd planned for years. She had thought it impossible to gain Robert's approval, but she had. If she could do that, nothing was impossible. It might be difficult at first at Bellevue, but in time she would come to think of this summer as a pleasant interval in her life. And Simon...well, she would always cherish his memory.

Anna took a deep breath and opened her eyes. "I'm going to New York. That's where I belong."

"You're sure this is what you want?"

She nodded. "I've always wanted this, and I can't give it up now."

Her uncle's weathered face revealed his disappointment. "What will you tell Simon?"

Simon. Her mind flashed with images of the man she had come to love. Simon smiling at her from his pulpit. Simon fighting a barn fire, his skin stained with soot. Simon in agony after Luke Jackson's death. Simon with his arms around her at Abram's Creek. Simon's lips on hers after little Anna's birth.

But she had already made her decision.

Anna looked up at her uncle. "I need to cook dinner. Then I want you to take me back to Granny's. I have to get ready to leave."

"Anna darling, please don't rush into this decision. Talk to Simon first."

She shook her head. "I vowed years ago I would make it to New York, and I can't give it up now."

He reached for her. "Anna, please."

She pulled away from him. "No, Uncle Charles. My mind is made up."

She began to cry then, her shoulders shaking. Uncle Charles wrapped his arms around her, and she cried for the empty years that stretched before her.

~

Something was wrong. Simon knew it. Anna had been quiet ever since her uncle arrived an hour ago. He had to find out what was troubling her, but she refused to meet his gaze across the dinner table. Doc Prentiss and John carried on a lively conversation all through the meal, but Anna remained quiet.

Anna looked up from concentrating on her plate and caught him watching her. With a scrape she slid her chair back from the table and stood up. "I'll check on Martha while all of you are having pie."

"What? No pie? I've never seen you pass up a dessert." Simon smiled at her, but she glanced away.

"I don't want any," she said, and disappeared into the bedroom.

John and Doc Prentiss plowed through the pie, but Simon couldn't muster the appetite. Soon the other men went out to the barn, and Simon got up and went to Martha's door. She and Anna were deep in conversation.

"But, Anna, you cain't leave this soon. I'll miss you so much." Martha's voice brought a frown to his face.

"I have to go, Martha. You're doing well now, and John and Simon can take care of you. If you have any problems, send John for Granny, and she'll find someone to come help out."

The bed creaked as Martha pushed up. "But I don't understand. Why do you have to go?" The baby cried at that moment. "She's hungry. I need to feed her, but, but..."

"I'll come back in before I leave." Simon backed away as Anna's feet tapped across the floor.

He reached out to her as she came out, but she backed away. "What's wrong, Anna? Where are you going?"

She closed the door to Martha's room, then hurried past him to the kitchen. She sank down at the table and covered her face with her hands. "I didn't mean for you to find out this way."

His heart raced, and he fell into the chair next to her. "Find out what? You're scaring me."

She pulled a letter from the pocket of her apron and handed it him. He smoothed the crumpled pages on the table and began to read. His mouth gaped wider with each sentence that he read. When he'd finished, he looked up at her.

"You're not going to New York, are you?"

She nodded.

He jumped up, grabbed her hands, and pulled her up. She looked at him with a startled expression. He clenched his teeth and glared at her. "How can you even think about doing this? Not after everything we've had together. You belong here with me."

She tried to pull away. "No, I can't stay with you. Please don't make this any harder than it is already."

He released her. "Anna, I love you. I want to spend my life with you, and you're throwing that away like it's nothing."

She balled her fists and held her arms next to her body. "There's no use arguing about this. I could never make you understand. I don't want to stay with you. I want to go to New York."

He recoiled from her words and backed away, shaking his head slowly. "I'm sorry. I love you so much...and I thought you returned my feelings. I guess I was wrong. Go on then, Anna. I hope you find what you're looking for in New York. It doesn't seem to be here in the Cove."

Tears stung her eyes. "Simon, please try to understand how much this means to me. It's my dream. I don't want to lose mine like you lost yours."

He blinked in surprise at her words. Did he want Anna to stay in the Cove and always wonder what it would have been like if she'd followed her dream? He couldn't stand it if one day she regretted staying and blamed him for the decision. He exhaled. "I don't want you to lose your dream either, Anna. I wish you the best."

Simon turned and strode from the house to the spot where he tied his horse earlier. He grabbed the reins, mounted, and galloped away without a backward glance. Since little Anna's birth, he had really thought he was making her understand how they belonged together. He'd been wrong. There would never be anyone for him but Anna, but her desires lay somewhere else. He would have to learn to live with that.

Chapter 25

Simon stared at the cold cup of coffee on the kitchen table in front of him and groaned. He pushed his open Bible to the side and listened for some sound outside the cabin. The morning silence overwhelmed him.

Many times during the past few months he had sat in this room and imagined Anna here, laughing with him, teasing him, pressing a quick kiss to his forehead. But she had ended that dream yesterday.

The sound of a buggy stopping outside caught his attention, and he walked to the front door. Doc Prentiss was climbing down, and Simon met him on the porch. "Morning, Doc. You're out kind of early. You just comin' by to visit, or can I help you with something?"

Doc Prentiss took off his hat and wiped the perspiration from his face. "It's Anna. She won't talk to me or Granny about this. She's mighty unhappy, and I thought I'd come see if there isn't something you can do to change her mind about leaving."

Simon shook his head. "I've tried, but it's no use. She wants to go to New York, and I can't fight that."

Doc Prentiss sat down on the steps and Simon settled beside him. "Simon, ever since Anna was a child she's talked of being a nurse in a big hospital. I always hoped she would follow me to the mountains instead. I have to confess there was an ulterior motive behind my bringing her to Granny's. I thought she would fall in love with the Cove and wouldn't be able to leave."

Simon laughed joylessly. "Well, it didn't work, Doc."

Doc Prentiss put his hat back on. "That's why I came to see you. I hope you'll try again to make her stay. Granny tells me Anna loves you and wants to stay, but she's too stubborn. Too determined."

Simon shook his head. "There's nothing I can do. Nothing I want to do. Not anymore."

A stunned expression flashed on Doc Prentiss's face. "What do you mean?"

Simon stared at the ground for a few moments before he spoke. "I want to tell you something, Doc. I've never told this to another soul except Anna."

For the next few minutes he related how his dream had crashed when he made the decision to stay in the Cove and pastor the church. When he began to talk of how he'd agonized for the past three years over why God ignored his pleas to let him serve in a large city where he would encounter many people without Christ, his voice trembled, and he rose to his feet.

Doc Prentiss stared at him for a moment before he stood and placed his hand on Simon's shoulder. "So you don't want to be the cause of Anna giving up her dream like you had to."

"That's right. I know what it's like to want something you can't have. I don't want that for her."

Sadness flickered in Doc Prentiss's eyes, and he shook his head. "Oh, Simon, how could a man of God be so wrong?"

"What are you talking about? Wrong about what?"

Doc Prentiss put his hand on Simon's shoulder and stared into his eyes. "When God called you to be His servant, He promised to equip you with what you needed to serve Him. He didn't ask to see a plan of what you were going to do during your ministry because He knew what He wanted you to do and where He wanted you to go."

Simon frowned. "But He had sent me to Milligan College, and all my teachers said I had the best speaking ability of any student they'd seen in a long time. They thought I had a great future ahead of me and would lead great numbers of people to the Lord. And I know I could have done that if I hadn't let the people of the Cove talk me into staying after my parents died. Nearly everybody in the Cove is a Christian.

They don't need me. I think about those outside these mountains who need to be told about Jesus."

Doc Prentiss chuckled. "Simon, you're looking at this thing all wrong. Even Christians who are mature in the faith need a shepherd. And just because they're believers doesn't mean they don't have needs. Everybody has problems. When trouble strikes a family in the Cove, who do they think of first? You, that's who. Because you've been there for them, and they know you'll help them. And they love and respect you for the kind of pastor you are. I don't think they'd know what to do without you."

Simon's heart dropped to the pit of his stomach. "So you're saying you think I'll be here forever?"

"Forever?" Doc Prentiss shrugged. "I have no idea what God has planned for you. Only He knows that. I thought I'd be practicing in a big hospital in Nashville or Knoxville, but God brought me to these mountains. Because that was His plan for me, I've never regretted it."

It was a long moment before Simon asked the question whose answer had eluded him for the past three years. "But how do I know what God's will is? How did you know?"

"I followed God's instructions."

Simon frowned. "I don't understand."

Doc Prentiss walked to his buggy, opened his medical bag sitting on the seat, and pulled out a well-worn Bible. When he returned to Simon's side, he had already opened the book and held it out. "I found the answer in a verse I have underlined. Read what it says."

Simon peered down at the page to the underlined scripture. "'If any man serve me,'" he read aloud, "'let him follow me; and where I am, there shall also my servant be: if any man serve me, him will my Father honour.'"

Doc Prentiss tapped the page with his index finger. "Simon, God didn't say we were to follow our dreams. He said we were to follow Him. If we do that and serve Him, He will honor us. Until you quit blaming God and surrender your will to Him, He's not going to honor you with the blessings He's ready to give you."

Simon bit his lip and nodded. "I'll think about what you've said."

A long sigh escaped Doc Prentiss's mouth. "Well, you better think in a hurry because Anna's leaving today."

"Today?" Simon's throat tightened. He tried to speak but couldn't.

"Anna said you read the letter. Didn't you realize today is August 10?"

He frowned and shook his head. "I must have skipped over that part."

Doc Prentiss smiled and turned back toward the buggy. "Whether or not you can make Anna stay, I don't know. But I do know if you don't get your relationship with God worked out, you're not going to be content with anyone—even her."

With that he climbed into the buggy and picked up the reins. Simon watched him drive away. He had never felt so helpless in his life. If what Doc Prentiss said was true, in all the time he'd been talking to God about his disappointment he'd failed to open his heart to what God was trying to tell him.

There was nothing more he could do to make Anna stay, but now he realized there was something else he had to settle: his relationship with the God he loved. He had failed his Lord—failed in the mission to which he'd been called.

He leaped up the steps and rushed into his house. His Bible lay on the kitchen table where he'd left it. Turning to the book of John, he sank down in his chair and began to read.

For the next two hours he didn't move from the table but searched Scripture after Scripture, trying to find a word that would give him an answer. Anything that might tell him why God had made him remain in the Cove at a small church. More confused than ever, he turned back to the Scripture Doc Prentiss had shown him. John 12:26.

He read the verse again. *If any man serve me, let him follow me; and where I am, there shall also my servant be: if any man serve me, him will my Father honour.*

In desperation he covered his face with his hands and cried out. "God, I don't understand why You seem so far away from me. I've stayed here and tried to do Your work here, even though I thought You needed me to do great things for You somewhere else. You don't answer when I pray. Why do You ignore my prayers? Tell me!"

A voice that began as a soft whisper and swelled like thunder flowed through his body. It was as if the speaker sat next to him, but there was no one in the room. Simon lowered his shaking hands from his face, stilled, and listened, for he knew the whisper was not of this world.

"Simon," it said, "the problem is not that I need you. It's that you need Me." Love. The words spoke love.

Simon pushed up from the chair and steadied himself on trembling legs. He wondered if Moses had experienced the same feeling when God spoke to him from the burning bush. God had a message for Moses that day, and He'd given one to him today.

Simon fell to his knees. "God, I'm Yours. I surrender my will to You. Wherever You want me to go, I will go. From this day forward I will serve You with my whole heart."

Simon stayed on his knees for long minutes. Gone were the dreams of yesterday. His heart was filled with love for the people of the Cove and how God wanted to use him to serve them. If only everyone could know the peace that he had found!

Anna. If only Anna could know that peace.

She was leaving today. He had to go to her and tell her what had happened to him. If she told him it was God's will for her to go to New York, he wouldn't try to persuade her differently. He only wanted her to be at peace about her decision.

The clock on the mantel in the parlor chimed twelve. It was already noon, and Doc Prentiss had said she was leaving today.

He rushed out of the house and toward the barn. Within minutes he had saddled his horse and was racing toward Granny's house. He prayed he wouldn't be too late.

～

Anna stood at the back door, the dishes she had been washing forgotten, and looked across the fields behind Granny's house to the mountains. A hawk was circling up above. How she would miss this view—the trees that sloped up the hillsides, the early afternoon sun-light, the blue haze that hung over the low mountains.

Robert would be here any minute now. Her trunk was packed and waiting in her room. Granny had been quiet all morning as she bus-tled about, and now she had disappeared. A squawk came from the direction of the henhouse, and Anna recognized the familiar protest of Jezebel, the new hen Cecil had given Granny. Granny emerged from the small building, her apron bundled up in front of her to form a pouch for the eggs resting inside.

Uncle Charles stepped up behind her. "Is your trunk packed?"

"Yes." She nodded without turning. "I missed you this morning. Where did you go?"

"I had to make a call, but I made it back in time to eat. I don't pass up an invitation to sit at Granny's table when I'm in these parts."

She took a deep breath. Granny's cooking was just one of the things she was going to miss. "I know what you mean."

"What are you doing?"

She smiled and turned to face him. "Just making some memories."

"Anna, it's not too late…"

Anna pushed past him and returned to the task she had aban-doned earlier. She plunged her hands into the soapy water and began to scrub the plates from their noon meal. "Did you sleep well? I didn't ask you this morning."

Her uncle sat down at the table. "I've slept in some mighty strange places in these mountains. A quilt spread on Granny's floor is almost like sleeping in luxury. I don't think I stirred once I settled down." He regarded her for a moment. "What about you?"

She finished drying the cup she was holding and stacked the clean dishes on the shelf on the wall. "Oh, I slept off and on. I was up early to pack." She untied the apron from around her waist, folded it, and hung it on the back of the chair. "When are you leaving?"

He stood up and stretched. "I'll head out as soon as you and Rob-ert get on the road." He pulled the watch out of his pocket and looked at it. "Robert said in my letter he would be staying in Pigeon Forge the night before he got here. He should be here soon."

"I suppose we'll stay at Mrs. Johnson's inn tonight. At least I'll get to see Naomi."

Her uncle nodded. "I saw her a few days ago. She and the boys are doing fine. She sends her love."

Anna tilted her head and listened for a moment. "I think I heard a horse. Maybe that's him now."

Together they walked out of the house into the front yard. Robert climbed from the buggy and smiled at her. He pushed his hat to the back of his head, stepped forward, and planted a kiss on her cheek.

"Anna, you sure are a sight for sore eyes. I've really missed my little sister."

Anna smile and hugged him. "I've missed you too. How is Mama?"

The corners of his blue eyes crinkled. "She can't wait to see you." He turned to his uncle and grabbed his hand. "Good to see you, Uncle Charles. Thanks for taking care of Anna while she's been here."

Uncle Charles pumped his nephew's hand. "Oh, she's had a lot of folks looking after her. Anna's come to mean a lot to the people in the Cove."

Robert looked back at her. "That's my little sister. She takes after Ma."

Uncle Charles nodded. "Yes, she does."

Robert's gaze drifted over the cabin before he glanced at Anna. "So this is where you've been living all summer? Where is Mrs. Lawson? I want to meet her and thank her for all she's done for you."

"She should be out in a minute. She saved some food from the noon meal for you."

Robert followed her to the front porch. "That's kind of her, but we need to leave soon."

Anna whirled to face her brother before stepping through the front door. Panic boiled up in her. It was really going to happen. She was about to leave. "When?"

Robert glanced at their uncle. "As soon as the horse is watered and has rested some. We need to get to Pigeon Forge before dark. Mrs. Johnson is expecting us."

Anna nodded and led him into the cabin. Granny was standing before the fireplace.

Anna pulled Robert toward her. "Granny, I'd like you to meet my brother, Robert."

Granny held out her hand, and he grasped it. "Thank you for your hospitality to Anna, Mrs. Lawson. Our family is very grateful for the time you spent with her. I know this has been a rewarding experience for her."

Granny's gaze flitted to her. "Not as much as for me. She's a smart woman, and I hate to be losin' her."

Robert nodded. "From what you wrote me, I believe she's going to be a good nurse."

"She already is." Granny glanced at Anna. "Take Robert into the kitchen and git that plate of food I saved him out of the pie safe. He's traveled a long way today and must be powerful hungry."

Robert grinned. "To tell the truth, I'm starved. I haven't had anything since breakfast."

Granny propped her hands on her hips. "You mean Miz Johnson didn't fix you no basket of food?"

"No ma'am."

Granny sniffed, her hands planted firmly on her hips. "Well, then you done come to the right place. There's nothing I like better'n feedin' a hungry man."

Anna trudged after her brother and Granny as they entered the kitchen. What was the matter with her? This was the moment she'd been waiting for all summer. As soon as Robert ate, they would climb in the buggy and begin the first step of the adventure she'd planned for years. She just wished she could be happier about it.

～

Simon urged the horse to move faster. The sun was getting high in the sky, and he hoped he wouldn't be too late.

Granny's house came into view, and he heaved a sigh of relief when he saw the buggy parked there. A man was holding a bucket up for the horses to drink from. If this was Anna's brother, then they hadn't left yet.

The horse trotted into the yard, and he jumped down just as Doc Prentiss came out the door with Anna's trunk on his shoulder. He looked up and nodded to Simon.

"Glad to see you, Simon. Come over here and meet Anna's brother."

Simon dismounted and tied his horse to the tree. The young man with the horse smiled as he approached. Simon could see the resemblance to Anna. He stuck out his hand. "I'm Simon Martin. I came to see Anna before she left."

The young man shook his hand. "Ah. Good. I'm Robert Prentiss, her brother."

Doc Prentiss settled the trunk in the buggy. "Simon's the preacher here in the Cove."

Robert's face broke into a big smile. "Oh, the preacher." He nodded toward the house. "Anna's inside getting the rest of her things. Just go on in and see her."

Simon swallowed and glanced at Doc Prentiss. "I think I'll do that."

He forced himself not to bolt up the steps as he approached the front porch. He had to be calm and composed when he talked with Anna. He walked through the open door and stopped at the sight before him. Granny stood with her back to the fireplace, Anna tight in her arms. Tears streaked Granny's face, and Anna's shoulders shook. Granny glanced over Anna's shoulder and saw him first. She gently pushed Anna away.

"There's somebody else here to tell you goodbye."

Anna turned, her eyes growing wide at the sight of him. She pressed her hand to her mouth. "Wh-why d-did you c-come?"

He stepped forward and glanced at Granny. She cleared her throat. "If'n you two will excuse me, I got somethin' to take care of in the kitchen."

He waited until she was gone before he stepped closer and spoke. "Anna, I had to come. There's something I have to tell you before you leave."

She shook her head. "No. There's nothing else to say."

He touched her arm and stopped her. "I have to tell you what has happened to me this morning. It's very important. Please hear me out."

She gazed up into his eyes, and he thought his heart would burst from the love he felt for her. She nodded, and he began.

"Your uncle came to my house this morning."

"My uncle?"

"Yes." He spoke slowly as he related the events of the morning, but he became more excited when he came to the part of how God had spoken to him. He ended by telling her of the peace that now filled his soul. "I owe your uncle a great debt for helping me see how I needed to let God direct my life instead of trying to do it myself."

Anna had not moved since he began speaking. After a moment she took a deep breath. "I'm happy for you, Simon. I know God is going to use you to do great things wherever He takes you."

"I think so too. But I wanted to tell you this because I want to make sure you're following what is God's will for you. Have you prayed about this, Anna? Or have you based your decision to go to New York on a childhood dream? If you can tell me this is God's will, I can be happy for you. I'll miss you, but I can let you go."

Tears trickled down her cheeks. "Simon, I…"

He took her by the shoulders and stared into her eyes. "I love you with all my heart, Anna. And there's nothing more I want for you than to know that you're right where God wants you to be."

She gazed up at him, and without warning she leaned close and pressed her lips to his. Before he could react, she pulled away and whispered, "I love you, Simon."

With that she ran for the door and out of his life. He'd never hurt so. He turned toward the fireplace and leaned forward. His hand clutched the mantel and his forehead rested on his fingers. "God, help me!" he cried. "I can't bear this alone."

Even as he said it, he knew he wasn't alone. The days ahead would be difficult, but God would be walking beside him every step he took.

Chapter 26

*A*nna rushed from the house and stopped at the bottom of the steps. Uncle Charles and Robert stood by the buggy, waiting. Her uncle walked toward her and wrapped his arms around her. He glanced over his shoulder at Robert. "I need to tell Anna goodbye. I'll just be a minute."

He steered her to the side of the house and faced her. "What did Simon say?"

"He told me about your visit this morning. He says you helped him see that he's doing God's will right here in the Cove. And he wanted to make sure I was doing God's will in leaving."

"Are you?"

"I want to go to New York," she said simply.

Her uncle frowned. "Life isn't always about what we want, Anna. God has plans for us that are so much better than the ones we think up for ourselves. Once I thought I knew what I wanted. I thought I'd be a doctor at Vanderbilt in Nashville, but God led me here to the mountain people I love. I've been at peace with that because it was God's will."

"But didn't you have any regrets?"

He shook his head. "No, because when I first entered medical school, I promised God I would go where He could use me most. I know He brought me here." He put his arm around her and pulled her close. "And God also blessed me with a wonderful family. You and

279

your brother are very special to me. You're like the children I never had. That's why I have to be sure you're following God's will in going to New York."

She stood wrapped in her uncle's arms, her mind whirling. "But wasn't it God who gave me this dream in the first place?"

He held her at arm's length and smiled at her. "Your dream to be a nurse? Sure He did. I just want to make sure you're going to be a nurse in the right place. Does God want you at Bellevue, or does He want you working out of a cabin in the Tennessee mountains? That's what you have to decide."

"How can I know for sure?"

"Well, I suppose we should look at both options open to you. If you go to New York, you'll live in a big city, become a great nurse, and help a lot of people. If you stay in Cades Cove you'll have a hard life, but the people here will love you for helping them. And then there's a young man who's surrendered his will to God and wants you to do the same. I know you love him, Anna. Together you could do great things in the Cove."

"How?"

Her uncle cupped his hand around her cheek. "There's a verse from the Bible I think holds the answer. Ezekiel was trying to unite his people, and he said, 'I will give them one heart, and I will put a new spirit within you; and I will take the stony heart out of their flesh, and will give them an heart of flesh.' Those words hold true for us too."

"But what does it mean?"

He smiled. "It means that God wants to take away your stubborn heart that is intent on doing your own will and replace it with one that's tender and responsive to His will. Have you considered the fact God may have sent you to Cades Cove so He could unite your and Simon's hearts into one that shares a singleness of purpose—to serve the people here? There's only one way to find out, Anna. Put aside what you want. Let God give you the blessings He has waiting for you."

Anna closed her eyes and covered her face with her hands. A prayer tumbled from her lips. "Oh, God, I've been so selfish and determined to get my own way that I've hurt many people around me. Take away my stubbornness. I want to follow Your will. Just let me know what it is."

Her uncle put his arm around her shoulders, and she leaned her head against his chest. The answer came to her, and it was as if she had known all along what she should do. She had been so intent on winning her battle of wills with Robert she had ignored what God was telling her. She raised her head and took a step away from her uncle, then whirled and hurried back to where Robert stood at the buggy.

He smiled as she came toward him. "Are you ready?"

She bit her lip and stared into the face of her brother. "You were right," she said.

A perplexed look flickered across his face. "Right about what?"

"I wasn't ready to go to New York, and you knew it. I'm sorry I behaved so badly about it. I should have known you were still looking out for your little sister. Please forgive me for doubting you and being angry with you."

He swallowed. "Of course I forgive you, Anna." He ducked his head, and for a moment it seemed that he was struggling to speak. "But there's something you must forgive me for. I should never have said you were spoiled and Poppa gave you everything you wanted. I spoke those words in anger."

"I realize that now."

"You're my little sister. I love you, and I only wanted the best for you."

She nodded. "I know that too. You knew what was best for me when I didn't. New York isn't for me. God used you to send me to Cades Cove, and I know this is where I belong."

He frowned and glanced at the cabin. "You want to stay here instead of coming with me? This place is so…How will I explain this to Mother?"

"Tell her I fell in love with the mountains and I fell in love with a preacher."

He grinned. "Is it the fellow who arrived a little while ago?"

"It is, and I want you to meet him. Will you stay tonight so the two of you can get to know each other?"

"There's nothing I'd like better, little sister."

~

A crunching sound of wheels turning on hard ground reached his ears, and Simon realized the buggy was pulling away from the house. She was gone, and with her went all the hopes and dreams he'd harbored since the day he walked around Granny's house and saw her jump from her uncle's buggy.

With a sigh he straightened his shoulders and shook his head. Getting over Anna wasn't going to be easy, but in time the heartache might start to fade a little. He didn't look forward to a future without her, but he knew God would be with him. All he had to do was remember God was in control, and he could make it through anything.

Behind him the door opened. Footsteps approached, and a hand touched his arm. "Would you help me bring my trunk back inside?"

His body froze at the sound of the quiet drawl he'd come to love. His eyes closed, and he wondered if he were dreaming. Slowly he turned, unable to believe the miracle of Anna standing before him. She smiled at him, and his mouth gaped open.

"Anna," he whispered. "I thought you'd left me."

She tilted her head, her hand caressing his cheek. "I couldn't leave, Simon. I love you too much."

Still unable to believe, he glanced past her. "But what happened?"

She smiled. "Uncle Charles made me see that God wanted me to surrender my will to Him too. I have done that, Simon, and I know God wants me to stay here and work with the people in the Cove. And I think God wants us to unite our hearts as one and serve Him with a singleness of purpose. What do you think about that?"

Simon's eyes grew wide. "I think that's a better plan than either of us could have dreamed up." He stared at her, still not believing what was happening. "But I heard the buggy leave. I thought you were gone."

"Uncle Charles left to make some visits, but he's coming back. Robert's taking care of the horse, then he'll come inside. He and Uncle Charles are going to stay tonight. I just wish my mother could be here to see how happy I am." She stepped closer and slid her hand to the back of his neck. "I'm ready to begin my life with you, Simon. Right here in the Cove."

His arms went around her, and he crushed her to him. "I love you, Anna Prentiss, and I'm not ever letting you go again." He drew back from her and stared down into her eyes. "Don't ever leave me. I'm not whole unless you're with me."

She smiled. "Neither am I. I promise I'll never leave."

He stared at her for a moment before his lips came down on hers. They clung together, lost in the wonder of the commitment they'd made to each other.

Simon finally pulled away. He grinned, then dropped to one knee in front of her, wrapped her hand in his, and gazed up at her. "Anna Prentiss, will you do me the honor of becoming my wife?" He hesitated. "Or do I need to ask your brother's permission first?"

Her face lit up, and laughter pealed from her lips. She dropped to her knees beside him and threw her arms around him. "I think he already knows. Simon Martin, I would be honored to be your wife."

He grabbed her arms and pulled her up as he rose. "Do you remember the first day you came here? We sat in front of this fireplace after supper."

She nodded. "You cut your finger that afternoon, and I bandaged it."

His hand dipped into his pocket and pulled out her handkerchief. "With this," he said. "I thought you were the most beautiful woman I'd ever seen, and I didn't even know you yet."

She smiled. "You were covered with dust the first time I saw you, but I couldn't forget about your eyes. They seemed to see right into my heart. I was so upset that night I cried because I didn't understand my attraction to you."

He laughed. "I guess God was letting us know then that He'd brought us together."

Footsteps stomped across the floor and stopped. Granny stood in the door from the kitchen, her hands on her hips. "I saw Robert puttin' his horse in my barn. What in tarnation's goin' on?"

They turned to face her. Simon held Anna's hand in his. "Granny, Anna has agreed to marry me. You're the first to know."

She stared at them for a moment before a big smile crossed her face. "Well, it's 'bout time. I done wore my knees out a-prayin' fer you two. I reckon I knowed that first day Anna got here the Lord had done sent the one I'd been askin' for."

Anna ran to her and hugged her. "Thank you, Granny. I shouldn't have waited so long."

Granny face beamed. "Don't matter none now. You finally listened to the Lord. That's all that's important." She looked past Anna and Simon. "Say, where's Doc? He already left?"

Anna nodded. "He had patients to see. He'll be back later, and Robert's staying too. Do you mind all the extra mouths for supper?"

"There's always room at my table for one more." Granny grinned and looked from one to the other. "A weddin'. Well, I cain't wait. I 'spect this gonna be the biggest shindig we ever seen in the Cove. When we gonna have it?"

Anna and Simon looked at each other and laughed. "We haven't even talked about that yet!" Simon said. "But the sooner the better as far as I'm concerned."

Granny frowned and walked toward the door. "Was that a wagon pullin' up?" She pulled the door open and called out. "Hello there, Joshua. Light a spell and come on in."

Anna and Simon followed Granny onto the front porch and watched Joshua Whitson climb from his wagon. He rushed across the yard and stopped at the bottom of the steps. He pulled his hat off and stared up at Granny, fear on his face.

"Granny, you and Miss Anna gotta come right away. Nellie done started havin' pains, and I reckon it ain't gonna be long 'fore the baby gets here."

Granny turned back to the house. "Let me get my things, Joshua."

As Granny reentered the house, Anna stepped down beside Joshua.

"Granny and I will do everything to make sure your wife and child get through this safely. And remember, we haven't lost a father yet."

Anna followed Granny into the house and Simon watched her go. "Want me to come sit with you while you wait, Joshua?"

"I reckon I'd like that, Simon."

Granny and Anna rushed back out the door. Granny headed to the wagon, but Anna stopped beside Simon. "I'm sorry to run off like this. Can you tell Robert where we've gone?"

"Sure. I'll bring him with me to Joshua's farm. He can see what your life is going to be like." He shook his head and smiled. "I guess this is going to be the story of our life. You take care of the mothers, and I'll distract the fathers. I think we're going to make a good team."

Anna's eyes beamed. "I think so too."

~

Anna could hardly believe a month had passed since she'd accepted Simon's proposal. The day she'd been waiting for had finally arrived. In a few hours she would be Simon's wife, and they would begin their life together. For the first time newlyweds would live in the honeymoon cabin Simon's father had built. Simon had worked hard for the last few weeks getting it ready, and she could hardly wait to see what improvements he'd made.

She twisted her body to get a better view of herself in the mirror Robert had brought her for a wedding present. The long white dress Martha made for her flowed to the floor and fanned out in a long train behind her. The veil her mother wore the day she married her father was waiting to be placed on her head.

A knock sounded on the door and her mother's voice called out. "Anna, may I come in?"

"Yes, Mama."

Her mother opened the door and stepped into the room. She pulled a handkerchief from her pocket and dabbed at the tears that pooled in her eyes. "Oh, darling, you're beautiful. I wish your father could see you today."

Anna grasped her mother's hand. "I do too. I think he'd be happy for me."

"He would. And he would have loved Simon. He's going to make you very happy."

The thought of Simon waiting when she arrived at the church sent a thrill through her. "Oh, Mama, I think I knew the minute I saw him, but it took me a long time to realize it."

"Sometimes we don't notice the blessings that are right in front of us." She cupped her daughter's cheek and smiled. "Come on now. We have to leave for the church or you're going to be late for your own wedding."

Anna picked up the veil. "Mama, will you put this on for me?"

Her mother took the delicate lace in her hands and positioned it on Anna's head, then stepped back to survey the effect. "Perfect. Ready to go?"

Anna let her gaze rove over the room she'd lived in for the past few months. She'd miss Granny, but she was ready to begin her life with Simon. She closed her eyes and sighed with happiness.

"Let's go."

They walked into the front room where her uncle and Granny waited. She glanced around for her brother. "Where's Robert?"

Uncle Charles laughed. "He went to keep Simon company. He said he couldn't have the groom getting cold feet and leaving his little sister at the altar."

Anna laughed and turned to her mother. "He likes Simon, doesn't he?"

Her mother patted her arm. "He's welcomed Simon like the brother he always wanted. I think they really got to know each other the night they waited for that baby to be born."

Anna smiled at the memory of the two of them keeping Joshua occupied while she and Granny helped usher his daughter into the world. "I think so too."

Granny cleared her throat. "Well, I 'spect we better git the bride to the church, or the groom may think she's not a-comin'."

Anna looped her arm through her uncle's and smiled up at him.

"Let's go, Uncle Charles. I can't wait to walk down the aisle on the arm of my second father."

His eyes misted, and he glanced at her mother, who smiled back at him. He squeezed Anna's hand. "This is the happiest day of my life."

~

Simon stood at the front of the church, his eyes unwavering as he watched the church entry. John and Martha stood with him at the altar as they waited for Anna's entrance. In the front row Anna's mother and brother beamed, and the preacher from Strawberry Plains waited behind him to administer the marriage vows. The organist Uncle Charles had brought from Tuckaleechee touched the keys of the organ, and its sweet strains drifted across the gathered audience.

Sometimes he almost had to pinch himself to believe this was really happening. Anna was going to be his wife. What had seemed like a dream a month ago was coming true today.

The door opened, and there she stood on her uncle's arm. They hesitated for a moment before they began the journey down the aisle. Her eyes locked with his as she approached, and his heart almost jumped out of his chest.

They stopped beside him, and he turned to face the preacher. Her uncle stood between them, her arm still in his. The congregation who'd risen as Anna entered sat down, and Anna's pastor from Strawberry Plains stepped forward.

"Dearly beloved," he began. Simon thought of all the times he'd stood before young couples and pronounced those words. Had the grooms been as excited as he was now? He hoped so. Anyone getting married should know the thrill of finally being joined to the one you love.

"Who gives this woman to be married to this man?" the preacher said.

"I do," her uncle said. He glanced down at Anna, kissed her on the cheek, then took her hand and placed it in Simon's.

Simon swallowed and closed the gap between them as Doc Prentiss went to sit next to Anna's mother. The words the preacher spoke drifted into his ears, and he concentrated as the ceremony progressed.

Finally came the words he'd been waiting to hear—"I now pronounce you man and wife"—and he thought he would explode with happiness. The preacher instructed him to kiss his bride, and he leaned forward to brush her lips with his. As he straightened, he caught a glimpse of the gold ring he'd placed on her finger. His finger rubbed the band as he smiled at his bride. She was his for always, and he was hers. The thought brought him the greatest pleasure he'd ever known.

~

Anna had tried to concentrate on the preacher's words throughout the ceremony, but she found it impossible. All she could think about was that she was about to become Anna Martin. Now she was someone's wife, and maybe someday she'd be someone's mother. But for now she basked in the glow of the love she felt for Simon.

Their kiss ended, and the preacher spoke out to the congregation. "Mrs. Martin's family is hosting a reception for all of you to wish the bride and groom good luck. Cake and cider will be served on the tables under the trees just outside the church. The couple hopes all of you will stay and celebrate their wedding with them."

The organ began the recessional, and Simon and Anna hurried up the aisle, their hands clasped tight together. They burst through the door and into the warm September sunshine. At the bottom of the church steps, Simon pulled her into his arms. "Hello, Mrs. Martin. I love you."

She wrapped her arms around him. "I love you too, Mr. Martin."

From behind them John nudged them forward. "This is no time to be stoppin'. The folks'll be comin' out any minute. Git out there and cut the cake so's you can visit with them."

Simon and Anna laughed and ran across the yard toward a table where sat the cake that Anna's mother had brought all the way from Strawberry Plains. Simon grabbed the knife, and together they cut the first piece just before the crowd descended upon them.

"Let me have that," Martha said, taking the knife. "Go meet your guests, and I'll serve the cake."

They moved away from the table and shook the hands of their friends as they filed by. Anna was struck by the smiles and happiness that were plain on the faces of Simon's congregation. She hoped she would be the kind of wife a preacher needed. That had been her prayer ever since she'd agreed to marry him.

After everyone had been served Anna and Simon moved among the people, stopping to talk to different groups. Suddenly John's voice boomed out above the crowd. "Folks, could I have your attention, please?"

Everyone quieted and turned to face John. "I been asked to get everybody quiet, so's a special weddin' gift can be given to my brother's new wife."

Anna looked at Simon, who shrugged his shoulders. She turned back to John. "Something for me?"

John motioned for her to join him. "Come on over here, Anna."

With a smile she left Simon's side and moved to stand beside her new brother-in-law. He pointed to his wife. "Martha's gonna tell you what it is."

Martha approached her, a coy smile on her lips. The other women of the church gathered in a tight group behind her. Anna let her gaze wander over the women.

There was Laura Ferguson, the first woman she had aided in childbirth, Gracie Long and Nellie Whitson with their babies, Pearl Davis holding Josie, Lavinia, Naomi Jackson and Mrs. Johnson who'd come from Pigeon Forge, and all the others standing behind Martha. Even Linda Mae Simmons's smile hinted at a promised friendship. Anna's gaze came to rest on Granny in the middle of the group, her back straight and her smile wide.

Martha stepped forward. "Anna, I won't never forget what you did for me when my little Anna was born. You saved her life and mine and gave me the sweetest little one I could ever have. I cain't never thank you enough for that."

All the women nodded their heads. Martha pointed to the women behind her. "Only a woman can know what it's like to enter that valley and come out alive. Ever since you been here, you've gone right there with us and brought us back. And we're not forgettin' what you've done."

Tears stood in Anna's eyes. "It's been my pleasure. I've been right where I wanted to be with the people I've come to love. I just thank you for letting me be a part of your community."

Martha took a deep breath. "Well, we all got together and made you a little present. We had to do it in a hurry, 'cause you and Simon didn't give us much warning. But anyway this is for you."

The women parted, making a path for Lucy and Ted Ferguson to walk through. A brown package rested in their outstretched arms. "This here's for you, Miss Anna," Lucy said.

"From all the women," Ted added.

Anna reached out and took the gift. She touched the cheek of both children and then glanced up at Martha. "Well, open it," she said.

With a laugh Anna tore the paper away and gasped at the sight of a patchwork quilt that lay within. She picked it up and unfolded it to get a better view of the workmanship. The squares embellished with embroidery and crewel each contained the name of the woman who'd sewn it.

Anna's heart filled with thanks for the women she'd come to love. "Thank you so much," she whispered.

Granny stepped forward and pointed to the center square. "Did you see this one, Anna?"

The words *Angel of the Cove* emblazoned in bold script leaped from the center of the quilt. Tears filled her eyes, and she clutched the quilt to her chest and buried her face in it. Granny's strong arms encircled her shoulders. "That's what the folks here call you, Anna. You done found a place in their hearts."

Anna raised her head and stared at Simon. His dark eyes held hers. *I love you,* he mouthed. The sweetest peace she'd ever known filled her. This was where she belonged. This was home. She smiled and walked toward her husband.

Discussion Questions

1. When Anna came to Cades Cove, she feared the people wouldn't accept her in their community. Have you ever felt like an outsider in a group? How did you cope with that feeling?

2. Simon questioned God about why he wasn't allowed to pastor a large church. How do you react when circumstances in your life prevent you from attaining what you wanted?

3. Although Anna wanted to become a nurse, at times she doubted if she had the courage and determination to acquire the skills needed in the job. What can you do when fear of the unknown makes you reluctant to work toward something you desire?

4. Even when Granny disapproved of a person's actions, she showed God's love for them by ministering to their needs. How do you react to the needs of the poor, the homeless, the hungry, and the unlovable in your community? What did Jesus say about helping these people?

5. Anna didn't trust Cecil Davis and thought him to be a cold, uncaring man. Are you quick to judge people before getting to know what they are really like? What does the Bible teach about judging others?

6. Anna and Simon became jealous when they each showed attention to another person. How can jealousy ruin relationships? How do you keep jealousy from taking root in your heart?

7. Anna feared she wasn't skilled enough to cope with a situation like the birth of Martha's baby. Have you ever been placed in an emergency situation that called for you to provide help for someone suffering? How did you react?

8. Anna and her brother had suffered a broken relationship because of angry words and actions. Have disputes caused problems in your family? If so, what can you do to heal relationships?

9. Anna and Simon found their fears and doubts vanished when they yielded their hearts to God's will. Have you put your faith in Him, and do you allow Him to guide you in all aspects of your life?

Sandra Robbins and her husband live in the small college town in Tennessee where she grew up. They count their four children and five grandchildren as the greatest blessings in their lives. Her published books include stories in historical romance and romantic suspense. When not writing or spending time with her family, Sandra enjoys reading, collecting flow blue china, and playing the piano.

~

To learn more about books by Sandra Robbins or to read sample chapters, log on to our website:

www.harvesthousepublishers.com